Celestial Voyages

The Moon

Jeff Provine

To Robert,
Edwardian Science Fiction

Jeff Provine

PublishAmerica
Baltimore

First printing

ISBN: 1-59286-010-9
PUBLISHED BY PUBLISHAMERICA BOOK PUBLISHERS
www.publishamerica.com
Baltimore

Printed in the United States of America

Dedicated to all my friends,
for always listening to my crazy ideas.

Chapter One,
The Beginning

My story begins on a lonely, dusty road deep in the farmlands of Ohio. I was just a lad then, barely nineteen years of age. I distinctly remember being dressed in a heavy red shirt, long brown pants, common boots, and a black hat; it was a chilly day in late October. The leaves had all turned to their dark yellows, reds, and browns and many had already fallen to the ground. The fields were yellowing, too. Soon the cows that dotted the summer pastures would be moved to winter lands and warm barns.

I was a doctor's son, the youngest of three. My two brothers had long ago moved away, the elder to New Jersey as an aide in the famous Menlo Park and the other to Dayton as a merchant's apprentice. I had stayed long at home, kept busy by helping my parents. My father, although he was a physician by profession, had a passion for farming and kept up a long list of chores for me. My mother also had me help her with chopping wood or other whatnot. In addition to chores at home, I would often help my father with his visits to check on the neighboring farmers in the evenings. I would drive the buggy while he quizzed me on European history or human anatomy or some other field of study. As night came and the sky darkened, the questions would grow less numerous and more spaced. Finally, he would just sleep, and I would guide our horse Bessie along the road toward the next appointment.

On top of all these errands and tasks, I sought an immense education. I attended a schoolhouse near my parents' farm until I had learned more than the teacher herself knew. I then began taking classes from my mother. She was a surprisingly stern educator and packed my brain as full as it could possibly be. I had continued this home tutelage to this very day of which I was speaking. I remember looking forward to trying my luck at a university the next year. However, it was not meant to be; fate had something much more interesting in store for me.

Before I mention what, though, I should explain why fate would hand this to me. I take a great interest in astronomy, although some may call it more of an obsession than an interest. Living out in the spacious skies, I could clearly see the stars, planets, comets, and other celestial objects. Without much more else to do with my free time, I gathered books about the heavens and studied. I purchased a small telescope by working small odd jobs for neighbors and thus furthered my view into the heavens. My passion continued to expand, and I accumulated one of the greatest stockpiles of extraterrestrial knowledge that Earth had ever known (or so I often liked to believe). Everyone who knew me knew of my affiliation with the skies. They would often approach me and ask where Saturn or Sirius was today. I would happily point it out for them, and they would give an amused chuckle.

One day when I was eighteen years old, a neighbor approached me with an advertisement in a mercantile catalogue. It told of a contest held by some shipping magnate in Britain challenging the best astronomers in the world. I was excited to find a chance to use my skills that were otherwise a mere novelty. I sent away for the packet of questions and desperately awaited its arrival. When it finally did arrive, I hastily began answering the questions, destroying several pencils in my frantic writing. Once I had finished the lengthy exam, I repackaged it into another envelope and mailed it back to the contest directors. Then I began my wait for the day of the announcement of results.

It was a lengthy interval of many weeks, but eternity would have been enough for the reward it gave me. When the letter finally came in the post, I was nearly too excited to open it. My hands were shaking with anticipation and I dropped the letter more than once before I finally managed to rip the envelope open. I read the first few lines, which were nothing more than formal remarks about how interesting the contest had been. Finally, I came to a column of percentages. The heading noted that the numbers were correct answers out of all answers and each row had a title such as "planetary coordinates" and "position calculation." I smiled widely as I saw the numbers that followed were all exceedingly high, none of them below a ninety-five percentile. I read on, finally coming to the bottom of the letter that stated, in large, bold letters, "CONGRATULATIONS, YOU HAVE WON FIRST PLACE!" Smaller words giving details about the contest and the signature by Mason Star, the eccentric industrialist who hosted the challenge, followed. However, I did not care about them. I tossed aside the letter and pulled the contest's prize from the envelope: a check for one hundred pounds sterling. It was more money than I had ever imagined that I would hold in my hand.

That check, in fact, was the reason that I was walking on the lonely, dusty road I mentioned before. I was on my way into Dayton to cash it and spend the night with my new money at my brother's room in the mercantile shop. I was light on my feet and the check in my shirt pocket seemed to be pulling me toward town.

Suddenly, I heard a strange noise behind me. I stopped and turned, first seeing a distant, small plume of dust on the road heading toward me. I stepped down off of the road and waited to see just what was approaching. As I realized what it was, I just stood agape in the ditch beside the road and stared.

It was a long, silver and black automobile. I had seen several of these horseless carriages before, though rare as they were then, but I had never even dreamed of one like this. It sped toward me, kicking up dust as it went. As it came closer, I could hear a strange, metallic whirring sound coming from its engine. All of the automobiles that I had heard before made roaring noises like a locomotive. It also had a very strange exterior. The sides of the motorcar were all silver, formerly brightly polished but now coated with a light glaze of Ohio country dust. The top portions of the motorcar's exterior were dark black, glossy, and looked to be made of small plates all aligned together. A uniformed driver sat in the front, steering the mechanical beast directly at me.

When it came close, it sped by me, suddenly stopped, screeching on its rubber tires, and then reversed with a deeper whirring sound flowing from the engine. I tried to look inside, but all of the windows aside from the front were covered with dark curtains. Finally it stopped right next to me and a side window near the back raised. A man with dark black hair graying at the temples stuck out his head and asked, "Are you Curtis Matricks?"

"Yes," I answered, trembling a little. The sight of the automobile had overwhelmed me.

"The Curtis Matricks who won the Star Astronomical Contest?" the man asked.

I nodded.

The window slid back into place and I stood aghast. Then the door suddenly swung open and the man stuck out his hand. He smiled broadly, showing twin rows of bright white teeth. His eyes were black and glistened with moisture so that they almost looked like the view of a star-filled night sky through a telescope. He leaned out of the motorcar, ruffling his black business suit. "My name is Mason Star, and I have a proposition for you."

I stepped out of the ditch toward him and extended my hand. As soon as he grasped my hand, he shook it vigorously and then pulled. I was taken by surprise by the tug and was hauled into the automobile under his strength. As I entered, I stumbled slightly and then fell onto a seat inside next to Star.

"Drive on," Star said, shutting the door. The driver nodded and the motorcar began whirring again as the scenery outside flew by.

I first looked out the window, a little anxious, and then examined the automobile. There was the driver's seat in front and then two couches in the back that faced one another. Each was covered in the finest leather that I had ever seen. Aside from the driver, Star, and myself, there was another person, a girl a few years younger than myself. She had long red hair that glimmered similarly to a warm fire. Her eyes were the same sparkling black as those of Mr. Star.

"This is my daughter, Mary," Star said, introducing us. Mary smiled slightly and nodded politely.

"How do you do?" I said, returning her smile.

Star immediately burst into speech, interrupting any answer she might have given. "As I said, Curtis, I have a proposition for you. Firstly, however, you must swear to secrecy despite what your decision is."

My curiosity took the better of me and I immediately promised silence.

Star smiled. "I'm much too old of a businessman to follow the word of someone I've never met before." He nodded to Mary, who opened a drawer from under her seat. She took out a legal folder and a pen and handed them to me.

Puzzled, I opened it to discover an affidavit that outlined my agreement to silence until the date of January the first, nineteen hundred and one. It seemed fair as all I had to do was not divulge any information given to me by Star until that day, which was only two and a half months away. I signed it and then handed the folder back to Mary. After examining the signature, she placed the folder back in drawer under her seat.

"Very well, then," Star said. "As I'm sure you know, you were the first place winner of my astronomy contest. You did exceedingly well, in fact. You scored two points higher on the exam than Dr. Alan Glen, the man who led the team that created it."

I smiled, very impressed with myself.

Star continued, "Dr. Glen was formerly the head of my personal astronomical panel. However, he had a very terrible accident on a hunting trip the day after the results of the test were sent out. Thus, he's not able to fulfill his duties for me any longer, and I need a new head of astronomy. I toyed with the idea of using one of my other astronomers, but I finally decided that you, with your exceptional... I might even say 'stellar,' eh? ... your stellar skills, would be the greatest choice for the position. And so I hurried across the Atlantic to find you and, well, to try to draft you."

I nodded and asked, "So, what exactly would I be doing for you?"

"You'll lead a group of six other astronomers scanning the skies, cataloging what you find, and, most importantly, examining the surfaces of the planets."

I raised an eyebrow in curiosity. I could understand someone with a massive shipping company needing to navigate by the stars, but the planets puzzled me. "The surfaces of the planets?" I repeated. "Why would we need to do that?"

The elder Star glanced over at the younger, whose mouth twitched slightly. He then leaned forward very seriously. The right corner of his mouth pulled up a bit, giving him a fiendish smirk. "We will need to know just where we're heading."

"Heading?" I asked, and then my mouth gaped. "You don't mean..."

"Oh, I do," Star said, nodding slowly. "Are you aware of Star's Tower? I'm sure it has been in the Colonial newspapers at least a bit."

I struggled to remember. Being from rural Ohio, I rarely heard international news. Finally a rough idea came to me. "Well, I've heard that it was some project of yours that just kept climbing into the sky. Workers were always going up and building more, but I'm not sure I know why." I then remembered snidely commenting that I doubted anyone knew what purpose it could possibly serve.

Star smiled. "That's good for a start. To tell you the truth, Star's Tower is essentially my own Tower of Babel, you might say. My effort to reach the heavens. Unlike the one of old, my Tower has been successful. It stretched out of sight, so most of those who saw it thought that it was nothing more than a giant pinnacle of a wealthy eccentric's insanity. Those I hired to work on its construction were sworn to secrecy, so the rumor of my lunacy stayed afloat.

"Oh, but it was much, much more. My Tower stretched up into an orbit around the Earth itself. As soon as it reached this height, it was six years ago, I ended work on the Tower and began a new project: a vehicle capable of travel between the worlds of our solar system. Workers still kept quiet and kept going up and down the Tower, just as they had since I had started building it in 1881. No one suspected that such a different, greater project was being performed.

"I've invested much time, money, and effort into this 'Starship' (I've named it after myself, of course) and in sixty-four days it will leave its port at the top of the Tower and become one of the greatest human achievements in the entire history of human achievements."

"Wow," I whispered. That one word of awe was all that I could utter. I had ten thousand questions running through my head, but they refused to come to my mouth.

"So, Curtis," Star said, sighing the words out slowly and leaning back into a comfortable position in his seat, "do you wish to be the astronomer of my expedition?"

My eyes were very wide with excitement. "Oh, very much so, sir! Who in their right mind would pass up a chance like this?"

"Good, good." Star smiled, nodding happily. "Jenkins," he said to the driver, "turn us around and head back to the Matricks farm. I believe Curtis will have some planning to do." The driver nodded and slowed the automobile.

Mary, silent and watchful up to this moment, handed me a yellow envelope. "Train ticket, pass onto the *Commencement*, and a note and check for your cab once you arrive in Liverpool," she said, outlining the contents of the envelope.

"You'll have one week to put your affairs in order before your train leaves from Dayton," Star said. "That ought to be ample time for goodbyes."

"Yeah," I agreed. I could not help but riffle through the contents of the envelope.

"You'll also need this," Mary said, passing me an enormous book. I took it, with much effort, and laid it heavily on my lap. The title read *Etiquette and Information for the* Star's Comet. I flipped through some of the pages, finding detailed sketches and thousands of words in small print.

"You should try to commit it to memory as soon as possible," Star said. I swallowed and glanced at the innumerable facts. Star seemed to have noticed and added, "If necessary, though, you may need to bring it with you."

My family's comfortable red farmhouse appeared in the window. I suddenly had the feeling that Star had been taking me home already, knowing that I would agree. The automobile stopped in the yard in front of the house, and my mother waved from the porch.

As I opened the door and stepped out, Star said, "You'll forgive us for not coming in with you. I've already explained this to your parents and they seemed overjoyed about it. Right now, we must be in Dayton as soon as possible to catch a train back to my ship."

He stopped me to shake my hand. "Good luck, and I'm looking forward to seeing you in a few weeks. And remember: complete secrecy!"

With that, he slammed the door, and the automobile began to move again. It turned and sped out of the yard and onto the road. Its whirring sound slowly died as I watched after it as it dashed away. I stood there for a long while, trying to sort everything out in my mind. It all was too much, much too much, for a young Ohioan farm boy. The time I stood there amazed seemed much longer than the next few weeks, at the end of which I found myself standing at the gates of Mason Star's astounding estate.

Chapter Two,
Arrival at Star's Manor

It was a dreary winter day in the English countryside when I arrived at Star's manor. I stepped out of the horse-drawn cab, pulled my coat tight around me, and waved farewell to the cabbie. He gave me a quick wave in return and then drove away, whistling happily over his ample payment for the distant trip.

I was now standing alone at the gates that led into the estate of Mason Star, the wealthiest eccentric that the world had ever known. Though the sky was overcast, I could see the faint outline of tall, thin metal tower that stretched up until I could see it no more. The gates were made of cast iron with twin giant 'S's imprinted on the two half-gates. Brick walls extended off of them and disappeared into thick forests in each direction. A small booth stood against the wall to the right of the gates. I looked through the fence, but could see nothing more than a twisting black asphalt lane that continued over a hill and out of sight. I could not hear anything but the wind blowing in the branches of the leafless trees on either side of me. The English world suddenly seemed very lonely.

The trip to England had been long, but fairly interesting. One week after Star and his daughter had left me at my family's farm, I boarded a train that took me directly from Dayton to the gigantic city of New York. I carried with me several cold lunches that my mother had packed for me and a single traveling bag. According to Star's *Etiquette* book, each traveler on the *Comet* was allowed one cubic foot of personal items and no more. Clothing would be provided, and I needed only to bring what I would wear on the voyage to England. I decided that the immense book would be one of my items and thus gave up one-fourth of my allotted volume. I then packed two blank books for keeping a journal and several pencils. That left room for several pictures of my family and friends, my toothbrush and other toiletry items, and a pocket watch given to me by my parents on my fifteenth birthday. The only other objects I brought with me were several changes of clothes and a wallet with my winnings from Star's contest.

Once I arrived in New York City, I made immediately for the harbor. I flagged a taxi and rode amazed at the colossal city around me. People seemed to be everywhere, pouring from the alleys and tall buildings onto the streets. The clothes worn by the multitudes were up-to-date, just like the expensive suits that hung in the mercantile shop in which my brother worked. Only the most impractical Ohioans wore such extravagances. I soaked in the city all the way to the harbor, and arrived with only minutes to spare before my ship, the *Commencement*, left port. I paid the cabbie out of my winnings and ran aboard the ship.

I spent the entire sea voyage pouring over the book of etiquette. Well, in reality, no, I did not. I actually spent the first two days quite ill from the constant rocking of the ship. Once I had gained my sea-legs, as they are called, I reviewed my book and nearly read the entirety of it. I rarely left my room, only for meals and when I could take staring at the book no more. When I did leave, it would be only a few moments before I returned to my study.

The book was simply amazing. It began with a history of Mason Star and his heritage. His father Maxwell had taken a small family-owned fishing fleet and refitted it for overseas trade. He had made a sizeable fortune in textiles before he died. At that point, Mason, who was quite young at the time, took over the trading company and further expanded it. By the time he was thirty, he had become one of the wealthiest men alive. He began to use his wealth with exceedingly large projects. He first spent five years adding to the family mansion, which, from the sketches provided, was simply massive.

In 1881, he began to build Star's Tower. It continued up into the sky for the next eight years. The Tower was an amazing piece of engineering. The French engineer Eiffel, with a team of radical but amazingly intelligent architects, designed the mammoth structure. The Tower itself was nothing more than a huge grid work that sprawled into the sky. Under the Tower was an abandoned coalmine that Star filled with supports spreading out from the base of the Tower. Not even high winds in the atmosphere could knock over the massive Tower. To combat stresses that might snap the Tower, electromagnetic locks were placed throughout the Tower. Whenever a strong wind pushed on the Tower, a current would automatically run through the magnets, thus reinforcing the Tower. I was amazed at the Tower and spent much time simply staring at the rough schematics with my mouth agape.

The epic continued with the construction of the Sky Train. As the Tower soared up into the sky, it became more and more difficult to deliver workers and materials to the construction site. Fortunately, Star had realized this from the first and construction of a special lightweight, electric vertical train had already begun. The wheels of the Train were cogs that fit exactly into a track with indents. As the wheels turned, the cogs would climb up the indented track and thus the Train would rise vertically up the Tower. Because the atmosphere thinned as the Train climbed, it was electric instead of steam, powered by a cable that ran from the powerhouse on Star's Manor.

When the Tower finally stretched into open Space, the workers capped it with a large platform. The platform, weightless as it orbited around the Earth, had several warehouses and a large main building at one end in which the Sky Train docked. The building was ornate and filled with seating, much like Grand Central Station in New York. The platform also had a large, open semi-oval, the docking place of the *Comet*, and soon other Starships.

Finally work began on the *Star's Comet* in 1894. The ship was immense, with numerous holds, bunkrooms, and open bays. I thought that the most amazing thing I had ever seen had been the drawings of the Tower, but now the *Comet* astonished me even more. I could not even imagine being on board such an amazing ship.

After the history came detailed maps and descriptions of Star's manor. I flipped through them, reading whatever caught my eye, but I did not have time to carefully review the manor as I had to move onto the study of etiquette onboard the *Comet*.

There were possibly a thousand listed rules, each detailing what one should or should not do. For example, only Star clothing was to be allowed onboard the ship, as the lack of gravity in Outer Space would make Earth clothing uncomfortable and possibly embarrassing. Both men and women would be on the vessel, but because there was only one room suited for toilets, entrance was determined by hour: males having access to the private room on even hours and females on odd hours. Even language was controlled by Star's rules. Any formal conversation must take place in English, which would stand as the primary medium on the ship, but private conversations could take place in whatever language the speakers deemed practical. A list of unseemly words in several languages that were not to be spoken onboard the *Comet* followed these rules. As I continued to read the lengthy list of practical, odd, and even bizarre set of laws, I often fell asleep in the gentle rocking of the ship on its way to England.

Now I stood outside of the gate, stunned for a moment. Finally, I took a deep breath and entered the booth to the right of the gate. Inside was a telephone with the Bell logotype planted firmly upon it. I picked up the phone and saw a light come on above me. Star certainly had a flare for technology. I spoke into the machine, "Hello?"

A moment passed and then a voice at the end said, "Ahoy?"

"This is Curtis Matricks," I said, clearing my throat, "here as a guest of Mr. Star."

There was a short pause before the voice replied, "Ah, yes, he has been expecting you. A car will be out shortly to pick you up."

"Thank you," I said. Since there was no further reply, I hung up the telephone and left the booth to wait outside.

The impressive English silence struck me again. Nothing between the winter grass and the gray sky made a sound, except for my own breathing and the slight rustling of the trees. I sighed and put my hands in my pockets to wait.

Suddenly, a soft whirring sound pierced the quiet. I looked through the gate and saw an automobile identical to the one in which I had first met Mason Star. The silver siding of this motorcar did not have Ohio dust, but the roof of the automobile and the top of its hood were covered with the same small black panels.

I had read about these panels in Star's book, in which he called them "the single most important invention of the expedition." These Solar Energy Collectors took in sunlight and converted it to electrical energy. An innovative electrician named Gregor van Sparchs had invented them for Star in 1883 and Star had immediately implemented them into use. The panels were actually quite sturdy against rain and made excellent roofing. After the article about the panels came another article in which Star outlined future plans to make these panels cheaply produced and sold throughout the world.

As the automobile approached, the gates opened wide. I stepped back to make sure that I was not in their way and watched the automobile slowly come to me. It stopped next to me and a back door swung open. Mary, Star's daughter, peered out and smiled pleasantly. "Hello," she said.

"Hi," I said, and then bit my tongue at the sound of my rural American accent. I stepped into the automobile and shut the door behind me.

"Take us back, Han," Mary said to the driver. He nodded and pulled the automobile into a wide circle to turn around. Mary turned to me and said, "I trust you had a nice journey."

"It went well," I said as the memory of my seasickness suddenly came back to me.

"Good," she said.

"Has everything been going well here?" I asked. I hated to make small talk, but nothing more would come into my mind.

"It has been quite busy," Mary said, rolling her eyes. "Father has been up late many nights barking orders and directing this and that. Unfortunately for me, he needs someone to take his notes for him." She paused, snickered, and added, "He has ghastly handwriting and so I attend him as a sort of secretary, I suppose."

I thought about that for a moment and did not reply. The automobile had reentered the gates and was heading up the hill toward the interior of Star's estate. As we approached the top of the hill, I strained my eyes to peer out of the front window. When the estate came into my view, my mouth gaped and I blinked several times in wonder.

The estate was more like a small city than a rich industrialist's abode. Star's large mansion, made of crimson brick and trimmed with bright-painted white, towered over the rest of the buildings that stood in front of it. The other buildings were numerous and in every thinkable shape. Several were cubes made from brick with chimneys and other columns sticking out from the interior. One curiously had enormous tanks on top of it. Others were small buildings that looked to be serving as houses. All of the buildings, however, had the same small black panels as roofing. Black asphalt streets were laid out among the buildings. Trees, all barren of their leaves, stood amid the buildings to add aesthetic pleasure to the scene. Several people strode around on the streets, but ours was the only vehicle in sight. Behind it all, and most impressive, was the enormously tall Star's Tower.

"We were just sitting down to dinner and we heard that you had arrived," Mary said. I turned from the window to face her. "I hope you would join us."

"Sure," I said, nodding. I dug my watch out of my pocket and checked the time. It was later than I had thought. The overcast English sky must have made the lowering of the sun nearly indistinguishable from noon.

Within moments the automobile had entered the village built around Star's mansion. I stared, soaking it all into my system. I had studied several maps of the estate from Star's book, but I had never imagined that it would be this impressive.

"I could take you on a tour of the manor tomorrow if you like," Mary said. She must have been observing my astonishment. I nodded, signifying that I would like a tour. I had planned on saying something as well, but the words would not formulate in my mouth. Fortunately, Mary continued by saying, "It will give me a chance to escape Father for a time."

Finally the driver stopped the automobile in front of the mansion. Mary opened the door and stepped out. As I followed her out, she said to the driver, "Thank you, Han. I doubt if we'll need you any longer tonight."

"Yes, Miss," the driver said. "I'll stow the car and head home then."

I shut the door behind me, and the driver drove away in the automobile. Mary began walking up the steps in front of the mansion toward the front door. I stood there a moment, staring at the enormous house. It was five stories tall and wonderfully decorated. Large white marble steps led up into a columned patio that served as an entry porch. Above the patio was a balcony with an enormous script 'S' surrounded in ivy cast from brass. A huge wooden double door with carved wooden ivy upon it stood impressively as the entrance.

"Aren't you coming?" Mary asked from the front door causing me to snap from my amazement.

"Oh, yes," I gasped. I hurried up the steps and to her. She pulled the door open and we entered into a small passage that served as an entry hall.

An elderly man dressed in a black butler's suit nodded as we came in. "I'll take your coat and bag to your room, sir," the butler said. Not used to being called "sir," I stared at him for a short moment before I realized that he was speaking to me. I then smiled apologetically and handed him my bag and, quickly removing my coat, gave it to him as well.

Mary then led me through a second set of doors at the far end of the hallway. As I passed through them, I could not help but gasp. The hallway that we had been in before was nothing more than a threshold to the true entrance hall. The room had an extremely high ceiling and its walls were incredibly far apart. Expensive furniture lined the walls and made clusters in some areas of the room almost like smaller rooms in themselves. A large red carpet led away from the entry to the left and right into hallways and then forward up an amazing marble staircase. At the top of the stairs was a huge balcony that led into the upstairs rooms of the house. A small polished wooden balcony was on each of the sidewalls and promised to be excellent for viewing or performing music. I felt completely overwhelmed and struggled merely to breathe as I gazed at the wonder of Star's mansion's entry room.

"You seem impressed," Mary chuckled.

"You could fit my entire house in here," I whispered. It was probably a true statement rather than hyperbole, too. The room was unlike anything I had ever seen, so massive and impressively decorated. I asked, "And you live here?"

"I'm sure one does used to it, eventually," Mary smiled. "Come now, they're waiting for us."

Mary turned to the right and followed the red carpet down a hallway. I followed, but had trouble keeping up with her pace, even though it was not quick. I kept pausing to look at paintings that hung on the wall or glancing at doors and wondering where they led. I even became so entranced with a suit of medieval armor that I stumbled on the carpet and barely recovered my footing before I fell.

Finally we arrived in the dining room and I once again found myself overwhelmed. The room was rectangular with a huge window studded with colored glass at one of the smaller walls and a gigantic fireplace at the other. The ceiling was high here, too, but not quite as high. Three huge electric chandeliers hung over the room. Ornate molding surrounded the edges of the walls and tapestries hung down the long walls. The main feature of the room was an enormous dining table that stretched for what seemed like miles. There was a cluster of people at the left end of the table near the fireplace, which was burning merrily.

"Ah, you've arrived, Curtis!" a loud voice called. I immediately recognized the speaker as Mason Star, a man one does not forget very easily. Mary and I walked briskly toward the voice.

As we approached, Star stood from his seat at the head of the table. He caught me by the hand and shook it with a strong grip. I smiled and said, "Hello, sir. I'm glad that I could make it."

"So are we, lad, so are we," Star said. He motioned toward the others at the table. "Allow me to introduce you. This is my wife, Alexis," he said, motioning toward a woman with fiery red hair very similar to that of Mary. She looked younger than Mason, but her sharp green eyes showed enormous wisdom. She was wearing a fashionable dress and amazing diamonds on her necklace and ears. She smiled pleasantly, surprisingly similar to the smile that Mary had given me weeks before in Ohio.

"And this is Mark, my son." Mark, a dark-headed youth about eight or nine years old, stood and shook my hand. He smiled and looked slightly fiendish. I imagined that Mason Star had the same look about him when he was a youngster.

Star then motioned to an elderly man in a gray suit with thin spectacles, the last diner at the table. "And this is Dr. Gregor van Sparchs."

Van Sparchs nodded and then stood to bow slightly. "It iz a pleasure," he said with a heavy German accent.

"The pleasure's all mine," I answered. "I've been looking forward to meeting the inventor of the 'single most important invention,' in Mr. Star's opinion."

Van Sparchs chuckled. "He'z read your book, Mason."

Star chuckled in return and then said, "Well, sit. I'm sure you're famished."

Mary and I took seats next to van Sparchs. In seconds, two maids entered and placed plates before us. I gazed upon the food, trying not to look too much like a bumpkin. There was some kind of meat (pheasant, I supposed), rice, and steamed vegetables, all covered with thin gray gravy. The maid who had given me the plate then filled my glass with a light purple fluid. Once Mary and I were served and Star had given a blessing, everyone began to eat.

I reached to pick up my fork, but discovered several dozen forks instead of just one. There were probably more forks next to my plate than my parents had in their entire silver set. I struggled to remember my mother's numerous lectures on dinner etiquette, but finally picked up the fork with which everyone seemed to be eating. Confident that I had gotten away with my ignorance, I cut and then ate a piece of meat. It was surprisingly moist and I was quite impressed with the eating style of the British elite.

"So how was the trip over, Curtis?" Star asked.

I swallowed the vegetables in my mouth and then hurried to answer. "Quite all right. I spent most of my time looking at your *Etiquette and Information for the Star's Comet*. I didn't quite finish it all, but I have studied the majority of it."

"Seriously?" Star seemed impressed. "I don't know of anyone that has spent that much time on it… You didn't read the entire thing, did you, Gregor?"

"Zertainly not," van Sparchs shook his head and grimaced. "You probably leveled a large forest printing each of those books."

"So no one knows the etiquette for the ship?" I asked Star, a little confused.

"Well, I'm sure they all glanced through the etiquette portion. I doubt very much that they studied any of the information or maps. And if they didn't learn the etiquette, I'm sure they'll pick it up very quickly. You did read the section on punishments, didn't you?"

I winced. Star seemed serious about running a clean ship. The book stated that he would assign punishments as he saw fit and then gave a lengthy list of possible punishments. One could be locked in the ship's brig, forced to do extra rounds of duty, or even made to read and then be tested over the contents of the book. "They seemed pretty creative."

Star smiled. "True, but I'm sure we won't have too many problems. I've hand-selected everyone who'll be on the *Comet*. They're the best and brightest that the Earth has to offer."

"Just remember, Mason," Star's wife spoke up, "you promised that you'd bring them home safely. If we lost them, progress could set back a century."

Star smiled more broadly. "I'll do my best."

The dinner conversation paused here for several moments. Finally, van Sparchs broke the silence with a joke about a Frenchman visiting Russia. The joke must have been limited to Europeans, because my American sense of humor could not find anything amusing about it at all. Still, I faked a pretty good laugh along with the others.

When we had finished our meal, Star called for dessert. We each received a small bowl of ice cream with a topping made from several fruits. The ice cream was refreshing, but I certainly thought that my mother's homemade cream that we iced during cold spells was much better.

Finally Star leaned back in his chair and contentedly sighed. "I hate to excuse myself, but I really must make sure that the Electrolysis Lab is functional again tonight."

He stood and began to leave the dining room. Mark stood from his seat and hurried to his father's side. "Will you be there for the next chapter tonight?"

"Definitely," the senior Star said and then left the room.

I glanced at Mary with a questioning eye. "They're reading Verne's *From the Earth to the Moon* before Father takes his own journey," she whispered. "Quite fitting, isn't it?"

I nodded and thought about nothing for a moment. I was brought back to reality by van Sparchs loudly scooting back his chair and standing. "I believe dat I will retire as well. I am sure dat Mason will have me very busy tomorrow inspecting de Electrolysis Laboratory."

"You should probably show Mr. Matricks to his room, Mary," Mrs. Star said. Mary nodded and we both stood. We left the room just behind van Sparchs, leaving Mrs. Star and Mark alone in the dining room.

Mary and I once again entered the intriguing luxury of the corridors of

Star's mansion. I tried not to let myself get too absorbed in examining the amazing items that decorated the mansion and to keep up with Mary. We went back to the main entrance hall and walked up the grand white staircase. When we reached the top, I paused to turn and look at the hall from above. It was still exceedingly spectacular, but I tore myself away from staring to follow Mary.

We walked down another hallway until we came to a small study. I say "small" relatively to Star's largest rooms here, as the study was certainly larger than the parlor in my parents' house. There was a polished wooden staircase that led up another floor. Mary and I climbed these stairs and came to another corridor. We walked down it and passed three doors, and then Mary stopped.

"This is your room," she said. She pulled a small key from the pocket of her dress and handed it to me. "The guest bathroom is down the hall two more doors. You won't miss it; the door has a porcelain brush for a handle."

I nodded and walked to the door of my room. I slid the key into the lock and turned until it clicked. As I swung the door open, my eyes once again widened at splendor. My bedroom had green carpeting and polished wooden walls. A table stood by the fireplace and had two comfortable chairs that faced toward the hearth. A desk with a leather chair was set in the corner by a large curtained window. A small electric chandelier hung from the ceiling and there were lamps on the desk and by the bed. The bed itself was the largest and most comfortable-looking bed that I had ever seen.

Mary giggled. "Is it satisfactory?"

I struggled to form a sentence. "Well, definitely. I mean, yes."

"Very well," Mary said. "Your bag is on the table and your closet has any other clothes you might need. If you need laundry or anything whatsoever, just use the telephone on the bedstand. When you're ready for breakfast tomorrow, call and someone will bring it to you. I'll take you on a tour after breakfast."

"Thanks," I said. She nodded and then left the room.

Now alone, I smiled to myself and jumped onto the bed. I stretched and sunk into the mattress. After sleeping on a thin bunk onboard an Atlantic liner, the bed seemed like something magical. Rather than even thinking, I just lay there for a moment, soaking in the comfort.

Suddenly there was a knock at my door. I groaned quietly, but then pulled myself up from the bed. I strode across the room and opened the door. On the other side was an average-looking man with brown hair and brown eyes. He wore a common brown suit and had a trendy hairstyle. Everything about him seemed normal except for a strange necklace. Around his neck he had a black vine from which hung the skull of some kind of rodent.

"*Salve*," the man greeted me. He smiled widely and caused his eyebrows to jump above his face. I immediately feared for my life. My first instinct was to slam the door, but before I could, he leapt into the room.

"Uh, may I help you?" I asked.

"Just a friendly visit," he said. He extended his hand and continued, "My name's Lukas Conners. Most just call me Luke. I've also been called *Mak'galla'heolea*, which roughly translates to 'He who speaks like the owl.' I was never sure quite why I talked like an owl, but that's what they called me."

" 'They'?" I asked.

"The Hagoola tribe of the Chihuahua desert. I spent two years with them while I was…" He trailed off and smiled nervously.

My jaw dropped as I suddenly realized to whom I was speaking. "Wait a moment! Conners? You're not the Conners who sabotaged the Amazon Tea Company's merchant fleet several years ago, are you?"

"Well… yes," he said. He crossed the room and sat in one of the chairs near the fireplace. I followed him, half-interested in his story, half-frightened and wanting to keep a clear eye on him. As I sat down in the chair across the table from him, he explained himself. "You see, though, I had almost no other choice. At the time, I was living among the peoples of the Amazon jungle. I was teaching several language classes at Oxford and had gotten a grant from them to study these tribes. A group of ten of us left London and had sailed directly across the Atlantic and then up the Amazon. When we first met up with them, they killed all of my assistants. Well, that's just their way, I suppose. It's definitely a way to keep out any Conquistadors or Portuguese invaders, right?"

I could not help but agree. Wiping out any strangers who came near would be an effective way of keeping out any potential aggressors.

"Anyway," he continued, "I basically threw beads, trinkets, and shiny things at them until I was sure they wouldn't kill me. Finally, I traded my shoes to the chief for a small hut to live in."

"How'd you do that?" I asked. "I mean, could you speak their language?"

"Oh goodness, no!" he said, tossing his hands into the air for emphasis. "They had a peculiar language that even their trade partners in the jungle didn't know. It was made up of clicks and hisses and whistles, no sounds from the vocal chords at all."

"So how'd they trade without speaking to one another?"

"Well, languages are all pretty much the same: some kind of thing doing something at some place and point in time, possibly to something else, and how it's doing it. So there you've got nouns, verbs, adjectives, and prepositions all rolled up. Conjunctions just fit between ideas, and interjections get tacked on for good measure."

I recalled the many, many hours I had spent dissecting sentences and memorizing rules of languages. It all suddenly did not seem fair with his simplistic description of communication.

Conners changed the subject away from language and continued with his story. "I simply used some gestures pointing out objects (houses, shoes, et cetera) and motions like offering my shoes to the chief. So once I had moved into the village, I could closely study them. We got along quite well as I traded this and that for some of their artifacts. Soon enough they accepted me and invited me on hunting expeditions and to their rituals. It was very fascinating. I wrote a book about it. Have you read *Treatise on the Peoples of the Amazon*?"

I shook my head.

"Oh, that's right," he said, slapping his head as punishment for forgetting himself. "Oxford took that out of print after the little incident with the Tea Company.

"Speaking of which, here's my side of the story: The Amazon Tea Company had been founded to level a huge area of jungle and turn it into a fabulous plantation for making tea. Unfortunately, they had chosen lands that served as the primary hunting ground for my tribe. If they succeeded in building this plantation, my tribe would starve to death."

He suddenly stood and his voice became angry. I swallowed, a little nervous, and hoped this man was not as insane as he appeared. He clasped his hands behind his back and began to pace in front of the fireplace. "And then think of it, lad. With some clever packaging, their tea would explode onto the market. Every businessman in London would then think, 'Oh my! Such a fortune to be made in the Amazon!' What follows? The leveling of the entire Amazon and the extinction of dozens, if not hundreds, of little-known tribes. Think of all the knowledge that would be lost!"

"So you had to stop them," I said in a quiet voice.

"Exactly," he said. His voice softened, and he kneeled next to my chair. "All I did was swim out and plant a few charges on each of their ships. When the explosives blew, everybody leapt overboard and then ran to safety, which for them was all the way back in Almeirim. Nobody that I could tell was killed, except for the company. Its investors were shocked and seized the assets to be liquidated. I guess you could say I was the Knight of the Amazon or something to that extent."

"So what happened next?" I asked.

He stood, apparently calmer. "Well, the authorities came looking for me, but I hid in the jungle as long as I could. With the help of my tribesmates, I made it to a port where I could get a boat away from Brazil. I finally ended up in Chihuahua as an interpreter for a group of geologists looking for minerals in tribal lands."

"So how did you get attached to Star?" I asked. Conners was strange, albeit very intriguing.

"Star found me in Mexico," he said, reseating himself. "When he started getting ready for this whole expedition of his a few years ago, he sent letters to all of the universities in the western world and asked about their best linguists. His letter to Oxford was never answered. Apparently, they didn't want it to be known that the best language professor that they had ever had was also a criminal in hiding. Makes sense, though. One of my former students, however, caught word of Star's questions at Yale and wrote a letter describing me. It must have been quite a portrayal, because Star went out and hired a group of professional detectives to find me.

"It took them a while to do it, but they finally tracked me down. I was quite impressed when they did. I had a cover name, a fake story, and I had even grown a pretty heavy beard, but they finally traced me to the Hagoolas. Star himself came to Mexico to speak with me. He said that he could pull a few strings and get England to grant me asylum. I agreed and left with him the next day. Ever since then, I've been living at Star Manor and trying to squander as much of Star's money as I can."

"Squander?"

"Delicacies, mostly. It'd be a shame to have all of his money and not enjoy it like one should. I had him redo one of the rooms in the mansion into a sauna. You should try it some time; it's very pleasant. I also had him add several hundred volumes to his library. He finally stopped allowing me to order books and threatened to take my purchases out of my salary."

I laughed and said, "You must lead a pretty interesting life." After I had said it, I thought about replacing the word "interesting" with "insane."

He leaned back in his chair. "Yeah, pretty interesting. And I've lived almost everywhere. England, Paris, Italy, Egypt, the Amazon, Tibet, America, Mexico, and probably some others that I don't remember very clearly.

"So what about you? What's it like being the hand-selected lead astronomer of the expedition?"

"I must admit, it feels amazing," I said, feeling quite proud of myself. "Just a little while ago I was on the farm in Ohio. Since then, I've been on a train to New York City, a trans-Atlantic steamship, and now here in England inside a mansion bigger than I could have ever imagined."

"And in a little while longer you're going to be farther than any human being has ever been," Conners smiled. "By the way, Star said you scored even higher than old Glen did on his own test."

"He told me the same thing," I said.

"All right then." Conners's smile melted into a fiendish grin. "Where's Betelgeuse right now?"

I paused, not having expected a test like this. I stood and walked over to the window to see if the clouds had broken.

Conners stopped me. "Nope, no visuals. Just point out where it would be."

"Oh, okay," I said. I took out my watch and checked the local time, then paused. "Which way's north?"

Conners pointed toward the door to the hallway. I thought for a moment, recalling the coordinates of where I was. Finally, I pointed. Conners stared at me for a moment and pulled a piece of paper from his pocket. He studied it and then looked up at me with a gaped mouth.

"How in the world do you know that?" he asked, dumbfounded.

I shrugged. "Well, all I had to do is remember where Betelgeuse is, then translate for latitude and the time."

"Wow," he said, putting the paper back in his pocket. "It took me nearly an hour in the library to figure all of that out. I must say that's very impressive."

"Thanks." I smiled.

Conners stood and stretched. "Well," he said, "I suppose you'd probably like to be alone to get settled. I guess I'll see you some time later."

He headed for the door. As he opened it, I said, "Goodbye." With a slam, he was gone, and I was alone once again.

I yawned, feeling the fatigue of lengthy travel. My bag was on the bed, but I decided to check through my closet to see just what Star had provided for me. I opened the door and pulled a cord to ignite the electric light that hung from the ceiling.

The closet was narrow but quite deep. One side had clothes hung on hangars while the other had drawers. At the far end of the closet was a full-length mirror to make sure that one was properly attired. I rummaged through the drawers and found shirts, socks, shoes, and finally a set of pajamas. They were made of a warm black material and had a silver 'S' in script on the left breast.

I changed into the sleeping clothes and shut off the electric chandelier. I crossed the dark room and then climbed into the bed. The pillows were extraordinarily soft and were already fluffed to perfection. The blankets were warm and fit snugly around me. Before I could realize it, I was in a heavy, peaceful slumber.

Chapter Three,
The Tour

When I awoke, the room was filled with a soft light. I sat up and stretched and then wondered what time it was. I crawled out of the bed and crossed the room to the closet to dig my watch out of my pocket. Surprisingly, it was nearly ten o'clock in the morning. I had slept much later than I imagined I would.

I now looked through the closet, seeing what clothes I could find. Star had stocked it well with several suits of differing colors and some less formal clothing. Behind them all was a strange full-body suit. Curious, I pulled it off of the rack and held it up to the light.

The suit was like a glove for an entire body. It had the legs, arms, and torso all together in a single article of clothing. It was made of a thick black material, almost like canvas, but much softer. The edges of the sleeves and leggings had elastic bands within them that would make the suit fit quite snugly. The torso had a long open slit where one could step into the leggings and then pull the rest of the suit onto his body. Numerous buttons lined the slit and promised to close it tightly. Pockets were everywhere on the suit: on the upper arms, thighs, and chest.

And, of course, a silver 'S' was stitched on the left breast of the suit. His signature script 'S' seemed to be on everything he had. Star was a man with a gigantic ego, but he also had the ambition and resources to match it.

I placed the strange bodysuit back into the closet and chose a nice-looking black suit. After changing into it, I noticed the mirror in the back of the closet. I smiled and struck a dashing pose. I scanned the mirror for a moment and then laughed at myself. It was not often that I was able to wear such dignified clothes.

I then went through my bag until I found my comb and tamed my mop of hair. I poured water from the pitcher on my desk into the washbowl and washed my face and neck. Finally I deemed myself worthy to reenter society.

Remembering what Mary had told me the day before, I picked up the telephone from the desk. After a moment, a voice said, "May I help you?"

"Uh, yes," I said, not very used to calling for service. "This is Curtis Matricks. I was told that I should call for breakfast."

"Very well," the voice replied. "I'll take your order and send it to the kitchen. What would you like?"

I had not expected this much service. I struggled to think and finally came to a decision. "I would like some waffles. Two, I think. With orange juice and a slice of toast."

"Would you like syrup?"

I had forgotten syrup. "Uh, yes."

"What kind would you like?"

The sheer volume of possibilities was beginning to unnerve me. Aristocratic living must take some getting used to. "Maple."

"Very well. It will be sent to your room as soon as it is ready."

"Thank you," I said and hung up the phone.

I then slumped into the chair by the desk. I had not expected the task of calling for breakfast to be so exhaustive. All of this rich living no doubt had its effect on people.

After sitting for a few moments, I stood up and decided to inspect the bathroom before breakfast. I left my room and entered one of the enchanting corridors of Star's mansion. The wooden floors had long running red carpets upon them. The walls, all painted a vivid white, had paintings or tapestries hung on them.

I walked down the hallway, passing doors to probably other guestrooms. Finally I came to a large wooden door with a porcelain brush. I smiled, amused at the decoration's appropriateness as the doorknob to a bathroom.

I turned the brush and entered the bathroom. Instead of finding the normal interior of a bathroom, it was a short hallway with several doors off to the right side. I chose a door and opened it, revealing a small room with a tub, sink, and toilet. Only Star would have turned a single guest bathroom into a hallway full of bathrooms.

When I came back to my room, I found an elderly maid standing next to the bed. She was tucking the sheets and blankets into their correct positions and mumbling to herself. I watched her for a moment before she noticed me.

" 'Morning, gov," she said with a thick Cockney accent.

"Good morning," I responded. I then spotted a tray of food on the table near the fireplace.

"Rough night?" she asked, trying to disguise her annoyance as polite conversation. I had apparently kicked around some of the sheets as I got up, and she had found picking them up for me slightly frustrating. I concluded that she must be upset with Star's numerous guests and then wondered if Conners might have had anything to do with distressing her.

"No, it was fine," I said. I sat down to the table and began to eat. The waffles were very good, but the toast had been blackened a little too much. A copy of a London newspaper was set next to my tray, so I opened it to read while I ate.

The maid finished with the bed and approached me. "Miss Star said that she would be up to see you at the half hour. Is there anything else you need?" She eyed the open closet and my clothes lying in a jumble on the floor.

"Uh, yes," I said, swallowing a mouthful of waffle. "Could you have my clothes laundered?"

"Certainly, sir," she said. She picked up the clothes from the floor and then marched out of the room, shutting the door rather loudly behind her.

I turned back to the newspaper and my breakfast. The headline read of some train accident near London, but the paper was rather dull in itself. I quietly finished my breakfast and then flipped through the paper to check for any political cartoons. Suddenly I was interrupted by a knock at my door.

I jumped from my chair and hurried to the door. When I opened it, I saw Mary standing there, dressed in a dark green casual dress.

"Good morning," she said. "Are you ready?"

"Yes," I nodded. She turned and walked down the hallway, and I hurried after her. She always seemed to have a quick step.

We first toured the immense mansion, which was simply amazing. The first floor was entertaining the numerous guests of the Stars. The vast dining room and entrance hall were just two of many large, open rooms. The mansion also had a marble ballroom, several smaller music rooms, a theater, and then numerous studies and billiard rooms where smaller get-togethers could be held.

The second floor, designed for business affairs, followed. Star had a suite of offices that occupied nearly the entire second floor and ran his shipping company right from his own home. There were dozens of office boys and accountants who were running from desk to desk, calculating figures and making records. The entire floor had an air of frenzy about it. It seemed as if the people in the offices all thought that the world was about to end and that by working quickly and intensely they could postpone the date of Doomsday.

After seeing the second floor, we returned to the third, which was for guests and family business. Rooms were much smaller and cozier here. Most of the floor had guest rooms similar to mine as well as studies and miscellaneous quiet rooms. The rest of the floor was a collection of rooms that served as the private rooms of the Star family. Mary only took me into the Star living room and dining room, and I marveled at their simplistic nature. It was like a small home hidden within the gigantic mansion.

The fourth floor was a conglomeration of extra room and furniture. Most of the rooms were decorated with furnishings that the Stars had collected during their trips all over the world. The immense library occupied a large portion of the fourth floor. Books surrounded the walls and several shelves stood on the floor by themselves. I decided that given a thousand years, I might be able to skim over most of the books in the library.

Conners was in the stacks, buried in a pile of books. He was so wrapped up in his reading that he did not even notice us when we spotted him. His face had an angry expression on it, as though he was furious with what he was reading. I imagined him as a kind of insane Hamlet, scurrying about the library and fanatically reading books. Mary and I chuckled at him and then moved on to the fifth floor.

The fifth floor served as a large storage area. Vast rooms were filled with tarp-covered furniture and boxes of this or that. It also held many of the utilities of the house. Huge storage tanks filled with water took up much of the fifth floor to supply the mansion with water: hot, cold, and tepid. The hydraulic engines for the elevators and dumbwaiters also found their places here. Numerous wires ran down from the solar panels that roofed the house. The wires led to several large batteries and from there the energy supplied the mansion's abundant electrical devices.

After seeing what there was to see on the fifth floor, Mary and I took an elevator down to the basement of the vast Star mansion. Here there were the kitchens (lined with stone and placed deep in the cool earth to prevent possible fires) and the cellars of wines and foodstuffs. There was even a suite of cool rooms for people to retreat to in the case of unusually hot weather.

Finally, we climbed a set of stairs and reappeared on the first floor behind the staircase in the entrance hall. I felt exhausted, but also exhilarated. The house was utterly amazing and I could have spent weeks exploring every nook and cranny in it.

"Now we can have a lunch and tour the grounds afterward," Mary said. Her voice seemed slightly hoarse, which was understandable since she had spent several hours telling me tales of what one room was and from where certain items in the house came.

"Sounds good," I agreed. She then led us back into the enormous main dining room. With only two of us in it, it seemed even larger than before.

She opened a cabinet next to the fireplace and pulled out a telephone. I shook my head in disbelief. Star had rigged his house with the most modern conveniences in every room of his gigantic mansion. She soon finished the call for lunch and we seated ourselves at the edge of the table near the fireplace.

"It kind of seems like too much," I mumbled.

"What does?" she asked.

"Well," I began my explanation, "using this huge room for just a simple lunch. I mean, we could fit maybe a hundred people in here, but there's only the two of us. There's practically an echo from the emptiness of the room."

"Oh," she said. "Are all Americans so distressed by living a little extravagantly?"

I chuckled. "Not at all. We have our fair share of lavishness, believe me. I guess I'm just a practical Ohio farm boy."

"Well, if the house is unnerving, we could find a cottage on the grounds for you to move into," she offered.

"No, that's all right," I declined. "It's an interesting change of pace to live in a place where my former house could fit in a single room."

A maid suddenly walked into the dining room pushing a small cart with a silver cover. She pushed it to the table and removed the cover to reveal twin trays of sandwiches, soup, and glasses of water. Mary thanked the maid, who bowed and left us to our meal. We ate quickly, I wishing to see the rest of the manor and Mary keeping up with my pace.

When we were finished and ready to move along, Mary called the maid to clean up the dishes while I struggled to contain my anticipation. She then led the way out of the dining room and down several corridors in the mansion. At last we came to a door that led outside.

"We'll see if we can get a car," Mary said, opening the door. "That way we won't need to walk too much." We stepped through the doorway and into the wintry English air. The sky was still overcast, but the world was brighter than yesterday. We walked down a long sidewalk with a pillared roof over it. It led to what seemed to be a large coach house. When we entered the coach house, however, it was much more than I imagined.

It was a long building with many doors, exactly like a coach house would be. However, instead of holding coaches and horses, it held a small fleet of automobiles. At least a dozen were identical silver-sided automobiles like the one that Star had ridden in the first day we met. There were several trucks for freight and large loads. Many of the marked spaces for parking the automobiles were empty.

"Wow." I whistled. I had only rarely seen a single automobile before, and now I was gazing at several dozen.

A tall, gaunt man in a derby and dirty clothes approached us. He smiled at Mary, checked me over, and then asked, "What can we do ya for, Miss?"

"Is my car available, George?" Mary asked.

"I set it to recharging last night," he said. "It should be good to go."

Mary smiled fiendishly, a mark that seemed to run in the Star family. "There aren't any available drivers, are there?"

"Nope, Miss," George winked. "We've got a big order coming in, so most of the trucks and nearly all of the drivers are down at the train station picking it up. I suppose you'll just have to drive yourself."

"Too bad," she said. "Make sure you tell Father that I requested a driver."

"Will do," he said and tipped his hat. He turned and walked to a desk in the near corner of the automobile house. He then opened a drawer and began riffling through it.

"What was that about?" I asked.

"Father doesn't approve of me driving on my own." She smiled. "George and I have an understanding, though."

George found what he was looking for in the drawer and hurried back to Mary. He handed her a pair of keys and warned, "Don't go too fast, now; he may spot you."

"All right," Mary said. She turned and hurried to the far corner of the automobile house. I followed after her, smiling as I sensed her excitement.

We finally came to a particular automobile. It was painted a cheery red and was much smaller than the other automobiles. It only had two seats and looked to be designed to be compact and charming. The roof of the automobile was made of a thick black tarp over a metal frame.

"Help me lower the cover," she said. "Trust me, it's quite exhilarating."

We grabbed opposite sides of the top and pulled back on it. The tarp at first refused to move, but then budged and slid back as the frame folded into a small stack. We then opened the doors to the motorcar and sat in the seats, Mary behind the steering wheel.

She took the keys that George had given her and unlocked a small panel on the dashboard of the automobile. The panel slid out of place and revealed a set of complicated controls. Mary expertly flipped several switches and the automobile came to life with a familiar whirring sound. Mary then drove the automobile out of its parking place and out through a door opened by George. She waved to him and then accelerated wildly.

I gripped the side of the seat, not knowing what to expect. She seemed to know what she was doing, so I relaxed a little bit and tried to enjoy the ride. Without the top, the wind whistled around the front window and passengers. It created a strange feeling, but was very intriguing.

"It's amazing to see so many automobiles and not a single horse," I said.

"Father hates horses," Mary explained. "I think he has an allergy to them, but he never admits to it."

We drove down the streets of the small village around the mansion. Most of the buildings were small houses, but a few were large structures that looked almost like factories. They were all very similar, however, and seemed to match the motif of the mansion with bricks, white trimming, and black energy panel roofs.

The little automobile sped along until we arrived at a large building with large metallic tanks on top of it. Mary stopped the automobile with a jerk in front of it. "This is the water plant for the village. It has storage tanks that holds the water, which flows through pumps and then out to pipes throughout the village."

I nodded to show her that I was listening. She asked, "Do you want to go in and look around or just move on?"

"I'd like to take a look," I said. She nodded and we left the automobile. We met up with a man named Nash who supervised the water plant. He was a large, jolly man who showed us everything with great interest. By the time we left the plant, I felt that I could have written a dissertation about the water system of Star Manor.

We continued on throughout the manor, seeing everything one could imagine. Star had an enormous laboratory designed specifically for electrolysis, the changing of water into hydrogen and oxygen gas. Mary explained that the laboratory was the most expensive building to keep in operation. The electrodes that ran electricity through the water constantly needed to be replaced. In addition, the large quantity of explosive gasses required extreme vigilance, but even so the laboratory had suffered its share of costly explosions. When I asked why all of this hydrogen and oxygen were needed, Mary simply said, "Fuel." I did not quite follow, but she said that I would understand when I saw the *Comet*.

We left the electrolysis laboratory and came to the electrical house that managed the electricity in the manor's village. Van Sparchs was there, barking orders, some in English, some in German. Whenever he made an aggravated German order, the workers would look at one another with questioning faces. Van Sparchs would turn red and repeat the order slowly in English. This happened not just once but at least five times while Mary and I were touring.

After a few more buildings, none of which were very exhilarating, we finished our tour of the village. We returned to Mary's automobile and as we got into it, she turned to me. "The only remaining thing to see on the Manor is the train depot. It's several miles away, so driving there would take some time. Do you want to see it?"

Something about the way she asked the question made it seem like an imperative. "Sure," I said. She smiled, a fiendish little smile apparently sparked by her desire to drive, and activated the small red automobile.

When its electric engine began to whir, she reversed the automobile onto the road and then accelerated forward wildly. She did this at every stop and I had gotten used to it; I even began to enjoy it.

We left the village behind and came into the open countryside. Sheep grazed on both sides of the black asphalt road and kept away from danger by a wire fence. The forest that grew on the manor could be seen spreading through the fields and making an outline around the edge of the manor. Aside from the whirring of the engine, there were no sounds. As opposed to yesterday where the silence was lonely, today it was peaceful.

I relaxed in the comfortable automobile seat and rested my heavily toured feet. Then suddenly an idea came into my head. I thought about it for a moment, measuring whether or not I should follow it. Finally, I decided to pursue it. Turning to Mary, I asked, "How fast can this automobile go?"

She looked at me for a moment before turning her eyes back to the road. She then said, "Right now we're going thirty-five miles per hour. I've gotten it up to fifty before. But we can always try for a new record."

I looked over at the speed dial on the dashboard, which indeed indicated to thirty-five miles per hour. Its maximum was forty, showing that Mary was already far beyond the limits of the suggested speed of her automobile.

"You may wish to hold onto something," she said and then immediately pressed as hard as she could on the accelerator. I gripped my chair just in time to keep from losing my balance and slamming into the back of my seat.

We accelerated wildly down the long, straight asphalt road. No one was in sight, only the green landscape flying by us. The engine whirred loudly, whining against the sheer velocity it was being forced to produce. I winced as the rushing air began to bend around the front window.

"Fifty-five!" Mary squealed in excitement. Her red hair was streaming behind her head, looking like a horizontal jet of fire.

I looked over at the speed dial again. It pointed to fifteen, but I assumed that it had spun around and began its second lap around the measurements. I watched it steadily rise to sixty miles per hour, a speed where one could cover the distance from my home to Dayton in fifteen minutes or go completely around the Earth in less than seventeen days.

Red lights began ignite on the dashboard. Mary sighed and took her foot off of the accelerator. The automobile began to slow and the force of the wind lessened. We finally came to a halt and Mary switched the automobile's engine off.

"What happened?" I asked.

Mary gripped the steering wheel tightly. "We started to overheat." She reactivated the engine and began flipping other switches. The whirring of the engine restarted, but then subsided as a windy whistle came in its place. The thermometer on the dashboard, formerly running high, slowly began to lower.

"I'll have to run the cooling fan for a bit," Mary explained. She leaned back in her seat and sighed. We sat in the automobile silently, waiting for the engine to recover.

In the distance, a black truck appeared over a hill, moving toward us. Another truck appeared behind it and another followed that. As the convoy approached, I recognized the trucks as identical to those in Star's coach house.

"Is this the delivery that George talked about?" I asked.

Mary nodded. "It's the last big one, too. After this, the only things coming in will be for the christening."

The trucks began to pass. Each of the drivers waved to us, but none stopped. They were going slowly, obviously trying to be extremely careful with their cargoes. I watched them go by and recognized an interesting symbol of the side of several crates.

"Mary," I asked, "isn't that the insignia for the Edison Company?"

"Yes," she nodded. "Father has taken a great shine to your country's Thomas Edison. He says that his ingenuity and expertise can't be beaten. Most of our orders for things we can't make here on the Manor come from

Edison's company."

"My brother works for Edison," I told her. "He never mentioned anything about Star in any of his letters, though."

Mary smiled. "You know how Father is about secrecy."

"Why is that?" I asked. I immediately bit my tongue, hoping that I did not sound too invasive. Curiosity about the subject had come into my head several times, but I had not yet asked anyone about it.

Mary did not seem to mind. "He's strange like that, I suppose. I think that he is trying to avoid too much public attention. Right now, everyone thinks that Star's Tower is just an eccentric work of art, perhaps. If they knew that he was working on a tower capable of reaching the stars, he'd be swamped with people trying to interview him or get a view of the Tower or who-knows-what."

I nodded and reviewed that idea in my brain. It seemed to make sense, but something seemed not completely right about that suggestion. We waited in silence until the convoy passed by us. Mary then began changing the switches on the dashboard until the engine whirred again. She smiled and the automobile began to move once again.

In a few minutes we arrived at the train station. It was a simple set-up with only a dock beside a stretch of railroad tracks, a watering and coaling tower, and then several buildings for storage. A train, sitting quietly, was waiting as people loaded and unloaded crates. Once parked near the dock, Mary and I got out of the automobile and climbed up onto the platform.

Mason Star was standing next to a conductor and giving orders. The workers bustled around them, pushing carts and loading crates onto the train. We watched the bustle for a moment before Star spotted us and waved us over to him, exactly the same motion he would give for any of his workers to whom he needed to speak.

"How's the tour, Curtis?" he asked, shouting above the noise from the busy workers.

"Everything's amazing," I shouted to him. He smiled with a shot of pride. "What's all this?" I asked him, looking at the workers as they passed.

"Party favors," he shouted. I looked at him, confused. He nudged the conductor, who took his place ordering the workers, and stepped toward us.

"The christening of the *Comet* is on the first of January," he said, beginning to explain. He threw his arm around my shoulders, pulling me close so that he would not have to shout. "I'm inviting the leader of every major nation and corporation in the world to the festivities. I even got an affirmative response from your President McKinley in the Colonies. He will probably be interested in meeting you.

"But because the christening itself will be orbit, we won't have the gravity we would for a normal celebration. Thus, I am supplying all of my guests with Star-made clothing and magnetic shoes which will supply a good amount of 'Earthness' to the christening."

I nodded, understanding his situation. I wondered how much it must have cost to supply such gifts to people all over the world. It must have been an astronomical amount, but I was sure that Star would be capable of affording it.

Star released my shoulders and went back to his directing duties. Mary and I looked at one another and decided to move along and get away from the intense bustle. We got into her automobile again and began to drive up the road from which we came.

We sat in silence for a moment, Mary concentrating on driving and I looking out at the stretching green of Star's Manor. As soon as I got the nerve to break the ice again, I asked, "So when do I get to see the Tower and the *Comet*?"

"Tomorrow, if you like," Mary said. "The Sky Train ascends every morning at six o'clock and comes back at five in the afternoon."

"I think I would very much like to go tomorrow," I said.

"Very well, I'll make the arrangements," Mary replied.

The conversation was left at that until we arrived back in the coach house next to the mansion. Mary drove the automobile into its allotted parking space and gave the keys back to George. He winked and asked, "You didn't do anything I wouldn't do, did you?"

Mary smiled. "Certainly not."

We left George and the coach house and returned to the mansion. Mary walked me to my room and then left me, saying that I would surely like to rest. I closed the door after her and sat in one of the chairs by the fireplace. I did nothing but think and review the day that I had had.

It certainly had been an amazing day. Star's Manor was almost like a mystical land of technological advancement. Everything was up-to-date, and possibly even ahead of it. He may have been a bit eccentric, but I definitely liked his style of romanticizing the Industrial Age.

Thinking like this, I fell asleep in my chair. It was hours later when I was awoken by a strange ringing sound. I sat up, completely confused, and looked for the origin of the ringing noise. Finally I realized what was happening and hurried to pick up the phone on the desk.

"Hello?" I asked.

"Mister Star has invited you to dinner this evening in twenty minutes," a voice said. "Do you wish to accept or would you like to have dinner in your room?"

"I, uh… Sure, I'll accept," I said.

"Very well," the voice responded. "Mister Star will meet you in the main dining room."

I rubbed the sleep from my eyes and opened the closet. Pulling the cord to activate the electric light, I looked at myself in the mirror. My clothes were wrinkled and my hair was disheveled. I gasped, but calmed down as I smoothed out my suit. I took my comb out of my bag and straightened my hair. Then I presumed that I was ready for dinner.

By the time I found the correct staircase and came across the dining room, I was at least two minutes late. Star and his family, along with van Sparchs and Conners, were at the table chatting.

"Fancy enough to meet us finally?" Conners asked. I knew that he was teasing me, but I had a feeling that he was actually a little upset by being forced to wait to eat.

I apologized for my lack of punctuality and took a seat next to van Sparchs. The dinner was short and conversation was fairly limited. The only interesting point of the evening was Conners telling a story of his time in Venice. He had ventured there as a young man, two years older than I, he said, without knowing any Italian and only elementary Latin. He eventually ended up in a prison for accidentally stealing fruits from a vendor's cart. There he began speaking with the other prisoners until he finally learned enough Italian to apologize to the fruit merchant and to offer to repay him three times over.

After dinner, I returned to my room. Since it was night and the room was growing cold, I lit the fire and looked for something to do before retiring to bed. Finally deciding, I took the journal from my bag and began to write in it. I wrote about all of the wondrous things that I saw on my amazing tour and scribed some thoughts of what I might see in the future on other worlds. I wrote until I finally tired out myself completely and crawled into bed.

Chapter Four,
Star's Tower

I awoke the next morning fairly early. Having figured out what to do in the morning yesterday, I bathed, dressed, and ate breakfast smoothly, and all well before six o'clock. I had picked another suit out of my closet, a brown one, to wear today. Looking at myself in the mirror, I thought it looked quite becoming on me.

At half past five, there was a knock at my door. I put down my journal (I had been reading over what I had written the night before) and answered it. When I opened the door, I recognized Mary Star, although in a very different outfit. Her hair was gathered behind her head into a tight bun and she was wearing a black bodysuit almost identical to the one in my closet.

Before I could say anything, she looked at me and asked, "What are you wearing?"

"What?"

"Your suit," she said, making a face as if I had answered the door in a Roman toga. "If we're to go up the Tower, you'll find it very uncomfortable."

I finally realized about what she was speaking. I had forgotten that Star had ordered everyone who went to the station to wear his bodysuits and not normal clothing. "I suppose I should change, then," I said, blushing from embarrassment.

"Quite," she said, turning away. "Come to the entry hall when you have. I'll meet you there."

I shut the door as she left and hurried to my closet. Grabbing the black bodysuit with the silver 'S' on it, I ripped myself out of my normal clothing and leapt into the new clothes. I pushed my hands and feet through the elastic sleeves and buttoned the torso together. The suit was surprisingly comfortable, though it did feel rather strange. I supposed that it was a similar experience would be giving a modern tuxedo to an ancient Greek.

After observing myself in the mirror for a moment, I hurried out of my room and down two sets of stairs before arriving in the entry hall. Mary was already there, sitting in a large, comfortably stuffed chair and reading a book. When I came near, she finally noticed me and stood. She slipped a bookmark between the pages and laid the book on a nearby table.

"Ready?" she asked.

I nodded. As we walked down the left hallway, I asked, "What were you reading?"

"*First Men in the Moon*," she said. "Father got it for me, and I decided to read it before the *Comet* left."

I smiled. It was a very appropriate book for the times. I had not heard of it, but I could imagine from its title that I would experience something very much like it in a few months.

We continued through the house's cavernous interior until we came to long, narrow hallway that looked newly redone. The wooden paneling on the walls still had a slight odor of stain. The floor was tiled with alternating dark and light marble squares, much like a chessboard. At the opposite end of the hallway was a wall made out of glass that gave a clear view of the base of Star's Tower. Several workmen were outside, talking to one another and looking at something at their feet.

We walked down the hallway and through a glass door in the far wall. The men looked up as we passed and nodded to Mary. Mary stopped and looked at them.

"It's not quite ready, Miss," one of them said. "Still getting some kinks out of it."

I looked at them and then down to what they were discussing. A small panel had been removed from the sidewalk and gears were lying beside the hole in the ground.

"Guess you'll have to walk, then," another told us.

"Very well," Mary said. "Thank you."

We began to walk down a strange pathway. It was made of a thick black canvas that stretched from the edge of the mansion to the base of the Tower. Both sides were surrounded with bricked gardens that were cultivated for flowers to be planted in soon.

"What were they working on?" I asked Mary.

"It's an automatic sidewalk," Mary explained. "The sidewalk moves on rollers as the canvas rotates like a belt. The original idea was to use it as cargo, but it is just now being built. Father thinks that the guests for the christening will find it impressive."

"I'll bet they will," I said, walking on the heavy canvas and trying to imagine a sidewalk that did the walking itself.

We walked down the strange path until we came to the base of the Tower, which was not quite as I had expected. The sidewalk led to another, which had a slow decline down below the ground. From what I could see above ground, the Tower was an interlacing of steel extending vertically until it disappeared high into the air.

I gawked at the Tower for a moment and then hurried after Mary, who had already begun to go down ahead of me. As I came to the underground portion of the Tower, I stopped, completely overwhelmed. The Tower extended underground into a huge docking area. There were at least four large elevators lowering into what looked like a large open mineshaft. Mary stepped into an elevator and then waited for me to catch up with her. I stumbled along, trying to take in everything at once.

As we descended, I leaned over the railing of the elevator to get a better look. The shaft continued downward for several stories, but was well lit with numerous electric lamps. There were several platforms and on each workers were loading crates into the Tower. I squinted to see exactly what they were doing, and I realized that they were not loading the crates into the Tower itself, but the vertical train that was inside the steel scaffolding. As we approached the first platform, I could make out the large cogged wheels that were grasping onto the track inside of the Tower and allowed the train to climb into the sky.

The elevator stopped at the second platform. Mary and I stepped out and walked across the platform toward the thick scaffolding of the Tower. We boarded the Sky Train through a large, heavy steel door that was swung wide on enormous hinges. Nearly all of the Train seemed to be made out of metal, probably aluminum. The door led to a very high-ceilinged room with a small ladder that led downward. The room was filled with crates, which were all tightly tied down with cords.

Mary led me to the ladder, and we climbed down to a smaller room. This room had seats in it for passengers instead of freight. Several workers dressed in black bodysuits nearly identical to ours were sitting, bound to their seats by straps that went over their shoulders and around their waists. They were chatting with one another, waiting for the Train to begin its ascent. When

Mary entered, they all nodded to her.

We chose seats and then strapped ourselves to them. The straps were made from strong fibers that were designed to pull snugly over your body. Not used to the straps, I left them fairly loose for comfort.

Within a few minutes, someone from outside of the Train shouted, "All aboard who's going aboard!" I then heard the massive door shut and lock firmly into place. A whirring sound, much like those in all of Star's motorcars only louder and deeper, ran through the cabin. The Train jolted slightly and then began to climb.

Mary pointed to a thick-glass window to my left. I gazed out just as the Sky Train rose out of the underground station. The world was passing by vertically, much like when one looks out of a glass-walled elevator. I first saw the walls of Star's mansion, then the roof, and then I could make out the whole of the village below us.

We continued on our ascent and the world below continued to shrink. It was not long before the village became a collection of black spots amid a large expanse of green that made up the meadows and forests on the manor. Finally, we passed through a thick fog that made up the clouds in the sky. After a time of being able to see nothing, we broke into the clean air above the clouds.

"Wow," I whispered. I could see for an unbelievable distance. Below us were clouds and patches of green and blue where the clouds broke to expose England and the ocean.

I grew tired of seeing the gray below us and leaned back in my seat. Mary tapped me on the arm and then handed me a small paper bag. "You may want this soon. Some people become nauseous when we leave Earth's gravity."

I accepted the bag, but mentally swore to myself that I would not get sick. I then turned back to the window, staring absently.

As the Sky Train continued higher, it began to grow dark outside. The atmosphere was thinning and stars were beginning to appear. I narrowed my eyes, trying to make out which stars were which. When I orientated myself, I leaned forward to see what else I could make out.

When I did, however, I found there was no gravity to stop me. I fell forward after I shifted my weight and the straps caught me and jerked me back into the seat. Mary smiled amusedly and watched me try to resettle myself. Finally I grabbed the straps and pulled them tightly around me so that I would not bounce. By this time, I had caught the attention of the other passengers, who were all chuckling at me.

I began to feel my organs move around in my body, freed from the heavy pull of gravity. My stomach seemed to rebel against me, but I swallowed and kept it under control as best as I could. All of my bodily fluids were beginning to float as well. It was an interesting experience, but not one I would wish on too many people.

We rode on until the Train finally came to a stop. Before it did, the wheels slowed, lightly pushing us all upward through inertia. I looked out of the window and saw nothing but a wall very close to the window.

When I looked back at the compartment where we were sitting, everyone seemed to be retying his or her shoes. I checked mine, and, though they were floating slightly, the laces were tightly strung. After they tied their shoes, the workers unstrapped themselves and stood up from their seats. Despite the lack of gravity, they all seemed to stand quite firmly on the metal floor of the Train.

As I unstrapped myself, however, I immediately fell up off of the floor and floated in midair. It was one of the most amazing situations in which I had ever been, but also one of the most embarrassing.

All of the workers began to laugh out loud. Mary stared at me and turned red. "When you changed your clothes, you did change your shoes as well, didn't you?"

"No," I said as innocently as I could. I looked carefully at her shoes, which were steadfastly planted on the floor, and noticed that they had very thick soles and the ever-present 'S' symbol on the ankle.

Mary buried her face in her hands. Finally she said, "I'm sure they have an extra pair of boots or two in the administration office. Come on."

She took me by the hand and pulled my floating body behind her. She led us past the laughing workers and up the ladder. Just as we came into the cargo room, the large metal door was opened by workers from the outside. When they saw me, they stared curiously for a moment and then let us pass without a word.

We walked down a narrow corridor that connected the Train with the station. As I was pulled along, I noticed that Mary was walking strangely, as though her feet were sticking to the floor. I finally realized just what was happening. The thick soles of the Star shoes had magnets that stuck to the metal floor, thus allowing one to walk on the floor and, presumably, walls or ceiling. My shoes, without magnets, were quite useless without gravity.

Mary entered a large elevator at the end of the corridor and pulled me in behind her. Two workers followed us, but when they saw Mary's expression, decided to wait for the elevator to return. The doors of the elevator closed tightly with a hiss. The elevator began to lower, and I floated higher as it did, finally hitting the ceiling.

"Ow!" I said as I bumped it. "What happened?"

"The elevator moved, but you didn't since you're floating," Mary explained. She pulled on my hand, causing me to come back to my midair stance.

The elevator soon stopped, and because I was now moving and it was not, I hit the floor. Mary made a noise like a half-laugh, half-sigh of frustration. As the doors opened, she pulled me up from the floor and left the elevator.

We came into a small corridor made of heavy glass. At the end was an open door with rubber pads along the parts that came in contact with the corridor's walls. I remembered reading that Star called these "airlocks," devices to keep the vacuum of Space around the Train away from the rest of the station.

As we passed by the open thick metal door, we entered a huge, open room. The ceiling, which was at least two stories above us, was made of thick glass so that one could look up and see the stars unhampered by the atmosphere. I whistled with awe and turned so that I could face up as I floated along after Mary. I stared at the stars as we crossed the room and was quick to recognize each.

Finally I had to tear my attention away from the ceiling. I looked around, noticing the strap-covered benches and ornate floor tiles. Lights, which were off because the Earth was facing the Sun, were strung on thin wires that easily spanned the great room in the lack of gravity. There were a few other people in the room, most of them heading either toward or away from the elevators.

Looking behind us, I saw that the elevator we had come from was just one of many. Each car of the Sky Train had its own airtight door that, when in position in the station, led to its own small corridor and elevator. All of the elevators lined the wall next to the Train and looked extremely complex and impressive as they moved up and down to unload passengers and cargo.

Mary began to turn to the left, heading for a shiny metal wall with the word "Administration" written on it in red script and a watermark of Star's silver 'S.' Another wall opposite to it had the word "Boarding" written on it. Several doors were open in each, and workers and men with clipboards were walking in and out.

Looking to my right, I caught my first glance of the *Star's Comet* through a glass wall. I muttered an impressed exclamation and squinted to make out the main details. It was majestic, like nothing I had ever seen before. The only things that I could compare to it were the enormous transatlantic steamships I had seen in New York harbor. I stared at it until Mary entered the administrative offices of the station, pulling me behind her and taking the *Comet* out of view.

The administration area of the station was quiet, but full of office noises like murmurs, coughs, telephones, papers, and heavy writing. There was a central room with a long desk at the far end and doors leading to independent offices all along the sides. Mary approached the main desk and waited for someone to meet her.

A young woman stood from a chair behind the desk where she had been operating a switchboard and hurried to help Mary. "Yes?" she asked. She smiled at me, inwardly laughing.

"I would like to see Mr. Edwards," Mary told her.

"Yes, Miss Star," she said. She pointed to an open office door to the right. "He's not busy right now and should be able to get to you right away."

"Thank you," Mary said and pulled me to the office of Mr. Edwards. She knocked at the open door and then stepped in.

"Ah, Mary!" Mr. Edwards said, unbuckling himself from an office chair and standing. He was a large, jolly man and wore a black suit similar to those we wore, but had a business tie stitched to the front and a slightly different cut on the shoulders and sleeves. "I'm glad you could make it and bring…"

He trailed off and began to look for a piece of paper. His metallic desk was covered with dozens of piles of papers, all held in place with paperweight-like magnets. Finally, he pulled a small slip from under one of the magnets and read it, "Mr. Curtis Matricks. Pleased to meet you. I'm Jackson Edwards, administrator of this station."

"I'm glad we could make it," Mary said, "but we've also got a little problem."

"So I see," he said, scratching his chin. He motioned to two smaller chairs on our side of the desk, which were bolted to the floor. We sat in them and buckled ourselves to them. Trying to sit in a chair without gravity was not an easy task, much like trying to sit on a chair on the bottom of a pond.

When we were finally in place, Edwards sat himself. "Well, this ought not be too hard to solve."

After buckling himself into his seat, he then took off his magnetic shoes and tossed them to me. Tossing is much easier without gravity than with it.

All he had to do was position the shoes in the air and then give them a slight push toward me. "These ought to fit."

I took the shoes and put them on my feet. They were slightly too large when I tied the strings, but it felt much better to wear proper shoes. I found a small switch on the outer ankle of each, and throwing it, they stuck firmly to the floor. I then gave my shoes to Edwards so that he would not have to go about in stocking feet. "Thank you," I told him as he finished tying my shoes on his feet.

"Always glad to oblige," he said. "You kids ought to feel lucky. Back when we first got the station built, they hadn't yet come up with these magnetic shoes. We had to float about and swim best we could. Sometimes I feel like those were better days, though."

"You've been here since the first?" I asked. Star had not included many biographies of people other than himself in his book.

"Yes, sir." Edwards smiled, leaning back in his chair to better remember the long-ago days. "I was in charge of the construction project, just under Mr. Star. He trusted me to get the job done, and I did it best I could.

"I actually was the first person to sleep in Space. It was back in '90, when we were first getting the station finished. Back then, everybody left when the train left and came back when the train came back. The doors could be opened from the inside back then. Not quite as safe as now, but that was the way it worked.

"Anyway," he said, finally getting back to the story, "one night I needed to test about a million rivets to make sure that a bunker was airtight so that we could open it. Instead of taking the train and doing it the next day, I decided to stay and finish that night. After I did, I ate a few crusts of bread I had left from lunch and wrapped up in a tarp. I remember it getting quite cold that night; we've got heaters now, though. Still, it was pretty interesting sleeping in midair. I suppose it was as close as you can get to sleeping in the womb again."

"Wow," I said, fascinated. Mary was not quite as interested as I was in his story; most likely she had heard it many times before.

"I guess you kids need to get on with the tour," Edwards said. "You're lucky to get such a guide, Curtis. Mary probably knows just as much about this whole thing as Mr. Star himself."

We unbuckled ourselves from our seats and, after a few farewells, left his office. Mary then showed me the administrative offices. Right now, they were just for relaying communications from the ground and a kind of middle management. When the station was open to the public, however, it would be used to organize travelers and the arrivals and departures of Starships. I imagined the office full of patrons awaiting a ship to take them to Mars or to Venus or possibly even to the most distant of planets, Neptune.

After seeing the offices, we reentered the main room. I seized the opportunity to walk closer to the thick glass wall that stood between the *Comet* and me. It was facing me, its prow showing a large window and two odd cylinders poking out like horizontal tusks. Two large wings, covered in black panels, extended from the sides of the body. On top of it was a large, round antenna.

"Amazing," I said. Mary agreed.

We then walked across the main room and went through a door in the wall that was labeled "Boarding." There were several doors, each leading to a thick-walled tube with glass ports every ten feet.

These tubes led to different places on the station. Some of them led out to small toolsheds and storehouses built on the platform for workers to store their tools and equipment when not using them. Other tubes led to bunkhouses and small apartments for workers who did not commute every day on the Sky Train.

Mr. Edwards had a rather spacious apartment where he and his wife had lived for the past three years. Mrs. Edwards was large and jolly much like her husband. She was in her apartment when Mary and I came by and eagerly invited us in. We sat and chatted for a bit, and she served us hot chocolate and sandwiches for lunch. The drinks came in strange cylindrical glasses that were completely closed except for a small hole on the upper edge. To drink from it, one had to suck out the liquid with his mouth. It was an interesting experience, but one had to be careful not to let liquid escape from the glass and float about as a liquid ball in the air.

After our visit with Mrs. Edwards, we finished the tour of the buildings that dotted the station's large platform. We were in the main room of the station once again, looking at the one tube we had not yet explored. It was the largest, most luxurious tube and had been designed for travelers to use when boarding a Starship. The tube led directly to the *Comet*, and I could barely contain myself as we walked down the tube and approached the Starship.

We entered the *Comet* by an open thick door. The corridors were metal and gleaming from their newness. There were several workers about, mostly walking to and fro on magnetic shoes and carrying weightless crates.

"This is Deck C," Mary said. "It is the middle deck of five, all designated alphabetically, beginning with the upper."

Our tour also began with the uppermost deck. We climbed up a stairwell, passed by Deck B, and then exited at the top. Deck A began with the pilot's station, where the *Comet* would be guided. There was a huge, reinforced glass window that showed the windows of the main room of the station. I imagined seeing the stars and planets moving around me through the window. There were several seats in the room. The foremost, meant for the pilot himself, was surrounded by dozens of levers. When a lever was pulled, as Mary explained, a corresponding rocket would fire, redirecting the ship. The other seats were meant for diagnostics and internal controls.

Port (I say 'port' here to give the Starship a feeling of an extraordinary sea-going vessel) of the pilot's station was a smaller room designated for the navigator. There were many charts and tables in boxes welded to the walls and a desk with many mathematical tools and measuring devices placed upon it with magnetic holders. I asked Mary about the navigator.

"Father needs someone to ensure that the ship is moving correctly," she said. "He picked the best, fastest mathematician he could find, Katherine MacPherson. She should arrive any day now. You'll meet her then."

We crossed the pilot's station and entered the communications room. The room was almost a mirror image of the navigator's room, but had a set of headphones, a series of telephones, and a telegraph key instead of mathematical instruments and charts.

We left the pilot's station at the foremost of the ship and headed aft. The ship's library was a rather small, but very inviting room. Shelves of books (strapped in, so that they would not escape from their places) lined the walls and broke only for the door and a large viewing port on the far side of the room. In the center was a long conference table, bolted to the floor and surrounded by magnet-footed chairs.

Deck A held the massive tanks that would supply the ship's water needs. Between the main tank and a secondary tank, there was a set of pumps to supply pressure in the pipes of the ship. Without gravity, the ship would need to pump the water continuously or it would merely float in its pipes.

The scientific laboratories were also on Deck A. The most advanced scientific gadgets that I had ever seen filled all four of them. One laboratory was fitted as a physician's office and held surgical tools, medicines, and an assortment of medical devices. The other three laboratories were more generalized, holding tools for geology, chemistry, physics, and all other fields of science.

In the need of external repairs on the ship, it would be necessary to send a team outside into the cold vacuum of Space. There was a small room dedicated for any such exits next to the fourth laboratory. Several heavy brown suits that looked somewhat like diving suits hung on the wall. Behind a thick wall and hatch was an airlock where those leaving the ship would wait while pumps recaptured all of the air to prevent any leak of precious atmosphere. Another hatch led into the void beyond the ship's walls.

At the rear of Deck A was the large electrical control room. Wires leading from the Energy Collectors that covered the wings and roof of the ship converged here and charged gigantic storage batteries. There were several stations with switches and current-describing dials that controlled electrical power of the ship.

There were also several bunkrooms, tight quarters which held four bunks each, and a freight elevator which we took to the second deck of the ship. Deck B mainly held bunkrooms, each nearly identical, and also the ship's bathroom, kitchen, and cafeteria.

The captain's room, obviously meant for Star himself, was amid the bunkrooms. Mary, very cautiously, as if she were not to be in the room, showed it to me. It was separated into two rooms, a parlor and a bedroom at the back. The room was stylishly decorated with magnets on every item and straps on every seat. When we finished looking through the room, Mary discreetly closed the door and we moved on.

In the front of Deck B, directly under the pilot's station, was the gunnery room. Two large cannons, the two tusk-like cylinders I had seen, poked out of the room into the outer vacuum. They had been specially designed for the ship to operate in Space. There was also a large Gatling gun that stood between the cannons. According to Star's book, the cannons were for shooting asteroids and other objects that stood in the way of the ship. Aside from the ship's artillery, the gunnery room held vast amounts of ammunition and firearms. I pitied anyone who decided to meet the expedition with hostilities.

At the rear of Deck B, there was a quaint theater. There was a stage with curtains that had magnetic strips at the bottom and rows of strapped benches for the audience. Assemblies would take place here, both for the amusement and education of the crew. On Sundays, the chaplain of the ship would hold services here, but there would also be plays and performances on the stage to liven the days of travel between worlds.

Two rooms, the chaplain's quarters and a storage room, were behind the theater. The chaplain had a room to himself, but only to promote privacy to anyone who met with him. It was spacious compared to the bunkrooms, but nowhere nearly as elegant as the captain's room.

After seeing all of Deck B, we took a rear stairwell to Deck C, where we had entered. We first looked into the rocket control room, which directed the massive propulsion rockets of the ship. Then we came to a large storage room, which was busy with workers loading crates in preparation for the ship's departure. This room also held a small brig, which Star mentioned in the "punishment" section of his book. I crooned when I saw it and hoped that I would never have to see out from the inside.

We next came to an agricultural laboratory, which was meant for animals. Though no animals were on the ship yet, there were places for goats and many kinds of fowl, as well as ample room for any alien animals we might acquire.

Next we saw the environmental control room. Here there were heaters and coolers and dozens of pipes that led in every direction to feed the ship with fresh air. Oxygenated air would be pulled up from the botany laboratory and then carried to the rest of the ship. Other pipes would pull the old air out of the ship and feed it back into the botany laboratory to be reoxygenated.

Finally we came to a room that made me more ecstatic than anything I had seen thus far. It was one of the two astronomy laboratories onboard the ship. It held a few charts, but mainly blank papers to be filled with discoveries. More importantly, it held the largest telescope that I had ever seen.

"I could probably map out the surface of Mars with this!" I shouted gleefully.

"Actually," Mary said, not quite as excited as I was, "that will be one of your duties. As we are heading to each planet, you will tell us as much as you can about them."

I smiled. The duties seemed more like pleasures. I could not wait for the expedition to begin.

Eventually, Mary tore me away from the astronomy laboratory and we continued down to Deck D. There were only three rooms in this deck, another astronomy laboratory (which I explored in depth just as I had the other, even though they were nearly identical), the botany laboratory, and the engineering room with the rockets that would propel the ship.

The botany laboratory was nearly empty at this time. There were multitudinous pots and beds filled with rich soil that were ready to be planted. The lights were brighter in this room than the others in the ship, most likely better illuminated for the plants' sake. In the middle of the gardens were several benches. Apparently, Star had also designed the botany laboratory to be a place to relax.

The engineering area of the ship served as a repair bay as well as the container for the enormous rockets of the *Comet*. There were tools everywhere, lining the walls and floor, all put in place with magnets. Chests filled with repair parts took up the remaining space in the room. Because of the amount of technology on board this ship, I imagined that the repairs would be numerous and difficult. However, with an engineering bay set like this one, Star probably had very little to worry about.

Behind the engineering area were the colossal fuel tanks and rockets. Twin tanks, one of hydrogen and one of oxygen, were lined with thick, reinforced steel meant to protect the ship from any kind of mishap. The tanks led into a small reaction chamber, and from there, the explosion of the gasses would be channeled out of the ship with tremendous force. All that I could see from the engineering area was a tall wall of steel with several ports for refilling the hydrogen and oxygen tanks and a small crawl space for emergency repairs between the two gigantic tanks.

We finally came to Deck E, the lowest deck on the ship. The deck was mainly for storage, but also held the ship's photography laboratory. Any pictures taken on board would be developed in the small darkroom in the middle of Deck E. There was also a large glass port for a camera to take detailed pictures of the surfaces of planets while in orbit around them.

There were massive bay doors that opened into vacuum on the floor of Deck E. They were in a room by themselves, surrounded by air pumps to create an airlock just like in the personnel airlock on Deck A. These doors were much larger, however, and meant for vehicles, not just people.

The vehicles of the *Comet* were in a room next to the airlock bay. There were several electric trucks and then three large dome-like transports. These last transports, as Mary explained, were for going to the surface of a planet. They would drop out of the bay doors and then fall through the atmosphere with parachutes and reverse rockets until they landed on immense pads underneath them.

"Have they been tested?" I asked, a little nervous at the idea of parachuting from orbit.

"Once," Mary said. "They worked fairly well, but all those aboard suffered minor injures. Don't worry, though. Earth has the highest gravity of any planet that we'll be landing on. If the landers nearly work here, they'll work quite well elsewhere."

I did not feel very encouraged. Fortunately, however, I was an astronomer and I doubted that Star would want to take me down to the surface of a planet when I could be in the astronomy laboratory with the telescopes.

I asked, "How do they get back up to the ship?"

"The rockets," Mary replied. She pointed to four thick cylinders on each of the landers. "On the way down, they slow the landers. When fully ignited, though, they launch the landers up into orbit, where the *Comet* can catch them and bring them on board."

While I continued to look at them, Mary pulled a timepiece from one of her pockets and made a little gasp.

"What is it?" I asked, a little concerned.

"Nothing serious, it's just later than I thought it was," she said. "There is a ship that will depart in several minutes, so we might wish to get to it."

"A ship?" I asked.

"Yes, another Starship," she said, turning to leave the *Comet*.

I followed her down the corridors of the ship. "This is the only one I saw on the platform. Where are the others?"

"The others are far from the massive size of the *Comet*," she began to explain. "Father calls them '*Meteors*.' I suppose the name is rather fitting."

We marched quickly through the ship, and I paused to examine interesting pieces of equipment only for a short second. I would then jog a little, quickly pulling up my magnetic shoes and planting them again in a long stride. Mary finally led me out of the ship and to a new area of the station that I had not seen before.

It was a large open room, similar to the room that had held the landers. There were a dozen or so men in it, all working skillfully without gravity. They surrounded three oddly-shaped vehicles and were apparently some kind of mechanic. One of the vehicles was complete, but the other two had large panels removed and the mechanics were working to insert and extract pieces.

"Mr. Varsley!" Mary called.

One of the mechanics looked up, saw Mary, and then knocked on a small window on the side of the vehicle that was whole. A man quickly crawled out of a hatch on the top and waved to us. "Over here, Miss Star!"

"Hello, Mr. Varsley." Mary approached the small ship and smiled at the man. She turned toward me and said, "This is Curtis Matricks. He'll be the head astronomer on the *Comet*."

"Pleased to meet you," the man said, shaking my hand as I followed Mary to the small ship. "I'm Edmund Varsley, test pilot of these contraptions."

"It's a pleasure," I said.

I carefully scanned the machine, not remembering anything like it in Star's book of etiquette. It was small, about the size of two carriages put together. The back half of it was completely enclosed by thick metal, and the rear consisted of the ends of two rockets, similar to the back of the *Comet*. The front half, on the other hand, had the ends of several periscopes looking out of it, as well as three small windows, one in front and two on the sides.

"This is quite a machine," I said, whistling slightly. "I don't remember seeing any descriptions about it before."

"They're still fairly experimental," Varsley said, climbing out of the hatch and pushing himself to the floor from the top of the vessel. "Star just organized them a few months ago. Everything is based off of the old test ships that we built when we were designing the *Comet*. The test ships were quite a bit smaller than the real thing, but it really gave the pilots a feel for flying in Space."

"So what is Mister Star's plan for them?" I asked.

Varsley turned to Mary, wanting her to answer the question. "My father wishes to create some kind of tour service. It was not quite necessary before the *Comet* started, but now he thinks it is time for it to be created."

I nodded and began inspecting the ship more closely.

Varsley approached me, beginning to explain more in depth. "They're very different from most of the things Star puts together. No Energy Collectors, no plants to replenish the atmosphere. Everything's run off of battery and stored air."

"Wow," I whistled. "How long does it last?"

"We could probably live in it for a full day or so," he said. "It certainly doesn't have the range that the *Comet* does, but it can accelerate faster. All it needs to do is make a loop around the Earth."

"Thus being a tourist ship," I concluded. Both Varsley and Mary nodded.

"I'm scheduled to head off for a quick test flight," Varsley said. "And I suppose you two would go with me?"

"Certainly," I said. Mary nodded in agreement.

"Very well then," Varsley said. "We best be off."

He helped us up onto the top of the ship and then down through the hatch. The interior of the ship was comfortable, with two couches: a longer one for passengers and a smaller one for the pilot. The front window was for the pilot to use and several periscopes extended to give him ample views. The two viewing ports on either side of the vessel were for the passengers to see out.

When we were in the ship, we quickly fastened ourselves to the couch. It felt strange to have to be locked into place, but without gravity it was certainly a necessity. Varsley climbed through the hatch, locked it closed, and then strapped himself onto the pilot's seat.

He quickly adjusted all of the various eyepieces for the periscopes, checked over the controls, and then smiled. He gave a sign to the mechanics outside, who unclamped the ship from its place in the bay. They pushed it into a smaller room, an airlock that would provide access to Outer Space.

As they locked the door behind us, the pumps were activated, sucking out all of the air in the room. Varsley tapped on the control console, waiting with the same amount of patience that a child waits for his birthday.

Finally he turned his head so that he half-faced us. "Ever read *Around the World in 80 Days?*"

Mary and I both nodded. He smiled and said, "We should be able to make the whole orbit in ninety minutes. What do you think Verne would think of that?"

"He'd probably be pretty amazed," I said. Mary nodded. It would take a very creative mind to surpass even Verne in forming such a fast journey.

"The key to the speed of the *Meteors*," Varsley said, "is that there isn't anything in Space to hit. I mean, sure there are dust particles that scrape things up a little and maybe an asteroid or two, but you can dodge around those pretty easily. Since there isn't anything slowing you down, not even a real big pull from the Earth, rockets will get you up to a real quick speed."

"Amazing." I smiled. The long journey I had traveled from Ohio could have been done in a mere half of an hour. It was something that I could barely even imagine.

Suddenly the pumps stopped. We could not hear the end of the pumping since there was vacuum around us, but a helpful light appeared on the door in front of us. It began to open noiselessly, revealing the star-filled darkness beyond.

Varsley quickly began fiddling with the controls. He first ignited the rockets, which caused the ship to rumble slightly. I gripped the seat, not knowing what to expect. Mary, however, seemed completely at ease with the eccentricities of the ship. The ship moved slowly out of the small airlock and then quickly began to accelerate. I could not tell how fast we were moving since all we could see were stars, but a dial registering speed spun more and more rapidly.

"Let me get up to a good velocity…" Varsley trailed off at the end as he moved several levers smoothly. Each lever controlled a small jet of air, which helped drive and position the ship. We waited patiently until Varsley was comfortable with the ship's movement.

Finally, he smiled. "That should be good enough. I'll turn the ship on its side so that you can get a view of the Earth below."

Just as he said that, we felt a jet of air twist the ship. Another jet stopped its rotation, causing us to be positioned so that the Earth filled the viewing port next to me. It was a majestic sight: vast green masses of plains, gray mountains, white clouds, and huge spans of blue oceans. Mary and I both gaped.

"We shouldn't have to worry about this," Varsley said as he skillfully piloted the ship, "but if the air starts getting stale to you, let me know. I'll let some fresh oxygen out of the storage tanks."

I did not hear much of his statement, though. I was too busy staring down at the world below. There was a large gray patch over most of England, but France and Spain stood out magnificently. We were quickly crossing over the enormous Atlantic Ocean, and I could see the white Arctic capping the world.

The minutes flew by as quickly as we did. We soon came into the shadow of the Earth, and I could see the twilight outline of the eastern coast of America before it disappeared in the darkness. While we flew through the sunless darkness, Varsley used a lamp that was mounted on the front of the vessel. Whenever it detected a large rock that was floating in our path, he would dexterously dodge around it and resume our flight.

We soon came to the edge of the darkness and saw the sun appear. It was the strangest sunrise that I had ever seen, but it was amazing nonetheless. The Pacific was lighting up beneath us, and we watched as Asia appeared. The islands of Japan and then the massive bulk of China shone beautifully in the light. We soon crossed over the barren steppes, and then finally returned over the continent of Europe.

"Well, that's the tour," Varsley said, trying to keep his tone nonchalant. Even he was excited by the flight, however, and his voice betrayed his exhilaration.

He twisted the ship back into a parallel position with the Earth. I was upset to see the Earth disappear from view, but had my memories to keep me content. Varsley slowed the ship considerably as we neared the platform.

The station seemed very small from the outside, but still amazing.

"Now for the tricky part," he whispered, sticking his tongue out of the side of his mouth. As the *Meteor* passed over the platform, he turned the ship completely around and fired the rockets. The ship came to a stop and then headed slowly toward the small airlock from which we had left. I grew anxious, wondering if he would crash the vessel into one of the walls, but he safely placed the *Meteor* into the airlock. Soon the air had returned and the mechanics placed the ship back in its place with the others.

Mary said that it was time to head back to the surface of Earth, and, though I was a little upset, I followed her away from the *Meteors*. We quickly bid farewell to Varsley, who waved politely and then fell to talking with one of the mechanics about the flight. After leaving Mr. Edwards's magnetic boots with him and borrowing a spare pair, we hurried to the elevators that would take us to a compartment on the Sky Train. We found seats and strapped ourselves into them. Two of the workers in the room with us recognized me and chuckled to themselves. I blushed and tried to ignore them.

On the way down, I was very quiet. I sat in my seat, eyes half closed, remembering the events of the day. Gradually the gravity gripped me once again and pressed me into my seat. After spending the day without it, I thought that gravity seemed to be a very cumbersome thing.

When we finally reached the Sky Train station on Earth, we stretched and unstrapped ourselves. After I stood, I found my feet stuck to the floor. Suddenly I remembered that I had left the magnets in my shoes on, turned them off, and walked with ease in Earth's gravity.

As we left the base of the Tower, a maid approached Mary. "Miss, Mr. Star has asked that you join him in the dining room."

"Thank you," Mary said. The servant left, never even seeming to notice me.

We walked through the house once again until we came to the dining room. Star and his wife and son were there, as well as Conners, van Sparchs, and a thin woman whom I had not seen before. We took seats, Mary next to her mother and I between Conners and van Sparchs.

The thin woman caught my gaze and held it. She was probably about thirty-five years old, but still held very youthful looks. Her face was lean, but not quite gaunt. She had black hair that barely hung to her shoulders. Her dress was as black as her hair and very stylish.

Star must have noticed me and said, "Curtis, this is Madam Elissa Rosiet. Elissa, Curtis Matricks."

"I'm charmed," she said, her accent very French. I nodded politely.

"Elissa will serve as our chief Agricultural Engineer on the *Comet*," Star said to me. He then turned to the thin French woman. "Curtis is our new chief astronomer."

"Such a young man for such a large position," she said.

"I'm sure he can handle it," Star said.

"He will," Conners cut in. "I gave him a little quiz yesterday and he passed quite well. I think that we could probably fire the rest of the astronomy team and just have him work around the clock."

"You would kill the poor boy, Luke," van Sparchs chuckled.

I swallowed, not from the suggestion that I work myself to death, but from being the subject of the conversation. Fortunately, maids and butlers entered with trays of food and broke up the dialogue about me. After a blessing from Star, we began eating.

"So, Mason, what exactly is Elissa's job on the ship?" Conners asked before placing a fork full of meat into his mouth.

"If you had even glanced at my manual, you would know," Star said, giving him a false-stern look. Conners rolled his eyes as if he were a rebellious son of Star. Ignoring the look, Star began to explain. "Elissa will be in control of the gardens on the *Comet*."

"Gardens?" Conners asked, surprised. "What kind of pleasure yacht is this?"

"Ze gardens are for much more than pleasure, monsieur," Elissa said, rolling the last word sarcastically. Her tone was stern, like she was preparing to lecture to a rambunctious child. "Ze plants in ze agricultural laboratory will supply ze oxygen necessary to stay alive in ze deep vacuum of Outer Space. I've spent much time collecting and breeding ze best plants for ze job. I will also keep ze plants and animals zat you will eat to supplement your packaged rations. I'm sure zat when you drink fresh milk or eat eggs or oranges, you will be very glad zat I am zere.

"In addition, I will inspect any plants or animals zat we come across on our voyage. For zat position, zough, I am in debt to Monsieur Star for supplying such an opportunity." Star nodded his head once as a sign of appreciation for the comment. Elissa finished her statements with, "So, Monsieur Conners, I will do much more zan keep fresh flowers at ze table onboard the ship."

"Indeed," Conners said. He smiled broadly; perhaps thrilled to meet someone who seemed a challenge or maybe a perfect target for his taunting.

"Elissa came in by train this afternoon," Star said, beginning to change the subject. "The rest of the party will soon be gathering, as well. I expect that the last member of the expedition will arrive on the twenty-ninth of December."

"How many people are you expecting?" Conners asked.

"Once again," Star said, eyeing him amusedly, "if you had read the manual, you would know."

"How can you demand that I read your voluminous volume when your library is stocked with classics?" Conners pleaded.

"Very well," Star agreed. "For your information, there will be seventy crewmen on the *Comet*."

Conners nodded and took a mental note. Dinner continued quite well until a discussion of the German Kaiser came about. Van Sparchs, a natural German and very proud of his country, argued with Conners, whom I was not certain truly did oppose the Kaiser's principles or was just teasing van Sparchs. The debate worsened nearly to the point of personal insults. Finally, Conners demanded that the argument should take place only in Arabic, as not to offend anyone present. He rattled a long line of words, after which van Sparchs turned red and went silent. Conners smiled at his unfortunate debate partner.

The conversation was then silent until Star had the dessert brought in, and we resumed speaking on less political matters. Finally, the long meal was over and we each went our separate ways. I retired to my room and made notes of what I had seen that day. Star's amazing manor was only the beginning of the wonders that I would see.

Chapter Five,
The Christening of the *Star's Comet*

I stayed in England until the first of January. I always seemed to have something to do, and the days went quickly. Much of my time was spent in Star's immense library, often discussing philosophy with Conners. I also went up the Sky Train several more times to visit with Mr. and Mrs. Edwards. Every day more and more pages of my journal filled with amazing events.

I did not see much of Mary during this time. She was usually following her father, taking notes and relaying orders. Whenever I did see her, we chatted for a few moments, but never very long. Usually, I only saw her at meals in the main dining room with her family, where the adults controlled the conversation.

Christmas time was special to me at the Star Manor. Since I was still practically a youth, Star took particular interest in me and invited me to his family's Christmas celebrations in their private suites. Locked away from the rest of the world, the Stars were actually a very common family during the holiday. On Christmas Eve, Mason Star read *A Christmas Carol* by Dickens aloud while his wife Alexis herself made hot chocolate for the family (all of the maids had been allowed the holiday off). Mark, like all young boys, stared out the window, waiting for Saint Nicholas. He was probably old enough to know that there was no such thing, but he held on to the romantic idea. Mary watched him, probably wishing to herself that she were still blissfully ignorant. The evening was quiet and personal, which seemed very much against the Star family's usually very social conduct.

I slept that night in an extra bed in Mark's room, where we stayed up late telling ghost tales to one another. Unfortunately, it seemed that Mark's stories scared me more than my stories did him. Finally, both frightened out of our wits, we went to sleep with the blankets over our heads.

The next morning we exchanged gifts. I had gone to the general store on the manor and picked out gifts for each of the family members. They were nice, but nowhere nearly as amazing as what the Stars gave to each other and me. Mason gave Alexis two astounding ruby earrings that would have made my mother weep with awe just to see them. When most of the gift-giving was over, Star then handed me a package he had received from my parents. There were two gifts (a new wallet and an interesting tie), and a long letter, which I read several times over the next few days.

That afternoon Star held a huge Christmas banquet and ball for all of his acquaintances and employees. An enormous tree, decorated from tip to trunk, had been set up in the main entrance hall. Twin music groups played carols from the balconies above the dancers. When we ate, the guests filled the entire dining table, and we all ate more than we could hold. Conners attended the ball, but spent most of his time in a study arguing with old gentlemen.

Star ended the evening with a toast to the expedition. "In exactly one week," he said, "mankind will leave the touch of Earth and, for the first time in all of history, travel among the planets." At this, everyone cheered uproariously. This was the first non-secretive proclamation made about the expedition. When news about it trickled out into the world, people took Star as more of a genius than a madman.

The next week was an incredibly busy one. I spent my time meeting and organizing my team of astronomers. In my charge were a young woman from Switzerland, two Frenchmen, a Brazilian, an Italian, and a British man from London. I reacted to responsibility as best I could and created a timetable for each of us to have as much time at the telescopes as possible. I also tested them, making sure that each were as good as they were supposed to be, and satisfied myself that they were the very best team of astronomers that Earth could muster.

Meanwhile, the rest of the manor was extremely busy. Madame Rosiet complained again and again that her plants were not being handled gently enough in the transit from the Sky Train station to the ship itself. Only Conners, nearly always tucked away in the library, seemed at ease.

"My duty does not come until we find someone to converse with," he once told me. Then, with a wink, he added, "Maybe we'll have bad luck, and I'll never do a lick of work."

Dignitaries from around the world gathered at Star's manor, taking up nearly all of the luxurious guest rooms and cottages. There were numerous heads-of-state and notabilities living very close to one another. More than once duels and challenges broke out over small mishaps. Fortunately, Star always persuaded the rivals to put aside their arms for now and wait until they returned to their home countries to declare war on one another.

Finally, New Year's Eve came upon us. Nearly all of the guests for the christening of the *Comet* had arrived. Star threw a midnight ball for them all to celebrate the coming of the New Year. He gathered key figures of his crew away from the ball for a final briefing about the expedition in a secluded office on the second floor.

There were twelve of us around a table with Star at the head. He looked very serious, and I doubted that he planned to sleep at all that night. Mary sat at a small writing desk behind her father with a thick pad of paper and several pens, ready to record anything that came up in the meeting. She yawned slightly, obviously tired by the busy week of preparation.

To Star's right was Lang Kahn, the Chinese rocketry engineer. He was a dignified Chinaman with close-cut hair and a small beard around his mouth. When Star had first begun his project, he had toured China, hoping to learn something about rocketry, with which he could propel his Starship. He had discovered Kahn doing a demonstration for a visiting Italian merchant. Star had immediately hired Kahn to design rockets for his ship and eventually brought him to England to oversee their construction. Kahn had been back to his native China for several months making a last visit before going on the expedition.

Next to him sat Dr. van Sparchs. I had learned from stories told by van Sparchs that Star had come upon the idea of Energy Collectors through a little-known technology journal. I supposed that if Star had not discovered van Sparchs and his invention, it would have disappeared without the world ever knowing of it.

Phillip Wellis, a Texan chemist, sat next to van Sparchs. He had devised using hydrogen and oxygen for the propellant in Kahn's rockets. The two had worked countless hours planning and designing the best possible propulsion system for the *Comet*. Being a fellow American, he and I had had several conversations about the United States. He was a mirthful man and continually told me the wonders of Texas.

Next to him was Katherine MacPherson, the navigator of the *Comet*. Like myself, she was a young person who had won first place in one of Star's contests and thus a position in the expedition. She had exceedingly bright red hair, nearly the color of shined copper, and thick glasses. Her English had such an Irish accent that it was almost easier to understand Conners when he tried to teach me one of the Slavic tongues than her in conversation. She was amazingly good at mathematics, especially at swift mental calculations. She tried to explain to me her duties on the ship, but I became lost somewhere between gravity calculations and distance as an integral.

Giovanni Tarsini, the head medical doctor onboard the *Comet*, sat next to Katherine. Dr. Tarsini was a tall, large man with very nimble fingers. When I had met him, he explained to me how playing the piano was analogous to surgery and proceeded to play an Italian folk song with an extremely fast tempo. I had wondered whether to be impressed or disturbed by his performance.

At the end of the table, facing Star, sat Lukas Conners. He had with him a small puzzle box and toyed with it during the meeting. He never seemed to pay attention to whoever was speaking, but could always recite what they had said if asked. Conners was a jester, but often found only himself laughing at his gags.

Louis Pierre, the communications controller of the ship, sat next to Conners across from Tarsini. Pierre was a quiet Frenchman, but very knowledgeable and spoke loudly and clearly when he did. Star had told me that Pierre had grown up as an orphan in Paris and had found employment as a telegraph operator. Eventually, he became one of the most skilled operators in all of Europe, sending detailed messages and capable of repairing nearly any type of communication equipment. According to Star, he had familiarized himself with Bell's telephone by buying one, taking it apart, and reassembling it scientifically.

I sat next to Pierre, nearly as quiet as he. My eyes were wide and I was very attentive. The night was growing late, but I focused on the meeting and resisted any drowsiness. I was taking notes over the meeting, trying to discern what it was about. Finally, I decided that it was mainly meant as an encouragement speech, like a general addressing his commanders the night before battle.

Madam Rosiet sat to my right. Her hair had been stylishly done, and she had added several hairpieces to it. She had worn an elegant ballroom dress and planned to escape from the meeting as quickly as possible and join the ball. She had little to worry about now and had finally finished placing the plants and animals aboard the ship two days before.

Father Richard Piousse, who was to serve as the chaplain aboard the *Comet*, sat next to her. He was an elderly man, but his light brown hair showed very little gray. He wore thin spectacles at the end of his nose for reading. I had spoken with the Father many times, but I could never discern from where he had originally come. He had evidently lived in the Vatican, Paris, Canada, Australia, and Spain during his life, all in ministering positions. He was exceedingly bright, almost too bright for Conners's liking. After the Father had first arrived, Conners met him with a comment about the distressing conversion of Indians by the Spanish priests in the sixteenth century. The Father smiled and asked Conners if he would help him avoid such a tragedy. Conners, taken aback by such a pious reply, sheepishly answered that he would try.

Between the Father and Star sat Sergeant Juan Rodreguez, a former soldier in the Spanish army. Juan had commanded several artillery groups and had very often found himself in the action of battle. He was a brilliant soldier and refused many promotions so that he could stay with the troops on the field. During the Spanish-American War, he had sided with the Cubans after having married a Cuban woman. Spain labeled him as a traitor, but Cuban revolutionaries and American newspapers hailed him as a hero. Star had heard of his maneuvers in battle and offered him a position on the expedition, which Rodreguez immediately accepted.

After calling us to order, Star began listing duties and handed us each a projected daily itinerary. He explained to us how we were his inner circle of crewmen and leaders on the expedition. He told us of dangers we may face, but wonders we might also find. Finally, he ended by standing and saying, "Tomorrow is a big day, possibly the biggest day in all of history."

We all murmured in agreement and then went our separate ways. Several of the crewmembers went down to the ball, led by the ornately dressed Madam Rosiet. Conners retired to the library for one final night of reading. The rest of us, including myself, walked directly to our rooms to rest up for the next day.

The next morning everyone was woken early. Star was nervous and continuously barked orders, though they sometimes contradicted one another. Star's staff and the crew of the *Comet* were to go to the station on the Sky Train early in the morning. The guests were allowed to sleep later and come on a special second trip of the Sky Train. Star had planned for nearly all of the celebrations to take place in orbit, a festivity like no host had held before.

Just before the guests arrived on the station, Star single-handedly organized everyone in the main room of the station and gave us each a place to stand. We formed several lines, by nationality, with each line extending from one of the elevators. When the notabilities came out of their cars on the Sky Train, they would immediately be bombarded with hands to shake and greetings from crewmembers from their home nation.

I stood in a line with Phillip Wellis and two other Americans who were engineers on the *Comet*. I found that standing in place in Outer Space is not as tiring as on Earth. Instead of gravity pulling me down, I casually floated on my own, held in place by Star's magnetic shoes.

We were all wearing nearly identical Star bodysuits. They were not exactly formal attire, but they did make an impressive scene. It was almost like seeing a group of people from the distant future aboard a fantastic Space city. I wondered just how the guests would take the scene.

While we waited, Wellis pulled a slip of paper from his pocket and studied it. I leaned over toward him to try to see what it was. Noticing me, he smiled and handed it to me, saying, "It's the program for today's celebrations. I found it on the floor last night during the party."

I looked it over and then handed it back to him. The list started with "Greetings in the Great Hall," then a long list of speeches, a knighting ceremony for Star, the christening of *Star's Comet*, and, finally, the beginning of its maiden voyage. The day seemed long and formal, and I wished that I could escape from it somehow.

"I didn't know Star was going to be knighted," Wellis said as he looked over the paper again.

"He's tried to keep it quiet," Foster, one of the two other Americans, said. "I'm not sure if he did it out of humility or as a surprise for the crew."

"Knowing Star, it was probably not out of humility," Wellis said, chuckling.

Suddenly, the band in the center of the room stuck up a loud chord. Startled, I jumped a little and looked around to see what was the matter. Above us, the elevators had started moving. Star shouted, "It's time, everyone!" and moved to the head of the line of British crewmen.

The band began to play "God Save the Queen" just as the first elevator moved into position. I twisted around in time to see the doors of the elevator open and Queen Victoria herself stepped out. Her black dress was very nearly the cut for Earth, but was designed to be functional in weightlessness. Star knelt as she passed and took her hand formally. Other members of the royal family and English dignitaries followed her out of the elevator. The elevator then began to move back to the Train to pick up other passengers.

Several other anthems were played as dignitaries from other nations came into the room. Finally, "Hail to the Chief" sprung into the air and the line of

Americans snapped to attention. President McKinley led a small troop of American personages out of the elevator. They were all wearing formal suits and magnetic shoes that Star had provided for them, which were different from Earth garb but still quite prim.

Wellis, nearest to the door of the elevator, first shook the President's hand. Smiling broadly, he said, "I'm pleased to meet you, sir. Congratulations on your reelection."

"Thank you," McKinley replied. "Congratulations on being a member of such an amazing expedition." He left Wellis and then shook my hand, giving me a similar address.

As the President passed, Vice-President Roosevelt approached me. "It's a pleasure, lad," he said to me, shaking my hand so strongly that I thought that my knuckles would crack. "I trust that you'll do your country proud."

"I'll certainly try, sir," I told him.

"I didn't say 'try,'" Roosevelt smiled, "I said 'do.'"

The humorist Samuel Clemens followed Roosevelt closely behind. He winked at me as he shook my hand and whispered, "Don't worry about him, he's just jealous."

The final American dignitary was Thomas Edison. He shook each of our hands, but did not say much at all. He kept looking behind him, making sure that the two helpers that were following him were carrying his equipment correctly. He had brought a large moving-picture camera to record the events of today, but seemed more interested in the camera than the events.

As the four American celebrities and their aides passed, President McKinley came back to us for another chat. "You four have made headlines all across the United States of America," he told us. "The whole nation is proud of you and eagerly awaits the findings of the expedition. I became the first President to leave the country during his term to attend this christening and see you off. Every American is backing you. There's going to be an entire exhibit dedicated to the four of you and this expedition at the Pan-American Exposition. Do your country honor and uphold it throughout the stars."

We patriotically smiled and promised to support America. The President then left us and merged into the growing crowd of world dignitaries. We looked at one another, then, realizing that no more American personages were coming, followed him into the crowd.

The room was quite open and filled with people. All of the benches had been unbolted from the floor and stowed away. Butlers and maids, who had been waiting in the administrative offices, entered the room holding trays of glasses and hors d'oeuvres. Star had made all of the glasses especially for the celebration, and they must have cost him a small fortune. *Fortunately*, I thought, *he won't much have to worry about them being dropped and broken.*

I spotted Mary through the crowd and walked toward her. She was talking to a British man and carrying the book that she had read as she waited for me before my first trip up the Sky Train. As I approached, I heard their conversation. I waited out of their view until their dialogue paused.

"So you enjoyed it, then, Miss Star?" the man said.

"Very much," she replied. "You wouldn't mind signing it, would you?"

"Oh, no, I'd be happy to," he said. "Still, I can't help wondering why I bothered making it all up now that your father has done all of this in reality."

"It was quite a tale," she smiled. "I'm sure you did not waste your time."

He smiled gratefully and pulled a pen from his jacket. He tried to write on the inside of the cover of the book, but found that his pen would not function.

"We've found that ink does not work well without gravity," Mary said, giggling. She gave him a pencil and he sketched a large signature. As he handed her back the pencil and the book, I took my chance to approach.

"Ah, Curtis," Mary smiled as I came toward them. "Curtis, this is Mr. Wells, the author. Mr. Wells, Curtis Matricks, our chief astronomer."

"Pleased to meet you," he said, shaking my hand.

"The pleasure is all mine," I replied, beaming at the author. "I read your *Time Machine* about a year ago. It was very fascinating."

"I'm glad you liked it," Wells said. "Mary didn't share my *First Men in the Moon* with you, did she? It's technically not to be published for a while yet, but Mr. Star was very interested when he heard about it. I wonder if something like it may come true for your expedition." As he finished saying the last line, he took a long glance at the star-filled ceiling.

"I would much rather it come true than *War of the Worlds*," Mary said.

"True, very true," Wells agreed. "Perhaps, though, you may stumble upon a culture more powerful than ours. You might, ironically, lead to the downfall of Earth with its greatest achievement."

I nervously blinked with wide-eyes. I had never imagined such a downside that might come from the expedition. Finally, I reassured myself. "Still, there are no advances without a few risks."

"Quite true as well," Wells said. Mary nodded.

Wells pulled his watch from his pocket and held it up to look at it. "Well, if you will excuse me, I have a short speech to give."

He left us alone in the crowd and moved toward a temporary platform that had been erected in front of the window that faced the *Comet.* Star was there and, as he saw Wells approaching, came to the podium in the middle of the platform. The band ceased playing its soft dinner music and soon the murmur from the crowd died away.

When all was quiet, Star began his welcoming speech. It was not long and rather interesting. He welcomed each of the dignitaries by name, beginning with the Queen. After each there was an applause, some long, others short but polite. I recognized a few names, but many of them I had not ever heard before. After Star finished his welcome, he yielded the platform to H.G. Wells.

Wells made a few remarks, a joke, and then quoted from his yet-to-be-published *First Men in the Moon.* Finally, he bid everyone on the expedition good luck. "I would now like to introduce Monsieur Jules Verne," he said, ending his speech, though he quickly added, "The man who couldn't write his way out of a paper bag."

As the audience chuckled, a man with a thick beard and a limp approached the podium. "Thank you, Mr. Wells," he said with a French accent. "I trust that you'll always keep readers fascinated with your scientifically implausible ideas."

The audience now chuckled at Wells. Verne's speech was much longer, but did include several humorous lines to keep it interesting. Despite the lines, I found myself floating in my shoes nearly asleep. I had been up late the night before and early that morning, and I found that I needed something to keep me alert. I finally stared beyond the speaker and concentrated at the stars in the sky around the *Comet.* This kept me entertained through several speeches, but eventually gave way to drowsiness once again.

I felt a finger poke me in the back. I turned slowly, trying not to attract attention. Finally I recognized Conners, who had moved through the crowd toward me.

"Pretty stimulating, isn't it?" he whispered sarcastically. "I would have thought that you'd have been more impressed with the celebrities of the world."

"Quiet," I whispered, noticing that a German diplomat whose name I could not begin to pronounce was looking at us.

"Don't worry." Conners winked. "We'll be farther away from them than ever possible before in a couple of days."

The speeches continued. President McKinley's speech was warming to the Americans, and Clemens made several jokes out of it to appease the other nationalities in the room. Toward the end of the speeches there was a stirring discussion on the rights of women and praising Star for including females on his voyage. The final speech was a short address by Queen Victoria herself, which led to the knighting ceremony of Star.

By this time, Conners had disappeared from behind me. I looked around and soon spotted him near Pierre. They were both red in the face as if they were resisting laughing out loud. I smiled and wondered what Conners had said to bring about those expressions.

The knighting was rather long and full of dramatic pauses instituted by Star to prolong the moment. The sword used for the knighting was enormous and would have been quite heavy in gravity, but moved effortlessly in the Queen's hands here in Space. Finally, the newly knighted Sir Mason Star stood before the crowd and bowed his head to their applause.

Outside, two people in pressurized suits appeared, causing the audience to gasp. Their suits were similar to those of deep-sea divers and long cords that attached them to the station ran from their belts. They moved slowly, encumbered by their thick suits. One held a large wine bottle while the other carried a large lamp that cast a spotlight on the other.

The platform was cleared and everyone moved closer to the window for a better view. The brown-suited person with the lamp moved into a position where he could best illuminate the other Space walker. The person with the bottle hopped close to the side of the massive Starship.

Mason Star's voice came from behind us, "Ladies and gentlemen, I present to you the first ever Starship in the history of mankind, *Star's Comet.*"

At that moment, the person in Space was given a signal of some kind. The bottle was raised and then dashed against the side of ship, exploding under the impact. Tiny shards of glass cascaded into space along with small liquid spheres. As applause rang out from the crowd, the lamp was extinguished and the space travelers disappeared from view.

"That was quite a celebration," Mary said, her voice slightly shallow from quietly listening to speeches for so long.

"It was," I agreed.

Star's voice sounded out again. "All members of the Star expedition please report to the ship."

The dignitaries clapped as those of us in black bodysuits with large sliver 'S's began to march toward the large corridor marked "Boarding." Star moved as well, pausing to say farewell to his family and kiss his wife before entering the corridor. I came just after him in a small group of travelers. Just before I entered, I turned to see Vice-President Roosevelt smile and nod respectfully.

We walked down the corridor silently, all of us wondering just what might come out of this expedition. When we came to the entrance to the ship, Father Piousse checked us off of a list. He repeated "Welcome aboard" to each of us as we stepped on. The air was warm onboard the ship and full of an attitude of adventure.

As we passed into Deck C, we all went our separate ways. Star immediately headed for the pilot's station. I went to the astronomy laboratory on Deck C to see what I could from inside the ship. The protective screens were rolled over the telescopes, so I found a viewing port on the side to look out. The two French astronomers entered the laboratory behind me and moved to the viewing port at the other side of the room.

The Starship shifted slightly as the docking clamps were released. They had never let go of the ship since it had begun being constructed. When the ship was free, small maneuvering jets were fired, causing it to pull out of its docked position at the station. It rose above the station and turned about. I looked below the ship, seeing the station from above with the massive Earth spreading out below it.

A meager rumble spread throughout the ship as the rockets ignited. We began to accelerate, moving forward faster and faster. The Earth fell away behind us and soon we were on our way to the Moon.

Chapter Six,
Voyage to the Moon

I spent my first few hours of the celestial voyage in the astronomy laboratory. I sent one of the Frenchmen to gather the other astronomers. When they had all arrived, I set up a schedule for them to follow. We would work in eight-hour shifts, making the best of our resources and times. The six astronomers under me would work in pairs, one viewing and one jotting notes, while I oversaw them and used the telescopes whenever they were not occupied.

After an hour of deciding the best times and assigning duties, we set to work. The two Frenchmen were off duty initially, so they went to their bunks to rest. Hosea, the Brazilian, and Hertzel, the Londoner, stayed in the Deck C astronomy laboratory while Helga and Giovanni went down to the Deck D laboratory. I stayed in the laboratory on Deck C, making notes of our meeting and outlining a short report for Star.

Star had stated that one of our main duties as commanders would be to continuously report important data to him and relay the feelings of the crew. Thus far the crew seemed to be in very high spirits, and I doubted that I needed to report that to him. Still, I thought that an outline of the plans I had made was a good thing to report as soon as possible.

Finishing my notes, I looked up at Hosea and Hertzel. They were busy improving on the map of the Lunar surface that we had been given. Below us, Helga and Giovanni were making scans of the stars, trying to locate any new appearances. Hosea was at the telescope, memorizing details of a sector of the surface. Meanwhile, Hertzel was sketching out the details on a large map that was held on the floor with papermagnets. When Hosea was sure that he had the details correct, he and Hertzel would trade places and continue the process at the next sector.

"Anything yet?" I asked.

"It is quite an improvement," Hosea said. "We're finding fissures and craters that we could not have ever seen through the atmosphere."

"No cities, yet, though," Hertzel chuckled.

I smiled and left them to their work. Heading out of the astronomy laboratory, I went up the nearby stairwell to Deck Λ. I checked in the pilot's station for Star, but did not find him there.

"He headed back to his room," the pilot on duty said, lowering a book that he was reading. The ship was essentially flying itself, pointed at the Moon and blasting away with its enormous rockets. The pilot of the ship only needed to make adjustments every few minutes and thus was left with a fairly easy task.

I then went down to Deck B and knocked on the door of Star's captain's quarters. He answered, holding a glass and wearing the standard black bodysuit. He must have left the pilot's station soon after we left the station to change to a more comfortable setting.

"Ah, Curtis, what brings you by so soon?" he asked.

"I set up a work schedule with my group of astronomers," I said, holding a piece of paper out to him, "and I thought that you would like to see it."

"All right," Star said. "Come in and have a seat while I look this over."

I walked into the suite and strapped myself onto the sofa. It felt good to not have my shoes keeping my body on the floor for a moment. Star looked at the notes and strapped himself into a chair opposite me.

"It looks interesting, Curtis," he said. "You know, I think that you'll make a fine—"

He was cut off by a knock at the door.

"Excuse me," Star mumbled. He stood from his seat and answered it.

A man was standing there, holding a young redheaded girl by the arm. When Star saw who it was, the blood drained from his face despite the lack of gravity. He gasped, "Mary!"

"I went down to the storage room on Deck E to locate the extra bolts and I found her stowed away," the man explained.

"Thank you. You may go now," Star mumbled, his teeth clenched. The man nodded and left. Star pulled Mary into the room and shut the door loudly behind her.

"What do you think you are doing here?" the senior Star asked.

"It'll take a bit to explain, but I'm sure you'll understand," Mary said, trying to calm her father.

"I think you'll have to do an enormous amount of explaining before I understand!" Star roared.

I wanted desperately to escape from the room, but the two arguers blocked the door. Since it was the only route out of the situation, I was stuck. I tried to blend in with the sofa and pretend that I was not there.

"This is the chance of a lifetime, Father," Mary began. "I couldn't let it slip by without doing anything about it."

"We had a talk about your wanting to go on the expedition," Star said, "and I told you then that you were too young to do something like this."

"Father, how old were you when you took over your father's small trading fleet and turned it into one of the biggest mercantile companies in the world?"

"That was different," Star said. "I wasn't risking my life at all."

"It was still the earliest defining moment in your life, and I'm older than you were then."

"All right," Star sighed, knowing that he had been bested by his own history. He changed his strategy. "What is your mother going to think when she finds your bed empty tomorrow?"

"Nothing," Mary said. "She knows about this. Actually, when I came to her about it, she thought it was a good idea."

Star swallowed.

"Father," Mary began the end of her argument, "I've followed you around for the majority of my life. I know everything about this ship, just like you do. I could definitely be an asset to you."

"True," Star said, "but do you know what the penalty for stowing away?"

"It was never addressed in the book of etiquette. I've already checked."

"I knew I had forgotten something," Star said, clenching his fist and pressing it against his mouth.

"The only thing you could do is turn the ship around and force me to go home," Mary said. "And you know as well as I do that you would never turn the ship around."

"Very well, you may stay," Star said. Mary smiled.

"But," Star continued, causing Mary's smile to diminish, "you will be an asset to this ship, even if it means working more than you ever have before."

"All right," Mary said. She and her father embraced, ending the discussion.

"You'll have to stay here," Star said. "All of the other bunks are already occupied. I trust you did bring essentials with you."

"Of course." Mary's smile reappeared.

"I knew you would. I suppose you can sleep on the sofa, though the straps aren't quite designed for sleeping. We could probably adjust—" He stopped, noticing me as he turned. "Oh, Curtis, I had forgotten all about you."

"That's all right," I said, smiling nervously. I stood and made for the door. "I'll just be on my way."

As I left, Star called, "Thanks for stopping by!"

Once in the corridor with the door safely closed behind me, I sighed with relief. I did not know whether seeing that argument was a good thing or a bad one. I was rather worn out by watching the ordeal and decided to head back to my bunk for a night's rest.

The bunkrooms in the *Comet* were designed for four people. Each person had his own bunk and three drawers, two holding clothing and one containing personal items. The bunk was a body-sized enclosure with a curtain to block out light. There was no true mattress, but all of the walls of the bunk were padded with thin cushions in case a body bumped into them while sleeping. There was a long strap to keep the sleeper in place while resting so that they did not float away in the lack of gravity.

In addition to the sleeping and storage areas, each bunkroom was equipped with rubber exercise gear hung on the wall on magnetic hooks. Star ordered that all crewmembers exercise by stretching the rubber strands for two hours daily. Humans came from the terrestrial planet that theoretically had the strongest gravitational field, and Star wanted to keep that advantage strong. He had found that workers on the station grew weaker without gravity and eventually could barely function under Earth's gravity.

When I reached my bunkroom, I found the curtain around Wellis's bunk closed. Star had put the four Americans together in the same bunkroom. I assumed that he felt that we would be most comfortable grouped with as a nationality. When we had learned our bunk assignments, Wellis had joked that he probably wanted to keep us in a single place to be able to keep and eye on us "bloody colonials."

I moved quietly, trying not to disturb Wellis. I deactivated the magnets on my shoes and floated noiselessly to my bunk. Taking off my shoes, I slid them into a drawer below the bunk and then slid myself into the bunk by pulling myself along the strap inside. I strapped myself securely and tightened it to a comfortable position. When I pulled the curtain shut, the bunk became almost black inside. I wrapped the blanket inside of the bunk around me and within a few moments I was asleep.

*

Sleeping without gravity is an intriguing experience. No matter the position, I seemed to be comfortable. I am not quite sure if it is like sleeping in a womb, as Mr. Edwards described it, but it certainly is comfortable. I imagine that if one were allowed, he would sleep for days on end. Unfortunately, we all had small alarm clocks to awaken us when we needed to get back to work.

I floated in dreamless sleep for about eight hours before my alarm clock went off and woke me with its ringing. Hitting the alarm, I yawned and unraveled myself from my blanket. The strap connecting me to the wall had become taut as I had floated away from it during my rest.

With the continuous blasting of the rockets, everything on the ship felt a kind of pull, somewhat similar to gravity, due to the acceleration. According to Star's book, the pull would never be more than two percent of Earth's gravity. Over eight hours, however, one could float quite a distance, making us glad for the straps in the bunks.

I pulled back the curtain and blinked at the brightness of the bunkroom. When my eyes adjusted, I immediately reached for my magnetic shoes. Fumbling without gravity just after you have awoken is not an easy task, but I finally managed to find my shoes and put them on my feet.

"'Morning," I heard a voice say. I looked up and saw Wellis busily stretching the rubber belts.

"Good morning," I replied.

I turned back toward my bunk and saw that the alarm clock showed eight-fifteen. Since it was an even hour, I decided to head to the ship's bathroom. I dug my pouch of toiletries from the drawer under my bunk and left the bunkroom. The ship's corridors were rather quiet, only a soft vibration reverberating from the rockets could be heard.

The door to the bathroom had a small clock built into it and an inscription in English to remind the crew which gender was allowed in the bathroom at what times. I entered the bathroom and saw two men standing at the sinks shaving. Feeling rather grimy, I headed for the showers that lined the wall farthest from the door.

The showers in the bathroom were some of the most advanced engineering in the ship. They worked off of pneumatics, the physics of gasses. When one entered the shower, he first activates the pumps that create a strong wind from the ceiling down toward the floor. Then the water is turned on, which flows from a faucet in the ceiling. Normally without gravity the water would become globules and hang in the air, but with the strong airstream, it fell to the floor much like on Earth. When one's shower was finished, he shut off the water and waited for the airstream to dry nearly all of the water. The rest of the water would then be mopped up with towels left in the dressing stall outside of the shower.

When I had finished with my shower, I put on a fresh bodysuit nearly identical to my old one. I then left the showers and visited the sinks. When I finished, I finally threw all of my wet towels and dirty clothing into a hamper with a magnetic lid near the door of the bathroom. All of the crew's clothes had names stitched into them, so laundry could be done at the same time and sorted later. In a few hours, I would be able to pick up my newly cleaned clothes in the cafeteria.

After replacing my toiletries under my bunk, I headed for the cafeteria for some breakfast. The kitchens were quite busy cooking food for all three meals at the same time. The crew on the ship worked at very different schedules, meaning that someone would need food at any given time. I ordered some bacon and toast for breakfast and got some orange juice from a pressurized dispenser.

I had very little of an idea how the chefs were cooking without gravity. There was a large list of foods that could be prepared posted above the window that joined the cafeteria to the kitchen. I supposed that they had selected easily prepared items for which they had devised cooking schemes.

When my toast and bacon were ready, the chefs placed them in containers on an iron tray. The containers were magnetically attached to the tray and could be opened and closed to avoid potential spills. The silverware was the same in Space as on Earth, but spoons were nearly useless for scooping soups, which had to be sipped like drinks.

Breakfast was rather uneventful. There were only two other people in the cafeteria, both Italian and conversing in their native language. I finished my meal as quickly as I could and left, eager to get to the astronomy laboratories.

As I exited the cafeteria, I passed the gunnery room. The door was open, exposing the numerous cases of ammunition and guns. Sergeant Rodreguez was sitting in a chair, polishing a large, ornate rifle. I felt the impulse to walk into the room and speak with him.

"Hello," I said as I entered.

"*Hola*," he said, smiling through a thick beard. He pointed the rifle that he was cleaning at me, checked the sight, and then put it away, chuckling at my horrified expression.

"This is quite a bit of weaponry," I said, eying the artillery guns behind him.

"It may be necessary," he said. "Especially when we're going through the belt of asteroids beyond Mars. We'll have to blow some of the bigger chunks out of our way if we can't maneuver around them."

"You think we'll need so many small arms too?"

"I hope not, but you never know what we might face. You may be happy to have a good revolver at your side if you face some fierce little green men." He chuckled at the idea, but paused afterward as if he were looking forward to a firefight.

"We could face a lot of these little green men with all the ammunition we have."

"You know of the Lewis and Clark expedition in your country?" he asked me. I answered affirmatively, so he continued by saying, "They say that they never ran out of two things: paper and bullets. Paper is not my department, but I aim to follow their example of having enough ammunition."

I nodded, understanding his position. Rodreguez seemed to be trying to place himself between the crew and total destruction. Feeling the urge to move on, I said that I needed to get to the astronomy laboratories, so he bid me farewell.

I walked with a quick pace down the stairwell to the astronomy laboratory on Deck C. When I entered, I saw Helga at the telescope, peering with intense concentration. I tried not to disturb her and went to look over the charts that the people on duty had made while I had slept.

In a few moments, though, Helga looked up from the telescope and noticed me. "Ah, hello," she said.

"Hi," I replied. "How does it look?"

"It is beautiful," she said. "The Moon is so close! You can see the mountains and valleys unbelievably well." She backed away from the telescope and motioned for me to take a look.

I went over to the telescope and gazed through it. The landscape of the Moon was amazingly clear, but still fairly distant. The surface was a gray color and seemed to be the same all over it.

"We haven't seen any water," Helga said. Star had mentioned to the astronomers that he would be extremely interested in any bodies of water that could serve as a fuel source. He had also offered a reward for the first to spot such a find. "Just rocks," she mumbled.

"Is the other telescope being used?" I asked.

Helga nodded. "François and Jacques put up the spectroscope to look at the make up. They've been taking data for quite a few hours now. I checked on them a little while ago, but they said they had not even found an atmosphere worth speaking about."

I nodded and then went back to check over the charts. We had made some discoveries, but the Moon was so close to the Earth that astronomers had already done much of the mapping. Most of our finds would probably come from discerning new stars or other celestial objects.

The day passed quickly and rather quietly. I looked over the charts, spent much time staring through either of the two telescopes, and made markings of my own. I had a small lunch, only a sandwich and a glass of water, and was very ready for a dinner by the end of my day.

When I entered the cafeteria that evening (I say "evening" here as a point in time, not a twilight on the ship), it was nearly full of people. Most of them had come off of duties and a few had just gotten up from their bunks. The cafeteria was fairly noisy now, with all of the people chatting with one another in differing languages. Pierre's voice added to the noise as he read the day's news over loudspeakers situated at the upper corners of the room.

I took a tray of food, found Conners at a table reading a book, and decided to join him. When he noticed me approaching, he put down his book and smiled warmly.

"Busy day?" he asked.

"Fairly," I said. "Nothing too bad, though."

"My day has been extremely slow," he said. "I spent most of the day in the library, reading this and that. I finally couldn't stand it anymore and wandered the corridors for a while before I came here. This expedition seems to have brought along all the comforts of home, as well as a heavy dosage of boredom."

"You really don't have anything to do?" I asked.

"Nope," he said, smiling fairly smugly. "I'm pretty much free until we find somebody to talk to."

I rolled my eyes.

"I've got cleaning duty tomorrow, though," he sneered. "I suppose I shouldn't complain. If everybody doesn't take up their part, our little society here might collapse."

I nodded. Everyone had one day a week that they were to report for cleaning duty, which had been chosen at random. The only way to get out of cleaning duty was to be terribly ill or off-ship.

"I've just spent the day laying around," Conners sighed. "Eventually, I got to thinking about the rigid, unemotional names on this ship. I mean, 'Deck B,' where's the poetry in that? And what about 'pilot's station,' 'rocket control room,' and 'bunkroom 12'?" His voice grew more indignant with each example.

"What do you propose to do about it?" I asked, chuckling at him.

"First off, I think we should give the five decks nicknames," he said, leaning back in his chair and loosening the strap that held him in place a little. "For Deck A, we could call it the 'Administration' Deck, which it kind of is with the pilot's station and radio room and all. Then we could have 'Bunk' Deck, since that's where most of the bunkrooms are anyway. 'Cow' Deck would follow, since it has the animal Agricultural Laboratory. Then we've got the 'Danger' Deck with the rockets and all. And finally, we'd have 'Empty' Deck, since it's just for storage."

"Interesting," I said. "You know how they say that there's a thin line between genius and insanity?"

"Yes?"

"You like to jump across it, don't you?"

Conners smiled, pleased at being teased.

Just then a man approached our table. He faced me and said, "Captain Star has requested that you meet with him as soon as possible."

"All right, I will," I said.

As the man left, Conners chuckled. "So he's calling himself 'Captain' now?"

"He might as well," I said. "It is his ship."

"I guess it's better this than 'Sir' Mason Star," Conners snorted. I could not tell whether he was genuinely entertained by Star's tendency toward arrogance or extremely jealous of Star's achievements.

I ate as quickly as I could and said goodbye to Conners. After putting away my tray, I left the cafeteria and walked several steps down the corridor to Star's captain's room. When I knocked, the door was almost immediately opened by Mary.

There were three people in the room. Mary had been taking notes and was near the door to answer it in such a quick manner. Star and one of the engineers were leaning over a set of blueprints that was on the table, held in place by magnets.

"It's just not getting the amount of filtration we need it to," the engineer said. "Some of the purifiers must be blocked under the botany laboratory."

"See what you can do about it," Star said. "How does restored water compare to our water consumption now anyway?"

"It's at about sixty-five percent of our maximum," he replied.

"How long could we go at this rate?" Star asked.

The engineer scratched his head. "Probably about twenty days if we don't do any rationing. If we did some rationing, we could stretch it out quite a bit."

Star nodded. "All right. See if you can fix it as best you can and give me a little report tomorrow before we leave."

"Yes, sir," the engineer said. He then gathered the blueprints and left the room.

"Ah, Curtis," Star said, clapping me on the shoulder. "I've got a bit of a reassignment for you."

"Really?" I asked.

"Yes." He nodded. "When we get to Luna, I'm going to set up a research station. Not much for right now, but it'll be built up later. We'll be leaving a significant portion of the crew there."

"Are you planning to leave me on the Moon?" I asked, a little fearfully.

Star laughed aloud. "No, I just need you to be there to help set up the station. We'll come into orbit around Luna tomorrow evening and drop the landers within an hour thereof. You will wait on the landers until we get some of the Station set up. Just take what you need. Do you agree to go?"

"Yes, most definitely," I said, marveled by the idea of landing on the Moon. Still, something seemed amiss to me.

"Good," Star said.

"Uh, sir, I've got one question," I said.

"Yes?"

"Why me? Wouldn't I do better work on the ship with the astronomy laboratories and one of the other astronomers land?"

"You're one of a kind, Curtis," Star said quite seriously. "I personally would like to keep you rather close."

"Thank you, sir," I said, smiling at myself.

After that, I left his room and headed to my bunk. I spent several hours flipping through the intricate drawings in Star's book and writing the recent events in my journal. Finally I shut the curtain on my bunk and went to sleep.

*

That night I was awoken by a strange sensation. I was slowly being pushed in different directions by an unknown force. After being confused for a moment, I finally realized that the ship was turning around. The rockets had been stopped and the ship was being rotated on maneuvering thrusters.

I stretched and quietly felt the ship move around me. It was a novel experience and strangely relaxing. Soon the ship stopped rotating and was facing the other direction. At last I heard the low rumble of the rockets as they reignited. Lulled by the sound, I soon fell asleep again.

The next day was rather run of the mill on board the Starship. By now, everyone knew his or her places and duties. Star seemed to enjoy the status quo of the ship and toured the entire vessel several times, always beaming with a large smile. When not strutting on the ship, he sat in his captain's chair on the bridge, watching the distant orb of Earth shrink as the ship flew away from it.

When I came off of duty in the astronomy laboratories, I accompanied Star on one of his tours. We only shortly visited the laboratories on Deck A where scientists were busy working on experiments that were unhindered by gravity.

Star next watched the animals on Deck C for a few minutes. They seemed to be very content with their small corral and magnetic footings. The odor in the room was rather powerful, and a sign on the door recommended that it be closed whenever possible to avoid contamination of the rest of the ship's air.

While we were there, Elissa entered the room. She was wearing a transparent cloth over her mouth to block the odors of the animals. "*Bonjour*, Monsieur Star, Monsieur Matricks," she said through the mask, greeting us. She was carrying a sack of grain to feed the animals (by "carrying," I mean pulling the weightless sack on her shoulder).

"Hello," Star said. I smiled politely, but did not say anything.

Star cleared his throat. "So, everything has run smoothly?"

"Very," she said. She emptied the sack into specially designed trays by squeezing the grain out of it. The chickens, running awkwardly on their magnetic footings, hurried to peck in the small holes in a low tray that would supply them grain. "Ze hardest part is keeping ze air clean."

I nodded and continued to breathe through my mouth to avoid the smell of the room. Bits of grain and other farmyard debris floated merrily through the air. Elissa took a small net that was hung on the wall with magnetic straps and began to scoop them up.

"How are the supplies?" Star asked.

"A little less zan expected," Elissa said, packing the net's quarry into the empty sack. "Ze chickens are laying well, but ze goats' milk is lacking."

I watched one of the goats, which were stepping over the chickens on the way to another tray that was designed for them to eat. They were funny creatures, and supplied most of the stink that filled the room.

"Can we boost their production, perhaps?" Star asked.

"Monsieur," Elissa held up a finger and smiled, "one must let nature run itself."

"I think it's a little late for that," I mumbled. Star did not seem to hear me, but Elissa smiled slightly under her mask.

Elissa finished filling the bag and rolled the top on itself to seal it. She had cleared much of the debris, but several small bits and the stench still hung in the air. "It may not be ze most pleasant of fertilizers, but it certainly does wonders for ze botany laboratory."

She left the room and we went after her. I was glad to be away from the animals and wondered if any of the stink had clung to my clothes. We had only been in there a few minutes, so I doubted that I would reek of it too much.

We followed Elissa down the corridor to Deck D and into the botany laboratory. As badly as the agricultural laboratory smelled, the flowers in the botany laboratory more than made up for it. I inhaled deeply as I entered and was glad to be rid of the goats and chickens.

The laboratory seemed more like a lush garden than a crucial part of the ship and essential to the survival of the crew. There were several benches in the center of the room for weary crewmembers to relax. Three crewmen were sitting on them, two were chatting and the third resting with his eyes closed.

Elissa emptied the bag of refuse into a tube, closed the lid, and then began a small pump that would carry it out throughout the gardens. The beds of the gardens were netted so that no dirt would escape into the air. Numerous plants grew up through the nets and spread their broad leaves so much that passing down the paths was somewhat difficult.

"Excuse me," a short Indian crewman said, trying to get around me. I stepped out of his way as best I could and let him pass. He was carrying a small watering can to moisten the beds. The can had a small handle that he pumped to squirt the water out of it via pressure.

I stayed in the botany laboratory for several minutes. The air was very warm, heated by the bright lamps on ceiling that supplied the plants with ample light for photosynthesis, and also very humid. The atmosphere seemed much fresher in the botany laboratory than on the rest of the ship, almost like a piece of jungle or forest brought along from Earth.

Just before he left, Star clapped me on the shoulder. "You may want to get some sleep before tonight," he said. "We'll have an assembly at ten, then we'll go directly down to the surface of Luna."

"Wow," I said, then quickly followed it with, "Yes, sir."

I hurried to my bunkroom and jumped into my bunk. With my alarm reset, I strapped myself in loosely. I was very excited and wondered about what marvels I might see. Eventually, I forced myself to clear my mind and rest.

It could not have been more than a few minutes after I had closed my eyes, but my alarm woke me with a buzzing sound. I opened the curtain and tried to pull myself out of the bunk. Unfortunately, I had forgotten to undo my strap and slammed my body against it. After recovering my breath, I undid the strap and soon left the bunkroom.

The ship was noisy as I hurried down the corridor to the theater. When I entered it, I found that the assembly would soon begin, slightly ahead of schedule. Everyone who was not on essential duty was in the room, chatting with those around them. I walked down the central aisle, looking for a free seat.

Finally, I found one on the front row next to Dr. van Sparchs. He nodded politely to me, but did not start a conversation. I returned the nod and strapped myself into the seat.

In a few moments, Star appeared on the stage and the room grew silent. Star began by whispering off stage, and then returned to the audience. "The photography laboratory is preparing images of the Lunar surface. They will be ready soon. Until then, I have an address I would like to deliver."

Someone in the back made a noise that caused everyone to stir. I imagined that it had been Conners, but I did not want to look around to confirm my suspicions.

Star seemed unaffected by the disruption. "Ladies and gentlemen, this project has been one of many firsts. It began twenty years ago as a whimsical idea, but now has become the greatest step that mankind has ever taken. One might even call it a leap, something as momentous as the discovery of agriculture or the invention of the printing press. It is true that humanity will never be the same. Tonight we will land on the surface of the Moon, something man has wanted to do since he first looked up at the sky and saw the mysterious disk staring down at him…"

His speech continued, but my attention left him as a large white screen lowered behind him. Cords on either end pulled it slowly down until it was in the center of the stage. I could hear a slight rustling behind it, signifying some sort of activity. Now I was not able to hear Star's speech at all, instead only being able to think about what was happening behind the screen.

Finally Star's speech ended and he turned, raising his hand to point to the great screen behind him. "And now, the first pictures of the Moon from an orbit around it!"

The audience mumbled among one another as the lights dimmed. Suddenly, a huge, gray landscape lit up on the screen. We all inhaled in amazement and then stared at it as carefully as we could.

The landscape stayed the same for several moments, and then began to move. We watched as the gray, pockmarked surface passed slowly across the screen. The lunar scenery continued by until the image froze near a large crater.

Star's voice rang out, "This will be our landing site. Within a few hours, the landing party will begin building several structures that will serve as the Lunar Station. The *Comet*, meanwhile, will orbit above the Station, watching and functioning normally."

Several more images flashed on the screen, close pictures of the landmarks that had been before only viewed from afar. Finally, Star ended the assembly with saying, "All members of the lunar landing party please report to the landers."

In a few minutes, we began our descent to the Moon.

Chapter Seven,
The Moon

I was sitting in the first of the three landers that were destined for the surface of the Moon. There were eight of us all crammed into a small room at the front of the lander. Most of the lander's storage space was dedicated to parts for the Station, leaving only a minute amount of space for passengers.

The pilot and his instruments took up most of the small room, causing the room to be even more cramped. He had several levers that operated the rockets that slowed the lander's fall and controlled its path. Periscopes that allowed him to see in nearly all directions surrounded his head. A small window of heavy glass was in front of him to give him a view of what was directly in front of the lander.

The only space left for the other seven passengers were two small couches with seven sets of straps. We were all firmly strapped into place, anxiously awaiting our landfall. There was very little room between us, but we were more interested in the world outside than our comfort. Two small viewing ports allowed us to see the stars outside and the distant horizon of the Moon, which was growing closer and closer.

I sat between Conners and a geologist whom I did not know. The geologist was completely still, though I could not tell whether nervously frozen or motionlessly patient. Conners, on the other hand, was wringing a handkerchief in his hands with anxiety. I tried to look out the ports, but I could never gain a very good view.

Mary sat on the other couch, next to her father. She had a good view out of a port and continued to look out it. Star had mentioned to me that she had somehow convinced him to take her along in the landing party. He had looked over the crew list and eventually replaced a chemist with her, which had caused Wellis to complain about his extra workload. Still, when he finished his remark, he admitted in a mumble that she may be a good addition after all.

I sighed, barely being able to contain my impatience to land. Our descent to the surface had begun immediately after the assembly. We all gathered on Deck E and hurried into our seats on the landers. When the pilot was strapped into his place and sure of all of the controls, he gave a sign to several men outside in the lander storage room. The men lifted the lander and carefully moved it into the launching bay.

After the men left, a large door was closed behind us, which made us all jump a little. Then loud pumps began to suck the air out of the launching bay. As the air became less and less dense, the pumps grew quieter and quieter until we could not even hear them at all. When the room became a vacuum, the door underneath the lander was opened. The pilot pulled a lever and caused the lander to begin its fall toward the Moon's surface. After we began descending, the doors shut, and the process was repeated for the second lander.

Below us, the Moon rushed upward. I struggled to look out of the viewing ports, but could still not see well at all. Finally, I focused on the pilot, watching his actions. He skillfully straightened the lander, continuously checked each periscope, and led us safely to the surface. Finally, the lander's footpads touched the dusty Moon, and we stopped with a dull thud.

The seat pressed up against my backside, and much of the stress was taken away from the straps. As we grew closer to the Moon, its gravity slowly caught us. After nearly three days without it, gravity felt rather strange, but pleasant. The weak gravity, only one-sixth that of the Earth, gave the odd feeling like when one returns home after a long trip.

"We're here," the pilot said, pushing away the periscopes and turning around in his seat.

"Good piloting, Smith," Star said and clapped his hands together. "Gentlemen, let's go. Remember this time, eleven twenty-six on January the third, nineteen hundred and one, and tell your grandchildren."

Star unstrapped himself, as did two other men. They stood, then each bent down to deactivate their magnetic boots. I smiled, relieved that the boots, which had been our only source of stability on the *Comet,* would now not be needed.

The three men left the front room of the lander and moved to the large storage room. They sealed the door tightly behind them, disappearing from view. They were silent for a long moment, and then we heard a loud humming begin.

"Pumps," Conners whispered, even though we all knew what the sound was. The men had put on the thick Spacesuits and then activated the lander's pumps to remove all of the atmosphere from the room. In a few moments, the sound of the pumps would disappear and we would not hear anything from them for a long while.

We all sat there completely silent for several minutes. Finally, an excited gasp from the pilot jerked us all to attention. We unstrapped ourselves and moved in the feeble gravity to look out the front window.

Outside, there were three men in brown Spacesuits. The one in front, most likely Star, waved vigorously to us. We waved back, but I doubt that he saw us through the small window. One of the two men behind him was carrying a Union Jack, the other a camera designed to work in the absence of air.

Star motioned to the man with the flag to plant it, and when he did, they posed for several pictures. Then the two men stood while Star said the words that he had long planned, "From the heavens we came, to the heavens we return." He recited the words he thought quite poetic many times to me and other crewmembers onboard the *Comet*. He now finally was able to say them from the Moon, but unfortunately, since he was in a Spacesuit, he was the only person to hear them.

Moments later the second lander appeared above us and slowly came to a rest about fifty feet from ours. Five crewmen in Spacesuits soon came out of it and joined Star and the other two men. They signaled to one another for a moment, and then walked toward the back of the second lander.

There were only ten Spacesuits aboard the *Comet*, and eight of them had been sent to the Moon for the workers. Star, wanting to be the first human to ever set foot on the Moon, had taken one of the suits for himself. Unfortunately for him, this meant that he would be required to work along with the rest of the construction team setting up the first building of the Lunar Station.

While the workers began, we returned to our seats and resumed waiting. Conners played with the handkerchief he had been wringing before, folding it into different shapes. The geologist and the pilot began to chat. I sat still for a while, and then moved over to sit by Mary, who had been silent since we had left the *Comet*.

"Pretty exciting, eh?" I asked.

"Quite," she said. She looked at me only for a moment and then turned back to look out the viewing port.

I said nothing for a moment, then ventured to say, "Worrying?"

"Well, yes, a little, I suppose," she said, turning back to me. "Those suits aren't exactly our safest pieces of equipment. A rend in it or if their welding torch got away from them and…" She trailed off and looked out the viewing port once again.

"I'm sure they know what they're doing," I reassured her. She smiled slightly, but did not turn away from the viewing port.

Finally, Conners finished playing with his handkerchief and tucked it into his pocket. "How long is this going to take?"

"They should have the first building up in less than an hour," Mary told him. "The buildings are really just walls that need to be welded together."

"And with this gravity, it ought to be a pretty easy job," I added.

"So, I guess we're going to be stuck here for a while longer," Conners sighed. He looked toward the pilot and geologist, who were discussing rugby. Conners had no interest in sports (at least common sports; he often mentioned that gladiatorial combat always seemed intriguing), and looked toward Mary and me for conversation. "So, Miss Star, Mr. Matricks, have you enjoyed your little holiday from the planet Earth thus far?"

I smiled. "It's been pretty pleasant."

"I agree, it has," Mary said.

"As for myself," Conners said before anyone could ask what he thought, "I've had a rather bland time. The only duty I have on the ship is cleaning, and that's only one day per week. I've really spent most of my time in the library. Quite a fascinating collection your father brought."

"I'm glad you like it," Mary said. "He spent a long while picking out the best books to take."

"The light reading was rather lacking, though. He certainly does enjoy technical manuscripts and deep literature. I suppose he wouldn't allow a dime novel anywhere near his library."

"You're quite right. Father takes reading seriously. 'It's what separates us from the animals,' he always says." Mary made the quote in a funny voice mimicking that of her father.

Conners chuckled. The conversation paused, then he said, "It certainly must have been interesting growing up among such riches."

"I can honestly say I haven't had many dull moments." Mary smiled.

"What about you, Curtis?" Conners turned to me. "Always a shindig in Ohio?"

I rolled my eyes. "It was never terribly glamorous, but I enjoyed it," I told him, then asked, "How about you? How did you grow up?"

"Well," Conners began, "it's not much of a story, but I'll try to make it interesting. I was born in a neighborhood of Belfast that I'm fairly sure doesn't exist anymore. I was the second of six children. My father was a lawyer and my mother did some sewing on the side of taking care of us children.

"I led a pretty normal childhood: making trouble, running around with neighborhood boys, skating if we could find enough ice, and so forth. Everything changed when I was ten or so, though. My brother, who was about fourteen, made the announcement that he wished to go into the army. My parents were rather pleased at his decision and helped him get into a military academy.

"Still, my father wanted a son to follow in his footsteps as a lawyer. All of my younger siblings were girls, so I was the only one left to be his protégé, whether I liked it or not. When I was twelve, I was sent to a dormitory school designed to give children the education they would need to be a young man. I studied hard, unwillingly, and finally could no longer stand it. I slacked off on my studies and graduated at the age of eighteen with barely passing marks.

"My parents were upset with me, knowing that I could have done better, and tried to push me harder. I would not respond, though. Eventually they just decided that I was on my way to become a 'black sheep' and hurried to apprentice me to one of my father's lawyer friends, which they were certain would make me into a fine young lawyer. I stayed at it for three years, miserable all the time. Then, in a fit of frustration, I left the lawyer's house, marched to my own, and explained to my parents how I refused to become a lawyer myself. An argument ensued, and finally I stormed out of the house, never to return.

"I stumbled from place to place, doing odd jobs along the way to feed myself. One day I bought a ticket for a ship destined for Venice on a whim. I guess I've told you that story, though."

When he finished, Mary and I looked at him silently for a moment. Conners noticed our pause in conversation and immediately changed the subject. "That's all ancient history, though. Here's a better story…" He began to tell us a tale about a trip he took to Egypt under another grant from Oxford. Most of the tale was bland, but we all chuckled at his telling of a brawl in a cantina in Cairo that nearly ended the expedition.

As he began to tell of his effort to scale the Great Pyramid in Giza, he was interrupted by a hissing mechanical sound. Our conversation paused, as did that of the geologist and pilot. We all listened silently and waited for something to happen.

Finally, the door that led from our small room to the large storage room began to slowly open. There was first a metallic thump as the locks were removed, then a hiss as it opened. Star, holding his helmet in his arm, smiled at us as he poked his head through the door. "Lady and gentlemen, it's time to move into our new lunar home."

We glanced at each other, and then we stood and moved into the storage room. The air was rather thin in the room, some of it having been lost by the imperfect pumps. The two men who had left with him were there, each holding several Spacesuits each. With Star's direction, we each took a suit and dressed in it.

The Spacesuits were made of very thick, heavy cloth with several layers of india-rubber and looked very similar to diving suits. There was only one opening in the entire suit, which was at the neck and surrounded by a metal ring with locks in it. We removed our magnetic shoes and stepped into the suits through the neck hole. We then pulled them up over our bodysuits, barely squeezed our shoulders through the hole, and then put the helmet on our heads. By giving the helmet several turns, interlacing locks on the metal ring of the suit and the helmet screwed together to form an airtight seal. A small tank of atmosphere, connected with the helmet by a rubber tube, went on our backs. The tanks supplied fresh air to our suits, which replaced air leaked out ever so slightly of inevitable tiny holes in our suits.

The two men with Star then went around, checking the seal at the neck on each of our suits. When they were satisfied that we had dressed correctly, they put on their own helmets and gave Star a sign. Star nodded, put his helmet on, and then activated the air pumps. We heard a dull thudding as they sucked up the air, then silence once they created a vacuum. Star pulled a lever, stopping the pumps, and then another lever to open the door of the storage room, allowing us to move out onto the surface of the Moon.

The Moon was like an eternal beach of gray sand at night. Every step we took left a thick footprint, and there were already hundreds of footprints of Star and the other workers. The sky above us was full of stars, and the sun was a large, bright orb. There was plenty of light on the Moon to see the things around us, but the black sky made it appear like night.

We walked across the lunar sand, heading for the small structure that the workers had just erected. It was very simple, having only four walls welded together with an airlock room and a few viewing ports. It stood near the three landers (the third had landed out of our view while we waited for the building to be put together).

Walking on the Moon was a very strange experience. Every normal Earth-step sent one bounding along for several feet. The suits compensated a little because of their stiffness that restricted taking large steps. Star and the two workers had found that bouncing like rabbits was the best way to traverse lunar ground. We tried to imitate them, but found that walking on the Moon would take practice.

We entered the airlock of the building and closed the door to the Moon's surface. Star pulled the lever to open the atmosphere containers. We waited until the air pressure returned to a normal level, marked by a barometer that was on the wall, then opened the hatch that led to the interior of the building.

The building was actually quite comfortable inside. The first building erected was the common room in which the crew of the Lunar Station would spend their free time and eat their meals. There were comfortable furniture and pictures arranged in the main room, giving it a feeling of a home. Plants, soon to be placed in the Lunar botany laboratory, were everywhere, busily keeping the oxygen replenished in the air. The sixteen other crewmembers from the other landers were already there. With four and twenty of us in that single building, nearly all of its spaces were occupied.

"Well, we've all made it now," Star said, smiling at each of us. Those of us who had just arrived began to remove our Spacesuits and to place them on hooks on the wall next to the airlock.

"I think that we should decide what building to erect next," Star suggested.

"We should probably put up the water station as quickly as possible," one man with his legs tightly crossed blurted.

"I zink we should construct ze botany laboratory," the botanist Elissa said. Star had asked her to accompany him to help erect the botany laboratory of the Lunar Station as well as to examine any alien flora or fauna that were discovered.

"I agree, that'd get all of these plants out of the way," Conners said. Elissa looked at him, somewhat surprised. She and Conners rarely agreed on anything, especially since they continually irritated one another.

"What about our power capabilities?" van Sparchs asked. "We're running on batteries currently. We may need to place the Solar Energy Collectors very soon."

Several other suggestions went up, each one different. Finally, Star held up a hand, stopping the discussion. "Very well, people," he said. "Here's what we shall do. The eight of you on construction duty will immediately begin construction. Four of you work on building the botany laboratory, two others begin placing collectors, and the final two prepare the water station.

As for the rest of us, we'll wait until we can do anything. We'll relieve you in five hours with a fresh crew."

Everyone nodded. Star was a good leader and delegated tasks well. The eight workers immediately decked themselves in the Spacesuits and left through the airlock. We could see them through the view ports beginning to assemble a new set of walls, ceiling, and floor attached to ours. They welded them together using a special blowtorch designed for use in Space. There were two tanks, one full of oxygen and one of flammable gasses, with two hoses that led to a single nozzle. The oxygen and gas mixed and were lighted by a spark.

The rest of us sat in the room, each finding something to occupy his or her time. Star began dictating messages to Mary, who scribed them in French for Pierre to send later. Louis Pierre had been brought along to send messages back to the *Comet*, but he muttered that he was useless until the antenna was built. Instead, he, Conners, and four other crewmembers began playing cards. Others were watching and waited for a hand in which they could join.

I took my journal and a pencil, which I had stowed away under my bodysuit, and began to write down what had happened today. The journal was filling up quickly, but still had ample room for months to come. I often flipped back to my days on Earth in Star's mansion and read about them with a nostalgic smile.

Two hours later, the workers returned. We noticed them coming back by the chugging sound of the air pumps. In a few moments, they entered the room through the hatch and pulled the helmets from their heads.

"How goes the work?" Star asked.

"It is good," a Polish man named Sebastian said. "We have built the botany laboratory. All we need to do is cut out the doorway."

"Very good." Star smiled. "Begin cutting in here. The next eight workers can continue where they left off outside."

Eight people stood and took the Spacesuits from the former workers. Conners, one of the eight who were now to work, sighed as he left his cards. They checked their air tanks and, when they saw that they had plenty of air for their shift, left through the airlock.

Inside, Sebastian and two others took up blowtorches to the wall. There were marks on the walls where doorways were to be placed. To make the cutting easier, these doorways were not made as strongly as the rest of the walls. In only a half of an hour, they removed a section of the wall and exposed a dark new room. The air hissed into it, filling vacuum.

My eardrums popped from the sudden change in pressure. Star went quickly to several large air tanks in a corner and opened them, releasing atmosphere until a barometer on the wall read normally. The new air smelled metallic since it had been stored in tanks before we had left Earth and burned my nose as I breathed.

The workers began to shave the edges of the weld smooth while the metal was still soft. One of them entered the dark room and returned with thick electrical wires. He skillfully plugged them into sockets designed for the addition of rooms to the main power circuit. Van Sparchs assisted the worker and himself pulled the switch to supply electricity to the new botany laboratory.

We all watched as the bright overhead lights flickered on. The room was very simple and had heavy glass ceiling, much like a greenhouse. There was a thick mesh of wires above the glass, protecting it from any falling objects that might break it and spell doom for the entire station. There were numerous beds of dirt in which the plants would be set. Just like on the *Comet*, there were several benches in the middle of the gardens meant for relaxation.

"Monsieur Star," Elissa said, "I zink it would be best to plant ze flowers as soon as possible."

"Agreed," Star said. "All right, everyone grab a plant, and we'll get this taken care of."

Everyone stood, some more quickly than others, bounced in the low gravity of the Moon, and picked up a plant. Elissa handed out several spades and we all worked to place the plants. We had to be careful while digging, however, not to hit the pipes that led from the toilets, which watered and fertilized the gardens.

Just about the time we finished planting, the eight workers returned. When Conners removed his helmet, he sighed deeply and then yawned. "I don't think I was cut out for labor, even lunar labor," he mumbled to me.

The next group of workers, many of them from the initial group, prepared to head out. I was among them and not quite sure how working on the surface of the Moon came off. Still, I pulled on the Spacesuit, checked the air tank, and then screwed the helmet into place. In a moment, we were out of the airlock and onto the airless Moon.

The Pole Sebastian directed us all, waving his arms and signaling what he wanted done. I could hear nothing in my helmet but my own breathing and the low hiss of my air tank. Everything on the Moon was completely silent. Whenever hammers struck or blowtorches spit out flames, they did it without any noise at all.

I was assigned to assembling the energy collectors. The man with me hoisted me up to the roof of the first building and then passed up large sheets of collectors to me. I screwed screws on them into pre-made holes and then plugged the sheet of collectors into the electric circuit of the Lunar Station.

Several hours later, three more buildings had been erected and nearly all of the energy collectors were in place. We returned to the airlock and then trudged into the main room. Inside, several men were working on cutting new doorways into the new rooms. Other men were connecting water pipes and putting the water station in order. We were all very glad once the bathrooms were in operation.

The Station continued to be very busy for the next day. We slept only a little, because we did not exert very much energy in the low gravity and thus did not feel terribly tired. Our meals were mostly foods that had been prepared earlier and were stored in tin cans. We ate only when we were hungry and detested the flavors of the canned foods. Conners said that he would rather be sleeping with the animals in the agricultural laboratory than eating these foods for much longer. We were very glad when the Station's small kitchen was finished and ate a large meal prepared in it to celebrate.

After the meal was finished, eight workers again headed out onto the barren surface of the Moon. Until more of the laboratory rooms were finished, there was not much work to be done inside of the Station. Thus we were trapped indoors the station with only a few games to keep us entertained.

Finally Conners approached Star, who was dictating notes to Mary in the botany laboratory. I was in the laboratory as well, helping Elissa straighten the numerous plants. I watched as Conners politely waited for Star to come to a pause in his dictating (a strange act for Conners that easily grabbed my attention).

"Yes?" Star asked, looking up from his thoughts.

"Sir, we've been stuck inside this Station for quite a while," Conners stated.

"Would you like another shift outside constructing then?"

"No, that's not exactly what I had in mind," Conners said, raising his hands defensively at the suggestion of more labor. "Actually, what I was thinking was that… since the vehicle storage room has already been built… I could take out one of the lunar motorcars and do a little exploring."

"That's quite a thought," Star said slowly.

Conners continued arguing for his case. "We've been here for quite some time now, and yet we have scarcely gone out to explore. Man has been curious about the surface of the Moon since he first looked up at the night sky. Frankly, it seems an imperative to do some exploration firsthand as quickly as possible."

"Are you planning on going alone?" Star asked in a tone that directed a negative answer.

"Oh, no," Conners replied, detecting Star's suggestion. "I was planning to take one of the two-seated cars... Curtis had volunteered to go with me."

I did not recall doing any such thing, but I knew that with Conners objecting was out of the question.

"He would be able to do any navigating we should need by the stars," Conners said, turning to look at me. He mouthed a short phrase, but I could not read his lips. When I did not respond, he continued with, "We would return shortly, probably in time for the next shift."

Star stared vacantly in thought for a moment and responded just as Conners looked to be giving up hope. "Very well, you may go. Return by," he paused to check his watch, "five o'clock."

"Thank you, sir," Conners said, nodding happily. He took me by the elbow and dragged me out of the botany laboratory. When we had gone into the corridor that led to the newly built vehicle storage room, he stopped and looked at me.

"You need to work on your improvisation," he told me.

"But you didn't even mention anything to me about going out there," I pleaded, pointing out one of the small viewing ports. "The shock of the suggestion threw my mind off track."

"See, now that's better," Conners said, ignoring my comment. "If you could make up stuff like that on the spot all of the time, we'd get away with more mischief."

He began walking down the corridor again, and I hurried to catch him. "I was serious."

"Nice use of continuing sincerity," he smiled. I finally sighed and stopped speaking, deciding that he was just doing his best to tease me.

We came to the door leading into the vehicle storage room and quickly entered. The room was full of several kinds of strange vehicles, some looking very similar to automobiles from Earth and others looking quite bizarre. Numerous pieces of machinery were lined up next to the walls. There was a worker among the assorted vehicles, checking them over and recording results on a clipboard.

"Hey," Conners called. The worker looked up quizzically. "Got a lunar motorcar that works?"

"They all work," the worker told him. "What do you want with one?" He stressed the word "you" with a sneer.

"We're headed out on a little expedition for Captain Star, so we need a motorcar to drive."

The worker nodded, but seemed reluctant. Finally he pointed to a large-wheeled vehicle that stood next to the airlock. "That one should be good enough for you."

"Thank you much," Conners hissed.

He and I approached the automobile, but were a little perplexed by it when we saw that it had no doors. I stared at it for a moment, trying to remember what Star's book had said about the vehicles that he had designed for use on the Moon. Conners, meanwhile, tried to open the front window on the car.

Behind us, the worker chuckled. "You have to unscrew the hatch on top."

Conners sighed through his nose. He climbed up to the top of the vehicle, careful not to break any of the energy collectors that covered the roof. He came to the hatch and twisted several screws. Finally it opened, and he lowered himself into the vehicle. I followed him and was surprised at how easy it was to climb around in the low gravity of the Moon.

The interior of the vehicle was small, yet strangely comfortable. There were two seats, each with several belts hanging off of it. Behind the seats were storage batteries and long cylinders marked "Emergency Atmosphere." Conners sat in the driver's seat, behind a large wheel and surrounded by levers. My seat had fewer levers, but seemed important nonetheless.

"Lock up the hatch and then pull into the airlock," the worker said, walking over to us. "I'll let you out."

I closed the hatch above and tightened several bolts with my hand. When I was sure that it was airtight, I sat back down in my seat. Conners flipped several switches and activated the electric engine. It whirred quietly, the same whirring sound that all of Star's vehicles seemed to make.

Conners pressed the accelerator slowly, and the car moved forward. He put us in the middle of the airlock and then waited for the worker to send us out. The worker checked our hatch and waved merrily as he shut the doors of the airlock behind us. Soon the humming sound of the pumps began around us. As the hum disappeared and the atmosphere became a vacuum, the doors in front of us opened.

"Finally!" Conners sighed. He stepped heavily on the accelerator and the vehicle burst out of the airlock.

I swallowed and tightened my safety belts. The vehicle moved quickly over the gray rocks and sand that covered the Moon's surface. The sky was very crisp and clear, completely black except for glimmering stars. The Sun and Earth were above us, but I did not want to loosen by belts enough to crane my neck to see them.

Conners drove the vehicle quickly away from the small Station. Since I had volunteered early for indoor work, this was the third time that I had seen the Station from the outside, and it had grown a great deal since. In a few more days, I imagined that nearly all of the Station would be completed. Then the expedition would be a matter of scientific exploration from the surface of the Moon.

"It's good to get out of that tin can," Conners sighed, breaking me out of my thoughts. "I think I've played a few too many games of cards."

"You weren't becoming claustrophobic, were you?" I asked.

"Nah, just bored. My choices were working, sleeping, or struggling to find some kind of entertainment. I'm not terribly excited about labor, I'm not terribly sleepy, and the entertainment has been wearing thin. I just had the idea to get out of there, and here I am."

"And you brought me along for the ride," I added.

"Would you rather be here or moving plants?" he asked.

I thought for a quick moment. It was rather nice to see new scenery, even if we were still trapped in an enclosed space. And I had to admit that Elissa's chore was growing boring, though it was a simple one. "I suppose this is alright."

"You suppose?" he asked. "We'll see about that."

Conners suddenly accelerated the vehicle, enough to push me back into my seat. I looked curiously at him and then out the front window. The gray landscape was rushing up at us, especially a large crater in the distance. It grew closer and closer and Conners continued to accelerate, causing the engine to whir more and more loudly.

Finally we hit the outer edge of the crater. Lunar dirt sprayed out from under the tires as we came upon the incline that made up the outer ring of the crater. The vehicle jerked up into the vacuum as it came upon the lip of the ring and then sailed free of the ground. Conners shrieked enthusiastically while I gripped my seat and shouted with less enjoyment.

In the weak gravity of the Moon, the short ramp allowed the vehicle to make an extraordinary leap that it never could have made on Earth. Aside from the engine, the vehicle itself flew noiselessly, but Conners and I were both screaming enough to cover up any sound it could have made. I risked a look out of the window, saw the ground far below us, and then slammed myself back into my seat.

The vehicle then began a slow descent. I felt my stomach quiver, but I swallowed hard and did my best to hold onto the seat. Finally the gray ground rushed up at us, and we landed in the middle of the crater, creating a huge spray of sand and pebbles.

"How was that?" Conners asked me, panting to recover from his screaming. "Was that just 'alright'?"

"You're insane!" I shouted, throwing my hands into the air. "If we had landed wrong or kicked a rock into the window or anything, we'd both be dead!"

"Relax," Conners told me, rolling his eyes. "I know what I'm doing. I knew this thing was full of sand. And besides, Star's made all of his stuff quite durable." He knocked heavily on the front window, causing me wince with the idea of meeting Space.

"Do you know what happens when humans come into contact with vacuum?" I asked him. "It's not good!"

"Yeah, I read about it," Conners said. "The Vacuum Accident of 1890, right?"

I nodded. The terrifying catastrophe happened as the platform on top of Star's Tower was being built. Several workers accidentally punched through a bulkhead, immediately sucking out the atmosphere. The other workers in the station had no choice but to close the emergency doors. It was nearly a day before they recovered the workers, or at least what was left of them. Star had not recorded many of the details in his book, but judging from what he did include, it must have been a terrible way to go.

"So you finally read the book of etiquette?" I asked, calming down and changing the subject.

"I skipped through to the more exciting parts." Conners shrugged.

He pressed on the accelerator again, causing the engine to nearly roar. The wheels of the vehicle spun wildly, kicking sand high up into the dark sky. Finally it caught enough resistance to push forward. Soon we were out of the crater.

"So now what?" Conners asked. "Should we search for intelligent life?"

I shook my head. "There's not anything here. We stared at the surface for two days and we could not see a thing. I doubt anything could live in a place like this." I motioned toward the vast empty fields of gray dirt and rocks.

Conners drove the vehicle away from the crater and farther away from the Lunar Station. "You know, if we can't find anything with which to communicate, I'm not much good up here." He paused, and then added with a sneer, "I'll probably get put on Sebastian's labor team for the rest of our stay."

"Until we get the astronomy laboratory built here, I'm stuck on construction duty too," I said, trying to offer him some consolation.

We drove around on the surface of the Moon for several more hours. There were marvelous stone formations, created by impact by meteors or possibly some ancient volcanic activity. Mostly, however, it was a barren landscape, filled only with small rocks, sand, and larger rocks.

Eventually Conners stated the obvious, "Pretty bland up here, huh?"

I nodded. "There's no jungles or civilizations or anything. Quite a few authors would be upset by this."

Conners opened his mouth to agree, but suddenly stopped. He made a hard turn, suddenly throwing the vehicle to the right. I was tossed in my seat a bit, but was more shaken by the abruptness of the turn.

"What are you doing?" I gaped.

"I saw something," he whispered and drove erratically until he found what he had seen.

I strained my eyes to examine the thing in front of us. Finally I realized that it was a mouth of a cave. It was large and tucked underneath a wide outcropping. I was amazed that Conners had been able to detect something like that out of the corner of his eye.

We swiftly came to the gaping entrance. Conners flipped a switch on the control panel, activating lamps on the front of the vehicle. A sudden burst of light filled the cave, showing that it was quite deep.

"What do you think formed this?" Conners asked. "There aren't any rivers or anything up here."

"Maybe a meteor hit the surface at a horizontal angle," I suggested.

"Should we go into it?"

I was not completely comfortable with the idea, but there did not seem to be much to stop us. The floor was wide and looked to be drivable. The ceiling was certainly tall enough so that we would not risk hitting anything.

"I guess we could," I said, and then quickly added, "We should take it easy, though."

Conners nodded and pressed lightly on the accelerator. We moved forward slowly, examining the wide entrance into the cave. I flipped several other switches, activating lamps on the sides of the vehicle to give us a better view.

For the most part, the cave was simply a flat, sand-filled floor with a high arched ceiling. Every so often we would come to a small pile of rocks or some odd boulders that had slipped from the ceiling above them. There was certainly not much to the cave, but it was quite an interesting thing to see in the Moon.

The roof of the cave began to come lower and lower. I wondered if it would dwindle to a height too short for us, but I did not worry much about it. Conners stared out the front window and out the window on his side of the vehicle, taking in all of the various rocks.

"You didn't see this with the telescope?" Conners asked me.

I shook my head. "The outcropping over the entrance must have hidden it from view."

Conners made a sudden fiendish smile. "Then it must not be on any of the charts, which means it is not named yet. How does 'Conners Grotto' sound to you?"

I rolled my eyes. " 'Matricks Cavern' has a better ring to it."

Now Conners rolled his eyes. "That's very arrogant of you."

We rode on in silence for a moment more. Soon we came upon a division in the cave, one path leading right and another left. The left path seemed to go down quickly while the right path continued in a rather level direction. Conners stopped the vehicle and looked out at the two tunnels extending into the darkness.

"I guess we could split the name," I said.

"Alright," Conners agreed. "Do you want left or right?"

I thought for a moment, weighing the choices. Finally I decided that it did not matter and I ought to choose randomly. "Right, I suppose."

"Very well then," Conners said. He turned the vehicle and drove down the left tunnel. "Let's see what we have in Conners Grotto."

The tunnel led very steeply downward. Conners moved the vehicle slowly, not wanting to upset it in the descent. The sand often slid under our wheels, causing Conners to brake and hiss worriedly. Soon the sharp incline ended, and we came to a large room that had a tall domed ceiling.

"None too shabby," Conners muttered. "A few lamps and maybe a rug or two would really improve the place, though."

I chuckled. "You don't plan on moving in, do you?"

"Nah. I'll just rent the place out. There's bound to be plenty of people who want a little piece of the Moon for themselves."

We explored the room, driving around the edges and trying to cast as much light as we could. It was a very impressive space, probably much larger than a cavern on Earth could have been. Then again, I had heard tales of massive caves under the Appalachian Mountains with rooms larger than some towns.

"See any exits?" Conners asked.

"No," I responded. The chamber seemed to be the end of the cave. There was a massive pile of stones and dirt that could have been an exit long ago, but it was very much closed now.

"I suppose we should head back and see Matricks Cavern, then," Conners said. He turned the vehicle and headed for the sharp incline that we had just descended.

Just as we came onto the incline, we suddenly slid backward. The sand at the bottom had not provided any sort of traction at all. Conners grimaced, backed the vehicle up a long distance, and then pressed the accelerator heavily. The vehicle sped forward, and I winced, urging it to make the climb up the inclined tunnel. But when the vehicle struck the sandy incline again, it did nothing but cause a huge spray of sand in nearly every direction.

The vehicle then became stuck in the deeper loose sand. Its wheels spun, but they only kicked more sand out from under us. Conners finally gave up and stopped the vehicle completely.

"Well, this is quite good," he sarcastically hissed.

I pressed my face against the window, trying to see how badly we were stuck. Even from my awkward line of sight, I could tell that we were not going to be going anywhere without getting the vehicle unstuck from the outside.

I turned to Conners and, trying to cheer him up, said, "I don't suppose we should get out and push?"

The grimace on Conners's face quickly twisted into a small smile. He leaned back in his seat and sighed. "No, we should just wait until they come and find us."

"We have plenty of air for until then," I said. As I did, I turned back and released a little atmosphere into our air, which was beginning to grow stale.

"That's good. If they don't come to get us, we'll starve to death instead of asphyxiating."

"You don't think we'd die of thirst first?"

"We might. I guess we can wait and see."

After our initial jests, we grew quiet. We both knew that the situation was very unfortunate. We were lost in a cave under the surface of the Moon, something we were certain that no one else had ever done. They might be able to follow our tracks, but we could be lost forever.

"What time is it?" Conners asked.

I checked the watch that I kept in one of my numerous pockets. "About four o'clock."

"So we have an hour until they even start missing us." Conners sighed. He began to shut off the external lights and the engine, leaving only the one on the front of the vehicle. "I suppose we should save some energy since there's not any sunlight down here."

We both were quiet for the next hour. I began to doze out of boredom, and I thought that Conners fell asleep completely. With only the one light and scarcely any sound at all, the vehicle made a surprisingly peaceful resting place.

Suddenly there was a strange clicking sound coming from the dashboard. Conners and I both jerked and began searching for the sound. As I continued to search, Conners stopped and listened to it.

"Wait!" he shouted. "It's Morse code! It's saying... 'To... lunar... motorcar'!"

I finally came upon the origin of the sound. A small shelf near me folded down from beneath the dashboard to reveal a small telegraph key. Next to it, a telegraph sounder was quickly clicking out a message.

Conners furrowed his brow, trying to concentrate on deciphering the message. "'Arrival... not... seen. Where... are... you?' Quickly, change me seats!"

We struggled out of our seats and climbed over one another, trying to get into the other's seat. It was a vigorous task, since we were both so eager to hear a message. Conners finally sat up triumphantly in my seat and hovered over the telegraph key. His quick action, however, turned me upside down in his seat, and I began clambering back into a correct position.

Conners quickly tapped out a message. It seemed to go quickly at first, but then he began to struggle as excitement overtook him. Finally he finished and leaned back away from the key to wait for the response.

"You know Morse code?" I asked him during the pause.

"Sure," Conners said. "I'm a linguist. It's kind of a language, right?"

My reply was stopped by the sounder suddenly coming to life. Conners waited until the message was complete and then explained, "They know where we are. They should be coming to get us in just a few minutes!"

We both sighed happily, glad that we were now certain to be rescued.

Conners suddenly looked at me and frowned. "Why didn't you tell me that we had a wireless machine?"

I swore that I had no idea that the telegraph was hidden inside the vehicle's dashboard. We began jesting back and forth, blaming one another and creating silly mock-insults.

In less than an hour, a light appeared in the tunnel above us. Two figures wearing Spacesuits came down the tunnel carrying a long chain. They waved to us and then connected the chain to the front of our vehicle. We waved to them in return, very glad to see them, and then we made wishful thoughts as they climbed back up the chain to the top of the tunnel.

The chain slowly pulled taught, and then we began to climb. Conners reactivated the engine and pressed the accelerator, helping the vehicle on its way up the tunnel. We were soon back to the entrance of the cavern, next to a larger vehicle that had a massive wench on its back. The two men wearing Spacesuits unconnected the chain, used the wench to roll it up, and then climbed onto the back of the other vehicle.

Both vehicles quickly drove back to the Lunar Station. Conners and I were very relieved to be out of the cave and sang songs from popular musicals all of the way. The other vehicle went through the airlock first, forcing us to wait for a few more moments, but finally we were able to park in the vehicle storage room.

Conners quickly unscrewed the hatch and leapt out of the vehicle. I followed him and suddenly heard him make a funny squeak. When I came out of the vehicle, I saw what had made him squeak and nearly squeaked myself.

Star was walking toward our vehicle, looking quite perturbed. Mary trotted after him with a look that she was trying to apologize for what her father was about to do. Conners immediately began to spin an elaborate tale, but was stopped on the fourth word by Star's hand.

"Mister Conners, you and I will have a talk immediately," he sharply said to Conners, who struggled between remaining silent and saying something. Star then turned to me and said, "Curtis, I think that you should go on a couple of work shifts, beginning now."

I nodded and hurried out of the room. I met Sebastian, who had been one of the men to pull us out of the cave. He made a joke at me, laughed, and then slapped me on the back. For the next few hours, I worked diligently on the construction of the Station with the look that I had seen on Star's face to keep me motivated. When I finally returned to the Station after dual shifts, I was completely worn out and headed for my bunkroom. I had just enough energy to prepare for bed before collapsing onto the thin mattress and falling asleep.

On our third day in the Station, I awoke to a loud shrieking. I jumped out of bed, pulled on my bodysuit, and hurried out of the male bunkroom to see what was the matter. Conners, who was pouting in the common room at the time, bumped into me as we both dashed to see what had happened.

We both entered the geological laboratory at the same time, followed by two others. Star and the geologist were already there, the geologist excitedly explaining what he had found. Star tried to calm him and to get a careful explanation out of him.

The geological laboratory was one of the last rooms of the Station to be put together. It consisted of four walls that were sunk deeply into the Moon's dusty surface and a ceiling to cap them. There was no metal floor as there was in the rest of the Station, but one made of gray Moon dirt. The ceiling had a single small electric chandelier. There were several benches along the walls full of equipment for testing various samples that had been collected.

In the middle of the dirt floor was a small, but very deep, hole. The geologist had been taking samples from it, deeper and deeper, until he began to shriek this morning. He mumbled the words, "great, excellent discovery," several times before Star could calm him down enough to see what was the matter.

Finally, the geologist began to explain. He held up tubes of dirt to illustrate his findings. "See this sample from twenty-five feet below? There's a rather large moisture count. Then, this sample from forty feet? A larger moisture concentration. Then, this morning I got a sample from fifty feet, which was… this!"

He triumphantly held up a tube that had several small white veins running through it. Elissa, who had arrived just before Conners and I did, gaped. The rest of us stood perplexed for a moment and waited for an explanation.

"Zey are roots!" Elissa finally said. Her mouth had moved several times before speaking and it took a great amount of effort to form the words.

Now everyone was gaping and staring at the tube of dirt. We watched it carefully for a moment, and then the geologist interrupted us.

"And according to the samples I've taken, there's some sort of reservoir or possibly even a cavern directly below us," he said.

Star immediately gave an order. "Sebastian, go get the drill. We'll see if we can open this hole wide enough to see what's down there."

The Polish worker and several other men hurried to the Station's vehicle storage room and quickly returned with a large drill, which had been designed to take samples from all over the Moon. Star had hoped that he might find unexploited minerals that he could mine cheaply at one-sixth of Earth's gravity.

They positioned the drill over the hole and placed a gigantic bit on it. With a loud whirring sound, the drill began to dig into the ground, creating a three-foot wide hole. We all waited anxiously for several hours while it dug. The dirt produced from its digging had to be continuously carted away and stored in the botany laboratory.

Suddenly, the whirring stopped and there were several shouts from the geological laboratory. We all once again hurried to see what the matter was. When I arrived, Star was talking to the three men who had been inside.

"The bit suddenly freely fell," one explained. "It must have hit a pocket of air or something like that. We barely caught it on the emergency cord, too."

"Then we could feel a gust of wind coming up into the lab," another broke in. "We didn't know what it was, so we left and sealed up the room."

"Wellis!" Star called. Wellis, the chemist among us, hurried to him. "Take a sample," Star said. "See what that gas is."

Wellis nodded, and we were all pushed away from the geological laboratory. Wellis put on a thick mask and took a small air pump in his hands. He squeezed a needle through the seal and pumped a jar full of atmosphere. We all anxiously waited while he spent several hours finding out just what it was.

Finally, he left his chemical laboratory with a short paper for Star. "It's mostly nitrogen," he said. "Then oxygen and carbon dioxide, and I think some other gases. It's basically Earth's atmosphere. A little less nitrogen and a little more carbon dioxide, but still, it's amazingly similar."

"I heard a theory that the Moon was part of the Earth before the material was blown off of it somehow," one of the workers suggested. "That might explain it." The geologist nodded, though several others of us looked skeptical.

"Whatever caused it," Star said, "I'm glad to hear it's breathable. Sebastian, remove the seal and the drill."

The Pole nodded and motioned for some workers to help him. They quickly broke the seal and then drug away the drill. The geologist hurried into his old laboratory and looked into the hole. Star came after him and looked as well. They both stared at it for a moment, and then at one another.

"What is it?" Pierre asked. He was in the middle of sending a message when the drill was being removed and had just now arrived from the wireless equipment.

"There's a light coming up from below," the geologist said. We all made a collective gasp of surprise. Several murmurs broke out among us.

"Rodreguez." Star turned to the lead member of the gunnery crew who was in charge of the Station's arsenal. "Prepare some arms. We're going down to see what's in this lunar cavern."

Chapter Eight,
Into the Moon

In only a matter of minutes a group of us were ready to descend through the narrow hole. The expeditionary team consisted of Mason Star, Mary, Rodreguez, Conners, Elissa, Wellis, Tarsini, and five other men under Rodreguez's charge. Star had also chosen me to go along with them and given me a small pistol to protect myself.

Rodriguez was the first to go down the hole. Sebastian had rigged up a pulley system that lowered a small platform on an extremely long cord. A small electric motor controlled the platform's descent and pulled it back up. Rodreguez climbed onto the platform, strapped himself to it securely. He held a rifle on his lap and had pistols at each hip. When he armed himself, he winked at me and said, "You'll never know what you'll find down there, *chico*."

He took a deep breath and then nodded to Sebastian, who took the signal to lower the platform. The motor hummed merrily as Rodreguez disappeared down the hole. We all anxiously waited for several minutes. Then the rope was tugged, meaning that Rodreguez wanted to stop. A moment later there were two tugs, the signal that the platform was ready to be raised again.

When it came back to the top of the hole, there was a note attached. Star plucked it up, looked at it for a moment, and then handed it to Conners. "It's in Spanish," Star said, shaking his head at Rodreguez.

Conners immediately began to translate. "The cave is amazing. The plants glow like daylight. No danger. Come quickly."

By this time, Star was already on the platform, ready to descend. He gave Sebastian a nod and then disappeared. Moments later, the platform returned empty, and Conners climbed onto it.

I was the fourth person to descend into the lunar cavern. The trip down was rather unnerving and grew quite dark. All that I could see around me was gray Moon dirt and then nothing. Finally, the light returned, this time from below. I began to see roots and several worms around me. In a moment, I came out of the tunnel and found myself hanging thirty feet above the floor of an amazing cavern.

The cave was lit by plants on the ceiling that glowed. They were very bright, and I could not look at them long enough to study them. There were darker objects among them, large insects that appeared to be chewing on them.

Below there were trees unlike I had ever seen before. They had broad, circular leaves, but the branches were in strange patterns from the main trunk. The branches swayed, despite there being no wind in the chamber. Among the large trees were bushes with thick purple fruits hanging on them. In the distance, I could see a large pond near an edge of the cavern, which was probably three hundred acres in area.

I finally touched the ground, which was covered in vines and mosses much like the floor of a jungle. Rodreguez helped me off of the platform and then gave the cord several tugs to show that it was ready to go back up.

"Good ride?" he asked. I smiled and nodded.

Star had his back to me and was surveying the jungle-like landscape. He had a pith helmet on his head, but was still wearing his black bodysuit. He looked like some kind of insane jungle explorer. I chuckled under my breath and then approached him.

"What do you think?" I asked.

"It's simply incredible," he said. "I can only imagine what the newspapers back on Earth will say about this."

"Are we to stay here?" I asked.

"We'll set up a base camp, yes," Star said. "As soon as we all get together, a group of us will make a little expedition into the forest."

Rodreguez joined us. "The pond should supply plentiful water, *señor*. With access to an atmosphere like this and a water source, the Lunar Station will become more of a colony than a scientific post."

"You're right," Star nodded. "If we find some minerals, it might be a very productive industrial center. I just wonder if we will be able to find useful plants and animals, like Columbus found with the discovery of the Americas."

Rodreguez nodded and made a low comment in Spanish. I made a point to memorize it, and I later asked Conners to translate. He said that it meant something to the extent of "bloody capitalists."

In a few moments, Elissa joined us. She shrieked with amazement when she came into the light and was breathing quickly when she stepped off of the platform. She said an exclamation in French as she approached one of the trees and touched the bark. We left her to her plants and waited for the rest of the party to arrive.

In an hour, all twelve of us and a camp's worth of equipment had come to the floor of the lunar cavern. We quickly set up tents, organized our batteries and energy collectors, and readied the camp. Wellis had collected water from the nearby pond and checked it for purity while Dr. Tarsini looked at it under a microscope for any dangerous creatures.

Tarsini finally looked up and said, "I do not see anything terribly wrong with it, but we might want to boil anything we will drink just as a precaution."

"Do you think that there is any chance of finding some sort of disease here?" I asked, having the plague of smallpox on the Indians as well as Wells's *War of the Worlds* in my mind.

"In my experience, I've found that there's always a chance for anything," Tarsini smiled. "However, since anything here has never had contact with humans before, we probably won't run into a germ that is adapted to attacking humans. We should be on the look out for poisons, however."

"Nothing zat I have found is poisonous at all," Elissa said. She had filled several containers with plants and other samples and sent them up to the Station for storage.

"Neither have I," Wellis added. "We might see something like a sulfur pit or arsenic soon enough, but this water is purer than most of the wells in Texas."

"Aren't most of the wells in Texas for oil, though?" Conners asked.

Star interrupted any answers. "Since the camp is ready, I think that we should do some exploring. Volunteers?"

Rodreguez and one of his men stuck up their hands. Conners followed suit, and so did I. When Wellis nodded, Star stopped taking volunteers and said, "All right, let's go, gentlemen."

"What should we do here?" Tarsini asked.

"See what you can find out about this place around the camp," Star said. "If anything goes wrong, fire a shot into the air and we'll come back immediately. If you hear a shot, a few of you should come and check on us."

"Very well," Tarsini said. I supposed that he planned on assuming control while Star was gone. "Good luck!"

We left the camp, each with a light pack and a weapon. I had the pistol that Star had given me and a knife in my boot. We covered ground very quickly, bounding several feet with every step.

The underground lunar world was simply amazing. There were numerous types of insects, all of them very large: long centipedes as large as pythons, winged insects bigger than birds, and several beetles sized like dogs. We did not see any mammals or reptiles at all. A few insects we saw had strange feathers, and we thought that they were birds before closer inspection.

"The weak gravity must have given the insects an advantage and allowed them to be dominant creatures," Star mused.

"We haven't seen any bug-people yet, though," Conners said.

"Depending on what they're like when we do find them, we may not want to," Wellis added.

When we had toured the entire room, which was quite large, the only thing that we had seen with any intelligence that we could see was a huge spider-like creature. Conners and Wellis stayed to watch it, but the spider hid away in a domed structure that it had built for itself and refused to be seen. The rest of us continued on and mapped the room.

Star looked at the hand-drawn map and cleared his throat. "There are three tunnels that lead out of this chamber, one to the south and the other two to the north close to one another."

"We should probably report back to the camp before exploring them," Rodreguez said.

Star shook his head. "Things have gone well thus far. I'm sure it'd be all right to look at them, at least a little bit."

Rodreguez sighed and agreed. We bounded to the two tunnels in the north and peered down each one before entering. The left tunnel led to a straight wall that would have to be climbed before anyone could continue down it. The other tunnel turned to the right and descended.

"Rodreguez, Devon, take the right tunnel," Star said, "Curtis, you and I will go in the left one."

Rodreguez saluted Star and then marched carefully down the tunnel. Star and I entered the other and immediately faced the rock wall. From afar, it looked much higher than it really was. Still, it was nearly four feet above my head.

"See if you can jump up it," Star told me.

I nearly protested, but then realized that with such weak gravity, I should be able to make such a superhuman leap. I took a few steps back and then jumped with all of my might. Quite surprised, I flew up to the top of the cliff and caught onto it with my arms. With a quick pull, I was on top of it and standing triumphantly. Star soon leapt up similarly, and I helped him onto the top.

We turned around and looked at the other side of the cliff. The tunnel grew darker as the glowing plants became fewer and fewer, but there was a brighter light toward the end of it. We could hear a faint swishing sound, almost like running water.

"Think that there is a river near here?" Star asked. I nodded and we began marching toward it.

The tunnel grew quite dark, almost like twilight. There were five-inch-long worms that slid along the wall of the tunnel, burrowing in and out of the rock. I was tempted to touch one, but was afraid of what might happen if I did. Once, a bat-like insect buzzed by our heads and then darted down the tunnel. It squeaked several times and frightened us, but did not hurt us.

When we came to the end of the tunnel, we reached a large chamber. It was rather narrow, only about twenty yards across, but very long. There was a five-foot-wide river in the middle that had strange insects skittering over it on enormous footpads. One insect was swallowed whole by an enormous worm that was swimming in the water like a fish. The same trees and glowing plants were in the chamber as in the first, but the river gave it a very different feel.

"You see that?" Star asked, pointing to several creatures far away on the opposite bank of the river.

I nodded without speaking. They looked like black ants that were standing upright and were holding something that looked like a spider's web.

Suddenly, there was a dull thundering echo that ran through the cavern. Star and I looked at one another, and he mouthed the word "gunshot." We immediately left the river chamber and hurried as quickly as we could down the tunnel. We reached the cliff and leapt down it, easily landing in the weak gravity.

When we came to the mouth of the tunnel, we met Rodreguez and his man Devon, who were breathing hard. I doubted that they had exhausted themselves from running since Earthlings could probably easily run a dozen miles the weak gravity of the Moon. Instead, their wide eyes gave impressions of shock and fear.

"Did the gunshot come from you?" Star quickly blurted.

Rodreguez nodded. "It was incredible."

"What?" I asked.

"The insect-men," he said, whispering mysteriously. The words sent a shiver up my spine.

Conners and Wellis ran up at this time with the men from the camp. They asked what had happened as well, but Rodreguez and Devon were in too much shock to explain.

"Let's get back to the camp," Tarsini said. "Some tea will calm their nerves."

Star agreed and we all walked to the camp, continually looking over our shoulders. Rodreguez and Devon sat in chairs that had been lowered from the Lunar Station and sipped at some tea that Tarsini had been making when he heard the gunshot. Finally, they were ready to explain.

Devon began making a sketch on some paper supplied by Mary. Rodreguez struggled to put words together and explain what had happened. "We had continued down the tunnel for quite a while," he said. "The glowing plants were becoming less dense and the tunnel grew quite dark. Suddenly, three of these insect-men came at us. They seemed to be confused, as we were. We stared at one another for a while, and then they began to come at us. We could hear them chattering to each other, but we did not know what they were saying. They had satchels with them and they were carrying sticks that had metal points like spears. When one of them raised his spear, Devon shot into the air. Then all of the insect-men hissed and fled down the other end of the tunnel. We headed away from them and then met up with you."

Devon finished his sketch and showed us all. It looked like an ant that was standing on its back two legs and had two sharply clawed phalanges on each hand and foot. The two upper arms were large and muscular while two arms in the middle of its abdomen were small sticks poking out just above the hip. It indeed had a satchel hanging over its shoulder and was carrying a spear like a tribesman of a forgotten realm of South America or Africa. Its face was very much like that of an insect; it had small, black eyes, antennae on its forehead, and pinchers covering its mouth. It looked very similar to the ant-like men that Star and I had seen standing near the river. There were several gasps and a few murmurs about the picture.

"So we've met the first intelligent alien creatures," Star said. "It even has tools and a bag. Amazing."

"Much more so than the spider we saw," Conners said. "I imagine that it has about the intelligence of a monkey or very smart dog."

"So what is our plan now?" Wellis asked.

"We need to make a more civilized contact," Star said. "But not immediately. I think that we should rest up for a few hours, then we'll send a few men out to try and find some insect-men."

" 'Insect-men' sounds too scientific," Conners muttered.

"We could call them 'Selenites,' " Mary suggested. "It's the name Wells gives the Moon men in his book."

Conners smiled and heartily agreed. We all then went our separate ways and tried to rest. According to my watch, I hadn't slept in nearly twenty hours. I was beginning to feel tired, but because of the low gravity, I never became very worn out. Still, I went into one of the tents and slept as best I could.

In a few hours I was awoken by Conners. He shook my shoulder until I sat up and yawned. I looked up at him and asked what was happening.

"Star is ready to move out," he said. I nodded and followed him out of the tent.

Rodreguez was handing guns to each of his men and instructing them to fire only if necessary. Tarsini and Elissa were leading a conversation about the medicinal value of several plants that they had found. Star was at the edge of the camp talking to Mary. From what I could overhear, Star had said that Mary was not allowed to go with him on the expedition to see the insect-men. Mary was arguing with him, but obviously losing this round.

I ate a quick breakfast that Tarsini had prepared and then reported to Rodreguez. He handed me a second pistol and a belt of ammunition and asked me if I knew how to use them.

"My father was not a big fan of guns, but my uncle took me hunting several times," I told him. He seemed convinced that I would not accidentally shoot him in the back and gave me an encouraging pat on the shoulder.

Finally we left camp. Tarsini, Elissa, Mary, and three of Rodreguez's men stayed behind on careful watch. Star, Wellis, Conners, Rodreguez, Devon, another of Rodreguez's men, and I headed away from the camp and down the tunnel where the initial encounter had been.

We did not see anything for a long while. Rodreguez pointed to the spot that they had come face-to-face with the insect-men. We continued down the tunnel and saw nothing. We walked on until we came to a fork in the tunnel and stopped.

"Which way?" Star asked.

"Your guess is as good as mine," Rodreguez said.

We could not see down the tunnels very easily as the glowing plants became very thin. Star flipped a coin, which took a long while to fall in the weak gravity, and then decided to head right.

In a few minutes, we came to a new chamber. It was very bright and was even larger than the chamber that we had first come into. The tunnel was high above the floor, but there was a trail that led down the bottom of the chamber. We could hear strange drumming sounds coming from somewhere, but we could not determine where. There were also a few loud roars that sounded like they had come from animals.

We walked down the trail and entered the dense forest on the floor of the cavern. The trees were much closer together here than in our own chamber and their circular leaves made the underbrush fairly shadowy. We stepped lightly and tried to keep our eyes open for everything.

Suddenly, Rodreguez, who was in the lead, stopped and held up a hand. "I see one of them. It-it looks like it sees us, too."

I peered ahead until I recognized the black outline of an insect-man. It was about seven feet tall and carried a long spear. I clutched my pistol tightly and tried to control my breathing. Star touched Conners on the shoulder, and then they both walked toward the insect-man. The insect-man watched them approach, and then suddenly cried out with a loud hiss and click.

Several insect-men leapt from the trees above us. One tackled Devon, who fired into the air, barely missing the insect-man's abdomen. Another insect-man attacked Rodreguez, threatening him with its spear. The rest of them surrounded us.

Wellis, a Texan who shouted that he was not about to be beaten by a bunch of oversized cockroaches, opened fire with twin six-shooters. It was an amazing display of gunplay, much like in a dime novel about the American West. Two of the insect-men's carapaces cracked under the bullets and the insect-men fell.

The insect-men then went wild and attacked us all. Rodreguez was stabbed in the right arm and his man was run through with a spear. Devon soon fell under the insect-man as well.

"Let's get out of here!" Wellis shouted. He grabbed Rodreguez by his good arm, helped him to his feet, and they hurried away, bounding in the Moon's weak gravity.

I began to run after them, but I felt a sharp pain in the back of my head. I blacked out, my last thought being a hope that I was not dead.

Fortunately, I woke up several hours later. Unfortunately, however, I had a pounding headache and was completely bewildered. I tried to make sense of what had happened, but nothing would come to my mind.

"Sleeping Beauty awakes," I heard a voice say. I sat up and looked around me. Conners, whose voice I had heard, was sitting near a door made of a very strange light purple wood. The walls were made of black stone that was cold and moist. The dungeon was lit by a few sickly glowing plants in the ceiling. Star was in a corner, staring blankly.

I cleared my throat and asked, "What happened?"

"The Selenites got us," Conners said. "They must have been waiting for us. I'm not sure why, but they wanted to capture a few of us. When they dragged us off, Devon and what's-his-name were lying on the ground. Dead, I suppose. I think Wellis and Rodreguez got away, though."

Star said nothing, only stared directly in front of his face.

"What happened after that?" I asked.

"They brought us back to their fortress and threw us in here," Conners said. "It was a pretty nice fortress. Very reminiscent of a castle that I saw in western France one time."

"What are we going to do?"

"Not much we can do," Conners said. "They had a couple of dozen soldiers that I could see. Not even Wellis could take out that many, so I doubt that there's too much hope of rescue. Escape is not much of an option either. Still, I think we have a plan."

"Which is?"

"We'll find out in a few minutes. Wait, no, now." He held his finger up to his lips, telling me to be silent.

I listened intently, but could hear nothing. Suddenly, I heard a shuffling of feet, a few clicks and hisses, and then more shuffling. Conners smiled broadly.

"Okay, let's see if this works," he said. He began clicking and hissing loudly, repeating the same sounds over and over again.

Suddenly, there came some clicking from outside. There was another shuffling sound and then more clicking for several sources. The door swung open and two black insect-men entered. Conners clicked and hissed at them, smiling as he did. The insect-men grabbed him and took him out of the room. They bolted the door behind them loudly.

I watched after Conners for a moment, perplexed. Turning to Star, I asked, "What happened?"

Star made a deep sigh. "Well, imagine it like this: you are in a pound and one of the dogs begins barking the word 'hello.' What would you do?"

"I'd probably put him in a circus," I said.

Star chuckled at my answer. "Well, maybe eventually, but first you'd take him and try to find out why he can talk and see if he can say anything else. It's a pretty clever plan, if he can make it work. I would be amazed if he can pick up a language this foreign that quickly."

"So he's going to see if he can talk with them?"

"He's going to try. He got the idea when he heard the guards make high click, low click, hiss, low click noises whenever they changed. We discussed it while you were asleep."

I leaned back against the damp wall and rubbed my aching head. A large bump was forming on the back of it. I hoped that the cold wall would help keep down the swelling.

Star was silent for a long while, but eventually said, "You know, Curtis, when I began this expedition, I expected to be hailed a hero throughout. Imagine, traveling world-to-world exchanging knowledge and technology. Why wouldn't I be a hero?"

I could not answer his question. I certainly never considered that I would be locked away in a dungeon deep inside the Moon guarded by giant insect-men. Most likely no one would imagine that.

We were silent for a while again, and then I broke the quiet with a question. "Mr. Star, I've always about something. Why were you so secretive about the expedition before we left? I don't really understand."

Star stared at me for a moment, thinking deeply. I continued, "Mary said that she thought that you just wanted to avoid too much attention. You know, to keep snoops and such from impending your work."

Star smiled. "That's actually quite close to the truth," he said. He leaned back and sighed, showing that the answer was very personal. "The real reason is that I was afraid of failing. I did not want to make headlines for years, and then suddenly hit a barrier that I could not pass. I'd be the laughing stock of the world."

He paused and I nodded. Star, despite his amazing wealth and achievements, was only human. There were probably very few men in the world who would be able to face the entire world with such an amazing disappointment. I agreed that it was probably better to be viewed as an eccentric than a failure.

"Do you think we'll get out of this?" I asked him.

"Hopefully," Star said. He paused, swallowed deeply and began a new topic. "Curtis, I have something I need to tell someone before I go crazy from hiding it. Only about three people other than myself know this, and they are safely back on Earth amid numerous ledgers."

"What is it?"

"I am almost destroyed, Curtis," he sighed. "I've invested everything in this—more than everything. I am sure quite a few bankers will be calling me shortly."

"What do you mean?" I asked. His home was enormous and fantastically decorated. He had more wealth in a single room than my family had on our entire farm.

"Constructing a tower capable of reaching Outer Space is more expensive than one would imagine," Star said. "I've emptied out my own pockets and borrowed more money than many nations have ever seen." He paused, then continued. "If we don't make it back, my lawyer has orders to give my wife. She'll dismantle everything and sell it for scrap until the debts are paid off. By selling stock in the shipping company, I think she'll be able to produce enough funds to keep the estate together."

I could not respond. Star sighed contentedly, however. "It feels good to let someone else know. You know how it is keeping secrets."

We were silent for a moment, then Star suddenly whispered, "Don't tell Mary."

I nodded. Star certainly tried to protect his family, even though he had his own daring adventures. I could not help but wonder about what would become of him if we did escape.

We sat there for several hours, waiting for something to happen. The only thing to come about was the guard tossing us two pans of food. The food was strange ground meat that obviously had not been cooked. The sight of the meal immediately destroyed any appetite that I had.

Finally, the door to the dungeon opened. We both sat up in surprise and stared at it. Two guards pushed Conners through it and then locked it shut.

Even in the dull light, Conners was obviously worn down. His hair and clothes were very ruffled, and he took short, shallow breaths. He lay on the floor where the guards left him and only moved to roll into a more comfortable position. Star and I rushed to him, trying to help him in any way.

"What happened to you?" Star asked.

"Interrogation," Conners said, coughing as he spoke. "By Jove, that interrogation would give the Spanish Inquisition a run for its money."

"Easy now," Star said, patting him on the shoulder. "You don't need to tell us anything until you're ready."

"Okay." Conners nodded. He coughed several more times, and then lay still. Finally, he asked us to help him lean up against the wall. When we moved him, he looked much more comfortable.

He then began to tell us what had happened. "I'm not sure where to begin, so I guess I'll try to do it chronologically. They took me out of the dungeon and marched me around in their fortress. After going through several corridors, they took me into a large open room when they began my interrogation.

"They took me before a gigantic worm-like creature. I'm fairly sure it was a queen like in an ant colony. She was very big though, probably five feet high and twelve feet long. She may have just been a regional governor or a general or something rather than their absolute queen, I don't know. She popped out two eggs during the interrogation; they were about the size of a man's head. Anyway, the queen clicked and hissed at me rapidly. I couldn't make any since of what she was saying, but I did the clicking that I had heard the guards say. I think it's some kind of salutation.

"When I became lost in her clicks, I pointed to my head and then waved my hands, trying to sign that I didn't know what she was saying. She seemed to have understood and stopped clicking so wildly. Eventually, we began to figure out a way of signing simple things to each other. Somehow I got across the idea that I was a traveler from up above the rocky ceiling.

"When I had told her my story, I motioned to her, trying to say that I wanted to know about this world. After a few tries, she hissed at an attendant, who immediately brought paintings made on thin wooden tiles. I suppose it was some kind of Moon-book." He chuckled, then coughed. After a pause, he continued, "The book showed about their entire society. Most of the Selenites are infertile females, like with insects on Earth. I guess the 'insect-man' nickname doesn't really fit then for the ones we saw, huh? They form the lower bulk of the society, mostly as warriors and peasants. Then there were males, who were about two feet tall. I only saw one, who was sitting next to the queen and gave me the book. According to the book, the males are the keepers of knowledge, like teachers and clergy and so forth. Then the queens rule over all of the Selenites, working together in a feudal fashion. The book also showed this enormous 'empress,' who must have controlled a dozen or so queens.

"Then came wood tiles about their history. The book had images of great queens and several commoners who did amazing deeds. There must be several nations throughout these tunnels, and they've been fighting for untold generations. There is only a certain amount of territory in the caverns, so any growth in population means that somebody else has to die. Thus, they've been battling feudally since who-knows-when.

"I finally began to pick words up among the clicks and hisses. I asked them to send you some food, and it looks like you got it." He sneered at the pink ground meat on the small plates. "I guess it would have been better to have asked them to put you out of your misery instead, eh?"

Star and I chuckled. "So how did this happen?" Star asked, eying his bruises.

"The queen told me that they were very interested in our 'roaring spears,' which I correctly assumed were guns. They hoped that these new weapons would give them an edge that would allow them to conquer their enemies forever. When I said that I did not now how to make them, though, they tried to beat the information out of me. Eventually, I explained that I was just a linguist, an educator, not a gunsmith. They beat me up a little more and then cast me aside. I'm not sure what we'll be able to do now."

My ears pricked. "You didn't say that *we* knew anything about guns did you?"

Conners smiled. His teeth were pink. "No, I didn't. They asked me. You're lucky that I don't think you know anything about guns, because I would have confessed it quick as a wink." He then chuckled to himself.

We were silent for a long while after that. Star began staring blankly again. I tried to help Conners as much as I could, but my medical knowledge was limited and we did not have any medicines at all.

Finally, Conners resumed conversation with me. "You know, Curtis, it's actually not that bad of a civilization. I mean, it's no British Empire, that's for sure, but I think it's probably better than our Dark Ages."

"How so?" I asked. I had pulled the sleeves off of my bodysuit to use as makeshift bandages. Conners had several cuts, but I was sure that they would be all right if bandaged well.

"Well, first they have an established government based on the reproduction of the species. I mean, if you have a revolution and kill all of the rulers, everybody will be gone in a few years. This way, no one would dare to revolt unless they had their own rulers already lined up, which would mean that there wouldn't be such a period of revolutionary chaos, like we saw with the French a century ago.

"Still, I guess this doesn't mean that the queens can be complete despots, though. The underclass, the infertile females, is needed to care for the queens and keep them comfortable and making eggs. So they probably need to take care of the proletariat. At least, keep them happy enough so that an army can control them.

"Then the males are kept busy with the intellectual side of the society. They wouldn't have much else to do than keep the queens producing eggs, so they probably have quite a bit of time for studying and so forth. I guess it makes sense to give them charge of the education, bookkeeping, et cetera."

He paused, made a bit of a sigh, and then muttered, "I just wish I could learn more."

After this, we went back to absently waiting. I had never been in a prison before, although I was sure that Conners was fairly used to it. Star did not seem to mind the prison so very much, but he seemed very lost and depressed.

In a few hours (at least I assumed that they were hours; the Selenites had cleaned out our pockets and taken our packs when they had captured us, so my watch was gone), we began to hear gunshots. We looked at one another in surprise, then pressed against the door to hear better. There were very few of the shots, and they were spaced randomly.

"They must be testing the guns they took from us," Star mumbled.

We listened intently until the shots stopped. Conners guessed that there had been about fifteen of them, although I had counted around thirteen. Still, that meant that they only had a handful of rounds left in the guns. I wondered how long it would be until they learned how to reload them.

The silence returned for a long while. The guards were changed often and twice one of them stepped in and threw us a fresh pan of pink meat. We were not very hungry, most likely a side effect of exerting very little energy in the low gravity of the Moon. Conners, out of curiosity, tasted the meat, but immediately spit it out. He winced and compared the taste to that of an unwashed bald ape. I wondered how he knew what such a thing tasted like, but I did not want to ask him.

I began to doze and began to lose track of time. Conners had fallen asleep, completely worn out by his ordeal with the Selenites. Star continued to stare vacantly, and I imagined he too eventually went to sleep. Here we all lost track of time totally. I did not know anything until I woke up, fiercely hungry and groggy, to banging noises.

The sounds were gunshots again, louder and much more frequent than before. I asked, "What's that noise?" but no one heard me.

I shook Star, waking him. He too was very groggy and looked like he had not cleaned up in days, but as soon as he recognized the sound of gunshots, he became fully conscious. "What is it?" he asked me. "What's happening?"

"I don't know," I said. I pushed close to the door, trying to hear what was happening. I could hear wild gunfire, shuffling of the Selenites' feet, and loud clicks and hisses. Suddenly, I heard a different sound, a clack followed by another clack in a second or two. When I recognized it, I gasped.

"What?" Star asked. He was waking Conners. Conners's bruises looked to be nearly healed, and he seemed to be in much better shape. His face was covered with a scraggly beard similar to that of Star.

"Boots!" I shouted. He made a gasp similar to mine, and then hurried to the door. We banged on it and called at the top of our lungs.

The boot sound stopped outside of our door and there was a murmuring. Finally, we heard the lock being removed. We stood back and helped Conners to his feet. The door opened with a crack and Wellis appeared from behind it.

"Wellis!" Star shouted.

"Good to see you, Captain Star," he said. "We've come to rescue you."

"That's jolly good of you." Conners smiled.

Wellis helped us out of the dungeon and for the first time I saw where we had been. The dungeon was one of many that were in a shallow crevasse in the rock wall of a large cavern chamber. There were dozens of Selenites wearing armor plates over their abdomens that had red paint on them and rough helmets on their heads with their antennae sticking out. They were all running here and there, rescuing other prisoners.

We left the crevasse and entered the large chamber. Here there were several buildings, many of them destroyed, and a pile of rubble that had once been a protective wall. Several towers still stood while others had been fiercely knocked down. There were broken exoskeletons belonging to deceased Selenites lying amid the debris. I supposed that Wellis had charged in and planned on rescuing us with a battle. It certainly seemed to have worked.

I watched a group of Selenites lift a gigantic struggling worm, which must have been the queen Conners described, onto a sledge pulled by what looked like a cross between an ox and a praying mantis. The queen was bound with thick cords that kept her from escaping her captors. Behind her, several small Selenites in red robes (males, I presumed) were tied and being led with leashes.

A Selenite approached Wellis and clicked wildly. Wellis squinted and shook his head. The Selenite then nodded and pointed to another pair of Selenites, who were approaching with a wooden box. They opened it and revealed strange-looking treasure. Wellis nodded and made a clumsy click and hiss. The Selenites then left, toting the treasure toward the sledge with the queen.

"You can speak with them?" Conners asked.

"Not very well," Wellis answered. "Heck, most the time I don't even get English right. All I know are a few clicking words, like for 'home,' 'go,' and 'fire.' " He directed us to another sledge that appeared to be waiting for us.

As we got into it, Wellis made another click and the driver nodded. In a moment, he struck the beast that was tied to the sledge with a stick and it began pulling us with a jerk.

"Where are we going?" Star asked.

"To see the 'Empress of the Fire,' " Wellis said. We exchanged glances and then looked at him confusedly.

Wellis winked. "You'll see."

Chapter Nine,
The Empress of Fire

Our sledge carried us out of the cavern containing the ruined fortress and into a series of tunnels. We rode silently through the tunnels, dimly lit by a few glowing plants on the ceiling. Wellis was playing with his revolver, twirling it by the trigger guard on his finger, but we did nothing but sit and watch the rock walls pass. The Selenite who was driving clicked at the praying mantis that was pulling the cart, much like a carriage driver would chat at a horse in the streets of London.

The sledge pulled us out of the tunnels and into another open chamber. I recognized it as the one where we were ambushed by the Selenites. Formerly, it had been a dense forest nearly devoid of Selenites, but now was crawling with them. They were hacking at the lunar trees and digging great holes where the trees had already been cleared. They all carried primitive tools that consisted of long wooden poles with rocks tied at the top by wrapped bark. The rocks had been sharpened and made good instruments for chopping and digging.

"What's happening?" Star asked.

"The Selenites are harvesting wood, dirt, and stone," Wellis explained. "They've decided to build a city in the chamber we entered."

"Quite pleasant of them," Conners said. "A trading center?"

"Maybe someday," Wellis said. We passed by the Selenite workers and headed into the passage that led back to the first chamber we had seen inside of the Moon. "Right now, though, it'll be a political capital."

"Capital?" Star raised an eyebrow in wonder. "Why's that?"

Wellis smirked. "I think I'll let Mary explain everything. You've been out of it for quite a while."

The lighting grew dark as the glowing plants became thin on the ceiling.

Our progress slowed when we came up behind a large sledge loaded with trunks of trees. Several uncooperative mantises were pulling it and causing the Selenite driver to hiss and click wildly at them. Our driver made several clicks and then shook his head. We slowly moved through the tunnel and finally came into the bright light of the great chamber.

"Wow," I whispered. Conners nodded in agreement at my amazement. Star said nothing, but I imagined that he was thinking much.

The entire chamber was alive with action. There were Selenites moving about everywhere. They were moving dirt, stone, and wood, constructing numerous interconnected buildings, and carting away unneeded materials. The construction had apparently been happening for several days as many buildings had already been finished.

"It's something else, huh?" Wellis asked with a smile. He made a rough clicking sound at the driver, who nodded and turned the mantis toward the middle of the chamber.

The very middle of the chamber held a massive construction project. All of the plants had been cleared away, and in their places were wooden poles that acted as supports for soon-to-be-built stone walls. The first few layers of stone had already been laid, and Selenites crawled along them, building up more height with the stones.

We moved past the largest structure and pulled to a stop at the front of a smaller building that had already been finished. It was a simple four-walled building made of stone, mortar, and wooden beams. There were two tall Selenites standing by the door to the building, which was made of thick, dark blue wood. The Selenites carried large spears and had metal squares over their abdomens with red paint on it. When we came close, I noticed that the paint was in the shape of a flame. Wellis jumped out of the sledge and waved farewell to the driver. Star and I followed Wellis and helped Conners out of the sledge.

Wellis saluted the guards, who stepped out of the way of the door. He knocked three times and the door opened slowly. A Selenite with enormous muscles extending out from beneath the plates of her exoskeleton stared at Wellis and then let him enter. Star, Conners, and I followed Wellis into the house silently.

Inside, the house was brightly lit by freshly planted glowing plants. I winced at first, and then my eyes grew accustomed to the brightness. When I finally saw what the house held, I let out a small gasp. Conners made a similar noise while Star just smiled.

There were four beings in the house as we entered, two humans and two Selenites. Dr. Tarsini was clicking and pointing with a short Selenite male who was holding a thick book made of wooden sheets. Behind them, a tall Selenite worker was slowly moving a fan made of unfamiliar leaves. She was fanning Mary, who was wearing an awkward, yet certainly extravagant, red garment similar to a toga and sitting in a gigantic couch that dwarfed her. The rest of the room was covered with ornate tapestries and carpets, which practically covered all of the stone and wooden walls and floor. They all had images of red and yellow flames jumping upon them.

"Mission accomplished, your majesty," Wellis said, placing his hands over his eyes while facing Mary's direction. The well-muscled Selenite glared at the rest of us until Wellis motioned for us to follow his action. When we did, the Selenite stopped glaring and backed into a corner that held a large, vicious-looking harpoon.

Dr. Tarsini looked up from his troubled conversation with the Selenite male. "Captain Star! Conners! Matricks! Finally! Conners, maybe you can start making sense of these Selenites."

"I'll do my best," Conners said. "Last time I did, though, they didn't like it one bit." He pointed to a nearly healed bruise on his forehead.

Meanwhile, Mary had leapt from her chair and thrown her arms around her father's neck. "Father! Are you all right? It's been so long!"

"I'm fine, Mary," he said. "A tad hungry, but no worse for wear. Conners is the one we should worry about."

"He looks to be healing nicely," Tarsini said, leaving the male Selenite behind and examining Conners' wounds. "He'll probably be fine in a few more days."

"Speaking of days," Star interrupted, "how long have we been gone?"

"About a week and a half," Mary said, still clinging to his neck.

"It must have been quite a week," I said, glancing at the Selenites and then at Mary's dress.

"Yes, sir, it was certainly something." Wellis whistled. "I doubt anyone would have expected it to turn out like this."

"Like what?" Conners asked.

"Well," Wellis began, "Captain Star, Lukas, Curtis, I would like to present to you the Empress of Fire."

Mary stepped back from her father and blushed slightly. Her father stared at her quizzically, and she said, "Yes, I am an empress."

"H-how?" was all that Star could stammer out of his mouth.

"It all started several hours after you left a week and one half ago," Mary began. "We all waited for the greeting party to return, hopefully with new acquaintances. When Dr. Wellis returned with Sergeant Rodreguez, we didn't know what to think. We sent Rodreguez and Dr. Tarsini back up the lift to get his arm cleaned up. The rest of us debated whether to move the whole camp back up into the Station or holding our chamber. We decided to wait for one night and then see what had become of you. We sent a lander back up to the *Comet* to get more support.

"At about eight o'clock, some Selenites wandered into our camp. There were twenty or more of them, so we tried to back away toward the lift slowly. They began clicking and hissing at us, and we tried to speak to them ourselves, but we could not make any sort of conversation. Suddenly one of them came right up to us and started to poke at Elissa, who froze and waited for something to happen. Finally Elissa poked back at it, and the Selenite continued to stare curiously at us. They clicked back and forth, and then two of them approached me. I panicked and stepped back away from them. They clicked confusedly and hurried forward. Wellis moved in front of me, trying to deter them. They were interested in him for only a minute before moving toward me again. I grabbed the nearest thing I could to defend myself with: a blowtorch.

"When it ignited and burned, the Selenites were shocked. The two in front of me immediately covered their eyes and then backed away quickly. The rest of the Selenites then started clicking wildly and covering their eyes with their hands. In a few seconds, they had surrounded me while two others ran away, apparently to get other Selenites.

"After that, it was a fury of action. They dubbed me the 'Empress of Fire,' since I was able to call up flames from will. The only other fire that the Selenites knew was from lava creeping up from deep inside Luna. The Selenites were from a village nearby here and enemies of the Selenites that captured you. By this time, we figured that the Selenites were up to something good. Before we knew it, the Selenites had adopted me as their leader. Even their queen was amazed by my blowtorch. Since then, more and more villages have been swearing allegiance to the Empress of Fire."

"Amazing," I whispered. Star did nothing but smile.

"I suppose it's not so very amazing," Conners said. "Look at Cortez and Pizarro. They were both accepted as wonders... until they dominated and destroyed both the Aztecs and the Incas, respectively."

Star sneered at him. Mary merely laughed off his comment. "I'll do my best not to repeat the mistakes of the past, Mr. Conners."

"Good, good." He clenched his jaw and nodded his head.

"So you can communicate with the Selenites?" Star asked.

"We've only been able to exchange clumsy words and phrases," Mary told him. "Mostly, though, we've had to use pictures. Dr. Wellis put together his raid by pointing and sketching pictures in the dust."

"They're certainly quick learners, though," Wellis said. "I've taught a couple of them to wield rifles, which are very useful against Selenite spears. We've also brought down one of Rodreguez's cannons for heavy artillery."

"Quite intriguing," Star said. He smiled at Mary and moved to hug her around the shoulders. The muscular Selenite leapt from her position and intercepted him. The harpoon that had been leaning in the corner was now planted firmly an inch away from Star's throat. Star froze and struggled to breathe.

Mary made two clicks, one high and one low. The Selenite guardian puckered and then slunk back into the corner. Mary moved forward to comfort her father. "I'm sorry. One of the villages donated their greatest warrior, K't'whoo, to be my personal guard. She's very good at protecting me—almost too good, sometimes."

"Amazing reflexes, no?" Tarsini said. "They are capable of moving very quickly, like a skittering beetle on Earth."

"A few can even kick out some wings," Wellis said. "Not very many. I suppose it's some kind of elite group or something."

"Wow," I said. "Who'd have thought?"

"It's certainly not like Wells's book," Mary said, glancing at her own red toga. "This was another gift from a village. The Selenites are very skilled at textiles, among other things. I've been receiving tapestries ever since the first village made me their empress."

"So how far does this empire of yours go?" Star asked.

Mary smiled sheepishly. "I am not exactly sure. Many villages have taken me as their empress. We have been given several directions and we tried to get them to sketch out a map, but we have not had any luck thus far."

"Hmm." Star scratched his chin, which had developed a scraggly beard. "I have the plan. Conners, you and Tarsini go back up to the Station and make sure that you will be all right. Then come back down and see what sense you can make of everything. I will give you a note for Pierre to relay back up to the *Comet*. The *Comet* will unload all available crewmen and supplies, then head back to Star Port. Meanwhile, Curtis, you and I will survey the chamber."

Mary cleared her throat. Before she could say anything, though, the senior Star interrupted her, "Ah, yes, Mary. I suppose you have responsibilities here as the matriarch. Wellis, I'll leave you to attend her. Does everyone agree?"

There were no objections, mainly because no one dared to make a sound.

"Very well then," Star said. Tarsini and Conners immediately left the building with a slip of paper with Star's scrawled handwriting on it. Wellis motioned to the male Selenite, who followed him out.

The Selenite K't'whoo watched the rest of us carefully as Mary returned to her enormous throne. The seat was low and wide and the back was very high. It was made on a frame of wood with large, comfortable-looking cushions. The Selenite behind her continued to wave the fan as though nothing at all had happened.

"This was made for a Selenite queen," Mary explained. "Queens are much larger than humans and worm-shaped. Still, the seats are quite comfortable. Nothing is too good for an empress, I suppose."

"Mary," Star said, "I am not sure what to make of this. I imagine it is wondrous for you, but what are you going to do with it?"

"I'm an empress, Father," she said, sitting up as straight as she could, trying to make herself look impressive. "This is not something that happens every day."

"Exactly. But are you going to be an empress forever?"

"I-I do not know," she stammered. "I had not thought of the long-term effects of this. I suppose I was waiting—"

There was suddenly a loud knock at the door. Star and I both turned to look as the Selenite guard moved to the door and opened it carefully. When she saw that everything was fine, she opened it wide.

Two Selenite females entered, followed by a male. The first two were carrying a huge misshapen hat with long cloth extensions. The male had a large wooden book and immediately opened it to a blank page of wood. The Selenites all covered their eyes in salute and then handed the hat to Mary's servant. The servant raised the hat and placed it on Mary's head. She then used her main arms as well as her smaller mid-abdomen arms to spread out and smooth the long cloths.

Star and I both smiled, and Mary turned slightly red in the cheeks. The hat looked to be made of numerous yards of cloth in red, blue, and green. The cloths wrapped around the head and then hung down similarly to a cape. It made Mary look like some sort of Arab queen. The Selenite smoothed it until the cloth extensions nearly covered everything above her waist but her face.

The male Selenite then suddenly jumped forward. He held the book in his lower hands and used his upper hands to paint with a collection of brushes that was held in a belt over his shoulder. Each brush was a different color and he would take out the appropriate colored brush, lick it wet, and then paint the board with it.

"Another gift," Mary said. "They certainly are smitten with me. Humans would be, too, I suppose, if a Selenite suddenly appeared."

"Just look at Marco Polo," I reminded them.

"Very true," Star nodded. "Now, Mary, about this empire of yours…"

Before he could resume a conversation about it, Mary interrupted him. "Ah, yes, your inspection. In a few moments I will take you out personally."

Soon the male Selenite was finished with his portrait and clicked enthusiastically. Mary made a motion to the Selenite fanning her by walking her fingers across her opposite hand. The Selenite immediately left the fan and hurried out of the building.

While Mary finished diplomatic pleasantries with the three Selenites who had brought the hat, Star and I moved into a corner to wait. We said nothing for a long while, then I asked him, "Has it really been a week and a half?"

"Probably," he responded. "We must have fallen asleep and dozed for days on end in this low gravity. There certainly was not much to do in that dungeon."

"Oh," I said and fell back into silence, which was almost immediately broken by a comment from Star.

"Kind of humbling, eh?" he asked. "We men set off to make contact with the Selenites and end up in a dungeon, not to mention the poor ones who didn't survive the ambush. And here we have a young girl to becomes a queen's queen by accident."

I did not respond to his musings, thinking that it would be best to leave him to his own thoughts. He and I waited in silence from that moment until Mary was finished with the Selenites. As they soon left, the Selenite who had been fanning Mary returned.

She covered her eyes and then approached Mary, extending her arms to help her up. Mary rose from her chair, waved for us to follow, and left the building. K't'whoo and the other Selenite followed closely behind, still wary of Star and me.

Outside seemed much darker after having been in the brightly lit building.

My eyes soon adjusted, however, and we came to a very ornate sledge just outside of Mary's building. It was pulled by two purely white mantis creatures and driven by a Selenite who was also completely covered in white robes. The main sledge was made of strong purple wood and had white cushions in it and white tapestries hanging over the sides. The two Selenites helped Mary into the sledge and followed her into it. Star and I were left to fend for ourselves, but we managed to enter by making a little jump.

The gravity seemed much stronger than before. I mumbled as such, and Star made a humming sound. "Our muscles must be wearing down," he said, scratching at his chin.

Mary motioned for the sledge to move on. The driver bowed slightly and tapped a whip on the backs of the mantises to make them move. The sledge jerked and then rode smoothly along the dirt trails between the nearly constructed buildings.

"This is T'wha," Mary said, extending a hand toward the Selenite that had been fanning her. She stumbled on the last word, trying to pronounce the letters too carefully. "She had been raised to serve the queen of one of the villages... Whee'k'ch, I think. When word spread about me, though, she was given to me as a handmaiden. She is very good, too, especially considering that we cannot speak with one another yet."

"I'm sure Conners will figure that out soon enough," Star said. I glanced up and saw a platform ascending, holding two passengers and several boxes of materials. Conners and Tarsini were apparently already on their way back up to the Station.

My stomach suddenly rumbled. The two Selenites looked at me while Star rolled his eyes slightly and Mary smiled.

"Are you two hungry?" she asked.

"Quite," Star replied. I had forgotten about my hunger while we were in the building, but after mentioning it, I grew ravenous.

Mary nodded and pointed at T'wha. Once she had gotten her handmaiden's attention, Mary made a motion of feeding herself. T'wha nodded and leapt out of the sledge. Turning back to us, Mary said, "She will find you something."

We again passed in front of the gigantic building at the center of the chamber. "This will be the Imperial Palace," Mary said. "From what I understand, I will have an enormous nesting room. I believe that I have fourteen queens under me right now, but I am not quite certain. Once Conners can speak with them, we can find out just what makes up my empire."

I smiled at the thought of an empress so clueless about her own empire. Still, this entire adventure had been unbelievable from the beginning.

Mary continued to show us the city that was being constructed before our eyes. Foundations marked buildings to be used as barracks, markets, barns, and housing. The Selenites had taken the clean spring we had discovered and built up a remarkable waterworks of stone and wood. Even the Greeks and Romans would have been impressed by the large wooden tanks that were held high in the air and pipes that ran overhead into buildings. Whatever water did not go into storage for use in the city was left in stone-lined pools for baths. Several Selenites were working on creating marvelous mosaics on newly built walls.

T'wha returned to us with an armful of purple fruit. Star and I bit into them and found them good-tasting. Their juice, although refreshing, left an acidic taste in our mouths and made our tongue and gums fairly raw. Still, our stomachs were glad to receive the food, and we continued observing the Selenites.

We soon left the first chamber through the tunnel that Star and I had explored days before. The large cliff had been cut away and now only a smooth incline lay as a road. The tunnel was busy with sledges carrying supplies and new workers into the growing city. We then came to the long, thin chamber that signified the extent of our explorations. It was now very different than before, with a large wooden bridge covered with soil that extended across the river and connected to a ledge on the opposite cavern. We crossed the bridge and watched as dozens of Selenite fishermen threw out huge nets into the water. The nets soon returned, rich with worm-like creatures.

After crossing the bridge, we left this cavern through another tunnel into a new chamber. This cavern was very large, much larger than the first cavern that we came upon. The atmosphere here was peaceful, except for the numerous sledges going to and fro on a trail that led to another corridor. On both sides of the trail, enormous beetle-shaped creatures grazed on rich plants. There were a few Selenite herders among them, each carrying a large stick that they could use to guide the beetles away from the trail. There were also several watchtowers where Selenites holding spears watched the traffic and scanned for any wrongdoing.

We crossed out of this cavern and came upon a bustling Selenite village. Here there were large gates at the end of the corridor that led from the last chamber. The gates were open wide, but there were multiple guards on top of them, carefully watching the traffic that passed beneath. They all covered their eyes when they saw Mary's sledge approaching, and one gave a long blow a signal horn.

When the Selenites heard the horn, they all leapt up from their work and covered their eyes in salute. We paraded through the masses, Mary waving to them royally as a queen should. The Selenites seemed completely enamored with her. I imagined what it would have been like to have a Selenite riding in a horse and carriage on Earth and thought it would probably be fairly similar to this.

We toured the village very quickly and paid a short visit to the village's queen. The queen lay on her side in a throne similar to the one that Mary possessed. She was surrounded by Selenites, both male and female. After a few pleasantries, we reentered the sledge.

Soon we stopped again, however. Mary halted the sledge in front of a building that seemed to be freshly built. It had a plume of smoke coming out of the top and was guarded by two massive Selenites.

"This is a *ch'k'whoo'p*," Mary said. "Essentially, it translates into 'fire-house,' meaning this is a blacksmith's shop. Very few villages had shops like these, only the ones close enough to lava vents to get a fresh supply of fire often. We have taught them how to make fire and handed out many flints and lighters. Now every village in my empire has a metal shop like this. Selenites know of great deposits of ores, but before now they had not been able to use them. Already they have been able to begin making metal tools and creating armor for soldiers."

"Impressive, Mary," Star said. I nodded in agreement.

We toured two other villages that day before returning to the main city. The Selenites were still working as diligently as before. Mary told us that the worker Selenites never slept in their lives, though males and queens sometimes did. When Mary returned to her makeshift palace, she was greeted by a line of supporters. The senior Star and I left her to her rule and went up the lift back into the Lunar Station.

We were greeted at the top of the lift by Sebastian, who had taken a shift manning the lift. "It is good to see you, sir," he said, smiling.

"You too," Star said. The conversation was short, though, as Star hurried to speak with Louis Pierre in the radio room. When we came upon him, he was peacefully listening to a phonograph record while sitting by the wireless telegraph machine.

"Louis," Star said as he entered.

Pierre sat up and jerked his hands about as if to make the situation look very busy.

"Ah, you have returned, Monsieur Star!" he said. "I sent your message to ze *Comet*. Ze landers will be returning shortly wiz all of ze available men and resources."

"Good, good," Star said. "Have you sent a message to the port so that they will be expecting them?"

"I-I was about to do so," Pierre said. He pulled the telegraph close to himself and then twisted a knob. The lights dimmed slightly as more current went into the radio wave transmitter. Pierre began typing rapidly, sending a message back to Earth.

"As for you, Curtis," he said, turning to me. "I think it will soon be time to get the astronomical observatory put together. I'm sure you will be able to handle that. The pieces should be arriving when the landers return."

Before I could answer, Star had turned away and hurried off to give out more orders. Not knowing quite what to do, I went to the main room of the Station to watch the landers come back to the lunar surface. Almost as soon as I came to a window, they appeared, first as small lights, then as blocky craft with flames jetting out of nozzles on their undersides. When they landed, I waited for the crew to arrive.

The next few weeks passed busily. With the help of the other astronomers (who had little idea that they would be deposited on the Moon with so little warning), the work crew and I were able to erect the observatory rather quickly. It was fairly simple and consisted of a box-like room with a large telescope extending out of the roof. The lens was on a series of gears and levers able to position it to wherever the observer would like to look. Mirrors refracted the image through a lens into the observatory where the observer could look. A hand-crank operated shield would extend over the telescope to protect it in the case of a meteor shower or other potentially destructive event.

Meanwhile, everyone else was very busy working in the Lunar Station and below in the lunar caverns. Most of the labors were in construction and organization of Mary's newfound empire. Mary herself developed many programs to revolutionize the conditions of her Selenite subjects. She had taken to clean out Selenite dormitories and create communication systems. One of her ideas, a form of democracy among the Selenites, was met with confusion and disgust by her Selenite council. The males simply did not understand the idea that the workers might want a say in government, as it had never been done that way. The vast majority of the queens absolutely refused to give up any of their power. Mary had convinced them to try it in one of the smaller villages, with one of her more liberal queens. The Selenites of that village elected a small council to act as a voice to the queen. The council had rarely spoken, but was growing bolder in their opinions. The experiment seemed to be growing successful. Each day, Mary's empire grew larger and more powerful.

None of Mary's actions would have proceeded, however, had not Conners begun to figure out the Selenite languages. There were numerous dialects spoken inside the Moon, but according to Conners most were centered on seventeen sounds that the Selenites made with their pinchers and mouths, despite the lack of vocal chords. He created an alphabet for them, based on these sounds: 'f,' three 'k's' (one high, one low, and one middle), 'p,' two 's's' (one high, one low), 't,' 'th,' 'ch,' 'sh,' 'wh,' 'wha,' 'whoo,' 'whee,' and two other sounds, 'click' (which humans could make by clicking their tongues on the roofs over their mouths) and 'snap' (which humans could make by snapping their fingers), that humans could not explain with an English alphabet. Working with some of the smartest male Selenites, he created written characters for this alphabet. He hoped to soon create grammar books and outline the first lunar language. Though he had much work ahead of him, he had already been able to teach himself, Mary, and Wellis to be able to converse with the Selenites.

Father Piousse had worked closely with Conners, aiding him in learning the Selenite language. The Father had set up a small mission in Mary's capital city, though it was of little use until the humans and Selenites could communicate. The Selenites were familiar with religion, though it was primarily used as a method of worship for the queen. Mary had done her best to dodge away from a god-like position, and it caused the Selenites to love her and her humility even more. Conners seemed slightly uncomfortable in the presence of the pious priest. They had many conversations, some of which had become quite heated.

Elissa the French botanist worked with the Selenites nearly as much as Mary and Conners. She had begun the enormous project of categorizing all of the Selenite plants and animals and pursued it with great energy. Armed with dozens of libraries of wooden books and samples gathered by an army of Selenites, she had already organized a great deal of information. She studied the 'glowing plants' that grew on the ceilings of the lunar caverns. According to what she had observed, the plants broke down complex substances in the soil to create energy, much of which was given off as light. These unique plants served as the most important part of the Moon's underground biosphere and Elissa hoped to find great uses for them on Earth.

Louis Pierre, the radio operator of the expedition, remained especially busy. In addition to sending messages, each day he would receive a lengthy message from Earth containing worldwide news and, sometimes, messages from loved ones. Star had allowed each crewmember to send a short message home, and we all jumped at the opportunity to communicate with Earth. On January 23 (we kept our days according to clocks, even though there were never nights under the surface of the Moon), we received word that Queen Victoria had died, and Star ordered a day of mourning for all British crewmembers.

The *Comet* returned nearly a week after it left. Its holds were packed to their maximum with workers, explorers, and supplies. Star welcomed the new colonists and immediately levied them with orders. It was amusing to see the astonished looks on the faces of the new arrivals. I imagined that my expressions were very similar.

We began to fall into a workable routine. I would sleep for ten hours every forty hours or so, since we were able to go for longer days in the weaker gravity. The majority of my time was spent in the observatory, which could map both new stars and the Earth itself. I used my free time to go down below the surface of the Moon to visit and watch the construction of the city. I also did my best to record everything that I saw in my journal. Page after page filled up with small text and numerous diagrams. Selenites and humans worked together now, studying one another's cultures and abilities, and I recorded it to the best of my ability.

Not everything seemed to be growing toward perfection, however. The other queens and empresses of the Selenites had observed Mary's growth of power. They were becoming increasingly wary of the humans' weaponry. Rumors had spread of a grand alliance to destroy Mary and to wipe out the humans forever. Star merely scoffed at these rumors, but I was often a little upset by them. I had the feeling that something terrible would come of them.

Chapter Ten,
Festivities

The events began February third at eleven twenty-six. It had been one month since we first landed on the Moon, or Luna, as Star preferred to call it. Star had decided that since the expedition was going so splendidly (as one could certainly call it now that his daughter was an empress over a lunar empire), the crew would have a short celebration. His original plans included a short feast in the ever-expanding Lunar Station.

Mary had decided to upstage her father and throw a wondrous celebration throughout her empire. The feast in the Lunar Station would be followed by a larger feast in her new capital city with queens from all over the empire attending. After that, there would be a long parade from the capital to one of her newly acquired outlying villages known as Th'ch'click. Th'ch'click had built a large field for gaming long ago and had been a center for celebrations for numerous generations.

The senior Star was not told about his daughter's plans until the night before. When someone (Conners, I believe) finally let him know, he was inwardly outraged. After breathing carefully for a few moments, he said in a low voice, "Very well, then. Perhaps the crew should join in on such festivities."

I attended the feast in the Lunar Station accompanied by Helga, my fellow astronomer. The Station's common room and botany laboratory had been converted into dining rooms filled with black-suited crewmembers. Nearly all of the crew had turned out for the feast. The only missing people were a skeleton crew aboard the *Comet* and a few people who were below in the lunar caverns. Mary and Wellis had yet to come up the lift from the caverns, but I had overheard Conners giving Star their promises that they would be there.

Helga and I were seated in the botany laboratory, which had been rearranged and filled with tables. Many of the plants, which had grown to enormous heights in the low gravity, were blooming, giving the laboratory a feel of some sort of pristine garden. In spite of having to wear the same black suit as the rest of the crew, Helga had tried to dress herself up by fancily doing her blonde hair and adding flowers to it. In the end, she looked quite stunning from the neck up, but had the same Star suit from the neck down.

In a few moments, Conners joined us at our table accompanied by two short Selenite males. Several Selenites had gone up the lift to observe the realm above their caverns. We had shown them our technology, and they had been thrilled the entire time. There were plans to bring two or three interested queens for a tour in the future, but currently the lift was not quite large enough to accommodate them. Conners also wanted to take some Selenites out into the void that covered the Moon's surface, but none of the Spacesuits would fit correctly. Star had promised to enlarge the lift and make new Spacesuits several times, but had not yet been able to organize it.

"Salutations," he said, sitting. "Or should I say, *s'ch*."

The two Selenites with him were wearing fancy blue robes with white trim. Selenite males were the only Selenites to wear clothing out of habit, while the Selenite queens sometimes had blankets and cloaks and the Selenite workers rarely had more than a satchel or necklace. They both crawled up into their chairs and hissed out, "*S'ch*."

Helga and I nodded and did our best to try to imitate their word.

Conners smiled at our failure to do so and tried to council us. "No, no, it's all from the front of your mouth. Just use the tip of your tongue and your front teeth. And pucker out your lips and hold them so that they don't move."

We tried to follow his directions and came out with a word that very nearly sounded like the Selenites. Conners nodded approvingly, as did the Selenites with him.

"By the way," Conners said to us, "these are K'f'k and T'p'sh, two buddies of mine." He then turned to the Selenites and clicked and hissed. The only two human words in the sentence were "Curtis" and "Helga." The Selenites nodded and waved rather politely.

The first course, a salad, was suddenly served. The crew had held a lottery to see who would need to do the serving for the evening. François and Hosea had been two of the unlucky ones that I knew best. Hosea served our table and mumbled impolitely before moving to the next one. I took my salad and chuckled at the poor man.

The salads had been prepared by Elissa and a few other botanists, some human and some Selenite. They were a blend of Earth plants and plants from the lunar caverns below. There were lettuce, tomatoes, and cheese mixed with stalks and tiny leaves from plants I did not know. The whole thing was covered in a thick, creamy blue dressing that I could not recognize as either earthly or lunar.

While we were eating, Conners began a discussion. "The Selenite language is quite fascinating," he said. Helga and I glanced at one another, knowing that Conners had just dominated the dinner conversation for the evening. "Their words are really just slung together sounds, which build off of one another. For example, *th't'f'th't'f* means 'empress' or simply 'queen-queen.'"

"Then, for sentences, they line up words like we do. However, there are certain differences. They do not conjugate verbs, for instance, but stick in another word to mean past, present, pluperfect, et cetera. Somewhat like, 'Way back when, I run to the store.'"

"What do they do for persons, then?" Helga asked.

"Well, it gets a little tricky there." Conners chuckled nervously. I assumed he was still working out the rules of grammar himself. "Apparently, they imply first and second person by pointing antennae. So if I were to say, 'I am leaving,' I would point to myself, and if I were to say, 'you are leaving,' I would point to you."

Helga nodded, obviously a little more interested than I was in the Selenite language. "And for third person?"

"I would just state the name at the beginning of the sentence."

I glanced over at the Selenites, who appeared to be more interested with their salads than the conversation at hand. Conners had said that some of the Selenites were becoming able to understand English, even if they were not able to speak it. I wondered how much English these Selenites knew. At any proficiency, though, they spent more time stabbing at the salads with their knives and then munching on whatever stuck to the knife long enough to get to their ant-like mouths. When their knives came close to their faces, the pinchers on either side of the mouth would take over most of the work and push the food into their mouths.

"What about plural forms and singular?"

"I'm still not quite sure what to do with them," Conners admitted. "Some dialects may clip on an extra sound or two and others may use an entirely separate word."

The conversation was suddenly stopped by a soft trumpet blowing. We all turned to see what exactly was happening, and Hosea dropped a small bowl out of surprise. Fortunately, the gravity was low enough that he caught it long before it hit the metal floor.

Mary, Wellis, T'wha, and K't'whoo had come into the Lunar Station fashionably late and were now on their way to their places at Star's table. Mary was wearing a flowing white gown made by the Selenites and her hair was done with what looked like two wings from a gigantic dragonfly. Wellis was wearing his black Star uniform, but had a white mantle over his shoulders. T'wha and K't'whoo were scarcely dressed at all, as was common for Selenite females. However, they were each wearing a rich mantle similar to Wellis's, but far more elaborate. K't'whoo had her trusty harpoon with her as well as a large shell held by one of her small arms.

The two Selenites seated next to Conners immediately covered their eyes. Conners half-heartedly followed their salute. Helga and I glanced at one another, smiled playfully, and covered our eyes too. Mary soon crossed the room and sat down after being greeted by an impressed, but upset, Mason Star.

We uncovered our eyes and continued with our salads until the main course was served. Again, Hosea handed us our food, mumbled, and moved along. This time we each received several slices of roasted chicken, lunar vegetables, and ample bread. The dinner continued smoothly and Conners and Helga continued to discuss the Selenite languages. The male Selenites and I, however, continued to be more interested in eating than in speaking.

Finally the dessert, a wholly lunar production, was brought out. It seemed similar to a crust with berries and cream, but had an odd taste about it. The taste was odd, but certainly not bad, and I finished it very quickly. The Selenites did too, each using his spoon to quickly shovel the dessert into his mouth. Conners and Helga ate more slowly, continuing to discuss Selenites, the Moon, and recent news.

When we had all finished, Star stood from his table and began a long toast. He related many of the events of the expedition and made us all feel proud to be ourselves. Conners translated most of the toast for the Selenites, who nodded approvingly often. Finally, Star saluted the Moon and its future. There was a loud clinking of glasses and rumble of agreement throughout the dining rooms as he sat.

"I suppose we should head to the caverns," Conners said. "It would be a shame to miss out on anything down there." He tossed his napkin onto his plate, motioned for the Selenites to do the same, and stood. Helga and I left with him, just as Hosea came up to the table and muttered something in Portuguese.

There seemed to be a mad dash for the lift from among the tables. Our group came as the second table and was immediately shoved into a line. Sebastian chuckled at all of the excited people as he let down the first group that had come to the lift.

"I've never been a fan of lines," Conners said, shaking his head. Helga and I nodded in agreement while the Selenites struggled to translate what he had said.

When the lift returned, it was able to hold only two human passengers along with the Selenite guests. Conners asked who would volunteer to stay behind, the person obviously not being himself.

"Ladies first," I told Helga. "Go ahead."

"Are you certain it is fine?" she asked.

"Yeah," I smiled sheepishly. "I'll try to catch up."

Helga boarded the lift, on which Conners and the two Selenites already stood. They disappeared from view and I sighed as I prepared to wait longer. Sebastian worked the simple gears and counted out the time it would take them to reach the bottom.

Suddenly someone called my name from behind. "Hey, Curtis!"

I turned and saw Wellis waving for me. Giving up my place in line, I headed back toward him. He was standing with two of Rodreguez's soldiers, joking about the upcoming celebration. When I reached him he shook my hand and smiled broadly.

"I've got a proposition for you, Curtis," he said.

"What's that?"

"Have you heard about the grand race that'll take place tomorrow?"

"No, but what about it?"

"Well, the deal is that each village in little Miss Star's empire will have a team of two race about in sledges chariot-style as the climax of the games. Captain Star liked the idea and had Mary allow teams representing Earth's 'villages.' "

"So you want me to race with you?"

"You bet." Wellis smiled. "I think we can win this one for Uncle Sam."

"Why me though?" I asked. "What about Foster or that other guy?"

"Foster's a city boy from New York," Wellis said. "You've had plenty of horse-handling, and besides, you're lighter, too."

"All right then," I said, a smile creeping up on my lips.

I stood with Wellis and his friends for several minutes until it was our turn to head onto the lift. When we were all standing comfortably on it, the lift began to drop with a sudden jolt. We descended slowly and then more quickly as we lowered through yards and yards of dirt.

The lift had been upgraded considerably since the first time I had ridden it. There was now a battery-powered light at the top so that the trip would no longer be completely dark until the lift came into the light of the glowing plants below. In addition, the tunnel and lift had been expanded so that more people could travel at once. Star had told me of a grand vision he had of a great series of lifts that would operate out of a lifting station to go to and from the surface of Luna, and I imagined it to be quite similar to the elevators of the station above Earth.

We finally came into the bright caverns below. The capital city of Mary's empire spread out below us, still under heavy construction. Many of the buildings had already been completed, but there was still much work to be done, especially on the palace. The Selenites were masters of mosaics and murals and had promised to decorate the entire city with their best skills.

When we stopped, Wellis immediately leapt off of the lift, disturbing the man on the ground. The two other men and I stepped off more carefully, under the watchful eye of the ground controller. When we were clear, he sent a signal up the rope to Sebastian, who began to pull the lift back up to the Station.

We left the lift and headed out into the busy streets of the capital. There were many Selenites; all hurrying this way and that, looking amazingly like ants. Many were carrying food, others were driving sledges, and one group was even assisting a queen on her way to Mary's half-finished palace.

Wellis snagged a fist-sized fruit from one of the Selenites and bit into it, sending juices down his chin. "What's the plan, gentlemen?"

"I suppose there's a feast here, too," one said. "I hope I can hold this much food."

Wellis and his friends headed off after a juice-laden Selenite to fill canteens with the sweet liquid. I decided to walk toward the palace and see what kind of festivities I could find.

The streets became increasingly filled with performers. Selenites that once carried fruit set down their burdens at merchant stalls and began the festival by painting on their front carapace and putting strange masks on their faces. A group of young Selenites caught up with me and danced excitedly around the rare human. After a few minutes, they found another human to dance around and left me with a large, odd-looking mask.

The mask was made of dried wood dust that had been set in glue and felt almost like papier-mâché. It was red and green and had giant plumes made of dragonfly wings and two gigantic eyeholes that looked odd when placed on a human head. The mouth of the mask was also large, probably designed that way so that plenty of food could be eaten by the wearer.

I put the mask on my face, though it fit awkwardly, and continued on with the festivities. There were now clusters of small bands making odd, almost tribal-sounding music, acrobats whose exoskeletons were exceptionally flexible, and even a group of combatants who sparred with extremely long poles. At one point, two Selenites capable of flying zipped overhead and dumped confetti upon the streets.

I watched the flying Selenites with awe. They were stouter than most Selenites and much larger shoulders and backs. While all worker Selenites had wings under their posterior exoskeletons, most of them could not use them. I had seen several flying Selenites before, but just for a moment. They would break into a run, build up a good amount of momentum, and then leap into the air. Their wings would start to flutter from under their shells and they would zip through the air. I had heard that Wellis had taken a motion camera and recorded one of these flights and planned to send it on a tour back on Earth.

In a few more minutes, I came across a particularly interesting group of acrobats and musicians. Every time a Selenite would make a sudden leap, the musicians would strike a high, prolonged note. They built a tall stack of Selenites with repeated notes that would be impossible to make on Earth with heavier gravity.

I suddenly felt a hand on my shoulder and turned. My mask caught on my shoulder and rose so that I could no longer see through the large eyeholes. I tried to straighten the mask, but I finally just took it off.

When I could see again, I saw Katherine MacPherson giggling at me. I smiled in return, somewhat embarrassedly.

"Enjoyin' yerself?" she asked, her accent as thick with Irish as ever before.

"Yeah, I suppose so," I said. "This is certainly something else."

" 'Tis," she said, gazing at the Selenite acrobats.

We watched the acrobats for a few more minutes and then decided to move onto something else. There were dozens of clusters of Selenite entertainers all over the city, and we did our best to see each of them. I doubted that any were quite as amusing as the first group of acrobats that we saw.

We found ourselves laughing at a trio of Selenite clowns who spent hour after hour pretending to beat one another with wooden sticks. Despite not being able to understand their comical banter, their antics made both Katherine and me laugh hysterically. Suddenly, however, a loud trumpet interrupted the clowns. More trumpets resounded, stopping all of the entertainers around the chamber.

"What's all this?" Katherine asked as the trumpets died away.

The entertainers were all beginning to break up and the crowds moved toward the palace. The clowns shed their sticks and followed the disserting crowd.

"I think the parade's about to begin," I said. "Shall we go?"

"I suppose."

We moved amid the thick crowds of Selenites and soon arrived at Mary's half-finished palace. There were numerous sledges lined up and people boarding them. The humans, queen Selenites, and most males were to have a place on a sledge. Only the most respected Selenite worker would be allowed to ride in a sledge; the rest had to walk along the sides of the parading sledges.

Katherine and I were herded onto a small but comfortable sledge, on which the driver immediately whipped at the mantises pulling it. We started with a jerk that pushed us back into the cushioned couch. When the sledge had come into a constant speed behind the sledge in front of us, we resettled ourselves and sighed contentedly.

"What exactly happened?" Katherine asked, laughing with surprise.

"Efficiency, I think," I said. "They certainly are sticklers for getting things done in a hurry."

"Very true." She nodded. "How much time have you spent with the Selenites?"

I chuckled, remembering the week and a half stowed away in a Selenite dungeon. Katherine gasped slightly, realizing what she had just asked, and then nervously rearranged her glasses because of the shift of her face.

"I'm sorry, I didna mean..."

"That's all right," I said, trying to console her. "Aside from the initial adventures, I've only spent a couple of days with the Selenites. I've been up in the observatory for most of my time here."

"Oh."

"How about you? I heard from Wellis that Captain Star had given you some special job dealing with them."

"Ah, yes." She smiled. "Cap'n Star wanted me to work with the Selenites to see what kind of mathematical backgrounds they had developed."

She paused, so I prodded her with, "So, what did you find?"

"Oh, they're pretty basic," she said, then paused again. Finally, she realized that I wanted more information. "They've developed up to about the areas that the Ancient Greeks had done. It's mostly for counting and keeping records in their villages, I think. Only the males use any sort of math, though. They're not very good at it either. I guess the problem could be in the number system. They've got a different symbol for each value of eight, since it's a base eight system. The symbols are pretty complex too; there're all circles and each one's just a little different."

I did my best to understand her wild explanation. Katherine had a lacking when she tried to make sense of her thoughts. I wondered if it had something to do with her genius in mathematics. According to several stories I had heard, many such intelligent people had problems fitting into the real world.

The parade went quickly throughout Mary's empire. The Selenites were all in good spirits and gladly danced around the more privileged sledges as they went mile after mile through the various caverns. Katherine and I were caught up in watching the Selenites in the parade and did not discuss anything more. I was fairly glad to have the distraction and not to have to listen to Katherine's wild explanations.

We paraded through numerous caverns of varying shapes and sizes until we finally came to a large cavern that had been well-developed by the Selenites. A cluster of buildings and thick-walled gates made up the Selenite village of Th'ch'click. Outside of the village, there was a wide field that had been designed for Selenite games. There was a mass of elevated seats on each side of the main field, which consisted of a large grassy area and a circular track.

As we grew closer, I recognized that the seats were more complex than I had first realized. Most of the seats were simple stones that were stacked to make row after row seating. Above them, there were large, flat areas capable of holding queens and their entire courts. Numerous murals and mosaics covered the seating, showing various images of Selenite games and events. Gigantic flags made of bright colors hung over the seats and had more images upon them. I gaped at the ingenuity of the Selenites and the splendor of their handiwork.

"Amazing," I whispered. Katherine nodded enthusiastically, her red hair waving wildly.

A male Selenite behind us began clicking and hissing. Katherine and I both turned, quite surprised, and stared at him. After a moment of listening to his clicks, we both shrugged.

"He's trying to explain how they built it," we heard a voice say in English. Conners hurried up behind us and patted the male Selenite on the head. "The stones for the seats were quarried out of the walls in the village, which built… I'm not sure what that means."

The Selenite waved his arms and clicked out different words. Conners clicked and hissed back at him. Finally, the two came to an understanding.

"Apartments," Conners concluded. "They're quite comfortable and defensible."

The Selenite clicked again.

"Apparently, they've used the field and apartments for diplomatic purposes," he translated. "Quite clever."

Katherine and I nodded. The Selenite clicked a few more times, and then motioned for us to follow him. Conners smiled, thrilled at himself for successfully translating for a Selenite.

We followed the Selenite up the seating of one of the stands. Mary and her court had already arrived at the top and were preparing the platform for sitting. Star and a few of his command crew were filling up seats below the platform. When we came to the top, Katherine and I joined Star while Conners hurried up to speak with Mary. The short male Selenite disappeared from view; apparently his task had been to point humans to the right seats, and he was moving on to find other humans.

"Ah, Curtis," a voice said from behind me. I felt a hand on my shoulder and turned to see Star smiling at me.

"I haven't seen you in a while," he said. "Are you keeping busy?"

"Oh, yes," I said, returning his smile. "I'm glad Mary organized this little…" I paused as Star's eyes squinted and his smile became forced. He was obviously upset that his daughter was upstaging him. I tried my best to finish the sentence, but it ended up in a fake cough.

Katherine suddenly interrupted us by pointing at the field and saying, "Something's coming out!"

There was a loud trumpeting as two sledges loaded with Selenites entered the field between two of the seating stands. Most of the Selenites were carrying large spears and various other weapons. The sledges moved to the center of the field, stopped, and, after unloading the Selenites with the weapons, hurried off of the field.

"What is zis?" someone asked. I recognized the voice as Louis Pierre, who must have been excused from his radio duties for the celebration.

"It looks like they're preparing for gladiatorial combat," Star gasped. He stood from his seat, excitedly outraged, and hurried up to the platform where Mary was watching.

Katherine turned as he rushed by us and gasped slightly. I jumped up and ran to catch up to him. The British Empire was known for its properness as well as its reactions to barbaric behavior. I hoped that I could catch him and calm him down before he reacted too much toward Mary. Unfortunately, one of the *Comet's* engineers accidentally caught me by the foot and Star had burst upon the platform before I could get to him.

By the time that I arrived, Star had already begun the confrontation.

"What is the meaning of this?" he asked, marching toward Mary. Mary's handmaiden hunched protectively toward her while her bodyguard tightened her grip on her harpoon-like spear.

Conners jumped to answer his question, bodily placing himself between the two Stars. "It's an opening act for the games portion of the empress's celebration. I'm sure you're familiar with the gladiators of ancient Rome."

"The Romans were far from civilized, though," Star said. He brushed Conners aside and faced Mary. "Do you realize what is happening?"

As he asked the question, I heard a loud hiss go up from the crowd. They were cheering the gladiators, who had raised their weapons in salute to the crowds. Several of the platforms were filled with queens and their entourages and the majority of the seats were already occupied. Still, there were trickles of additional audience members piling into the seats of the massive arena.

"They're just games, Father," Mary said. She clicked to T'wha, who nodded slowly.

"Very well then," Star said and crossed his arms over his chest. "Let's watch."

We all turned back to the field, where several clumps of combatants were dueling. With each swing, the crowd would gasp and then hiss as it was blocked or dodged. There was a vast array of weapons being used, from nets and long ropes to spears and short clubs to slings and sharp, flat rocks meant for throwing. For defense, many of the Selenites were wearing rough metal breastplates, shields made from the shells of gigantic beetles, and even a few had helmets with their antennae pointing out.

The fights were rather exciting, and if one group fell to cautiously circling and observing their opponents, another group was sure to be launching attacks at one another. Once or twice, I found myself yelling out cheers and jeers at the combatants. They would spar back and forth, always checking one another for a weakness in their defenses.

Suddenly, however, most of the cheers from among the crew were replaced by horrified gasps. One of the Selenites had pushed another back with several attacks and then launched another vicious strike with her heavy spear. The defending Selenite tried to jump up and away from the attack, but the attacker repositioned her spear and stabbed it through the Selenite's abdomen. The Selenite jerked and then fell to the ground, where it quivered before laying still.

While most of the crew gasped in horror (though I think that some found the slaughter entertaining), the Selenites jumped from their seats and hissed excitedly. The victorious Selenite pulled her weapon from the body and waved it triumphantly. Another Selenite tried to take advantage of her luck and made a move for a surprise attack, which was skillfully blocked.

"Did you see that?" one of the botanists shouted above the crowd.

Star turned back to Mary, who was panting with shock. Her mouth hung open and her eyes were wide. Finally, she tore her gaze away from the field and buried her face in her hands. T'wha moved to comfort her, as did the senior Star.

"Mary," he said soothingly when he reached her side. When she did not respond, he called to her again, less soothingly. At last she looked up. Star patted her shoulder and said, "You need to stop this."

Mary's eyes were red. She tried to speak, but could not.

Conners stepped forward again. "You shouldn't stop this! It's their culture! They have a—"

Star glared at him until he stopped talking and backed away slowly. He sunk into the crowd of Selenites behind Mary and crouched to try to disappear.

Mary half-returned her face to her hands before halting. Her father whispered something to her and she nodded. She turned to K't'whoo and clicked out a message. Her bodyguard froze for an instant and then took up her shell. She blew a long, loud, low note, which was enough to quiet the crowd and cause the gladiators to pause.

"Tell them that I do not want any killing," she told K't'whoo, who clicked and hissed into her shell, which projected her voice for all to hear.

When they received the message, the crowd clicked and hissed at one another, and then fell to hissing at the empress. The gladiators on the field looked around, apparently confused. The senior Star smirked.

Mary frowned at the crowd's hisses and glanced at the blowtorch that was kept by her side. Finally, though, she turned back to K't'whoo. "Explain to them that every life is invaluable and it is wrong to waste like this. Can you do that?"

K't'whoo thought for a moment, then nodded. She took several minutes clicking and hissing through the shell. At first, the crowd continued to hiss, but they grew quieter as the speech continued. When it came to an end, they all made joyful hisses and began to cover their eyes in a massive salute.

"What's this all about?" I asked under my breath.

"Nobody cares about the common workers," a voice answered. Wellis, who was among Mary's council as an adviser, had heard my comment. "The queens are not going to like this speech, however. Mary's going to have trouble with them for a while, I bet."

I looked out over the arena and saw several of the queens waving in outrage. Two of them, however, seemed to be cheering along with the Selenite workers. Most of the male Selenites, who were the recorders of history that did not stray outside of the ways things were meant to be done, looked confused. Still, the majority of the people in the stadium seemed thrilled with the empress's new proclamation.

Mary stood from her small, portable throne and waved out to the crowd, which erupted in a loud mass of clicks and hisses. When most of the cheers had begun to die away, she turned back to K't'whoo and said, "Now tell the gladiators to spar, but not to hurt one another."

K't'whoo nodded and enthusiastically clicked at the combatants through her shell. The gladiators, excited over their newfound survival, eagerly began to fight in a playful way. The crowd cheered again, and the gladiators did their best to create wonderful entertainment for them.

Mary and Mason Star began to whisper between themselves. I caught a few words, and from them decided to let the conversation stay between a father and his daughter. Instead, I joined Wellis at the front of the platform to watch the mock-battle.

"She makes quite a ruler, doesn't she?" Wellis asked me, not looking away from the field.

I smiled and nodded, glancing back at the human girl who had become an empress over a vast expanse of lunar insect people. Even one month ago I would have thought such a thing to be impossible, and I would probably have called anyone who dreamed up such a thing crazy.

*

*

When the gladiators had worn themselves out, they left the field. Mary ordered a short service for the fallen warrior and made a stumbling speech through her bodyguard's shell. The Selenites hissed sadly at the fallen gladiator and cheered for their empress. The corpse was put on a sledge to act as a funeral pyre (a touch none other than the Empress of Fire would have done), and, when it was lit, the pyre moved off of the field to be extinguished.

After the pyre, the field was cleared and then filled with several cages holding wild lunar creatures. I tried to recognize them, but I had never seen anything like them in my visits to the caverns. They were as large as horses and looked fairly reminiscent of the mantises that pulled Selenite sledges. However, they had larger hind legs and much smaller heads, as well as two sets of enormous moth-like wings.

"What are those things?" I asked Wellis.

"They're called *snap't'f*," Wellis said. "I saw some Selenites bringing them from the east. They come from rocky, dry regions and are really ornery critters. From what they explained, I think we're in for some entertainment."

One of the creatures was led from its cage lead by two strong Selenites with hooks attached to a collar on its neck. A brave Selenite climbed onto the back of the creature and lashed a rope around the collar. She tied the other end around her abdomen and secured it. She then held on with both hands and gave a nod. The two Selenites holding the creature suddenly let loose, and one even thwacked it on the thorax.

The creature erupted with violent movements, tossing the Selenite in a vain effort to throw her from its back. The Selenite struggled to stay in at least a small amount of control, but was barely hanging onto the rope. After hopping along the ground several times, the creature suddenly leapt into the air and fluttered its wings. The whole crowd shrieked and watched as the creature spun in the air and dove this way and that.

"Wow!" Wellis shouted. I joined in his shouts, but I could not possibly catch up with his level of excitement.

The creature dove toward the ground and then suddenly fluttered back up into the air. The Selenite held onto the rope and used the collar to drive the creature back to the ground. Finally the creature gave up the use of its wings and returned to kicking and jumping along the ground. In a few more moments, the creature grew tired and began to walk casually. The Selenites on the ground caught it by the collar and led it back into its cage.

The victorious, although very dizzy, Selenite untied herself from the creature and dropped to the ground. Two other Selenites hurried to her and picked her up. The Selenite waved her arms happily, and the crowd hissed with excitement.

"Wow," Wellis repeated. He suddenly turned and dashed toward Mary and Star. He saluted them and said, "I request permission to ride one of those beasts."

Captain Star nodded, and Mary giggled at Wellis's excitement. He thanked them both and dashed down the seats and disappeared from view.

The crowd began to cheer again as a second creature came out of its cage. The scene was very similar to the first and similarly exciting. I was distracted from it, though, when I spotted Wellis dashing toward the cages. He was wearing his black Star suit as well as the white mantle given to him by the Selenites and also a wide hat common among cowboys of the West.

Many of the members of the crew began to laugh and to point, while the others cheered him on. He waved at us and then spoke with the Selenites below. They gave him a long rope, which tied around his waist. In a few moments he was waiting beside a cage containing a vicious *snap't'f*. When the second rider finished with her creature, the Selenites moved it back into its cage and prepared Wellis for his ride.

Finally a fresh creature was pulled from its cage and held down by the collar. Wellis stretched his neck to the left and then to the right, his cowboy hat flinging both ways. When he was ready, he climbed up onto the *snap't'f*, which shifted angrily under Wellis's weight. He waved to the Selenites, gripped the rope around the creature's collar, and grinned as the Selenites released their hooks.

The *snap't'f* suddenly leapt up into the air and beat its wings wildly. Wellis let out an incredible shout of surprise, which caused all of the Selenites to hiss excitedly. The creature stayed high above the ground, twisting and flapping its wings in a desperate attempt to remove its rider. Wellis hung onto the rope and did his best to keep his legs tight around the creature's body.

After making several turns around the air above the arena, the creature folded its wings tightly around itself and dove headfirst toward the ground. To an Earthling, the fall seemed to be quite slow, but the Selenites all hissed in amazement. Wellis grunted and struggled with the rope, pulling up and choking the creature. Still it fell downward, accelerating and gaining great momentum.

When the creature was a few feet above the ground, many crewmembers were on the edge of panic. I was petrified with astonishment and stood dumbly with my mouth open. Someone started shouting in French, excitedly trying to give directions to Wellis. Both of the Stars remained quiet and watched apparently calmly, though Mary was wringing her dress with her hands.

Wellis pulled so hard on the rope that he was leaning nearly flatly on the back of the creature. Realizing that the creature refused to stop falling, he brought out his legs and jabbed his heels into its sides.

The *snap't'f* roared wildly in pain and shock. It reflexively flung out its wings, which caught the air and dramatically slowed the creature. Wellis shouted out a victory cheer, and the Selenites immediately joined in on the cheer. The creature landed on the ground with a dull thud and struggled up on its feet. The fall had given the creature a hard knock and it now stumbled in a daze.

"Good show!" one of the crewmen shouted. Wellis smiled broadly and waved triumphantly.

As Wellis shifted his weight with a wave, the creature came out of its daze. It began kicking its hind legs and rearing back. Wellis skillfully held onto the creature, moving his body to counteract all of its movements. The Selenites and crewmembers cheered wildly in a single voice. I screamed especially loudly, cheering on my fellow American and his Texas wrangling abilities.

The creature tried to flip onto its back, but Wellis caught it by the collar and pulled its head the opposite way. It hissed at him and then leapt into the air again. After making an amazing loop, it spiraled to the ground. Wellis was wearing the creature down and had almost exhausted it. When it reached the ground, it kicked twice more and then tiredly sat down.

The crowd erupted with shouts and hisses. Wellis untied himself as the Selenites approached to catch the collar of the creature and jumped down from its back. He turned to Mary and saluted by covering his eyes, and then waved to the enthusiastic crowd. Several young Selenites ran out of their seats and were hurrying to surround the amazing human rider.

Behind him, though, the creature had not yet given up on its fight. It suddenly jumped up and threw out its wings, which knocked away the Selenite supporters. It roared at Wellis and then charged, using its wings to throw itself forward.

The crowd shrieked wildly. Wellis turned just in time to leap into the air, which was a simple task in the lunar gravity. He landed on the creature's back and threw his arm around its neck. He squeezed, trying to control the beast.

The young Selenites who had come out onto the field squealed and tried to race back to their seats. The enraged *snap't'f* charged at them, snapping its mouth. Wellis strengthened its grip and threw his body to the left, forcing the creature to turn or risk breaking its neck.

The creature leapt into the air again, a dangerous leap now that Wellis was no longer firmly attached to it. Mary shouted to T'wha, who relayed orders to a cluster of Selenite entertainers. The three Selenites nodded and rushed to action. They hurried to the edge of the platform, extended wings from under their shells and leapt into the air.

Above them, the creature was swooping randomly with Wellis bouncing on its back. His arm was the only thing holding him onto the creature and preventing a long drop, which would be life-threatening even in lunar gravity. Wellis kept tightening his grip on the creature's throat, but he could not bring it down.

The Selenites hurried to catch up to the *snap't'f* on their fluttering wings. They surrounded it and hovered, trying to get close without being hit by the gigantic wings of the creature. Finally they zipped into the fray and grabbed the creature. They stopped fluttering and added a tremendous amount of weight to the load.

The creature roared and did its best to flap its wings, but the added weight slowly began to drag it to the ground. It sluggishly lowered and finally landed on the ground, where Selenite gamekeepers pounced upon it. Wellis and the Selenite entertainers climbed off of the creature. The ordeal had stunned Wellis, but he did his best to stay on his feet.

Mary jumped from her seat and led a great mass of the crowd toward the field. I did my best to keep up with the crowd, but I somehow ended up near the end of the rush by the time it reached the field. As the Selenite tamers shoved the *snap't'f* into a cage, the crowd surrounded Wellis and the entertainers. Cheers broke out throughout the arena when they saw that Wellis was dazed but uninjured.

Several crewmembers and a crowd of Selenites, including Mary and her court, helped Wellis off of the field. He was led off of the field and taken to Mary's apartments where he could rest. Everyone whispered among themselves and stood dumbfounded until Mary sent T'wha back to the area to restart the games. T'wha climbed up to the platform and waved to the trumpeters.

When the horns sounded, the crowd slowly returned to its seats and the creatures, all safe in their cages, were dragged off of the field. In a moment, a vast number of Selenite clowns charged onto the field. The clowns all wore large, goofy masks and bright-colored ribbons that hung from their shoulders. A group of them played exotic instruments while the acrobats among them danced wildly. Within a few minutes the crowd had forgotten about Wellis's adventure and laughed hysterically at the clowns.

I was smiling at a small group of clowns came out and pretended to fight like the gladiators had, when I suddenly realized that Conners was standing next to me. I jumped a little, surprised by him, and then calmly said, "Hello."

"That was something else, huh?" Conners asked me. I nodded to him while paying half of my attention to the clowns below. Conners continued in a low voice, "The Selenites have quite a culture. Too bad Star's trying to ruin it."

"How's that?" I asked, cocking an eyebrow at him. "Are you still upset about the gladiators?"

"They were troublesome young ones who had been trained to fight," Conners explained. "T'p'sh had told me all about it. Now their whole social order will have to be rearranged since there's no punishment for bad Selenite youths."

"So death is a good punishment for young people who don't really work out like they're supposed to?" I asked.

Conners opened his mouth to explain how the Selenites depended upon social positions that were defined from birth, but stopped himself. I did not have to point out the similarities between his argument and his own childhood. Instead, he began to focus his dispute on the chaos and social change that this would cause.

I suddenly interrupted him. "Maybe it would be best to change their society. Isn't social reform something you'd like to see?"

Once again he stopped talking. It was not often that Lukas Conners was without something to say.

"You're just upset that Star got the better of you, aren't you?" I asked.

Conners sneered, sighed, and then nodded. "You're right. He was right. You know, I hate it when other people are right."

We both chuckled and then turned back to the clowns. They performed for a long while before another set of gladiators came out onto the field. Conners silently moved away from me and joined Louis Pierre and Elissa, who were discussing something in French. I decided to skip some of the games and headed out of the arena to see how Wellis was doing.

I left the seating and edged my way into the walled village. The streets were clogged with vendors and crowds. They were exchanging *k'whee*, the Selenite currency. Each village had its own version of *k'whee*, which ranged from carefully painted black stones to decorated cloth to bits of shells. Mary had been working to create a single *k'whee* mint and a single currency for her empire: durable metal coins. A building had been created for the mint, but her plans had been put on hold while new lunar ores were being mined for the first time and sent to new foundries for smelting and purification.

K'whee worked very similarly to most Earth currency, but had several differences about it. Taxes were a rarity in the lunar caverns, but the majority of the money was held by the queens of each village. Instead of paying monetary taxes, each Selenite worked for her queen for as much time as they wished. Time was exchanged for *k'whee* (the rate of exchange was controlled by the queens), which the Selenites traded among themselves in their own, small businesses. Most of the money, however, ended up in the queen's coffers again as the Selenites paid for rent of the queen's land, housing, and goods. Male Selenites rarely saw money and merely lived off of the queen's wealth.

I struggled through the crowds and came to the cliffs that had been quarried for apartments. I presented myself to the guards, who recognized me as a friend of the empress. The hallways were large enough for a queen to struggle through, but looked very safe and defensible. After passing by several more guards, I eventually entered Mary's apartments, the heavy wooden door of which was guarded by K't'whoo.

Wellis was lying on cushions on Mary's large throne. Only Mary, Star, Tarsini, and T'wha were in the room with him as the rest of Mary's court had been dismissed back to the arena to watch the games. They all huddled around him, Tarsini on his knees, checking over each of Wellis's joints and bones.

Wellis smiled when he saw me enter the room. "How was that for you, Curtis?"

"It was certainly entertaining," I said, greeting him.

"Stop moving," Tarsini warned him. "You have not broken anything, but I could easily fix that dilemma."

Wellis lay quietly while Star moved over toward me. "He's got a few bruises, but otherwise he's quite all right. Not many people could be as tough as a Texan cowboy, I suppose."

"Will he be racing tomorrow?" I asked.

Tarsini nodded. "I do not see why not. As long as he gets some rest beforehand."

"So there's not much to see here," I said, seeing that Wellis was frustrated by all of the attention. "I suppose I will head back out to the games, then."

"I'll go with you," Mary said. She smiled and added, "An empress should not disappear for too long."

Mary and I left the apartments and T'wha followed closely behind. K't'whoo joined us at the door and waved a group of guards over to us to complete Mary's security. We passed easily out of the apartments and strode through the crowds without being slowed. The crowds parted around the empress and all of the Selenites covered their eyes in salute as she passed. It had taken me a long while to push through the crowds, but we arrived back at the arena in only a few minutes.

When we arrived at Mary's platform atop the seating, a new group had settled onto the field. Massive blocks of stone had been pulled in on large sledges and a single Selenite was on top of each. They were pounding at spikes, racing to see who could crack the stone block first. The crowd was in a great commotion, though the event seemed rather boring to the humans. Despite some surprising similarities, there were still many differences between the humans and the Selenites.

After several more gladiatorial matches, short plays, and other events, I decided to leave the games and retire for a rest. I struggled back into the city and found one of the numerous bunkhouses designed for the servants of the guests of Th'ch'click. One bunkhouse had been set aside for crewmen of the *Comet* and had been separated into numerous compartments. I found an empty bunk and leapt upon it. After calling in a favor from a Swedish rocket engineer to make sure that I was awake well before the sledge races tomorrow, I fell asleep.

Chapter Eleven,
The Races

In a few hours, I found myself being shaken awake by a Swede. "Vake up!" he shouted.

"I'm awake! I'm awake!" I replied. He smiled at me and then left, glad that he no longer owed me a favor for looking after his duties.

I stumbled off of the bunk and might have hurt myself if the lunar gravity were not so weak. The shock from hitting the ground at an awkward angle woke me fully. Now certain of my bearings, I straightened my clothes, washed up in a stall next to the bunkhouse, and hurried out to the arena.

The games had continued for the hours that I had slept. Right now the Selenites were setting up for a new event and the field was empty. The field had formerly been pristine and perfectly level, but the numerous events had kicked up the dirt and left small mounds next to holes. The seats were as full as ever; I wondered how many of the Selenites had not left their seats since first sitting in them long ago. I began to climb up the seating to be near the empress's platform, but was stopped by someone loudly calling my name.

I turned to see Wellis, who was hurrying toward me. He looked to be in prime condition, like nothing at all had happened with the *snap 't 'f* yesterday. "We're almost ready, Curtis! Where've you been?"

"I was asleep in the bunkhouse," I explained. "I made it back for the races, right?"

"Barely in time," Wellis said breathlessly. "The races are in tournaments, and our sledge is in the first race. Come on, boy, we need to get down there."

I followed him behind the seats and to a large corral that held dozens of mantises. Dozens of sledges were waiting for their riders, who were all milling around the scene, preparing for the race. Each team was wearing a different colored cloak from their shoulders that designated from which village or

Earthly country each racer came.

Wellis and I hurried to Foster and a pair of Selenites, who were standing next to a beautifully decorated sledge. It was a short wooden sledge and had been painted so that its front was blue and the rest of the sledge had red and white horizontal stripes. I smiled at how much it reminded me of election campaign wagons that I had seen in Dayton when I was a child.

"All right, Yanks," Foster, our fellow American, said when he saw us coming. "Let's do this one for Lady Liberty." He handed us each a cloak similar in cut to the ones that the Selenite riders were wearing. The cloaks had a field of blue and red and white stripes that made a rough resemblance of the American flag.

Wellis and I helped one another put the cloaks around our shoulders. They had been made on the design for Selenite cloaks and fit rather uneasily on human shoulders. The cloth from which the cloaks had been made was quite strong, but light and waved beautifully in the wind. Selenite textiles were certainly amazing things. When we had the cloaks on as comfortably as they would be, we stepped into the sledge and waited as the Selenites moved our mantises into place.

The Selenites were hissing and clicking in our direction, though they were paying close attention to the harnesses that they were sliding onto the mantises. Wellis clicked and hissed in return, and I was amazed at his understanding of the Selenite language. I was able to make out several words, but I had yet to train my mouth to make the same sounds as the insect-like mouths of the Selenites.

Finally they stepped away from our mantises and covered their eyes in a salute. Wellis and I saluted in return, and then Wellis snapped the reins and clicked, causing the mantises to move forward in a slow trot.

"We should have a pretty good edge over some of the villages," Wellis said to me. "The empress gave us these mantises out of her imperial stables, and I've been told that they're some of the fastest in all of the caverns."

I smiled and said, "That's certainly good."

"Right," Wellis said. He passed the reins in his left hand and used his right to pick up a strange looking pole from the floor of the sledge. "This is your duty for half of the rounds," he explained, handing the pole to me. "You do your best to trip up the sledges and whack the drivers, as well as keep other riders from doing the same. It's illegal to touch the mantises with the pole, though. I think your position is called the *click'k's*. Since I'm the driver, I'm the *whoo'wh*. The race is counterclockwise for two laps, and we switch places when the first lap is over."

"Okay," I said, nodding. The idea seemed simple enough, though I suddenly had some apprehensions about the race.

Despite my unexpected stage fright, we soon pulled onto the track that surrounded the field of the arena. There were six other sledges on the track and we were spaced so that we would all have an equal distance in the circular track. Our sledge was second from the middle, meaning that there were numerous sledges slightly in front of us and a sledge a little behind. The other racers were all Selenites, who were hissing and clicking at one another, trying to scare one another with threats and boasts.

I glanced at Wellis, who was calmly gripping the reins and making clicking sounds to the mantises. He suddenly looked up, noticing my glance. Then he smirked at me and turned back to clicking softly at the mantises.

There was a short trumpet melody and everyone in the seats around the arena covered their eyes in a salute. Mary, wearing the same white gown as before, though her hair was set in a new style with strange-looking flowers poking out of it, was carried down the seats from her platform by a small group of Selenites. A large horn was carried behind her by another Selenite.

When they reached the ground, they marched across the track just in front of the racers. We all saluted, covering our eyes. The procession continued past us until they reached the very middle of the field. The Selenites carrying Mary gently set her down and the horn-bearing Selenite brought the instrument to her.

"Be ready," Wellis whispered to me. "When she blows the horn, we all take off like firecrackers. Brace yourself." I nodded and set my feet as best I could in the short sledge, ready for anything.

Mary took the gigantic horn from the Selenite, probably an actual horn from some lunar animal, and blew into it with all of her might. The mantises all hissed wildly and broke into fast runs. Every sledge jerked into a rush behind the mantises, and the drivers whipped at them and made loud hisses to urge them on. I nearly lost my footing and was glad that Wellis had told me to brace myself.

"That sledge on our left is gaining!" Wellis shouted.

I turned to my left and watched the sledge approach quickly. The Selenite driver was mercilessly whipping at the mantises, forcing them to go faster and faster. The pole-wielding Selenite behind him hissed at me and clicked its mouth menacingly. I sneered at him and did my best to call out a Selenite taunt.

When the sledge came close enough to ours, the Selenite and I began whacking at one another with our poles. At first we did not get anywhere, each blocking the other's attack with the pole. I suddenly stopped focusing on him and swung at the driver, making contact with the shell on the front of her abdomen. The driver hissed, and the sledge slowed and lost several yards before the driver recovered.

The Selenite with the pole took this time to whack me in the arm. I gasped and rubbed the arm, hoping that a deep bruise would not form. Despite being from a world with one-sixth the gravity of Earth, the Selenites were often quite strong and some even rivaled humans in strength. I ignored the pain as best I could and gripped my pole, deflecting another shot

"We're catching up on the right!" Wellis shouted. I grunted when I saw another sledge moving toward us as our sledge caught up with it.

The Selenite to the left took another swing at me, and this time I blocked and twisted, pinning our poles together. The Selenite hissed in surprise and tried to undo the poles. I gritted my teeth and continued the twist, finally throwing the pole out of the Selenite's grip. The Selenite clicked with horror and struggled to find something with which to defend her sledge.

I shoved my pole under the front of the sledge and lifted with all of my might, trying to upset it. I could not throw the sledge even in this low gravity, but I did do enough to turn it over on its side. The Selenites inside jerked as the sledge tipped, and spilled out of it into the field. The mantises slowed their run to a walk, and the sledge disappeared behind us.

I heard Wellis shout again and turned to see the Selenite in the sledge to our right poke at him with her pole. I twisted my pole forward and deflected another sharp poke at Wellis. The Selenite hissed and clicked, though I could not hear it over the ruckus from the sledges and mantises.

We sparred back and forth for a minute, and each time that I tried to catch the pole in a twist, the Selenite dodged away from it. The Selenite was very good with the pole and gave Wellis and me each several good slaps while I could scarcely touch her with my pole. I finally tried to slam down on her with my pole, and when she blocked it, my pole snapped and suddenly became tremendously shorter.

Wellis, observing our battle out of the corner of his eye, grunted at my shortened pole. I grimaced at him and returned to the fight in time to deflect a severe whack.

I tried to stab at the Selenite and made several good hits before being deflected. The shorter pole was harder to ward off than a full-length one.

After deflecting a stab, the Selenite hissed at me and then came down with a strong hit.

My reflexes overtook me and I grabbed the Selenite's pole with my hands, dropping my pole to the floor of the sledge. The Selenite yanked back on her pole, but I pulled at the same time, causing it to cancel our tugs. The Selenite pulled again, and this time I pushed, which made the Selenite lose her balance and stumble onto the edge of the sledge. The sudden movement of weight caused the sledge to tip. I picked up my stub of a pole and shoved, throwing the sledge onto its side. Again the Selenites spilled out and the mantises, no longer driven by whipping reins, slowed to a halt.

"The starting line is approaching!" Wellis shouted. "Get ready to change!"

We suddenly crossed the line at which we started, signifying that we had already circled the track once. I dove forward and took the reins as Wellis dropped them and twisted back behind me. I sat on the driver's seat and whipped at the mantises just like I would have done at home in Ohio.

The course ahead had four overturned sledges, meaning that only two other sledges were on the track. One was several yards ahead of us while the other had begun to lag behind. I urged on the mantises, doing my best to catch up with the other sledge. For the first time, I heard the crowd around us, hissing and screaming wildly as we raced around the track.

We finally began to catch up with them, but their *click'k's* was very much ready for us. As we approached, he began to swing at me with his pole, doing his best to upset my driving. I took the reins into my left hand and used my right to block the merciless attacks. I winced at each blow, knowing that I would probably develop numerous bruises. After three hits, though, Wellis was able to catch the blows with his shortened pole.

The two sparred, and our mantises dashed amazingly until we were even with the other sledge. The *whoo'wh* hissed at me, and I did my best to roar back at her. Wellis and the other *click'k's* continued to exchange blows.

As our sledges hurried along on the track, the wrecked sledges began to race up at us. I shouted back to Wellis as the first one came upon us, and he secured his footing just as the sledges split and dashed around the debris. When we passed the broken sledge, our two sledges came back together and the two poles once again began to whack at one another.

Wellis made a victorious shout that caused me to turn my head. He had somehow gotten the Selenite's pole, and the Selenite was fumbling with his short one. I asked him later how he had done it, but he just laughed and said that he was not quite sure himself.

He took the long pole and smacked the Selenite with it, causing her to stumble and fall on top of the driver. I suddenly jerked the reins, and our mantises turned right, spooking the mantises of the other sledge. The confusion caused the sledge to overturn, and we left them in a clicking, hissing pile.

"They're way behind us, Curtis!" Wellis shouted, noting that the other sledge had no hope of catching us. "Go for the finish line!"

I smiled and urged on the mantises. We finished the last quarter of the track and easily crossed the finish line. The crowd hissed excitedly as we slowed our mantises to a halt. Wellis and I waved to them, and then turned to salute the empress by covering our eyes. Mary just smiled at us and shook her head.

A flock of Selenites suddenly came onto the track and picked up the debris from the race. Wellis and I were taken off of the sledge, which was led away for the mantises to be changed. While the Selenites took care of our sledge, we hurried to the center of the field where Mary and her Selenite aides were watching.

"We've got a few races off," Wellis told me. "In a few minutes, though, we'll have to race the rest of the winners."

We approached the empress, who nodded to us and grinned excitedly.

"That was quite a race," she said.

"No kidding there," Wellis said. "We don't quite do it that way in Texas, but I suppose we could always learn."

"Good luck in the final race," Mary said, taking the enormous horn from one of the Selenites. We thanked her and then turned as the new racers were lining up.

There were seven teams of racers, as before, but this time two of them were from Earth. Two Germans had a darkly-colored sledge, while the French had colors similar to the American sledge. We cheered them both on, though I believed the Germans would fight more fiercely with their long pole painted black.

The race was quick and almost brutal. The German team, made up of an engineer and a botanist, upset two of the sledges and won a fast victory. The French had performed excellently as well, but had been beaten by a team of Selenites. The Germans proudly marched to join Wellis and me and whispered between themselves.

There were many other races that followed, but no other Earthly teams won. The Selenites were very skilled at their sport and hoped to beat the humans in the final round. When all of the winners had been collected in the center, the track was cleared and our sledges were lined up for us. This round, Wellis and I were third from the outer end and the Germans had gotten the very inside lane.

We all saluted the empress a final time and climbed into the sledges. Our mantises had all been replaced with fresh ones and Wellis and I had been given a new pole to replace our broken one. The Germans waved to us, wishing us luck, and we returned their wishes with the same. Mary suddenly was given the horn, and she blew a long, low note to start the final race.

The sledges all started with a sudden burst of speed. The crowd around us cheered and threw out flower petals of differing colors. The petals fell like confetti around us and made me feel like I was in some kind of bizarre parade.

Wellis, who was to drive first again, caused our mantises to veer left, toward the middle of the circle to cut off the sledge just behind us. The mantises of that sledge were frighteningly close, and I could hear them puffing and hissing as they dashed. I could have easily tripped them up, but I remembered that touching the mantises would mean disqualification.

Instead, I leaned out the back of the sledge and poked at the *whoo'wh*. The *click'k's* blocked several of my pokes, but was busy with another sledge on her left. Realizing that I could not accomplish anything like that, I retreated back into the sledge and tried to think of a new plan.

"Hold on!" Wellis shouted, meaning that he had a plan of his own. I ducked low for balance and gripped the side of the sledge. Wellis moved to the left a little more and then suddenly slowed the mantises. The mantises of the two sledges behind us squealed and tried to stop, upsetting their drivers. Both of the sledges became tangled up with their mantises and flipped. The Selenites crawled out of the wreckage behind us and tried to free the mantises that had become trapped under the sledges.

Wellis and I both let out cries of victory. We had eliminated two other sledges at the same time. He whipped the reins, hurrying the mantises along. For the rest of the lap around the track, we did not encounter any of the other sledges, and he and I switched places without missing a beat.

I tried to encourage the mantises to move more quickly, but they were already moving as quickly as their legs could carry them. There were only two other sledges on the track now: the Germans and a team of Selenites who had started in the lane to the right of us. Currently, the Selenites were in the lead with us very close behind them, but the Germans were quickly gaining on both of us.

"Come on, Hans!" Wellis shouted at the German engineer, who was driving the sledge. The German smirked and edged his sledge closer to us.

The Selenite sledge to our right slowed slightly as the mantises grew tired. I shouted back to Wellis, who turned to watch them approach. He answered my shout with another, signaling that the Germans were going to get to us at the same time we got to the Selenite sledge. The race was going to be very close.

The three sledges pulled into a tight group, with our sledge in the middle. Wellis worked busily to fight the Selenite and the German at his sides. The sledges came so close to one another that even we drivers began exchanging attacks. The crowd was very excited and struggled to get into positions where they could see what was happening. The seats on the opposite side of the track emptied as the other seats became overly crowded.

After a minute of close combat, the Selenites pulled away and then suddenly cut left again, slamming into us. We, in turn, slammed against the Germans, who were thrown to the left. The German *click'k's* tumbled off of his feet and caused the sledge to overturn, leaving only two sledges in the race.

Wellis and the Selenite *click'k's* attacked one another viciously. Every third blow or so would strike one of the drivers and cause the sledges to become dangerously unstable. The Selenite *whoo'wh* and I both struggled to keep our mantises under control and our sledges upright. We repeatedly slammed into one another, trying to tip the opposing sledge, but neither of us could knock over the other.

Wellis and his opponent both suddenly lost their poles and began swinging at one another with their fists. Finally, the Selenite jumped out of her sledge and tackled Wellis, causing them both to spill out. I barely kept the sledge from tipping and had to shift my weight quickly in order to maintain balance.

Behind us, Wellis grabbed his pole, smacked the other fallen combatant, and then made a mad dash for the sledges. The crowd roared wildly in support of Wellis, who was already very popular for his dangerous ride on the *snap't'f* earlier in the games. Making enormous bounds with every step, Wellis soon caught up with the sledge and jumped. Instead of leaping into our sledge, however, he landed in the other.

Wellis let out a hysterical war cry, slapped the *whoo'wh* with the pole, and then leapt out of the sledge, doing his best to upset it. As he came into our sledge, I pulled the mantises right and succeeded in overturning the other sledge. The Selenite jumped out of it just before it tipped and landed outside of the track.

Wellis and I both laughed with exhilaration and soon crossed the finish line amid great roars from the crowds. Many of the Selenites and crewmembers alike charged out of their seats and surrounded us. They lifted us both out of our sledges and high into the air. The crowd carried us off of the track to the middle of the field, where the empress was waiting with our trophies.

The mass of Selenites and humans deposited us just in front of Mary, who grinned at us both with excitement. Her troop of Selenites surrounded us and took our red, white, and blue cloaks from our shoulders. Mary then presented us with two new cloaks, both shiny and yellow. We covered our eyes and then bowed before her, while the Selenites draped the cloaks over our shoulders.

We turned back to the crowd and waved broadly to them. They pressed in around us, all trying to give us their congratulations at the same time. The next hour was nothing but a blur of faces, ranging from human to tall Selenite worker to short Selenite male to massive Selenite queen. Wellis and I both agreed that it was one of the most spectacular events of our lives.

Chapter Twelve,
Abduction

With the grand race the games were completed, and the Selenites began to return to their own villages. I returned to the crew's bunkhouse, excited but tired after the great ordeal. My plans to rest, however, were interrupted when I met Wellis, who insisted that we go out and celebrate. So Wellis and I went throughout Th'ch'click, having a victory party in every bunkhouse and tavern in the village. There I learned a large vocabulary of Selenite words and phrases, though most of them were synonymous with "congratulations."

Our final stop on our celebration tour was Mary's apartments. The guards, though some of them had not even been to the games, were eager to congratulate us and escorted us into Mary's rooms. Wellis and I were still quite excited from the race, but the celebrations had begun to wear us down. We stumbled every so often as we walked and had become quite giddy.

The guards left us at the door, and we burst into the apartments, which had been quiet when we entered. Mary, T'wha, and several male Selenites were looking over sketches on wooden tiles, deciding on some sort of governmental business. They stared at us as we came in and then burst out with congratulations, much like all of the other celebrations.

After congratulating us, the male Selenites were dismissed. They collected their wooden tiles and left, nodding excitedly and trying to cover their eyes in salute while not dropping their tiles. We thanked them, but were happy when they had left. Male Selenites were easily excitable, but their sense of celebration was rather boring compared to that of the Selenite workers we had met in the bunkhouses and taverns.

"Are you two still floating this long after the race?" Mary asked, giggling at us.

"You bet," Wellis said. I nodded and grinned.

"Well, you look terrible," Mary said, pointing to a mirror. "What have you been doing?"

Wellis and I walked over to a mirror that hung on one of the walls. The frame was made of beautiful, ornately-carved wood, but the mirror itself was cloudy and clumsily constructed. (I believe that it had been made as a gift in one of the deeper villages of the lunar caverns that had access to lava and therefore fire.) Despite its fog and warping angles, Wellis and I could see that we were messes. Our hair was disheveled and pointed in every direction. Our clothes had numerous stains and Wellis's even had a tear in it where he had caught it on a rough stone corner. The cloaks, however, still shone as brightly as they had when Mary presented them to us before.

I moaned at my appearance and said, "I suppose we've been doing a little much on the celebrating."

"I don't think you can ever have too much celebrating," Wellis smiled. He tried to smooth his hair, but it fought against his fingers and stayed as a mess.

"How much more time is my father going to give you to celebrate?" Mary asked. "I am surprised he hasn't demanded you in the Station already."

"I'm in your charge as long as I'm in the caverns, Empress," Wellis chuckled. "Supposedly, I'm studying Selenite alchemy and organizing a plan for educating them."

I cleared my throat. "I'm not quite so lucky. I should probably get back up into the Station as soon as possible."

There must have been something pitiful in my voice as I said it, though. Mary smiled and said, "Well, Father has been planning to create a study of astronomy among the Selenites. Perhaps you and I are discussing that?"

I retuned her smile. "That would keep me busy down here, wouldn't it?"

"She's quite an empress, isn't she?" Wellis asked, winking at me. He turned back to the mirror and examined the rip of his black suit.

"I could have T'wha stitch that up for you," Mary offered. "Father hates it when his suits aren't treated with care."

"I'll try better next time I win a Selenite sledge race," Wellis told her.

"You could clean yourself up in the bath, if you wish," Mary said. Wellis smiled and nodded, so Mary turned to T'wha and said, "Would you run a bath for Mr. Wellis and stitch his tear?"

T'wha made several clicks.

"Um... run a bath," Mary tried to clarify. She raised her hands, motioning out the explanation. "Fill it up with water."

T'wha nodded and took Wellis by the arm. As she led him out of the room, deeper into the apartments, Wellis leaned heavily on her shoulder, showing his exhaustion from the race and extended celebrations.

"He'll have some fun in there," Mary giggled. "The bathtub is large enough for a queen Selenite. I hope he can keep awake enough to stay afloat."

She moved up to her massive throne and sat. "In a few minutes, we could turn on the wave-maker. It is quite a soothing thing for queens, and I suppose Wellis would enjoy it very much, especially as a surprise."

I laughed at the thought of Wellis swimming for his life in a gigantic bathtub. Since the throne was big enough for several people, I joined Mary on it and leaned back into its multitudinous cushions.

"T'wha certainly seems to be mastering the English language," I said, trying to begin a conversation.

"Very much so," Mary replied. "T'wha is a very good learner, as well as a great thinker. She has been around ruling bodies all of her life and knows far more about lunar diplomacy than I can even imagine knowing. When I first began understanding the Selenites, she did her best to teach me about governing, but I'm afraid she will always grasp more than I do."

"Wellis and I think that you've been doing a great job," I offered. "You stopped the gladiatorial tournaments, and that was just a little while ago. I couldn't even begin to list all of the reforms you've started!"

Mary smiled humbly. "I suppose I am doing fairly well."

"The Selenites seem to think so. Not everyone can become an empress overnight. And at the games, they were cheering for you as much as any of the entertainers."

"Well, they celebrate you quite a bit too," Mary said. "And for good reason; the race was certainly impressive. I—what is that?"

Mary suddenly jumped up from the throne and looked up at the ceiling. I looked too, but had to shade my eyes against the brightness of the glowing plants that grew there. Finally I saw what Mary was watching; a small crack was forming between the plants and dust fell in a thin stream. The crack suddenly widened into a small hole. More cracks appeared, creating a spider web of fissures on the ceiling. The whole room began to vibrate and a loud noise like thunder rang out.

Realizing that the ceiling was about to collapse, I grabbed Mary by the waist and pulled her close to the wall next to the large throne. We ducked under the throne's edge as best we could and gritted our teeth as the ceiling caved in on us. The thunder became a loud crash, and the air was filled with dust and stone. We were both blinded for a moment, but then shrieked as we regained our vision.

The room was eerily lit by the fallen glowing plants and the floating dust. Ropes fell through the hole in the ceiling, and five black-robed Selenites swung down upon them. Each Selenite was wielding a hooked spear, which looked especially threatening in the darkened, dust-filled room. They hissed loudly and searched the room for us.

When one of the Selenites spotted us behind the throne, it clicked to the others. The five Selenites surrounded us and pointed their spears threateningly. The black robes covered them completely, except a thin red sash that covered their eyes, allowing them to resist any identification. As they moved closer to us, a powerful odor like sulfur swept into my nostrils, making it difficult to breathe.

Mary and I both screamed in terror. Mary shouted as loudly as she could for her guards, but the debris from the ceiling was blocking the bulky doors. We could see the doors bang against the rubble, but it refused to open. We continued to shout in a panic as the Selenites moved over the broken stones toward us.

I glanced over at Mary, who was gaping and trembling in terror. Overcome with a sense of chivalry, I leapt up from her and tightened my fists. "D-don't come any closer! The Empress forbids it!"

Despite my caution, one of the Selenites grabbed me by the throat and lifted me in the air. I struggled to breathe, but between the Selenite's clawed hand and their powerful odor, I began to lose my concentration. Finally I swung out with my leg, and felt my foot make contact with one of the Selenite's thighs. The Selenite hissed in pain and dropped me to the ground. Because of the low gravity, however, I was already in a fighting stance before my legs touched the debris-strewn floor.

I picked up a spear lost from the Selenite whom I injured and then pointed it at her as she clutched her leg. Turning to the other Selenites, I shouted, "Don't make me do this to you, too!"

Two of the Selenites hissed at the warning and charged me. I threw a fist at one, who dodged around the blow. The other tackled my feet, dropping me to the floor. Then the dodging Selenite jumped into the fray to help pin me to the ground. They would have easily caught me, but I had grown up on a farm where the forms of entertainment for my older brothers scarcely strayed from wrestling with me. I grabbed at one Selenite's leg and pulled, throwing her away from me. The other Selenite bit at me, making a deep scratch in my leg with her pinchers.

I groaned and continued to struggle with the Selenites. The other three had moved around me and surrounded Mary. She screamed as they grabbed her and tried to fight back, but they drastically outnumbered her. I glanced around for her as I pushed both of the Selenites away. They had bound her hands, feet, and mouth and were now heading back up the ropes.

"Mary!" I shouted. She struggled against the cloths that bound her, but she could not free herself. I tried to jump up one of the ropes after them, but a Selenite claw caught my foot. As I was brought crashing down on the debris-ridden floor, I saw the two Selenites who had fought me beginning to climb out as well.

"No!" I shouted and grabbed one of the ropes.

As soon as the Selenites climbed into the hole in the ceiling, however, they cut the ropes. I leapt off of it as it became limp, just in time to land safely on the ground. A cloud of dust rained through the hole with a soft crashing sound. The abductors had escaped, and I could do nothing about it.

I suddenly heard a loud bang from one of the adjacent doors. It was the door that T'wha and Wellis had left through, and now they were trying to get back in, but debris blocked the door. I hurried to the door and cleared away rubble until it would open.

Wellis and T'wha jerked through the door and panted with exertion from pushing on it. When they saw the room, they both stood stunned for a moment. T'wha scanned the room for Mary and then immediately dashed to the dust-covered throne. She fell onto it and gripped her head in grief.

The main door began to bang again, much louder than before. Wellis and I ran over to it, trying to avoid the large rocks on the floor, and began to clear the rubble away. Finally, with a loud crunch, the door swung in, revealing a heavy battering ram. Mary's Selenite guards charged into the room, waving their spears. The lead guard stumbled on the stone debris and fell. The rest of the guards froze in place, wondering what exactly had happened. When they saw that Mary was gone, though, they began to panic and to search wildly in the debris.

K't'whoo came into the room with a second group of guards. She observed the wreckage and then turned to Wellis, clicking something. Wellis clicked back, shrugged, and then turned to me. "What happened?"

"We were sitting here on the throne when the ceiling suddenly began to cave in on us," I explained. "Mary and I ducked away from the rocks, and then some Selenites in black robes came in after them. I tried to fight them off, but they kidnapped her!" My fists clenched as I finished my description of the abduction.

Wellis nodded and clicked at K't'whoo. The guard hissed and pointed some of the guards toward the ceiling. They leapt into the air and fluttered up the dark gaping hole where before peaceful glowing plants had grown. Within a second, though, they returned sorrowfully. They clicked at K't'whoo, who hissed angrily and then stomped her foot.

"What did they say?" I whispered to Wellis.

"The tunnel must have been destroyed after the kidnappers escaped," he translated. "We can't follow them and it'll take a while to clear out the mess."

"So what do we do?" I asked.

"I don't know," Wellis said, shaking his head. "Did you see anything on them that you could give as a recognizable symbol? Like body paint or a colored sash or anything?"

"Only a thin red cloth around their eyes." I shook my head, but then looked up and said, "They did have a weird stench, kind of like sulfur. Could the Selenites know anything about that?"

"I don't know the Selenite word for sulfur," Wellis explained with a sigh. T'wha tapped him on the shoulder and clicked, "Ch'k'sh'th'p'whoo."

"You've pretty well got English under your belt, don't you?" Wellis smiled at her. T'wha shrugged and clicked a short sentence.

"K't'whoo," Wellis called. The Selenite guard turned to him, and he clicked out a sentence including the word T'wha had given him. K't'whoo's large eyes went wider, and she clicked to the guards, who hastened out of the room.

When they were gone, K't'whoo and Wellis clicked back and forth in a hasty conversation. T'wha watched them quietly, trying to discern exactly what was happening. I merely stood there, feeling like quite an idiot for not understanding anything. Finally, K't'whoo nodded to Wellis and left the room hastily.

Wellis turned back to us. "She said that she might know what is going on. We need to get Captain Star and Rodreguez and Conners. When you find them, meet back here as quickly as possible. We'll figure out what to do then."

In less than an hour, two Selenites and five humans had come together in Mary's apartments. We were in a small bedroom off of the main room and gathered around a table. The door to the bedroom was open, showing the wrecked throne room as a gloomy reminder of what was happening.

Star was at the head of the table, leaning with his elbows upon it and his hands gripped in a fist in front of his mouth. Wellis had found Star and given him the news, and Star had not taken it very well at all. When he had entered the room, he was mumbling to himself that he never should have allowed Mary to come down from the *Comet*. He was serving as the lead tactician for the meeting, though I wondered how well he would do with his emotions in shambles.

Rodreguez and Wellis sat to his left, both looking over a notebook that Rodreguez had brought. It listed all of the weapons that were on the expedition and their locations, whether on the *Comet*, in the Lunar Station, or given to the Selenites as gifts of technology. They were discussing what would be available for any battles that might result from this event.

Conners and I were on the right side of Star, and we were both sitting very quietly. I had found Conners sitting in a Selenite tavern in Th'ch'click, telling a long story to several interested patrons. I whispered to him what had happened, and he immediately spilled his drink all over himself in surprise. We hurried to the meeting as quickly as possible, leaving the Selenite tavern patrons confused.

On the way back to the apartments, I mumbled my feelings on that first we had been kidnapped and now Mary.

"Selenite kidnapping is an interesting subject," Conners had told me. "According to K'f'k, Selenites prefer kidnapping and prisoners of war over just killing their enemies. Captured male Selenites can be interrogated for information, captured female Selenites can be turned into slaves, and captured queen Selenites can supply eggs for the village. Killing is reserved for straight battles, gladiators, and as execution for criminals, and these are only for female Selenites. Rarely, though, a group of rebels may kill a queen or male, but that hasn't happened for a long time."

T'wha and K't'whoo were on the opposite side of the table as Star. They were clicking to one another, trying to decide what needed to be done. I could not understand all of what they were saying, but I was quickly becoming accustomed to the Selenite language.

Finally, Star sighed and lightly slammed his fist on the table. We all looked up at him. He began the meeting with, "What are we going to do?"

K't'whoo clicked hastily. Conners translated, "We need to get the Empress of Fire back... very quickly. There may be riots of panic if she is gone... too long."

"So how do we go about that?" Star asked.

"I've been drilling a crack team of Selenites with rifles," Rodreguez said. "We could fight our way into any village in the entire Moon."

"That may not get her back quickly enough, though," Wellis said.

T'wha nodded and clicked. Wellis, who was not quite as skilled as Conners with the Selenite language, struggled to translate what she said. "The enemy villages may lose interest in her when they discover that she is not like the other queens of the Moon. If they cannot gain eggs from her, they will probably kill her."

Star turned pale.

"We could send a covert team after her," Conners said. "Curtis knows what they smell like, so his nose could lead the way."

I nodded. "I'll help with anything I can."

T'wha clicked at K't'whoo, who had become lost in all of the English. K't'whoo then clicked at us. Conners again translated. "She says that she can have a sledge ready to go within an hour. Curtis's description of the sulfur stench narrows it down a lot, so she knows where to begin the search."

"Where?" Star asked.

"Villages in the deeper levels of the caverns have access to lava vents, which supply fire to them, and them alone. The Selenites who live in these villages, though, develop a body stench that is similar to sulfur, though each village is believed to have a slightly different odor. Rumors say that they've felt threatened since the Empress of Fire appeared last month, so maybe they could have done it. It's a possible motive, anyway."

"I can arm them with enough weapons to take on any Selenite army," Rodreguez offered. "Most of our weapons are held in the capital city, though. It may take a while to get them to the sledge."

"Excellent, then," Star said. "What about your soldiers?"

"We'll be ready for anything that we're ordered to do, sir," Rodreguez told him.

"Very well," Star began to sum up the meeting. "Curtis, Conners, K't'whoo, and I will go on the covert operation in the sledge. Rodreguez and Wellis will wait here with the army and be ready to respond at any time. T'wha will act as Mary's heir, ruling the throne until she returns."

"Excuse me, sir," Wellis said. "I know the Selenite ways quite well. I think that I'd do better on the mission than with the army. And you would probably be more useful here, helping T'wha with the court and commanding the Station."

"She's my daughter, Wellis," Star said coldly.

"And that's why I dare enough to question your orders," Wellis said. "I don't know what would happen if you became tangled up with the Selenites."

Star squinted at him, paused, and then hissed through his teeth. "You're probably right, though I hate to say it. I'll stay here, while you accompany the sledge."

We all nodded in agreement and Star dismissed us. The next hour was a buzz of activity as K't'whoo assembled a perfect sledge. The front held the driver's bench, as usual, but the rear was large and covered with a large cloth sheet on several loops. It looked amazingly like a prairie schooner that I had seen in a newspaper picture when I was in Ohio. The floor of the sledge was quite low and perfect for hiding weaponry. Rodreguez sent two of his fastest men back to Mary's capital. They returned just before the sledge was finished with rifles, pistols, and ample ammunition. They even had a small crate of dynamite, in case we ran into something immovable. We worked as quickly as we could, lining the weapons in the floor of the sledge and hiding them under lunar grasses. We left places in the grass mound where Conners, Wellis, and I could hide in case the sledge was checked by enemy guards. Our story was that K't'whoo was just a farming Selenite who had been sent by her queen to carry hay as a gift to a village named Ch'k'ch't in the deep caverns. It seemed to be a simple but convincing story, and I hoped that it would get us to the place where Mary was held without a confrontation.

Before I knew it, we were off. K't'whoo drove the sledge, which was pulled by the two muscular mantises that had pulled the sledge that Wellis and I won the races in earlier. I wondered if it were just a coincidence, though I doubted that it was. Conners, Wellis, and I were packed into the back of the sledge under the cloth, and we sat waist-deep in the hay as we rode along. We each had a firearm ready at our hands in case of an emergency.

The first hour of the trip went quietly. Finally we grew terribly bored with the ride and risked whispering to one another. At first Wellis and I competed against one another trying to guess a number that Conners had thought up. That game grew old, however, and we finally came into practicing our Selenite language skills.

There were many, many dialects and possibly even totally separate languages, Conners explained to me, when I referred to lunar speech as "the Selenite language." Right now the only dialect that we humans had begun to learn was known as S'k'ch. This dialect was spoken in nearly all of the villages of Mary's empire and she had begun a plan to make it the universal language of it. Conners said that he had met with several male Selenites from a nearby village that spoke S'f'ch, which was very similar and shared many words.

We had gone for numerous hours before K't'whoo stopped the sledge. During this time I had nearly caught up with Wellis my the ability to communicate with Selenites. We were interrupted by the sudden halt and did not make a sound until K't'whoo stuck her head under the cover of the sledge and told us that it was safe. K't'whoo had decided to give the mantises a quick break and had undone them from their harnesses. They were grazing peacefully on some short shrubs, not knowing the importance of the trip.

Wellis opened the cover and jumped out of the sledge first. Conners and I quickly followed him, eager for a chance to stretch our legs. The spot K't'whoo had chosen for the break was a very peaceful, very secluded alcove a little way off of the main trail. It had a small pond of water that was fed by a trickling waterfall and had a small hole in the bottom where the water drained. The glowing plants on the ceiling were a slightly different variety than the ones that we had seen before, and had a bit of a green tint to them. The walls were certainly different than the caverns we had been in before; they were thick with purple quartz and twinkled under the light of the glowing plants. We washed up in the pond and found some red fruits to eat so that we did not have to go into our rations for food.

'How far have we come?' Conners clicked to K't'whoo.

'We are now quite far from the empire,' she replied, swallowing a large mouthful of the fruit. 'It is still a long journey until we reach the village of S'p'th.'

I smiled, pleased that I could make out nearly all of the Selenite words. Conners was an excellent teacher of languages, and in a few short hours I had nearly mastered it. I could not help but think that this was only a single dialect, and there were hundreds, if not thousands of more lunar dialects still to learn.

'What exactly is our plan for when we get there?' I asked, trying to discern for what I should be prepared in the future.

'K't'whoo can investigate the locals and find out if there has been any interesting business concerning the Empress of Fire,' Wellis said. K't'whoo nodded.

'Just don't make it look like we're too interested, though,' Conners warned.

K't'whoo finished her fruit and then said that we had better get on our way. We three humans climbed into the back of the wagon, secured ourselves, and Wellis retied the cover tightly shut. As soon as K't'whoo redid the harnesses on the mantises, the sledge began with a hard jerk.

"I think she needs to work on her driving," Conners said, reverting back to English because of the painful lurch.

"She's probably a little concerned for the Empress," I said. "Mary is her charge for life, remember."

"I suppose so," Conners sighed. "Still, next time maybe she'd want to give us a little more warning." He rubbed his backside where it had hit one of the guns below the hay.

We continued on for several more hours. Wellis and I both decided to rest and left Conners on guard. The sleep was very comforting, despite the hay being rather itchy. It was not as deep as I was used to in weaker gravity, however, and I dreamed several odd dreams. I could not remember many of them after I woke up, but I distinctly remember a short dream where I was surrounded by a circle of dancing Selenites with festival masks. If I tried to move, the dancers would pin me in closer and closer until the dream finally slipped away and was replaced by another.

I woke up with a quiet gasp when I felt the sledge stop moving. Wellis woke up too and looked over at me, then Conners. I whispered to him, "What is it?"

Conners shrugged. There was a tap on the front of the cover, the signal meaning "be quiet." We waited for a second tap, meaning "hide," but it fortunately did not come. We could hear Selenite voices outside, clicking back and forth. K't'whoo was speaking to someone, but we were not sure who. After short pause in conversation, the sledge moved forward again, but only a few feet.

When we stopped again, the three of us looked at one another nervously. Suddenly, the sledge moved again, but this time we felt it go down. We gripped the sides of the sledge as it jerked a little and then swung. Finally the sledge returned to a slow descent, which perplexed us all.

Conners began to move toward the opening of the cover, trying to peek outside. Wellis and I waved at him to stop, but he opened the cover just enough to see through a small hole. When he finished looking, he turned back to us. His eyes were wide and he mouthed the word, "Wow." He pressed his finger against his lips and then motioned for us to look.

Wellis tilted his head, offering to let me go first. I nodded and crawled over to the opening. As I pressed my eye against it, I became astounded. I could see out over a chasm, but I could not see how deep it was. We were on a small wooden platform that was being lowered by strong ropes made from strange yellow vines. The far wall of the chasm was at least one hundred feet away and lit with several green-tinted glowing plants. The wall itself was made of a dark purple stone which looked completely unearthly. When I had seen enough, I ducked back inside the sledge and gave Wellis a turn.

We continued to descend for a long time. I felt my ears pop twice as the air pressure changed and we went deeper and deeper into the chasm. We did not dare speak or even give K't'whoo the signal to ask if we were all clear. Finally, when we touched the bottom, we began to move again. We were all glad to have the chasm behind us and to be moving more horizontally than vertically.

In another hour, K't'whoo stopped the sledge. We waited until she poked her head under the cover. Instead of telling us that we could get out, she told us that we could move around, but it was not safe to leave the sledge. Conners moaned quietly and crossed his legs.

'Where are we?' Wellis asked.

'We've reached the Undercaverns,' K't'whoo said. 'We are in a rather empty grove, but I do not think that it is quite safe to be out of the sledge.'

She left briefly and then returned with fresh fruits and a gourd full of water. We thanked her and nibbled at the fruit. We waited until we heard the mantises hiss as they were reattached to the sledge. The sledge moved again, and we leaned back in the hay to wait.

Chapter Thirteen,
The Undercaverns

I had fallen asleep again, and was awoken by a Selenite head sticking through the cover. I sat up quickly and almost kicked at it before I recognized it as K't'whoo. Conners was already awake, and I shook Wellis until he was awake as well.

'I found these for you,' K't'whoo said, handing three small piles of blue robes to us. 'They will cover your body. If we are fortunate, no one will recognize you as not being Selenite.'

We struggled into the loose, royal blue robes that consisted of a long garment that hung from the shoulders to barely drag on the ground, a short vest that rested on top of the main garment, and a fancy head covering that looked like a turban with a cloth mask hanging off of it. When we had gotten them mostly around our bodies, K't'whoo motioned for us to step out of the sledge.

The sledge was standing in a dark alley of some sort of city. As I climbed out of the sledge, the air struck me with the strong odor of sulfur, very similar to the stench that I had smelled on the Selenite attackers. The whole area was very shadowy, and the only glowing plants that I saw were dark red in color instead of the bright yellow ones that we were used to in the upper caverns.

K't'whoo was wearing blue robes similar to ours, though hers seemed to fit better since she had the figure for such a garment. She helped us straighten and smooth our robes and correctly place the hat upon our heads. The hats had thin black cloths that covered the eyes while the turbans enclosed the antennae, meaning that every inch of flesh was completely covered. I looked at Wellis and Conners, and I supposed that if I were expecting a Selenite, I would certainly think that they were one. I hoped that I made a convincing Selenite as well, but there was no mirror with which to look at myself.

'These are the robes of the servants of the male Selenites,' K't'whoo clicked. 'We should not be bothered when we wear them. Be sure to travel in single file, and try to look silent and dejected.'

'So how'd you come about getting these?' Conners asked, trying to look at himself in the odd blue robes.

'I will leave it as the fact that the Empress will have some missing *k'whee* from her treasury,' K't'whoo said, making a clicking chuckle.

'Where are we?' I asked, almost missing the Selenite joke.

'This is Ch'k'ch't,' K't'whoo said, waving her clawed hand dramatically. 'Watch your step; I have heard that the streets can be rather rough here in the Undercaverns.'

We nodded and said that we were ready for anything. Wellis pulled weapons from under the hay and we split them among us. K't'whoo looked at the pistol that he handed her rather quizzically, but decided that she could use it. We hid the weapons under our robes, where they would be out of sight but still in easy reach.

As we left the sledge behind, K't'whoo gave us one last piece of advice: 'Do try not to speak; you have human accents.' Conners seemed rather insulted, but K't'whoo slung a satchel over her shoulder and refused to pay attention to him. She took a deep breath and stepped out of the alley into the street. We followed her carefully, Wellis directly behind her, myself behind him, and Conners in the rear.

Ch'k'ch't seemed like it had come out of the more horrifying parts of Dante's *Inferno*. There were numerous buildings surrounded by small alleys and wide, dirty roads. Selenites, stockier and fiercer than those from above, walked the streets wearing short skirts from their waists and often tall hats. Apparently, they had discovered more of a use for clothes than the Selenites from the higher parts of the caverns. Conners mentioned to me later that these lower Selenites do not have such wondrous textiles and wearing clothes is an attempt to show that they are well off or important.

We walked briskly between the Selenites and ducked away from anyone who looked at us. Several merchants offering coarsely-made metal baskets and various other metallic objects tried to speak to us, but K't'whoo ignored them with enough disdain to quiet them. There was a brawl outside one of the buildings involving five Selenites, which we did our best to walk around. Just after we passed the fight, soldiers wearing rough metal helmets and breastplates broke up the brawl and sent the Selenites in different directions.

K't'whoo led us through several more streets before we came to a large, walled citadel. We marched passed the guards, who snorted at us. The servants of male Selenites were apparently a scorned part of society in the Undercaverns. As we passed them, one of the guards spit on Conners's back. Conners struggled not to turn and to threaten them and followed without making much of a sound. Behind us, however, the guards were chuckling giddily.

We moved through the citadel quietly until we came upon another group of blue-robed servants. They were marching into a corridor that led deep into the citadel. K't'whoo tried to move around them, but a male Selenite came upon her and hissed until our line merged into the other line. We continued to march with them, unable to talk to one another and devise a method of escape.

Finally we entered a large library, filled with metal tiles. Each tile was painted with images just like the wooden tiles of the caverns above. Evidently trees were not very plentiful in these caverns, but they had the heat and metal to make up for the lack of wood. The lead Selenite stopped, causing us all to stop. Conners was paying more attention to the library than to the line, however, and bumped into me. He quickly realized his mistake and straightened up in line.

When everyone had come to a halt, the Selenite in the lead began clicking out orders. There were certain tiles to be gathered for recopying and others that needed to be taken out to be read by the males. K't'whoo hissed in frustration as she was given an order. The orders followed down the line through each of us. Wellis, Conners, and I moved as a mass toward the innumerable tiles.

"Can you read Selenite?" Wellis whispered to Conners.

"I don't have to," Conners replied. "They don't have a written alphabet, just pictographs and murals. The problem, though, is that I don't have a clue how the tiles are organized. We could be in here for a few days before we found the right ones."

I turned to K't'whoo, who was following behind us. "What do we do?"

K't'whoo paused, trying to think. Finally, she clicked quietly to us. 'I have a plan. When I give a signal, make a run for it.'

'Make a run for it?' Conners asked. 'Is that even a real plan?'

K't'whoo did not reply. Instead, she guided us near the door and, when we neared it enough so that we would have to turn to move toward the tiles, began a mad dash. We followed her, running as best we could in the odd robes and light gravity. The four of us quickly ran through the door, escaping into the corridor. Behind us, the lead Selenite servant hissed in confusion and outrage, but did not order anyone to chase after us.

Once we were a safe distance from the library, we stopped running and slid back into single file. K't'whoo led us down more corridors, deeper into the citadel. We seemed to be going in almost random directions: up stairs, left corners, right corners, and then down again. Most of the corridors were empty, and whenever we did come close to other Selenites, mainly armor-clad guards, they ignored us.

'Do you know where we're going?' Conners finally clicked out.

'Not exactly,' K't'whoo admitted. 'We need to stay in this wing of the citadel though. The mercenaries will be housed here somewhere.'

We three humans sighed, discouraged that our guide did not know her own directions.

The random searching must have continued for nearly another hour. If we were in stronger gravity, our legs would have been quite tired by this time, but fortunately we were in the deep caverns of the Moon. We had searched through dozens of levels and even sneaked through several barracks. There had been nothing similar to the abductors until we crossed a large room with a fountain and several groups of Selenites.

I gasped as I recognized two of the Selenites' robes and froze, causing Conners to bump into me again. "It's them!" I whispered excitedly, pointing at the black-robed Selenites.

"Are you sure?" Wellis asked.

"Yes," I whispered. I could not help but stare at them, wondering what they had done with Mary.

The two Selenites were sitting on the edge of the fountain, drinking from rough metal goblets. They did not seem to notice us at all, and were very interested in their drinks. We moved near a wall and stood in silence, trying to avoid attention. Finally, the two Selenites threw their goblets into the fountain and stood up. They clicked at one another and then left the room into a hallway.

'We'll follow them,' K't'whoo hissed quietly. She stepped away from the wall and led us toward the corridor that they had entered. We followed her as quickly as we could, trying all the time to keep a straight line. Fortunately, none of the other Selenites in the room seemed interested in a quartet of servants at all.

When we reached the corridor, we stopped using our short, dejected steps and dashed quickly after the Selenites. We hurried after them and finally caught up with them just as the corridor began widening to become a large domed room. They had gone out onto a bridge that spanned over something that emitted a dull red light.

'Halt!' K't'whoo hissed loudly.

The two Selenites paused, surprised that a servant would make such a shout. They turned back and looked rather quizzically at us.

We charged into the domed room. My nose burned at the powerful odor of sulfur that filled it. I looked over the edge of a bridge and saw a fiery red lake of molten rock. There were strange glowing plants floating in it, casting a red glow the color of blood that filled the room. We approached them and spread out so that we could all face them.

'What do you want?' one of the Selenites asked, hissing disrespectfully at us.

K't'whoo, sick of being insulted as a servant, jerked off her mask. The rest of us followed suit, and the Selenites hissed in shock as they saw that we were human. When they saw me, they hissed more loudly and pointed in disbelief.

'You! How did you come here?'

'Never mind that,' I clicked. 'Where is the Empress?'

The Selenites hissed in rage. They pulled their robes back over their hands and revealed menacing claws.

'Don't even think about it,' Wellis clicked. He pulled twin pistols from under his robes and pointed them at the two Selenites. They hissed, looked at one another, and then ran down the opposite end of the bridge.

"Get them!" Wellis shouted.

We dashed after them, moving as quickly as we could in the uncomfortable robes. They moved more quickly than we could and disappeared into the corridor on the other side of the bridge. We followed through the corridor, but lost sight of them. Finally, we heard a door slam in front of us and stopped to investigate.

'It is locked,' K't'whoo said, beating her fists against it.

"Not for long," Conners said, pulling a small stick of dynamite from under his robe. He took the match that was attached to it and lit it with on the rough stone wall. When the fuse was blazing, he stuck the stick into the edge of the door next to the wall. Then he, Wellis, and I ducked down the hallway. K't'whoo looked at the stick curiously for a moment and then followed us.

In a quick second, the dynamite exploded. There was a loud rumble and then a cloud of dust spewed out over us. Conners laughed with triumph and led us back to the now-broken door.

The door led to a small room where the Selenites had hidden themselves. One of the Selenites, who had probably been bracing the door, was blown against the wall and now lay unconscious and bled from several small cracks in her carapace. The other Selenite was tucked in a corner, shivering in shock from the explosion.

'Don't hurt me!' she pleaded.

'We do not want to hurt you,' Conners said, trying to calm her.

'But if you do not tell us what we want to know,' K't'whoo added, 'we will.'

'I'll tell you anything!' the Selenite said, trying to deflect our stares by holding her hands in front of her.

'Where is the Empress?' I asked, rather loudly. I was more than a little surprised that I could be so forceful.

'She is not here!' the Selenite said, quivering so much that it made it difficult to understand her. 'We were just hired to capture her. They paid us in dozens of bolts of cloth! We could not refuse!'

'Bolts of cloth?' Conners furrowed his brow. His theory that the villages of the lower caverns were behind the abduction had suddenly been undermined. Such a sum would have been unimaginable for them.

'Who hired you?' K't'whoo asked, skipping past any theories.

'They refused to say! We met them in Th'ch'click and they paid us when we had captured her. They sent a male and two servants to trade us the *s't'snap* cloth for her.'

'So who did it?' Wellis asked. We all sighed and tried to think.

Suddenly, Conners's eyes lit up with realization. "It makes sense."

"What makes sense?" Wellis asked.

"I will explain when we're back in the Empire," Conners said. "And if I'm right, we need to hurry!"

K't'whoo seemed to follow him. 'Let us move!'

We left the frightened Selenite and hurried down the corridor, which was riddled with pieces of wood and stone. When we left the corridor, we came upon the bridge, which was thick with guards who had been sent to investigate the loud explosion. They gasped at us and raised their spears fiercely.

"The masks!" I gasped, realizing that we had not bothered to put our masks back on our heads. The Selenites, few of which had seen humans before, were now probably very uneasy about us.

"No time now!" Wellis shouted. He took out his pistols once again and fired a warning shot into the air. The loud bang of the gun caused the guards to hiss, and several of the ones at the far end of the mass began to run away.

The more resolute Selenites started a charge toward us, their spears far out in front of them. Conners, K't'whoo, and I pulled out our pistols as well and joined Wellis in emptying their carousels. The first line of guards fell and many of the second collapsed under the further barrage. K't'whoo was struggling with the human weapons, and finally she dashed low and picked up a spear from one of the fallen guards.

When all of the ammunition was emptied out of the pistols, Wellis, Conners, and I fell back to reload. K't'whoo leapt in front of us and took a strong defending stance. Whenever a guard approached close enough to reach with the spear, she would stab at them. Being raised as a defender for a queen, her skills were quite exceptional, and none of the guards could get around her. She would stab them in unarmored areas, hit them with the blunt end of the spear, or launch them over the side of the bridge into the fiery lava below. She would often fight numerous guards at a time, kicking and clawing them in addition to using her spear.

Despite being distracted by K't'whoo's skills, I managed to reload both of my pistols. Conners and Wellis too reloaded and nodded to me than we were ready. By the time that we had prepared another barrage, however, K't'whoo had eliminated most of the guards and sent the rest of them fleeing.

"Impressive," Conners said and whistled.

'Thank you,' K't'whoo said, pulling her pinchers back in a Selenite grin. Her robes were ripped in many places, and she had several small gashes, but for the most part she was in remarkably good condition for the battle that she had fought.

We raced down the bridge and followed the corridor back into the large room with the fountain. The Selenites inside had seen the fleeing guards pass them and were watching to see from what they were running. When they saw us, many of them panicked and dashed into other corridors. Some simply sat in terror, amazed at the human heads that they saw poking out of blue servant robes. Several of them, trying to be heroic while others fled, charged at us, but they were all put down by either a human pistol or a Selenite spear.

After fighting our way through the main room, we dashed down hallways, trying to remember where the entrance to the citadel had been. All of the way we could hear horns sounding as the emergency call went throughout the citadel. At several corners, we met with masses of Selenite guards, though most fled at the sight of us. We finally came to the library, where the servants were shocked at us.

'This way!' K't'whoo said, finally having her bearings. We followed her until we came to the entrance of the citadel, and then she stopped, causing us all to stumble over her.

'Wait,' she clicked. She motioned for Conners to take off his robe, which he did gladly. She took the large blue cloth and threw it out of the door. A spear immediately fell from above and pinned it to the ground before it had a chance to fall. Two more spears rained down on it before they realized that it was an empty robe.

'Spear throwers on top of the citadel. They'd kill all of us before we could make it into the streets.'

"So what do we do, fearless leader?" Conners asked. With his blue robe gone, I could see the amazing amount of ammunition and explosives that he had tied around his body. There was even a second set of pistols hanging from a loosely holstered belt around his waist.

K't'whoo scanned the room, trying to think of a plan for escape. I followed her gaze, but the entrance hall only had thin metallic tapestries, a table with sickly red glowing plants on it, and several ornamental spears hanging on the opposite wall. Just as I sighed and began to give up hope, she clicked happily and ran over to the table. After knocking the plants off of it, she tried to lift it.

Wellis and Conners hurried over to her, realizing her idea. They helped her lift it and finally placed it on their shoulders. I gaped at them for a moment, and then understood that they meant to use it as a shield. The table was made out of metal and was quite thick on top, most likely thick enough to block a spear. I dashed over to them and squeezed under it behind Conners.

"Think this will work?" Wellis asked.

'It should,' K't'whoo answered. 'Go over to the door. On the fourth count, start running. Don't stop until we are safely inside the village.'

We moved to the door, skittering like an eight-legged beetle. It was hard to move wedged under the table, still in the odd garments and low gravity. I hoped that we could run more easily than walk under it.

At the door, we waited as K't'whoo counted out a first click. I glanced around Conners and the others and swallowed nervously as I saw the long distance between the door and first alley. Seeing the blue garment pinned to the ground by a spear did not help the situation for me any either. K't'whoo counted a second and third click, and we all set our legs, ready to make a mad dash.

When she made the fourth click, we shot out of the door and into the open courtyard. There was a loud hissing from above, and then a thud on top of the table. A spear hit it, but did not pierce through the thick tabletop. The force of the spear pushed us down a little, but we were able to keep the table in position over our heads. More spears came at us, hitting the table and striking all around us. Wellis howled excitedly, exhilarated by the dangerous sprint.

As we came halfway to the beginning of the village, one of the spears successfully punctured the table. It stuck through the bottom, just between Conners's head and mine. We both gasped, though mine was much louder since I could see the implement of death hanging just a couple of inches in front of my face. This spurred us to run faster, bouncing up and down in the low lunar gravity.

We finally reached the village and dove behind a building for cover. We dropped the table, checked our weapons, and then continued on sprinting through the crowded streets. Behind us, we could hear horns blowing, alerting the village soldiers of the emergency. The crowds all pushed back and gazed at us, amazed at the humans who were racing down the streets.

As we passed the tavern where there had been a brawl, many of the patrons came out to see what was the matter. When they saw us, half of them ran back inside, dumping out their drinks as they went. The others made a vicious shout and vowed to come after us. Wellis halted long enough to fire two shots, one from each gun, into the leading Selenite. All of the Selenites dropped out from the pursuit, shocked at the thunderous ringing of the guns. The crowds around began to panic and ran hissing into the alleys.

We quickly came to our sledge, which had been waiting for us in the first dark alley that we saw in Ch'k'ch't. The mantises were anxious and clawed at the ground, ready to run. Wellis, Conners, and I dove into the back of the sledge while K't'whoo undid the ropes that held the mantises. She then quickly leapt into the driver's bench and whipped the mantises, causing them to dash even more excitedly than they had in the races before.

We flew through the streets of the city. The sledge would bounce off of the ground whenever it hit a bump, causing it to toss us about in the back. Wellis, Conners, and I dug through the hay beneath us, trying to get to the heavier weaponry that Rodreguez had packed for us. Wellis was the first to come upon one of the repeating rifles and smiled as he held it in his hands. Conners and I found similar weapons and quickly checked to make sure that they were well-loaded.

K't'whoo clicked excitedly from the front. Conners untied the cover and stuck his head out the front. When he did, he cursed in Mongolian and sat back into the hay. As he did, I peeked out the front, trying to see what was the matter.

The massive gates that led from the village to the trails outside were shut. Two rows of Selenite guards stood in front of it, making sure that no one would be able to escape. I groaned and tightened my grip on my rifle.

Wellis crawled past us and joined K't'whoo in the front of the sledge. "Conners!" he called back, creating a plan. "Get a couple of sticks of dynamite ready!"

Conners immediately dug into the hay, pulling out two sticks of explosives. He handed them to Wellis, who began to light the fuses. He clicked at K't'whoo, telling her to get ready to turn away.

We approached the wall of guards as quickly as ever. Conners and I each took several shots with our rifles, taking down two of the guards. Their heavy metal breastplates made shooting them difficult, however, and worked to deflect some of the bullets.

When Wellis was ready, K't'whoo suddenly pulled back on the reins of the mantises, causing them to slow and to turn to the left. Conners and I fell forward due to the sudden change, but caught ourselves on the sides of the sledge. Wellis threw the sticks of dynamite, planting them close to the gates and deep inside the lines of steadfast guards. The sledge turned around and began dashing away to a safer location.

All at once, the dynamite exploded, throwing guards in every direction. One of the doors of the gates fell completely, while the other swung open and broke its hinges. The guards who had survived the explosion were terrified by the sounds and scattered.

We all hissed victoriously, and K't'whoo turned the sledge back toward the ruined gates. We crossed through them quickly, leaving behind the village and quickly escaping toward the upper levels.

Chapter Fourteen,
Treason

The return trip to Mary's empire went much faster than the travel away from it had been. We no longer needed the story that we were visiting Ch'k'ch't; now K't'whoo could use the truth that she was the Empress's guardian and needed to return to her side. Conners, Wellis, and I still stayed in the back of the sledge, but we did not need to be so quiet. We stopped only once, to feed the mantises and to stretch our legs.

When we returned to the capital city, we found everything to be very still and quiet. Word had gotten out about the capture of the Empress, and the Selenite workers who had been so enamored with her were mourning her loss. Many of them were wearing red sashes around their necks, showing their patriotism as members of the Empire of Fire.

We rushed to the palace, where T'wha and Star had been holding court. The guards let us in without a word, and our weary mantises were taken to the Empress's stables to be cared for. There had been much construction on the palace since I had last seen it, and there were still Selenites painting murals and placing pebbles in enormous mosaics.

When we came to the throne room, K't'whoo threw the doors open violently. Everyone inside looked up, shocked as we marched quickly into the throne room. T'wha was sitting on the throne, dressed in ornate black robes that Mary had ordered be designed for her. On both sides of the throne, two guards stood, protecting the surrogate empress. Around T'wha there were numerous male Selenites who had been sketching on wooden tiles, but now stood frozen.

'Did you rescue the Empress?!' T'wha shouted at us as we came toward her. She half-stood from the throne, anxious for an answer.

'No, we did not,' K't'whoo answered, covering her eyes quickly in a quick salute. The four of us stood in front of T'wha in a half-circle, still armed and breathing heavily.

'Then where is she?' T'wha asked. She slumped back into the numerous cushions that lined the throne.

"We do not know for certain," Conners said, 'but we have a very good clue.'

'What is it?'

'The kidnapping was nothing short of treachery,' K't'whoo told her, hissing out the last word viciously.

The male Selenites around us all gasped in horror and whispered to one another. Even the guards on both sides of T'wha looked stunned, though they struggled to stay at attention. T'wha leaned forward as if the air had been knocked from her lungs. Treachery was one of the worst crimes in the Selenite world, even more serious than on Earth. Their feudal society depended on everyone staying in their places; deviation only caused the shattering of the social order and turmoil.

'Who?' T'wha asked, her voice shallow with shock.

'It must be one or more of the queens,' Conners clicked, trying to avoid emotion. 'The abductors were mercenaries hired out of Ch'k'ch't, paid with bolts of *s't'snap* cloth.'

Everyone in the throne room hissed in disbelief. Conners had explained to us that *s't'snap* cloth was native only to several of the villages of Mary's empire. While anyone else from the upper levels could have paid them with the cloth, it would have been ludicrously expensive. The queens who controlled the cloth growth in their villages, however, could have given them the cloth out of their personal stores and not even missed the revenue.

'I understand,' T'wha whispered. 'Servants, leave us!'

The males stood to go, but Wellis stopped them. 'Hold it!'

The males froze, eying the guns that Wellis had hanging on his belt. "I think we should keep this to ourselves until we find out who is behind it."

T'wha nodded. Most of the males looked at one another quizzically, wishing that they could have understood the human language. T'wha called for more guards, who took the males to holding rooms so that they could not make contact with anyone outside of the palace. The guards, who were all very loyal to the Empress, swore silence.

Just as the males left the throne room, Star, who had been in another part of the palace, dashed into it. "I heard that you had just arrived," he said, out of breath not from the run but from excitement. "Where is she?"

"We do not know yet, sir," Wellis said, shaking his head.

Star stopped and gaped. "Then shouldn't you be looking for her?"

"We need an idea where to start," Conners said. "T'wha, has there been any suspicious activity lately?"

T'wha nodded slowly. 'The time that you have been gone has been one of great turmoil. Within the empire, six of the queens have stopped trusting the humans, blaming them for the disappearance of the Empress. They have demanded that any human who comes within the proximity of their villages be escorted by Selenite guards. In addition, any and all human weapons have been outlawed within their villages. There is now a division among the villages of the empire. I have done my best to keep the empire together, but the anti-human queens are sowing distrust among the other villages as well.'

We all listened intently as she explained the fracturing of the empire. I glanced at Star, who had been here to witness all of the events. He nodded several times, showing that he was beginning to understand Selenite speech. Learning even such an alien language as this was almost simple since we had spent so much time around it.

When T'wha finished, Star spoke up. "It gets worse."

'How could it?' K't'whoo asked, closing her claws in rage. 'Civil war is upon us! Our empire will crumble unless the Empress returns!'

'There is another empire that has grown up since the humans first came to our caverns,' T'wha said. 'They call themselves the *Sh'k'wha Th't'f'th't'f'click.*'

I glanced at Conners, unfamiliar with the word. He noticed my glance and whispered, "The Empire of the Selenites."

I nodded and then looked at the ground. The whisper made the name sound forbidden or evil. I fought off a shiver that tried to go up my neck and concentrated on listening to the matter at hand.

'They have banded together against the Empire of Fire,' T'wha explained. 'Their entire existence is to bring down our empire and destroy all humans. I have heard tales from scouts that they have amassed a great army on the border of our empire, very near the villages that are growing quite anti-human themselves.'

"What've you done about it?" Wellis asked, his voice rising. "Is Rodreguez ready to fight them if they try anything?"

"Rodreguez has his army ready," Star said, trying to calm him. "We hoped that when you returned with Mary, though, we would not need to use the army."

'Now it appears that war will be necessary,' T'wha said, shaking her head. 'We have begun to—'

She was suddenly stopped as the door to the throne room opened and a guard hurried up to us. Before T'wha could scold her for interrupting them, the guard saluted and clicked, 'There is a fight among the males. What are your orders?'

T'wha was speechless for a moment. Finally, she came to her senses. The stress of the times appeared to be wearing her down. 'Take me to them.'

The guard saluted and turned, walking quickly out of the door. T'wha hurried after her, and the rest of us followed. We rushed through the hallways, dodging around groups of guards who where also coming to the scene of the fight. As we came closer to the room where the males had been locked away, noises of loud hisses and crashes began to grow louder and louder.

We came to the massive doors that led to the room, which was locked shut with a large wooden beam and was surrounded by guards. Several of the guards were wishing to open the doors and stop the fight immediately. Others merely wanted to look in on them, interested in the idea of seeing male Selenites fight one another.

When T'wha approached, the guards all stepped back respectfully. K't'whoo hurried beside the surrogate empress and lifted the heavy beam. They both pushed, opening the doors wide. When they did, they both hissed in shock.

I struggled to a position where I could see into the room. As I looked in on it, I could not help but giggle. I immediately slapped a hand over my mouth, however, and turned away from the scene. My hand pressed tightly until I was able to control my laughter.

The room was filled with two-foot-tall insect-men, all scurrying around and trying to punch one another. Their robes, all brightly done in differing colors and often too large for their small bodies, made the scene look like it belonged in the sideshow of a circus. Something had gotten them so excited that they began to fight, though the male Selenites often considered fighting to be beneath them.

'Halt!' K't'whoo hissed with amazing volume. The males all suddenly stopped in their tracks. Several continued to grip the robes of each other, not even wanting to move enough to release their opponents. The entire room went absolutely quiet immediately.

'What is the meaning of this?' T'wha asked, jerking her clawed hands in a manner that conveyed outrage.

All of the males began to click at once. Several hurried up to her, waving their arms to get her attention. Others in the back began to argue again, hissing and clicking with their faces very close together. One even threw an awkward punch at another, but missed so badly that the other did not retaliate.

'Halt!' K't'whoo hissed again. Once again, all of the males froze in silence.

'T'p'sh,' T'wha said, pointing to one of the males. I recognized him as one of the two that had accompanied Conners to the banquet long ago.

'Esteemed substitute Empress,' he began, half-covering his eyes in a slow salute. 'The battle began with a disagreement between my collegues P'f and Wh'f'click. P'f had made a statement many of us found inappropriate—'

'That is a lie!' one of the males interrupted. He suddenly went quiet as T'wha glared at him angrily for speaking out of turn.

'Continue,' she told T'p'sh.

'Wh'f'click rebuked him for such a comment, and then P'f said that Wh'f'click had no room for rebuking since he came from such a worthless village.' T'p'sh began to shake his head sadly. 'We all began to join into the argument, and insults arose, and we then started this terrible brawl.'

T'wha nodded. 'What was this statement?'

'A disparaging one toward our human friends,' he said. There was a slight rustle in the short crowd behind him. 'He stated that life had declined into doom for us all since the humans had arrived.'

'P'f!' T'wha called. The male sheepishly emerged out of the crowd and saluted with shaking hands. One of his antennae was bent, and his robes were very ruffled.

'P'f, who is your Empress?'

P'f first answered that T'wha was, but after seeing the glare she gave him, changed his mind and said that Mary was his true Empress.

'And who is your queen?'

P'f gave a long series of clicks in which I became lost. I wondered how many of the sounds belonged to the name of the queen and how many were other words, though I new that queens' names had been subject to substantial growth over the generations.

'What are her feelings toward the humans?'

P'f swallowed nervously. He gave an honest answer, but one that seemed very dark and disturbing to me.

'And how much *s't'snap* cloth is in her treasury?'

P'f recited a figure. T'wha rubbed one of her pinchers with her claw.

'That seems a little small for such a queen who has so many *s't'snap* fields," she hissed quietly. She turned away from P'f. 'Guards! Take him to the dungeons and interrogate him about the location of the Empress.'

P'f squealed. Many of the other males hissed, not amused at all with the idea of being tortured. Conners himself shuddered, remembering his short interrogation a month before.

Two guards walked toward P'f and caught him by his ruffled robes. He began to hiss in a high-pitched scream, which continued as the guards dragged him out of the room and down the hallway. All of the other males stayed quietly in place, not wanting any suspicion on them.

T'wha then left the room and asked for it to be locked back. The guards replaced the heavy beam, and all of the males inside were very calm. I doubted that any other fights would break out among them for a long, long time.

When we arrived back at the throne room, we were ready to resume discussing our options. Just after we came into the room, though, the two guards and P'f entered. I was amazed that an interrogation could take place so quickly, though P'f looked to be no more damaged than he had when he left us moments ago.

'The male has something he wishes to report,' one of the guards told T'wha. She shoved P'f forward.

P'f stumbled and barely kept his footing. He buried his eyes under his hands, making an extremely strong salute. To the humans in the room, it looked as if he were weeping uncontrollably and trying to hide himself. 'I know where they took her.'

His voice was quiet and blanketed with fear. Still, we could all tell what he meant to say.

'Where is she?!' K't'whoo demanded. She stomped, and the sound seemed to knock P'f to his knees.

'I delivered the *s't'snap* cloth to the marauders,' he explained. 'They handed the Empress over to me, tied in a heavy sack. I took her back to my village and presented her to my queen immediately. After that, I quickly returned to the palace so that I would not be missed. The queen traded her to the Empire of Selenites for a large number of soldiers, *k'whee*, and a huge mass of *k'k* fruit. The deal was that the Empire would protect the queen and the village in case it was ever discovered.'

'Where is the Empress?!' K't'whoo could no longer contain herself. She gripped the male by his robes and hoisted him to her face. Wellis and I jumped to her side, pulling on her arms to make sure that she did not strangle the defenseless male.

'The Empire is holding her in the fortress below Snap'ch'sh!' he screamed. 'That is all I know, I swear it!'

K't'whoo dropped him on the floor. Wellis and I let her go as she walked angrily toward the exit. T'wha called to her, stopping her just before she left through the door.

'What are you going to do?' T'wha asked.

'Find the Empress,' K't'whoo hissed.

'We need a plan first!' T'wha pleaded. K't'whoo turned and sighed, frustrated.

"Here is what we shall do," Star said, taking command of the situation. T'wha yielded to him, as people usually did when he flexed his muscles of command. "K't'whoo, Wellis, Conners, and Matricks will all repeat their covert operation and penetrate into the fortress. Rodreguez and I will follow with the army, in case we require a battle. T'wha, you will stay here and prepare to rally the Selenites."

I was surprised to be called Matricks. Before, I had always been known as Curtis, but now I supposed that I had grown in importance or at least maturity. It felt quite nice to be included with men like Lukas Conners and Phillip Wellis by being referred to by the last name.

Everyone nodded to Star, agreeing with his tactics.

"What about him?" Conners asked, pointing to the male who was still sitting on the floor and shivering.

'He knows the punishment for treason,' T'wha said calmly. 'I will wait until the Empress returns to allow her to pass judgment.' The male winced.

In only a matter of minutes, we were once again in the sledge, charging along the trails in search of Mary. While we were in her empire, we three humans did not hide under the cover of the sledge. Instead, we rode quickly and proudly, surrounded by a small escort that T'wha had dispatched for us. Because our former mantises were still worn out, we had been given completely fresh ones who were certainly strong enough for any task.

When we came to the border of the villages still loyal to Mary, though, we had to hide away. The escort continued with us, since it would be allowed in a realm that was ruled by the Empire of Fire, even if it did not allow humans and their weapons. We were stopped by several patrols, but the escort always earned permission to hurry on our way almost immediately. As we came to the border that led to regions outside of Mary's empire, however, the escort left us, wishing us good fortune as we disappeared into the corridors of a foreign, hostile nation.

We remained tucked away in the hay. Wellis had a rifle in his hands during the entire trip, though Conners and I thought that we did not need to hold weapons, just keep them well within reach. I tried to remain focused on our mission, but a small voice kept causing me to worry that harm might have come to Mary.

K't'whoo acted very coolly every time that we were stopped. She told the Selenites that checked her that the sledge was on a mission from one of the queens who had betrayed Mary. Security was much tighter than it had been going to the Undercaverns. Once one of the checkers even demanded to see the wagon and poked into the hay with his spear. I felt one of the pokes stop just next to my leg, but I did not make any sound at all.

We were silent for nearly the entire journey. Only once did Conners speak up, whispering, "You know, it makes sense that some of the queens would rebel against Mary. She had been altering their societies, giving more freedoms and powers to the Selenite workers and making all kinds of advances that would decrease the power of the queens. This may even be an attempt to avoid self-destruction."

"Well, they're certainly going to be destroyed now," I said. "Once Mary is back, the whole empire will rise up against them."

"True, true," Conners replied, and the conversation ended.

We rode in silence, passing through several checks easily. Suddenly, however, we were stopped for a final time. The guards who stopped K't'whoo were insistent that they could take the sledge and deliver it for her, while she was very enthusiastic in offering to deliver it herself. They became suspicious and forcibly removed her from the driver's bench. Finally, one of the guards struck K't'whoo, who immediately struck back.

The guard flew through the air with the force of her punch and landed on the cover of the sledge. It collapsed under her weight and ripped as broken poles poked through the cloth. As the guard moved to stand up, she felt Conners's body through the canvas and hay.

'There is someone hiding!' she shouted, just before Wellis unloaded his rifle into her abdomen. Conners shrieked as the Selenite slumped and struggled to throw her off.

Meanwhile, K't'whoo had dealt with the other guards. She took their spears from them and immediately jumped back onto the sledge. She kicked the mantises, which hissed and lurched forward. Wellis poked his head out of the hay and asked what had happened.

'We have been discovered,' K't'whoo said, hurrying the mantises onward. 'In a few moments, they will be after us. Prepare your weapons.'

Wellis ducked back under the canvas and began loading the extra ammunition under the hay onto his body. Conners and I struggled to see through the mess of hay and torn canvas, then loaded ourselves with weapons just as Wellis was doing. I had to struggle to remember to breathe, and I could hear nothing other than my loudly beating heart.

Behind us, we heard a distant horn blowing. K't'whoo sighed and clicked softly, 'That was the alarm. We are almost to the city. Perhaps we could escape in the streets as we did in Ch'k'ch't.'

"We'll follow your lead," Wellis said, spinning the carousel of a fully loaded pistol. "Tell us when we need to pop out and start shooting."

We drove on, scurrying away from the fight scene. I could imagine several Selenites looking at the guards confused and then charging after us angrily. I hugged one of the pistols and prayed that we would get away in time.

Suddenly I heard the rhythm of the mantises' legs go awry, causing my heart to slow in wonder at what it was. As I listened, I realized that it was not a loss of rhythm, but the sound of more mantises. In front of us, K't'whoo shrieked, probably seeing what I had heard. Wellis sat up out of the hay, brushed aside the canvas, and started firing with his rifle.

Conners and I soon joined him. When I saw what was chasing us, I nearly dropped my gun. We were in a tall, narrow chamber of the caverns with a long trail along its floor. There was a mass of Selenites riding on the backs of mantises, which were jumping high as they ran fast enough to catch up with us. Under Wellis's first barrage of fire, two of the mantises and riders dropped, but more seemed to appear to take their empty places.

As Wellis began to reload his weapons, I pulled up my pistol and continued the assault. I glanced at Wellis, hoping that he would be finished reloading by the time that I had run out of ammunition. I also saw Conners, who was not firing, but seemed to be counting to himself.

"What are you doing?" I shouted at him, firing as I said it.

"You'll see!" he shouted back and pulled a knife from his pocket. He took a stick of dynamite from the hay below him and worked at cutting the fuse.

I struggled to concentrate on the crowd of riders behind us. Finally, my gun clicked, showing that it was out of ammunition. I tossed it aside and picked up a fresh gun, which immediately began blazing at the riders.

"Here we go!" Conners shouted, lighting the dynamite. He dropped it out of the wagon and began to count in a whisper.

I fired another shot and then watched as the mantises charged over the dynamite. Just as the bulk of the mass of riders went over it, the dynamite exploded in a bright flash and thunderous boom. The mantises and riders were tossed by the explosion and struck the walls of the narrow cavern. Of the riders who were left on their mantises, only two were courageous enough to continue their charge after us. The others pulled to a halt and then retreated.

Wellis finished reloading his weapons and jerked back to the fight. He picked off one of the riders with a rifle bullet and then wounded the mantis of the other rider. The rider was thrown as the mantis halted in pain and was left in no condition to follow us. Wellis shouted in defiance at the ruined riders and shook his rifle above his head.

K't'whoo drove the sledge quickly through the rest of the chamber and into a tunnel. 'Once we get through this tunnel,' she said, 'we will come upon Snap'ch'sh.'

The tunnel grew dark as tunnels usually did. I finished reloading my weapons and sat back in the hay, waiting until we came out of the tunnel. I wondered what would happen once we reached the village, but I doubted that it would be as easy as our adventure in Ch'k'ch't, if one could call that easy.

Suddenly, there was a fluttering sound, and K't'whoo shouted in shock. I turned, but in the dark I could only see large black objects that dropped from the roof of the tunnel. K't'whoo was another dark object who was striking out at the other dark ones.

"What are they?" I shouted.

"I don't know, but they're in trouble!" Wellis shouted back. He immediately began firing into the air and struck one of the objects, which hissed in pain.

"Flying Selenites!" Conners shouted. He himself picked up a pistol and fired wherever he could see a dark object.

'Help me!' K't'whoo shouted.

I immediately clambered over the hay and wrecked canvas. I felt one of the Selenites strike me and gasped as the pain spread through my body. When I was able, though, I leapt back up and jumped onto the driver's bench next to K't'whoo.

My gun blazed, and one of the black objects twisted in the air and fell to the ground. I fired several more shots, but the flying Selenites were very fast and stayed away from the guns.

Conners and Wellis were being battered by the Selenites behind us. They shouted in pain as each black object hit them. Fortunately for K't'whoo, I was successfully intercepting many of the hits from the Selenites. She whipped at the mantises, causing them to dash through the tunnel as quickly as they could. Blasts continually rang from three guns, and though they were injuring us, the Selenites were losing the battle as they disappeared one by one.

The black objects pounded us all, included the fleeing mantises. It was a very discombobulating experience, for every time I thought that I could make out one of the Selenites, it would disappear into the shadows and another would strike me. The fluttering wings of the Selenites and resounding explosions from the guns did not help the situation as they filled the tunnel with chaotic noise.

I shot into the air and took down one of the objects, which fell directly into my lap. These Selenites were quite different from the ones I had seen before. They were very small, about the size of the male Selenites. They were infertile females, like the workers with which I was familiar. Its back shell was much larger in comparison than the other Selenites, and the shell held enormous wings. Not able to reflect on this new kind of Selenite at this moment, I threw the flying creature off of my lap and returned to shooting.

Finally Wellis blasted at the last flying black object. K't'whoo slowed the mantises a little, not so panicked now. As we came under one of the few glowing plants in the tunnel, I observed our battered crew. Wellis and Conners were both bleeding from the jaw and moved like they were already forming bruises. K't'whoo's exposed flesh seemed fairly beaten, but the strong exoskeleton armor of her body must have protected her from many of the strikes.

We suddenly came out of the tunnel and into a wide street thick with Selenites. Wellis, Conners, and I immediately dove under the canvas, doing our best to make sure that we would not be seen. Unfortunately, the Selenites had gathered quizzically at the loud sounds coming from the tunnel and had been watching as we left. They had clearly seen us even before we got a chance to hide ourselves.

Many of the Selenites hissed hatefully at us, others remained quiet and gawked, and still others fled fearfully from us. K't'whoo clicked at them, trying to calm them down, though it was a vain effort. Wellis came out from under the canvas and fired a shot up into the air, which made the Selenites panic just as they had in Ch'k'ch't. The crowd suddenly vaporized from around us, with the Selenites diving into alleys or merely running up the street to get away.

"That seemed to work well enough," Wellis smiled, happy with himself.

'It will be moments before the village guards are upon us,' K't'whoo said, causing Wellis to stop smiling and return to reality. 'We must move quickly.'

She whipped at the mantises, which began to dash down the street. The buildings in Snap'ch'sh seemed to be neat and prosperous, similar to the newly built ones in Mary's capital city. Everywhere we went, though, the Selenites were already fleeing from us, running through the streets, shutting their windows, and cowering in corners. I almost felt terrible frightening them simply by being in their city.

Horns and drums began to resound in the air above the village. K't'whoo whipped the mantises, trying to urge them to move even more quickly. Already, I could hear the clanking as the guards were working to put together their ranks for defense. I wondered how far away they were from us, but decided that I would probably rather not know.

K't'whoo suddenly stopped the mantises, causing us all to lurch forward. Wellis nearly tumbled out of the sledge, but caught himself on the side of it with his hand. Conners and I looked at one another, and then we looked forward and strained our eyes to see why K't'whoo had stopped us.

Distantly in front of us there was a tall wall placed high in the streets. Around it, several dozen Selenites were standing guard, waiting for our sledge. They must have started preparing the defense when they heard the horns. There was no way to go through it, and the guards would probably attack us if we tried to blast our way with dynamite.

Instead, K't'whoo led the sledge into an alleyway. We drove though the tight alley for a short distance, and then K't'whoo stopped it completely. Wellis, Conners, and I looked at her questioningly, but she jumped down from the driver's bench without a word.

She began undoing the harnesses that held the mantises. When she had completed half of her work, she finally began to explain. 'We cannot go by street any longer. We must abandon the sledge and head toward the fortress on the rooftops.'

'Are you sure?' Wellis asked.

'Yes,' K't'whoo said. 'They are searching for us as we speak.'

'How do you know?' I asked.

'*K'snap'click*,' she said. 'You can hear them if you listen.'

I strained to listen as she finished detaching the mantises from the sledge. In the distance, I could hear rustling, but I could not determine its source. Then I heard a far away, howling hiss. I shivered, not wanting to know what had caused it.

K't'whoo released the mantises, which immediately dashed away. She then turned back to us. 'We will have to leave the sledge, though I do not know what they will do with it once they capture the weapons inside.'

I nodded. There was a sizable arsenal hidden beneath the hay, far too much for us to carry. Human guns were superior to Selenite spears in combat, and allowing them to gain the guns might lead to something terrible.

"They don't necessarily have to capture it," Conners said in English with a smile. He once again pulled several sticks of dynamite out of the hay. We all smiled with him and then hastened to leave.

In a moment, we were all loaded with as much ammunition as we could carry, though K't'whoo was still wary of human weaponry, especially in hand-to-hand combat. There was still a substantial amount of weapons in the sledge, but we were not able to put them on our bodies. When we left the sledge, climbing up the wall of the building next to us on a grappling hook K't'whoo had brought, we looked like dime novel descriptions of vicious banditos.

The climb was simple in lunar gravity, despite the weapons, which hampered our movements more than dragging us down by weight. We reached the top of the building and regrouped on the roof. As K't'whoo retrieved the rope we had used to climb, Conners lit a stick of dynamite he had been holding in his teeth.

"Let's see what they think of this," he said, and dropped the explosive down into the hay-covered bed of the sledge. We dashed to the other end of the building, hurrying to escape the blast. When we came to it, K't'whoo, who was leading us, leapt and made an incredible jump across the next alley onto the next building. Wellis, carrying multiple bandoliers across his shoulders, followed her, waving the rifle in his hand as he jumped. Conners and I reached the edge of the building at the same time and leapt out over the alley.

When I first pushed off from the roof with my feet, I closed my eyes, wondering if I could make such a jump, even in lunar gravity. I felt myself flying through the air, almost floating, and opened my eyes. I could see the alley below, far below, and my stomach tightened at the sight of it. The other building approached me quickly, however, and I landed safely on the other roof. When I touched, though, my foot slipped, and I would have fallen backward had K't'whoo not caught me.

Just then we heard the loud explosion from the sledge. It was actually several explosions, as the first stick of dynamite set off the others. I knew that the sledge must be destroyed by it, and all of the weapons inside were now useless slag metal. The building, too, must have sustained a fair amount of damage, as it rumbled and leaned slightly toward the ruined sledge.

'Now we will have a fair bit of chaos to cover us,' K't'whoo clicked calmly. She began to dash across the building, her insect-like feet clacking on the tiles of the roof. We hurried after her, doing our best to follow her fleet footing.

We were fortunate that Snap'ch'sh was a wealthy and powerful city, enough so to have the majority of its buildings roofed with stone or tiles. Many villages in the caverns were much poorer and fashioned their roofs with thin planks of wood or dried grasses.

At the edge of every building, we jumped again. Each time we leapt, my heart either stopped or beat with such fervor that I could feel nothing else in my body. We came to one building that was taller than all of the rest, but used K't'whoo's grappling hook and rope to climb it easily.

Behind us, I could often hear the strange howling hiss of the *k'snap'click*. They were growing closer, probably told of our position by the explosion in the sledge. I wondered how long it would be until they caught up with us or if we would move too quickly and lose them again.

We finally came to the last building, where K't'whoo stopped so suddenly that we all stumbled and fell onto her. When we were sorted out, she pointed out over the ledge of the building. We crept up to it and peeked over at the scene beyond. There was an open area surrounding a short, round tower. I assumed that the area was usually used as an open-air bazaar since there were multiple colored stalls, now devoid of any merchants. Patrols of guards were circling the tower, bristling with long spears and other weapons.

'This is the entrance to the fortress,' she told us. 'We will jump down to the merchant booth below, and wait for a chance to storm it.'

"You certainly know a lot about Snap'ch'sh," Conners said, just before we prepared to leave the roof. "Have you been here before?"

'Once,' she clicked. 'I was young, then, however.' She then leapt down from the building to the ground below.

"She must have a good memory," Wellis said and smiled at Conners. Before Conners could reply, though, Wellis jumped and followed K't'whoo.

"You know," Conners told me, "that's not very comforting." I shrugged and jumped, landing on a pile of tapestries that had already been deformed slightly by Wellis and K't'whoo. Conners came after me, falling very slowly through the air and landing almost silently in the tapestries.

We crawled to the edge of the booth, staying very low to be out of sight of the guards. We then peered over at them, trying to calculate their maneuvers. There were two layers of guards, the outer one going clockwise around the tower and the inner one moving counterclockwise. Beyond them, the tower stood with spear throwers on the top of it. Its door faced us, a large door made of layers of heavy wood. Eight guards stood at attention in front of it and looked like they would refuse access to anyone at all.

"What's the plan?" Conners asked.

'I am thinking,' K't'whoo replied.

After a pause, Conners whispered, "I'm ready for anything just as long as it is not 'make a run for it.' "

K't'whoo smiled, pulling back her pinchers slightly. Selenite smiles seemed strange to humans and might even frighten young children. I suddenly wondered what Selenites thought of the human smile, pulling our faces back and baring our teeth and mouths. A human smile suddenly seemed like a very strange thing indeed.

"What if we made a diversion?" Wellis suggested. His voice brought me out of my thoughts and into the reality of the situation.

'That might pull away some of the guards for a moment.' K't'whoo nodded. 'We could perhaps then destroy the door with your crashing sticks.' (Selenites had no word for explosion, though I thought that "crashing" made a good description of them.)

"It would be tricky to do," Conners said. "But I think that we could pull it off."

'Very well,' K't'whoo said. 'Here is what we will do. I will sneak around the tower and cause a crash with one stick. When you hear the crash, one of you will run out with another stick or so to destroy the door. The other two of you can provide cover with your weapons.'

"Sounds like a good plan," Wellis said.

He and Conners quickly versed K't'whoo in lighting a match and then igniting the dynamite. They told her how to count down for the explosion. Finally K't'whoo nodded, said that she was ready, and sneaked out of the booth. She disappeared around the corner of the building we had just left and began the long trip to the opposite side of the tower.

"So," Wellis whispered, "who's going to run it out there?"

"Don't look at me," Conners said, pointing at his legs. "Bad knees."

I looked at him in confusion. "You told me a week ago that you considered yourself to be the best runner in Oxford."

"Well, we're not in Oxford, now are we?" Conners rolled his eyes, realizing that lying was no way to be discounted for the run.

"Let's just draw straws," I said, picking at loose strings on my suit, which had been very tattered in the past few adventures. I quickly found three, two of the same length and one much longer. Turning my back to them, I arranged them in my hand so that they appeared to be the same length. I turned back to them and allowed them both to choose strings.

"Not me," Wellis said, holding up his short string.

"Me either," Conners said, comparing his string to Wellis's.

My heart sank as I opened my fist and saw the longest string sitting in my palm. "Well, I guess I'll do it, then."

"Here's what you do," Wellis said, holding out a stick of dynamite to me. I took it, my hand shaking a little. "When the guards turn away, I'll light the fuse. When you hear the fuse lighting, start running. Conners and I will fire at the Selenites, keeping them well away from you. Count to three as you run, and then throw it. Then do your best to hurry back here, away from the explosion."

I nodded. I tried to say something, but no words would form in my mouth.

We quickly moved into positions, ready for K't'whoo's explosion. I was at the open end of the booth, ready to run. I had shed many of my weapons and held the dynamite out toward Wellis. Wellis and Conners kneeled at the edge of the booth, weapons ready. Wellis had a match in his hand, and was ready to strike it when he heard the explosion.

Finally, it rang out. There was a plume of dust and everything seemed to tremble just a bit. Wellis lit the match and held it. The patrolling guards, perplexed by the explosion, all hurried toward it. The guards at the door remained at their post, but looked to be a little shaken. Wellis held the match for a long while, waiting for the guards to move as far away from the door as they would.

When we were satisfied, he lit the dynamite. "Go!" he shouted, and I immediately dashed out into the open bazaar.

I ran more swiftly than I had in my entire life. Each step I took sent me bounding up into the air, and I landed a long distance from where I had left the ground. I counted out three seconds, then I threw the stick at the door. It sailed through the air, flying a long distance in the lunar gravity, and hit the door just above the heads of the guards.

Just as they noticed me and began to hiss wildly, I fell down, stopping myself, and then began to dash back toward the merchant booth. A spear flew at me, but it must have been a hasty throw as it missed me terribly. When I had taken my second step on the way back to the booth, the dynamite exploded, throwing the guards in all directions. The explosion picked me up, too, and tossed me into an uncomfortable position just in front of the booth. The guards at patrol who had gone to inspect the other explosion now hurried back toward me.

Wellis and Conners were firing wildly. I could see the spear throwers hiding behind the stone walls, which were being cracked and chipped by bullets from Conners's guns. Wellis, meanwhile, fired powerful rifle blasts into the crowd of rushing guards, who were resolute in their charge. When I looked back at the door, where the dynamite had exploded, I could not believe my eyes.

The explosion had certainly injured it. There was a large crater-like depression in it, with splinters of wood lying all around. However, the door's inner layers had withstood the blast. Despite the dynamite, we still could not get through the door.

"No!" I shouted and climbed over the edge of the booth. I picked up my guns and turned back to the bazaar, firing at the guards, still dismayed at the door.

"What do we do now, Wellis?" Conners shouted over the noise of our gunfire.

"I don't know!" Wellis shouted back.

"We can't stay here!" I said, firing at the mass of armored Selenites who were charging across the bazaar at us.

"Then let's make a run for it!" Conners shouted. He emptied his guns' chambers, stowed them in holsters, and pulled out fresh ones from behind. While he did this, he edged toward the open end of the booth, ready to run.

"Sounds like a great plan!" Wellis said. He provided cover while I reloaded all of my guns and bandoliers of ammunition, and then we both followed Conners out of the booth.

Finally we fell to sprinting down the street, firing behind us only when we could turn away from concentrating on running. The guards continued to pursue us, sounding horns to alert the rest of the guards in the whole village. We had nearly outrun the initial guards when a new group came running at us from the other direction of the street, the guards who had been stationed at the wall we had dodged before.

Conners made a Latin curse and led us down an alley. Wellis and I followed him without question, even though he had no more of an idea where to go than we did. We dashed through the city, dodging groups of guards and bounding high in the air with each step.

After fleeing for a long while, we came to an empty building whose door was open, and we dove into it. Wellis shut the door behind us and wedged it shut with the furniture inside. He panted from excessive running for the first time since we had come to the Moon. Conners and I quietly began reloading our guns and discarding spent cartridges. Wellis made sure that all of the windows were blocked and then began reloading his own weapons.

We could still hear the sounds of the guards outside. They had lost us moments before we hid in the building and were probably searching wildly for us. I heard the hissing cry of a *k'snap'click*, which made me swallow nervously. There were even fluttering sounds, as if they had called out more of the vicious flying Selenites.

"How long to you think we'll hold out here?" I whispered.

Conners shook his head while Wellis shrugged and said, "We'll see."

Chapter Fifteen,
Rescue

We waited silently in the empty building for a few minutes before we began to grow restless. Conners began pacing, mumbling to himself in a language that I could not remember ever hearing. Wellis continuously looked out the window, checking for any sign that the guards had traced us to this building.

Finally, I had a thought and spoke. "I doubt that door could withstand another blast of dynamite."

Both Wellis and Conners looked at me.

I shrugged. "I mean, the guards are looking for us in the village. They're probably thinking that no one is crazy enough to attack the tower like that again."

Conners grinned fiendishly. "Well, they've never met us, have they? So how do we get over there?"

"We could take the rooftops again," Wellis suggested, peeking out one of the windows. "Check the second story. See if we could punch our way up to the roof."

Conners and I nodded obediently and headed for the small ladder in the corner of the room. We crept up it into the room on the second floor of the empty building. It was quite dusty in the room, which was filled with boxes that were covered in tarps. Conners hoisted me up to one of the beams, and I pushed on the tiles above me, looking for any loose ones.

One suddenly gave under the pressure of my hand and popped out of place. I grabbed it and twisted, pulling it down into the room. It left a small hole, and I calculated that three more removed would allow us to escape. "Catch," I said and tossed it down to Conners.

Conners caught the tile and set it down on the floor. He watched as I wiggled three more, removing them and opening up a hole large enough for us. I tossed the tiles down to Conners quietly, then motioned for him to get Wellis. He nodded, impressed, and disappeared down the ladder.

Wellis came up the ladder with him when he returned. Wellis whispered that I had done a good job and motioned for me to look out. I poked my head out of the hole, saw that it was clear, and then moved my whole body out of the hole. I waited on top of the tile roof until Wellis and Conners followed me out of the hole.

"Which way?" I asked.

Wellis pointed past my right shoulder with a pistol. Without a word, he ran past me, picking up speed. At the edge of the roof, he leapt, easily landing on the next roof.

Conners was about to jump, but there was suddenly a low, howling hiss. We both turned and saw a large spider-like creature crawl over the edge between us. I gaped, finally seeing the *k'snap'click*. It was sized about like a large dog, but had the hideous appearance of a spider. I recognized it as the creature Conners and Wellis had watched long ago when we first came to the caverns, though this one was much more ferocious.

The creature hissed and climbed closer to us. It was certainly more aggressive than the creature we had seen before and looked to have been trained for hunting. It lunged, but was stopped in midair by a bullet from Conners's pistol.

Every Selenite head in the village turned at the sound of the shot. Conners winced, realizing what he had just done. The guards were all now heading toward the building, ready to kill us where they found us. We glanced at one another and then followed after Wellis, who had already begun to run down the next rooftop as quickly as he could.

The three of us raced across the rooftops, faster than we had before. In the distance, we could see several clusters of the small flying Selenites like the ones that had attacked us in the tunnel. Fortunately, they did not seem to spot us. I wondered if they were able to see us or just did not want to admit to seeing us since we had defeated the other flying Selenites already.

In only a matter of minutes, we arrived back at the building where we had paused before jumping down into the bazaar. We crouched there for a moment, checking over the scene. Nearly all of the guards were gone; only a few stood in front of the damaged door. A long sledge had been moved into the bazaar, filled with lumber. A few Selenite workers were beginning to lay out pieces of wood to repair the door.

"Plan of attack?" Conners asked.

"Let's charge in," Wellis whispered. "Conners, you do the honors with the dynamite this time. Matricks and I will run with you this time, providing cover as we go."

"Sounds good," I said, checking to make sure the pistols on my hips were freshly loaded. Conners and Wellis jumped down off of the building into the merchant's booth once again. I looked out over the bazaar and, once satisfied that the guards had not seen us, hurried down after them.

Conners was already preparing the dynamite. "This is the part where K't'whoo left. I wonder what's happened to her."

"I'm sure she's all right," Wellis whispered.

"She is the Empress's guardian, after all," I said, reassuring him.

Conners lit his match and moved it close to the fuse. "Ready?" he asked.

Wellis and I nodded a single time, and Conners ignited the fuse. Wellis and I both began shooting right then, Wellis hitting one of the guards in the thorax and me causing the spear throwers above to dive for cover. Conners then ran out holding the dynamite out in front of him. We followed him, firing as we went.

The guards, who had seen the injuries of the guards who had stood by the door last, ran in differing directions. Some of them charged at us, hissing a battle cry, but most of them simply ran away from the door. The workers who had been preparing to repair the door immediately ran away as well, disappearing from sight almost instantly. A few of the spear throwers lobbed spears at us from above the tower, but the spears missed badly as they did not risk aiming in such a hail of bullets.

Conners threw the dynamite and then dove to the ground. Wellis and I dropped into kneeling positions, but kept firing as long as our weapons would last. All of the guards who charged at us were cut down by our bullets, and the spear throwers stayed in the protection of the tower defenses.

The explosion washed over us, knocking me down. Wellis cringed against the force of the blast, but stayed on his knee. When the shockwave passed, we looked up. Conners shouted victoriously at the completely demolished door and jumped to his feet. He pulled the pistols from their holsters and fired at the spear throwers. Wellis and I followed him, firing as quickly as we could.

When we reached the door, we leapt inside and stopped. Wellis pressed his back against the stone wall and quickly reloaded his weapons. I joined him in reloading, pulling ammunition from my numerous belts. Conners jogged deeper into the tower, judging that he hand not fired enough shots to need to reload his guns.

Just after Wellis and I reloaded, we saw several guards come into the bazaar. Wellis fired at them, taking down one of the guards with a lucky hit. He then jerked his head to the side, motioning for me to run after Conners. I nodded and headed deeper into the tower, hoping that he would be all right by himself.

I reached the end of the short hallway and came to a large circular room. There was an enormous hole in the middle of the room, and it had a spiral staircase cut from the stone and a primitive lift to move transports. Doors led to more rooms around the exterior of the room and a ladder on the opposite side of the hole went up to the roof where the spear throwers had hidden. Conners was at the bottom of the ladder, pointing his pistols up it and shouting wildly.

"I'm holding the spear throwers here!" he said, seeing me as I came in. "Head down into the fortress! I'll catch up!"

"Wellis is holding guards at the main door," I told him as I jumped onto the spiral stairs and began to hurry down. "They're going to be here any minute!"

"That's great news," he said sarcastically, hissing through his teeth.

I did not reply to his comment and rushed down the stairs. Twice I lost my footing, but it was easy to catch myself in the low gravity before I fell. The stairs spiraled at a sharp angle and descended a great distance. It took me several minutes of simply running down them before I came to a landing, which quickly became an open room with hallways and doors leading in a dozen directions.

There were two Selenite guards in the room, standing at attention in the middle of it. When they heard me jump down the last few steps, they quickly snapped up their spears and pointed them at me. I pointed my guns at them, one trained on each.

The Selenites looked at the guns fearfully, and their body positions loosened as they clicked softly to one another, trying to decide what to do.

'Drop your spears!' I clicked.

They looked quizzically at me, probably surprised that I was able to speak. They both obeyed and threw their spears into a corner of the room.

'Where is the Empress of Fire?' I clicked fiercely at them.

They did not move, so I pulled back the hammers on the pistols. I hoped that they would understand that the motion was a threatening one. I do not know if they realized it, but the clicking of the weapons certainly unstrung them.

One of them pointed to a door on their left. I moved slowly to it, not taking my eyes off of them at all. Finally I decided that it would be best to take them with me.

I motioned my guns for them to move in front of me and clicked, 'Open the door.'

The Selenites moved slowly, watching me as carefully as I had watched them. The guard who reached the door first opened it wide. I then moved toward them, pushing them down the corridor beyond the door.

'Take me to the Empress,' I commanded. They cringed slightly and began to walk down the corridor.

Suddenly there was a loud shout from above and then a booming sound. I turned, wondering what was happening. Just then I saw the lift in the middle of the shaft come crashing down, holding Wellis, Conners, and the body of a guard who must have come too close to them. They must have jumped onto the lift in an effort to escape the guards who had charged us after we punched through the main door.

I felt a heavy punch in my back. I lurched forward and dropped one of my guns. When I was able, I twisted and shot, hitting one of the Selenites. She had used the distraction in an effort to disarm me. The other Selenite had begun running down the corridor in an effort to escape from me.

Wellis and Conners picked themselves up from the destroyed lift. The rope that had held it fell from above and landed behind them. The end was frayed like it had been cut suddenly. They were covered in dust, still had bruises and cuts from the fights before, and now had new ones that had just begun. I grunted, wondering if I looked as badly as they did.

"Now that I think about it," Conners said, rubbing a sore spot on his leg where he had landed awkwardly, "that was not the best escape route."

"It got us down here quick enough," Wellis told him. He looked up and moaned, "They're coming down! Don't they ever stop?"

"This way!" I shouted to them. Seeing my gun on the ground, I stooped to pick it up quickly.

When I was sure that they saw me, I began hurrying after the Selenite who had escaped from me. Conners immediately began running after me, while Wellis stayed behind and tried to take shots at the guards who were now charging down the stairs. When spears began to be thrown at him from above, though, he dove out of the bottom of the hole and hurried after us.

The corridor did not have any doors on the walls, so we continued to run down it. It was very long and it took us a long to reach the end of it, the Selenite guards chasing after us all the while. I could see the guard who had escaped from me and ran as quickly as I could to catch up with her, but she was too fast.

At the end of the corridor, she disappeared totally. We came to a small, square room that had three new corridors. Two of them had strong glowing plants, like the corridor we had just left, while the other was quite dark.

"What do we do?" I asked.

"Split up?" Wellis suggested, not even sure of his own idea.

"I suppose so." Conners nodded. He immediately ran down one of the bright tunnels.

"Good luck," Wellis called to me and hurried down another well-lit tunnel.

I winced at the dark tunnel, but ran into it despite my better judgment suggesting that I follow Wellis or Conners. Behind me, I heard the distant footsteps of the Selenites approaching, which made me hurry down the tunnel, despite how dark it grew.

I followed the tunnel for only a few steps before it began to slope greatly. At some points, I nearly had to slide down it, carefully using my feet to guide me. The slope continued for many yards before the tunnel leveled again. I was glad to see that I was not descending any longer, and then sighed as the tunnel sloped downward again.

Finally the tunnel ended, opening up into a large circular room. It was lit much better than the tunnel had been, but was still very shadowy. The room was stacked with boxes, and I wondered if it was some kind of storage area. I heard clicking inside, and I recognized it as Selenite speech. I gripped my guns very tightly as I entered, scanning the room for any sign of guards.

Suddenly I heard a hissing shout and a spear flew at me. I ducked beneath it, but it clipped my shoulder, leaving a shallow scrape. I squinted away the pain and fired a shot in the direction from which the spear had come. The clicking suddenly became louder, and I knew that there were at least three Selenites hidden in the room with me.

I ducked behind a small stack of boxes and peeked out above them. I saw a pair of antennae poking up behind another stack and shot at the boxes. The pile tumbled under the force of the blow, causing the Selenite behind to make a high-pitched hiss in shock. There were two other hisses, coming from other stacks of boxes.

I made two more shots, knocking down the other boxes. Finally, the

Selenites leapt up and began to run. One charged at me, brandishing her large spear viciously. I emptied my guns into her abdomen, causing her to drop to the ground. The other two Selenites fled out of the room, dashing into the corridor from which I had just come. I holstered my empty guns and pulled a fresh one from a holster behind my back. By the time I began to chase after them, however, they had already disappeared in the darkness of the tunnel.

Scanning the room, I looked for another way out. There were several doors leading off of the room, one on the far end and three on each side. I opened the far door first, wondering where it might lead. I stepped through, but paused as I heard the sound of rushing water. The door led to a short cliff that hung over an underground river. There were numerous filthy pots that lined the cliff, causing me to wonder if this were some kind of Selenite sewage system.

I stepped away from the cliff and back into the room. There was a distant clicking and hissing coming from the tunnel, signifying that the Selenites were still after me. There was another sound in the room, a soft banging coming from the middle door on the left side of the room. I could almost hear shouts coming from it too, and though the door muffled them, they sounded like English.

I hurried to the door and pulled a thick wooden board that had been holding it in place. The board struggled against my pull at first, but then slid out of its position. When the door was freed, I tugged at it and opened it wide.

"Curtis!" I heard a voice scream. It sounded like Mary, but I had never heard her voice so breathy and exasperated.

Before I could respond, Mary charged out of the dark room. Her dress was dirty and tattered, but it was still recognizable as the dress she had been captured in so long ago. Her hands and feet were bound with thick cords, but she hopped along easily in the low lunar gravity. She made a quick jump and threw her arms around my neck.

I nearly fell backward in surprise. Mary leaned on my neck heavily, as if she did not have any strength in her legs at all. I tried to say something, but I could not make any words come out of my mouth until I finally said, "Are you all right?"

She nodded, but I was not very convinced. She had dried blood on her forehead, and her face was very dirty. Her hair was filthy as well and terribly mussed. Her eyes, though, were the same starry darkness that they had always been.

"Cut me loose!" she said, tugging at my neck until her bound wrists were in front of my eyes.

I did not have a knife with me, but I turned to look for one. As I turned, Mary, who clung tightly around me, twisted with me. Just as I began to search for something with which to cut the bindings, I heard a group of Selenite guards charging through the tunnel. In a few moments, they would be in the room.

"No time for it!" I told her.

I thought as quickly as I could, trying to find an escape route. Finally, it occurred to me and I winced, not liking the idea. Still, it was the only thing I could think of. I quickly picked up Mary, who still clung to my neck, and dashed to the cliff overlooking the river.

As we came to it, Mary twisted her head, trying to see where we were going. When she saw the river, she squeezed my neck in shock. "What are you doing?" she screamed. "Don't jump!"

I struggled to breathe under the pressure of her arms on my neck. "It's the only way out."

Behind us, the first Selenite guard leapt into the room. I gasped, but I did not edge toward the edge of the cliff.

Mary screamed when she saw the Selenite. "Jump!" she ordered, urging me to move quickly.

I leapt, leaving the cliff behind. We floated slowly at first, and our fall gradually grew faster and faster. Falling on the Moon is a very intriguing experience; in the first few seconds, it almost seems like one is flying. That sensation does not last long, however, and we suddenly found ourselves crashing into the water below.

We sank beneath the water as we struck it, but almost immediately bobbed back up. The Selenite guards ran to the edge of the cliff above us and hissed angrily as they saw the river. Its current was quickly pulling us away from them, and none seemed to want to chase after us in the water. One threw her spear, but the shot was more to quell frustration than to hit us, and it missed us by several yards.

Despite our limited ability to swim, we seemed to stay easily on top of the water. The river moved fairly quickly and was very brown from the mud it was moving about in it. Mary shifted into a more comfortable position next to me, but still clung tightly around my neck and shoulders.

The river continued to carry us deeper and deeper. It twisted often, snaking through long, thin chambers of the caverns. There were not any shores on either side, just sheer cliffs where the river had worn through the rock. We seemed to be stuck traveling on the river until we came to a place to escape from it.

We floated in silence for a long while. Finally, I wondered aloud, "Was this a good idea?"

"I didn't see much other choice," Mary said.

I nodded slightly in agreement. The conversation paused again as we passed a large onyx formation on the side of the river. It was very pretty, but neither of us was in the mood to appreciate something pretty.

When we passed it, I struggled to resume the conversation. "Are you all right?" I asked. "They didn't hurt you, did they?"

Mary shook her head slowly. "They didn't want to injure an Empress too terribly. I got a few scrapes, but I'll be alright."

"What happened after they took you?" I asked. Memories of the abduction were still very vivid in my mind, almost like how a very real nightmare stays in the mind after one wakes.

"I don't really know," she said. "I was blindfolded for the longest while. I think I must have changed hands a couple of times, though. Every so often I would be taken from one sledge and dumped into another. Finally they pulled me out of the final sledge, carried me a long way, and then locked me in the dungeon."

"You've been there all this time?"

"Most of it, but not all. I was taken out several times to speak with a couple of queens, who spent their time telling me that there was no hope of rescue, that the Empire had been defeated, and that all of the humans were either killed or driven out of the caverns. They must have been trying to break my spirits. I held onto hope as long as I could, but they were very horrible in their talks." She turned away from me, hiding her face.

I swallowed and did my best to cheer her. "Well, we did come for you. And your empire is certainly not defeated."

"That is good to hear," she said, turning back and smiling a little. "Tell me about it."

I took a deep breath and did my best to explain everything that had happened, from the initial chaos, to the adventures in Ch'k'ch't, to our return, and then finishing with the rescue here in Snap'ch'sh (though I could not make the correct snapping sound since my hands were too busy guiding us through the water). The tales seemed to cheer her up, and I did my best to make the adventures seem exciting and amusing. She giggled each time I mentioned Conners bumping into me when we had disguised ourselves as servants in Ch'k'ch't.

When I came to the point where I had opened her door and she leapt around my neck, I stopped the story. It had taken a while to tell it all, and we were still floating in the river without a means to escape. The river did not seem to matter as much as it had before, though, and we both were much happier than before.

"So what happened to K't'whoo?" she asked me. "And Conners and Wellis?"

"I don't know." I shook my head. "I haven't seen K't'whoo since we first blasted the door to the fortress and the others since we split up in the corridors."

"Do you think that they are alright?"

"Probably. K't'whoo certainly knows her way throughout the caverns, and Conners and Wellis can each take care of himself well enough."

"Do you think that they're still looking for me?"

"They wouldn't give up until they found you," I told her. She smiled, pleased to feel important.

Mary was about to begin another question, but stopped as we began to hear a distant rumble. We both looked at one another quizzically, but did not say anything. The current of the river carried us quickly toward it, and we would find out what it was very soon. As a precaution, I swam to the edge of the river, hoping to be able to grab at the rock walls in case we needed to stop suddenly.

After a wide arc in the river, we came upon the source of the rumble. Mary and I both screamed, and I did my best to claw at the wall and stop. Directly in front of us was a large circular chamber, where the river seemed to stop. The water drained in the middle of the chamber in a huge whirlpool that sucked down anything that came near it.

I tried several handholds, but they all seemed to break away under my hand. The current of the river was increasing, and Mary was gripping at my neck very tightly again. I continued to dig at the walls until I finally grabbed a large piece of gray stone that held. We stopped with a jerk, and the water pulled at our bodies, trying to drag us away.

"Don't let go!" Mary shouted to me. Even though she was very close to my ear, the rumble of the whirlpool nearly drowned out her voice.

I gritted my teeth and did my best to hold onto the rock. Pieces of wood that had been floating in the river rushed quickly by us and disappeared into the whirlpool. The current was very strong and my muscles were beginning to become sore.

Suddenly the rock began to give way beneath my hand. We were quite near the whirlpool and I was certain that this rock was our last hope. However, it had been constantly weakened by a rushing river and was simply waiting for the time when it would break free. Unfortunately, that time seemed to be very soon.

"The rock's breaking!" I shouted at Mary. "Hold on tight!"

She pulled tightly around me just as a crack appeared on the edge of the rock. I watched it, helplessly, as it slowly pulled away from the stone wall. Finally it left the wall completely, and we were swept through the river. The whirlpool rushed up at us and swallowed us down.

I took a deep breath just as our heads were pulled under the water. I struggled against the current, but finally succumbed to it. We were sucked down through the water and entered a fairly large tube at the bottom of the chamber. It pulled on us quickly, forcing us deeper and deeper. As I tried to guide us through the tube, Mary kept completely still, her eyes and lips clamped tightly shut.

My lungs were beginning to burn as the tube widened. It seemed to change its angle and soon we were traveling at a slant instead of straight down. Just as I was beginning to give up hope, I heard another rumble through the water. At last the tube gave way, and we found ourselves falling from a large waterfall.

Sensing the air, we both took a much-needed breath, though we both inhaled plenty of water with it. We then screamed, feeling the fall. Just after the scream, however, we splashed into a large pool of water again. The waterfall rained down on us, but I swam out from under it and finally pulled us onto shore.

Mary let go of my neck and coughed deeply. I coughed as well, spitting out some of the water that I had taken in. We finally finished coughing and collapsed onto the shore, worn out by the experience. We breathed deeply, trying to replenish the oxygen in our bodies.

Suddenly Mary sat up and turned. I lay a moment more, but I saw what she had seen and immediately jumped up as well. There was a small crowd of Selenites next to us, staring quietly. I grabbed for my right pistol from my hip holster, but it was missing, probably lost in the river. Fortunately, the one at my left was still in place. I rested my hand on it, ready for anything the Selenites might do.

Strangely, they just seemed to stare at us, trying to figure out what exactly we were. Several more Selenites came from behind and joined the others in staring at us.

"*S'ch*," Mary hissed, holding up her hands peacefully. Several of the Selenites returned the greeting quietly, but most of them remained quiet.

One of the Selenites had a small, oddly-shaped spear with her. Mary motioned toward it and clicked calmly. The Selenite nodded and passed her the spear. As she handed it to me, she said, "Now we can cut these bindings off."

The Selenites whispered to one another, amazed at Mary's speech. I wondered if they were from one of the villages that had not seen a human yet. They watched us carefully, inspecting everything about us and all we did.

Mary held out her hands to me, pulling apart her wrists as far as the bindings would let them go. I used the spear to cut through them, slowly and carefully. When I had freed her wrists, she took the spear back from me and freed her ankles. Finally she handed the spear back to the Selenite from whom she had borrowed it and thanked her.

'Where are we?' I asked the Selenites.

They looked at me amazingly, and it was a long while before one answered. 'T'k'k'whee.'

I looked at Mary, who shrugged, unfamiliar with the name. We stood, water dripping from our clothes. Mary's formerly white dress was now soaked through with muddy water and stained brown, and she was missing both of her shoes. Even my black Star uniform showed signs of brown stains. It seemed to hold water very well and weighed down on my body even in lunar gravity.

Once I stood, I could see beyond the Selenites. We were in a large chamber filled with bright glowing plants. The pool led to irrigation ditches, which spread out throughout the chamber. There were numerous crops growing between the ditches, and it looked like enough food to feed all of London for a year or more.

"They're farmers," I realized aloud. I looked at the spear again and recognized it as more of a shovel or hoe than a weapon.

Finally one of the Selenites stepped sheepishly out of the crowd. 'What are you?' she asked, quivering a little.

'We're humans,' Mary explained, 'from the Empire of Fire.'

The Selenites all suddenly hissed in shock. The crowd fled away from us, terrified. Several were loudly hissing, 'Human! Human! Run for your lives!'

"I don't think that I expected that kind of response," I muttered. Mary shook her head.

We followed them slowly through the fields, heading toward a small cluster of buildings. They were rather poorly built, having grass and cloth roofs over baked mud bricks for walls. I wondered just where we had ended up here beneath the surface of the Moon.

As we reached the first building, we saw a small group of guards marching slowly toward us. I gripped my pistol, readying it for a warning shot into the air. When I pulled the trigger, however, it did nothing more than click. The water in the river must have destroyed the gunpowder or soaked the gun enough that it would not fire. It would be a long while of drying before it would fire.

"What do we do?" I whispered, replacing my useless weapon in its holster.

"I do not know." Mary shook her head.

The guards came to us, carrying spears but not wearing the armor that the guards of Snap'ch'sh would wear. They certainly must have been from a poorer community.

'Halt!' the lead guard ordered, though we had both stopped walking before they came to us.

'S'ch,' Mary said, bowing slightly.

The guard seemed shaken by the courteous salutation. 'We are the guard of T'k'k'whee, a member of the Empire of the Selenites. As humans, you must be arrested and sent to Snap'ch'sh for execution!' She grew bolder as the last words came out of her mouth.

We both backed away suddenly. Mary took a deep breath and stepped forward bravely. 'Who makes such a law?'

'The council of the queens of the Empire,' the guard said.

'Why do you follow such a heinous decree?' Mary asked. 'Was your queen in the council that made it?'

'No, but it is the mandate of the council.'

'Was your village forced into this empire?'

The guard looked at Mary, trying to measure her. I was simply watching with a bit of awe as she used diplomacy to save our skins.

'Our village joined the Empire by request and a show of arms of Snap'ch'sh,' the guard explained.

'Such an action is merely bullying,' Mary told her. 'Your queen should have a choice, as should you.'

The sudden addition of democracy confused the guards. Several conversations began whispering back and forth between them. I smiled as the ranks of the guards fell slightly apart. Several of the guards began arguing with the others, trying to reestablish what had always been. Tales of Mary's efforts in democracy must have spread at least this far into the lands outside of her empire.

The lead guard fell back away from Mary to discuss this with the rest of the guard. They hissed at one another, and I did my best to listen in on their conversation, even though it was in a slightly different dialect than I was used to. Some wanted to release us, some wanted to turn us over to Snap'ch'sh, and one even wanted to kill us outright.

As they were arguing, another Selenite hurried from inside the town and hissed loudly at them. 'The Empire of Fire has attacked Snap'ch'sh!'

The conversation stopped and they all looked at the messenger. They stared silently for a moment, then the one who wanted us dead clicked that this was a good reason to kill us now. The other guards began arguing with her again, and soon even the messenger became embroiled in the squabble.

I looked at Mary, who smiled at the news, and said, "I guess your father and Rodreguez are just about here."

She nodded and interrupted the arguers. 'Perhaps you should take us before your queen and allow us to plead our case.'

The Selenites studied her comment for a moment, and then fell back to arguing. I realized that they were not going to decide anything very soon, and that we did not have too much about which to worry. Mary and I moved slowly away from the guards and sat down.

Suddenly there was a loud cracking sound. Mary and I recognized it as gunfire, but the guards had never heard such a sound. They looked at one another and then marched off to investigate. The guard who wanted to kill us tried to stay behind, but the lead guard made her move with the group. The messenger quickly followed after the guards, muttering about the woe to come.

"What should we do?" I asked.

"Let's go and see what is happening," Mary said, just as another crack of gunfire rang through the air.

We both stood up and hurried after the guards, bounding in gigantic steps. We soon crossed through the village, where villagers had closed all of the doors and windows in an effort to hide. As we crossed to the other side, we saw the guards standing very still with their spears on the ground.

In front of them was a group of ten or twelve Selenites wearing battle armor. They had large red plumes coming from their helmets and red paint that showed the emblem of a flame. Each one was carrying a rifle, something I had not seen a Selenite with before. Mary screamed happily when she saw them and rushed toward them.

The leader, who immediately recognized Mary, dropped to her knees and covered her eyes. The others covered their eyes too, but held their weapons to keep the other guards from moving. Meanwhile, the guards did their best to hold still, even though they were amazed that it was the lost Empress of the Empire of Fire that they had just seen. They hissed quietly, all rebuking the one that had wanted to kill us.

I followed after Mary and, as I grew closer, recognized the leader as K't'whoo. She seemed overjoyed at the sight of the Empress and clicked too excitedly to be understood. Mary hurried to her and hugged her tightly. K't'whoo stood up as I came to her and hugged me too, her massive muscles squeezing me more tightly than Mary had when I had opened her prison.

We left the guards behind, marching quickly toward the exit of the large chamber. The soldiers with K't'whoo all hissed a merry song, celebrating the return of the Empress. Mary did not march with us, however, as the soldiers had hoisted her up to their shoulders to carry elegantly, as an Empress should.

As we came to a short tunnel that led away from the chamber, I asked K't'whoo how she had found us.

'Remember I was on the other side of the fortress?' she explained. 'I waited after the explosion to follow you in, but when I saw you run away chased by the guards, I decided to wait. Soon, I saw you return and then successfully enter the fortress. I sneaked in behind the guards and stole armor off of one of the bodies so that I could blend in with them.

'I hurried after the guards, following the mass that chased after you. They were shouting that you must be after the Empress, so I decided to wait and rescue you when the guards found you. When we came to the dungeons, the guards began reporting that you had jumped into the river. That must have been quite an escape.'

'It certainly was,' I said, still very wet from the muddy river water.

'We knew about the whirlpool, so we did not think that you would survive. I rushed out of the fortress and hoped that I could get down here to T'k'k'whee… to rescue your corpses.'

'I am glad that you had so much confidence in us,' I clicked jokingly.

'Not many are foolish enough to go into the river,' she told me, 'and very few of those that do survive.'

I grimaced, realizing that we had been very fortunate to come out of the whirlpool.

'But now with the story,' K't'whoo said. 'I met up with the army, which was already on the march to Snap'ch'sh. They had decimated everything in their path and now looked to destroy the heart of the Empire of the Selenites.

'They nearly shot me, but I quickly threw off the enemy armor and surrendered. When they realized who I was, they took me to the generals. The Empress's father gave me a small group of soldiers and told me to rescue you, which I suppose we just did.'

'Yes, you certainly did,' I sighed happily.

We marched out of the tunnel and into a larger chamber. Here we climbed up a large stone formation, finally reaching the top, where Star, Rodreguez, and the Army of the Empire of Fire waited. The entire army broke out in a joyous hiss when they saw the Empress. Star immediately ran to his daughter and hugged her tightly.

Meanwhile, Rodreguez came to my side and clapped me on the shoulder. "Quite a feat, *señor*. Very few men I have trained could have done such a mission."

I thanked him and joined with the army as it began to march victoriously back toward the Empire.

Chapter Sixteen,
Return

We quickly marched back to Mary's capital city, which had formally been dubbed Th't'f'click Th't'f'th't'f'ch'k, or "Village of the Empress of Fire." At the request of the crewmembers that were not so familiar with Selenite languages, it had also been given a nickname of Star City. I was not certain whether the "Star" in the name signified Mason or Mary, though it probably stood for both of them.

As we marched, I could see the path that the army had used on its way into enemy territory. Many of the scenes were very similar to that I had seen when Wellis freed Conners, Star, and me in the Selenite village a month or more ago. Any wall or tower that had stood in the way of the army had been smashed by cannons and gunfire. The armies had been decimated, just as K't'whoo had described.

Two other armies had followed in the main force's path, forming the new guard of the devastated villages. Mary promised to hold elections to restore the governments of the villages, but until then, there would be martial rule. Mary ordered that all of the queens who had either rebelled against her or joined the Empire of the Selenites were to be removed and imprisoned.

Mary saw to it that the prisons were not dungeons, as she had experienced for so long. Instead, the queens were kept in large, comfortable "nurseries," as Mary liked to call them. They would still enjoy luxury and hold the task of producing the next generation of Selenites, but the queens no longer had any political power at all. All power was transferred to the Empress, who promised to return it to the Selenites as soon as they formed a working democratic council.

When we entered the first village that had remained loyal to the Empress of Fire, we were greeted by hordes of Selenites that cheered wildly. They all took off their red sashes of patriotism and waved them excitedly. Mary, who was riding atop a small platform covered with pillows that the army had carried for her, waved to all of the Selenites and enjoyed the impromptu parade.

The march continued through several more villages, each more excited than the last. First they waved their sashes, then they began throwing flowers and fragrant seeds, then the Selenites themselves joined in on the parade, marching and hissing the victory songs that the army hissed.

We finally reached the capital, where the grandest celebration occurred. Messengers had run ahead of the army and given out the information that the Empress had returned. The Selenites were very quick to prepare a festival, an idea that T'wha condoned and reinforced. As we came into the capital, we were swamped with congratulations, presents, and praise from the crowds.

I was marching next to Rodreguez, who tried to say something to me. However, the music from the singing soldiers and instruments all around the city drowned out his voice. I shrugged and asked him to repeat what he had said, but he only laughed, amused with the victory parade.

The longest part of the march was from the outskirts of the city to the palace at its center. Several times the army was brought to a standstill as the crowds pressed in to congratulate it. Rodreguez allowed the army to stand for a moment and then issued the order to march forward, which was slowly carried out as the army moved a few steps before being stopped again.

When we finally reached the steps to the palace, T'wha and Mary's entire court (those who had been loyal, anyway) rushed to the Empress. Mary seemed to be instantly surrounded by several servant Selenites, numerous males, and even two queens who had come from their villages to greet her. I did my best to push my way out of the crowd, as it seemed to overcome me.

Suddenly, however, K't'whoo saw me and shouted, 'There is the one who rescued the Empress from her dungeon!'

The Selenites around me all shrieked with glee. I was immediately hoisted up into the air and they carried me along toward the palace. As I passed by them, the Selenites covered their eyes at me and clicked great compliments to me. I could not help but feel excited, and the whole parade became a blur of exhilaration. I finally found myself on top of the steps of the palace, being led by the hand by K't'whoo. She pulled me through the large palace doors just before they were closed.

Outside, a festival resounded loudly. Inside, however, things grew quieter and more serious. Mary wanted to know everything that had happened since she was abducted. T'wha, who was still wearing the ornate robes that Mary had provided for her, was quick to have Mary sit on the large throne and tell her the entire tale.

I did not listen very carefully as she explained what had happened while we were at Ch'k'ch't, but then my ears perked as she began telling about the things that had happened while we were in Snap'ch'sh. T'wha had led an empire-wide investigation, finding out who was loyal and who was not. The male Selenites were very responsive to their questions, as each of them greatly feared the possibility of torture. Once she knew where the alliances stood, she sent out the armies of the loyal villages to retake the rebellious ones. Because the treachery was from the queens and males, many of the armies of the villages merely stood back and let the queens be taken. As they did, the soldiers were reported to be repeating, 'All hail the Empress of Fire.'

Mary was pleased to hear that the queens had already been captured. She explained her ideas of holding the queens as prisoners to T'wha, who wholeheartedly agreed to it and relayed the commands.

When Mary was well informed, she leaned back on her throne and sighed wearily. "It is good to be back here."

The court all smiled and hissed amongst themselves.

'Do you wish to clean up?' T'wha asked.

Mary looked down at her torn, mud-stained dress and nodded enthusiastically. 'I will go to my quarters now,' she told her court. 'Go and celebrate in the festival.'

The various Selenites around her covered their eyes in a quick salute and then left the throne room. Only Mary, T'wha, K't'whoo, Star, Rodreguez, myself, and several guards (now always present as they feared another abduction) remained in the room.

"With your permission," Rodreguez turned to the senior Star. Star nodded, and Rodreguez followed the court out into the busy festivities.

Mary stood from her throne and walked toward me. "I suppose that you should be cleaned up as well. I'll send a servant for you in a moment." Then she, K't'whoo, and T'wha left the throne room through a door that led directly into Mary's luxurious apartments behind the throne. The guards followed her, keeping a careful eye on their beloved Empress.

Star sighed and clapped me on the shoulder. "Good show, Mr. Matricks."

"Thank you, sir," I said, looking sheepishly at my destroyed uniform. "I apologize about the suit, but it was necessary."

"That's quite alright," Star assured me. "I'm not one to hold a dirty suit

CELESTIAL VOYAGES: THE MOON

against the man who rescued my daughter. Thank you."

I nodded as humbly as I could. A servant appeared from another door and led me out of the room just as Star moved over to the throne to sit. I could not imagine the amount of relief he must feel knowing that his daughter was safe and sound once again.

The servant took me to an empty room where the court stayed and pointed to a hot bath that had been run for me. She also brought me a suit of fresh clothes, though they were not like Star's uniform in the least. After washing off all of the mud that had caked on my body, I tried on the new clothes. There was a short skirt that wrapped around the waist as an undergarment, and then a large red robe that covered the rest of my body. A yellow mantle went over my shoulders and had two red flames stitched to it, making it known that I was an important figure in the Empire of Fire. To finish the outfit, I had a red and yellow turban placed on my head. There were small holes where antennae were meant to stick out, but it still fit fairly well.

I laughed at myself as I looked down at the garment around my body. I wished that I had a mirror to see exactly what I looked like in the Selenite robes. The servants who surrounded me, however, seemed to think that it was quite stunning.

A though occurred to me while I was putting sandals made of wood and thin vines onto my feet. I asked the lead servant, 'Have you heard anything about Wellis and Conners?'

The Selenite clicked and explained that they were in an infirmary on the second level of the palace. I thanked the servants and hurried to find out what had happened to Wellis and Conners. I hoped that they did not need an infirmary, but I could not be sure what had happened to them after we split up in the tunnels beneath Snap'ch'sh.

I dodged around a pair of patrolling guards and hurried up a narrow staircase up to the second level of the palace. After gaining directions from another pair of guards, I soon came to a small door that led to the infirmary. I knocked, and the door was opened by a small Selenite male.

'I am looking for Wellis and Conners,' I told him. He nodded and opened the door wide so that I could come into the room. As I passed him, he complimented my garments. I thanked him with a chuckle.

Both Conners and Wellis were lying on thin mattresses that had been placed on the floor. Dr. Tarsini was in the room with them, though he sat in the corner of the room reading by the light of several glowing plants. They all looked up as I entered and smiled widely.

"So here's the big savior of the Empress of Fire, huh?" Wellis asked me. He had a bandage on his forehead and several more on his limbs. There was a large bandage on his shoulder, and it appeared that he was doing his best not to move his arm.

"Lucky you took the right tunnel," Conners said. He was in a similar condition to Wellis, but seemed a little less cheerful. "That's all the doctor's been able to talk about for the past hour or so." He grimaced at the Selenite, who sheepishly left the room.

"What happened?" I asked.

"Well, whose story do you want first?" Wellis asked.

"I suppose either," I said, sitting in a chair next to Tarsini.

"I'll go first then," Wellis said, looking over at Conners. Conners nodded rather apathetically.

"When we split up down the different corridors, I found that mine seemed to zigzag around quite a bit. It had a lot of doors on each side, and I did my best to check them all. Finally I came to a Selenite guard and questioned her at gunpoint where Mary was kept. The guard tried to tell me that she did not know, but finally said that she was down the dark corridor you had gone in.

"I decided to turn around and head back that way, leaving the guard tied to a crate of food or something. I hiked back up the tunnel and then hit a huge mass of soldiers. At first they did not see me and I heard them saying something about the Empress jumping into a river. I wondered what it was all about, and then they spotted me. I did my best to run and hide, but quite a few of them caught up with me. When my guns ran out of ammunition, it turned into a big brawl. Fortunately, I held out long enough for the guards to hear the cannon shots from above. With some swift talk, I got them to surrender. I led them up to the surface, where we saw the army. The soldiers took the guards prisoner, and then Rodreguez sent me back here to have my wounds looked at. I don't think I'm very hurt, though. I should be able to get up right now, but old man Tarsini won't let me."

Tarsini made a noise in his throat and looked up from his book. "You will heal better if you stay in one place."

Wellis rolled his eyes. "I suppose I'm stuck here for at least another hour or so."

"At least one day," Tarsini corrected him. Wellis sighed and muttered something under his breath.

"So what about you?" I asked, turning to Conners.

"There's not too much to tell," Conners said. "I went down the tunnel, which kind of sloped upward. In a few steps, I came to a door, opened it, and found myself in the middle of a barracks full of guards. We exchanged some blows, and then I ran down the tunnel, hoping to come back toward the other tunnels. It was a few minutes before I realized that I had taken the wrong turn as I left the barracks. By then I had no choice but to keep running and shooting. I finally came to a kind of open room, which had a couple of dozen guards in it. They did their best to dodge around me, and I finally escaped out a door that led into the city. It must have been some kind of secret entrance or something. Anyway, by that time Rodreguez and company had begun demolishing everything, so I did my best to get found and brought back. Then they locked me up here with Wellis and Tarsini and a couple of Selenite doctors, though they've all left. Something about a festival."

"Yeah, there's quite a celebration going on now that Mary is back," I told them.

"Is that where you got the clown suit?" Wellis asked.

I chuckled. "No, this was a gift from the Selenites. You'll probably get one too as soon as you're out of here."

Wellis sighed, not liking the idea of Selenite clothes. Conners, though, made an interested sound. I left them to themselves after chatting for a few more minutes and then headed out onto the streets to celebrate.

The next day was a very busy one. The wild festivities had continued without stopping for many hours before Mary and T'wha began to instill more formalities into them. Soon the celebration began to slow as Mary requested that the Selenites return to work and serve their Empress there. The workers left the streets and returned to their various duties, but all were still very excited.

There were now only a few processions given by several villages. They were small, rarely more than five or six sledges, and usually proceeded laden with gifts toward the palace. They entered the city with loud noise, and all of the Selenites who could hear them pulled away to watch as they passed. When they arrived at the palace, they courteously delivered their gifts, which Mary graciously gathered. After the delivery, the sledges went quietly out of the city, returning to their own villages proud to be a part of the Empire of Fire.

The only form of celebration left was an awards ceremony that Mary had planned. I rested a long while before the ceremony, then met up with Wellis and Conners, who were to receive the same award that I was. Mary had created a medal for K't'whoo and us, as a special award for our heroic efforts in rescuing her.

Wellis and Conners were both on their feet by the time of the ceremony. They had cleaned themselves and wore new clothes. Wellis had gotten a fresh Star uniform, but we wore a white mantle and short cloak around it to appease the Selenites. Conners had a very ornate set of robes made in five distinct layers, as he told me proudly. The robes seemed heavy, even in weaker gravity. I hoped that he would be able to move as well as we could as we came to the ceremony.

I had worn the robes that I had been given before, though I had abandoned the headwear. I was growing to like the garments very much. They were made of strong material, but it was still very flexible and smooth. They were quite comfortable, after I grew used to them.

The throne room served as the stage for the ceremony. Star had gathered all of the crewmembers he could to attend it, and Mary had no problem filling the room with the members of her court. The winners of the awards were to stand outside of the throne room and would enter when their award was called.

Wellis, Conners, and I stood outside of the throne room, anxiously waiting for our award, the last of three, to be called. K't'whoo had not yet appeared, but we expected that she would be ready in time. Star and Rodreguez were waiting in line ahead of us, dressed quite nicely in their black uniforms. T'wha and a group of male Selenites had already gone into the ceremony, receiving awards for their service in government during the time of crisis.

Star pulled a piece of paper from his pocket. He had written an acceptance speech and was taking a few moments to review it. Rodreguez looked at him, then shook his and started pacing in front of the door to the throne room.

"It's taking them quite a while to accept the thing," Wellis muttered.

"I suppose each one of the males had a speech to give," I said. "They may be short, but they're longwinded."

We waited quietly for a few more moments, and then a loud applause rang out from the throne room. We looked at one another and at the closed doors, waiting to see what was happening. Star put the paper back in his pocket and straightened up. Just as he did, the door opened, and a pair of guards motioned for Star and Rodreguez to follow them. The two men disappeared into the throne room and the guards quickly closed the door behind them.

Conners stepped forward, trying to look through the door before it closed, but the guards were too quick for him. We were not certain why, but Mary had ordered that the winners should not see into the hall before they were given entry. Conners stepped back from the door and sighed. Just as he turned back toward us, his sigh turned into a long whistle.

Wellis and I turned to see K't'whoo approach us. She was wearing ornate dark green robes that hung very slightly off of the ground. A gold-colored ribbon was wrapped around her head and matched the trim on the robes. I was amazed to see K't'whoo in such garments, since the only other clothing she had worn were the blue servant's robes she had gotten in Ch'k'ch't.

"Quite a getup," Conners commented.

K't'whoo looked at him, not exactly understanding the words. However, she could guess about what he was speaking. 'Yes, clothes seem to be growing in popularity a great deal. I thought that this would be fitting for such a ceremony.'

'It looks quite good,' Wellis clicked.

'They are not terribly comfortable, though,' K't'whoo said, shifting slightly in the robes. 'Why would humans want to wear such things?'

'Earth's atmosphere is quite a bit more variable than the caverns,' I said. 'If a breeze came through all the time, you would want to wear them too.'

'I suppose so,' K't'whoo nodded.

We waited quietly, not knowing how long it would be until Star's speech would be over. I remembered back to the long speeches that had been given in the station before we boarded the *Comet*. It seemed like so long ago, and I supposed that a great deal of things had happened since then. It was even longer since I had been home in Ohio, walking on a dusty road toward Dayton.

The loud applause rang out again. We all jerked to attention and moved close to the door. The door was wide enough for us all to walk through it shoulder to shoulder.

"Stand up straight," Conners whispered to me and tapped on my lower back. I shifted my posture, and wondered if I did indeed look more dignified.

The door suddenly jerked open and the two guards motioned to us. We stepped forward all at different times, but then fell into a synchronized step. I swallowed, slightly nervous, and did my best to keep my footing with the others.

As we stepped past the doorframe, I was overwhelmed with the glamour of the throne room. It was much brighter than before, showing freshly planted glowing plants. Lively marching music played from several clusters of bands that sat on balconies above. Around them there were numerous banners hanging down from the walls, each showing the emblem and colors of a village in Mary's empire. At the front, above the throne, was a gigantic banner that hung with reds, yellows, and oranges and looked like a tall flame emenating from the throne. I could now see why Mary wanted to hold the ornate throne room as a surprise for the winners.

We walked down an aisle in the middle of the room. The mosaic floor had been covered with a long red carpet, making the room look much like a palace from Earth. There were crowds of Selenites on each side of the aisle, all members or servants of Mary's new and growing court. In the front on the right side was a large mass of black where all of the humans stood, dressed as neatly as they could be in Star's uniforms.

I saw Louis Pierre standing next to Elissa. They both must have left their important positions to attend. Deeper in the crowd I could see Sebastian, the lead engineer on the Lunar Station, who smiled broadly at us all. Even Dr. van Sparchs seemed fairly interested in the ceremony.

We soon neared the throne, where Mary stood with several handmaidens and the winners of the other awards. Each of them, from T'wha to Rodreguez, each had a large stone disk hung on a ribbon around their necks. We all looked at one another and smiled.

When we arrived at our places in the front of the room, Mary began a short speech. She outlined our adventure, telling a short bit about our secretive journey, the escapades Ch'k'ch't, and then our success in Snap'ch'sh. As she finished, the audience all hissed and clapped uproariously.

Mary then began handing out the medals, which the handmaidens had been patiently holding. They were all stone disks that were carved ornately with different images hung on brightly colored ribbons. First she gave one to K't'whoo, saying, "For your loyalty at my side always."

Next she gave a medallion to Wellis, saying, "For your selfless skills and bravery." As I watched Mary put the ribbon over his neck, I thought that I saw Wellis blush a small bit.

Conners bowed low, making it simple for Mary to put the medal on him. "For your courage and proficient tongue." Conners thanked her and fiddled with the stone disk that hung around his neck.

Finally Mary turned to me. As she gave me the medal, she whispered, "For rescuing me." I smiled and nodded thankfully.

When the medals had all been given out, we turned to face the crowd. They applauded again, even more loudly this time. One of the crewmembers dashed out of the crowd with a large camera and took our picture. The bright flash from the camera stunned me for a moment, but I was glad to think that the moment would be recorded for posterity.

As the crowd quieted, Mary resumed the ceremony. 'I have created the Legion of Honor of the Empire of Fire, which begins with this group of heroes. All Selenites who show themselves worthy will join the ranks of the Legion of Honor and these great beings. To commemorate the members of the Legion,' she paused long enough to motion to a Selenite in the front row, 'this plaque will record the names of all those within it.'

A Selenite came out of the front row and held a large black plaque that our names had already been inscribed upon it in either English or the new Selenite written language. The crowd leapt up from their places with applause. Everything seemed to be drowned out in their shouts and hisses.

After the ceremony, I returned to the Lunar Station, which had grown significantly since its first days as a small plant-filled room. Mary was busy with her empire, Wellis aiding her and teaching the Selenites the secrets of chemistry, and Conners both learning from and teaching the Selenites about languages. There did not seem to be very much deep in the caverns for an astronomer.

Things seemed to be much quieter on the surface of the Moon. I returned to my bunk, which had not been used since before the games. The sheets had been straightened, though. I wondered who had been careful enough in their cleaning duties to attend to my bunk. I ignored it, though, and pulled out the drawer that held all of my things, which the crew of the *Comet* had brought them down by request.

I quickly pulled out my journal and tossed it onto my bunk, hoping to record all the things that had happened to me over the past few days. Beneath it I could see several photographs of my family sitting atop Star's enormous book of etiquette. I looked at the pictures carefully, and then replaced them in the drawer.

The next few hours were spent writing in the blank pages of my journal. The memories and ideas came to me so quickly that I gave up making real sentences and merely outlined the things that had happened. When I finished, I flipped back over it and chuckled, thinking that it looked like an explorer's journal with diagrams, short paragraphs, and numerous jotted notes. I supposed that in a way I was an explorer and that my book had good reason to look like that. After folding the book up, I placed it carefully in the drawer.

I yawned, worn down by the numerous deeds that I had done. I took off the outer layer of the robes, folded it neatly and tucked it away with my Star uniforms. Then I crawled under the thin blankets, closed the curtains around the bunk tightly, and fell into a deep sleep.

The days that followed seemed very docile compared to the ones that had passed. I spent the majority of my time in the Lunar observatory, mapping new stars and watching the skies. One time during my shift at the telescope, I watched the *Comet* come back from Earth, bringing new supplies and settlers for the Moon. It seemed to glide to smoothly, its bright bursts from its rockets lighting up the sky like stars. Star had mentioned to me that the newest crewmembers were more like colonists, since they were probably going to stay on the Moon for a very long time.

One day Star himself came into the observatory. Hosea and I were mapping out a small cluster of stars, trying to distinguish among them when he interrupted us. He dismissed Hosea for a moment, saying that he wished to speak with me privately. As Hosea left for the galley, I swallowed, not sure about what he would want to speak.

Star moved very smoothly to a seat next to the charts we had been sketching. He examined them for a moment before speaking. "This is very good work, Curtis," he said.

I thanked him softly and tried to make myself look comfortable.

"You've certainly proven yourself," he told me. "When the *Star's Comet* leaves in two days, it won't be making a return trip for some time. It is going back to Earth to be refitted and restocked for another journey."

"Another journey?"

"Yes. I've lived a long while and I'm certainly not getting any younger. I think that I would like to get on with the expedition before I waste too much time."

"So, where are you planning on heading?"

"Venus, Curtis. I was tempted much by Mars, it's true. I've even had a few requests that Mars be my next destination. Still, I've always had a sort of fascination with Venus. We'll be leaving for Venus on the first of July. But don't let that get out too much."

"We?" I asked. My stomach squeezed, excited already.

"I have a position waiting for you onboard if you want it," Star said, smiling. "You do want it, don't you?"

"Oh, very much so, sir!" I said, making a Selenite salute by covering my eyes slightly. I could not help but add, "Who in their right mind would pass up a chance like this?"

"Good," Star said. He turned to leave. "You are off duty until we leave. Check with Pierre to determine the departure times. Until then, you're free for the next few days. That ought to be ample time for goodbyes."

As Star left, I waited patiently for the door to close. When it did, I jumped with excitement. I was destined for another celestial voyage, a whole new set of exploration and adventure. I hung in the air for a moment in the weak pull of the Moon, tightening my hands into fists excitedly.

When I came to the ground, I immediately stepped out into the corridor. My first destination was my bunkroom, where I made certain that I would be ready to leave in a moment's notice. When I was sure, I left the bunkroom and headed toward the lift and the caverns.

The lift operator seemed to act in slow motion as he prepared it to carry me down to the caverns below. I assumed that it was just my excitement, but I could not help myself. The journey down the lift seemed even longer than the first time I had gone down the dark tunnel. Finally the lift came to a stop on the floor of the chamber. I waited for the Selenite lift operator to open the lift and then I hurried off to Mary's palace.

As I came to the door, the guards granted me access and saluted me. I smiled, pleased by their courtesy. When the gate was opened, I left the guards behind and scurried through the corridors.

I first found Conners sitting in a small room with five Selenite males. They were looking over wooden tiles, taking the images and scribing them with text from their new alphabet. I waved to Conners from the door, and he smiled when he saw me. Leaving the Selenites to their work, he stepped out of the room and greeted me.

"Hey, Curtis," he said, shaking my hand. "I haven't seen you down here lately."

"I've been fairly busy in the observatory," I said. "I decided to stop by, though, as I'm headed back to Earth."

Conners nodded. He brought his face close to mine and lowered his voice. "Star taking you to Venus, huh?"

I nodded. "Apparently I've done a good job."

"I would say so," he smiled. "Star gave me a similar speech yesterday, or maybe the day before that. It's so hard to keep the days straight down here.

"Anyway, he said I had certainly shown myself worth my salt. He and I agreed that I had done enough around here. There's a new linguist coming on the next arrival of the *Comet*. I'm supposed to show him the ropes for a few weeks and then head off to Venus."

"Stay here?" I asked. "I thought that the *Comet* wouldn't be coming back in that short of time."

"It's not. Star told me about another ship, the *Luna I* or something like that. They've almost completed it back at Earth's station. He said that it was just a little cargo ship to be sent back and forth from the Earth and to the Moon."

I smiled at the last few words in his sentence. A few decades ago the Moon was nearly totally in the realm of fiction. Wells had just finished his book about the Moon before we left. Now, however, it was a very real situation, though it seemed at times almost fictional.

"I suppose I will see you in a few weeks then," I said, shaking his hand again. "Good luck."

"You too," he said. He reentered the room full of Selenite scholars and I journeyed down the corridor to my next destination.

I entered the throne room, admitted by two guards who treated me similar to the ones who had let me into the palace. The throne room still had its amazing decorations. Mary and her court, which included Wellis and K't'whoo, were around the throne, discussing political business. They all looked up as I came into the room, wondering what had brought me to the throne room.

"*S'ch*," I said, covering my eyes as I approached the throne.

"Hello, Curtis," Mary said.

"I have come to say a short goodbye, I suppose," I told them. "I am on my way back to Earth for a few months."

"Ah, of course," Mary smiled. She turned to her court and said, 'Leave us for a moment.'

The entire court left her. She caught Wellis and K't'whoo before they left as well. The four of us stood facing one another quietly for a moment.

"Back to Earth, eh?" Wellis finally said. "Planning on visiting home?"

"I suppose I could," I said. "It depends on just how much Captain Star plans for me to do."

'Good luck on your journey,' K't'whoo clicked. 'I hope to visit your world one day as well.'

"Do you know when you will return?" Mary asked.

"No, I don't. It could be quite a while."

Mary nodded.

Wellis suddenly took K't'whoo by the arm, muttering something about needing to see T'wha. They quickly left the room, taking the pair of guards with them. The guards at first refused to abandon the room, but Wellis finally talked them into leaving. Mary and I stood alone quietly.

Suddenly she jumped at me and hugged my neck. I was surprised at the action and found it somewhat similar to when she had first come out of her dungeon. After clutching me for a moment, she let go of me and said, "We will miss you here in the caverns."

"I'll miss it here too," I nodded. "I'll see if I can send some messages through Louis Pierre."

"That would be nice," she said. Her dark eyes seemed more starry than usual.

She opened her mouth to speak again, but the door of the throne room opened at the same time. T'wha stepped through it and clicked, 'The emissary from P'whoo's is here. He wishes to meet with you as quickly as possible.'

Mary smiled at me. "I suppose I should meet him. An empress's work is never done."

"Right," I returned her smile. "I'll see you soon."

I turned away and left her throne room. As I passed, I said farewell to T'wha, who wished me a safe and enjoyable journey.

Wellis caught me as I passed by the crowd of the court and shook my hand. "If the President calls you, put in a good word for me, okay?"

I told him that I would and pushed past the court. They all greeted me with salutes and compliments, still amazed at my saving the Empress. I thanked them all and exited the palace. In a few more minutes, I was already back in the Lunar Station, bidding farewell to others from the crew.

The *Star's Comet* left orbit of the Moon at noon on March 1, 1901. I had taken one of the early landers up to it and made sure that everything was in order to return home. Landers seemed to be going up to it nearly around the clock, filling its holds with Selenite artifacts. I wondered why Star was packing so much into the *Comet*, but I could not find him to ask.

I found myself in the first astronomy laboratory, where I had a clear view of the Earth. With the powerful telescope, I could see the clouds and the top of Star's tower. Beneath it, I traced the image of England, Europe, and waited to see the Ohio. The clouds were broken above the state, and I imagined the bright day they must be having.

I heard the door of the laboratory open and turned to see who had entered. Katherine MacPherson came through the door and smiled under her large glasses. "Are ya headin' home?" she asked.

I nodded. "If Star will give me enough leave, I hope to."

"He will," she said. "He canna say no to you."

"I suppose that's true," I said, thinking of Star's generally very positive attitude toward me.

There was a sudden jerk, and a rumble went throughout the ship. The rockets had gone from their dormant orbital mode to full blast. I gripped the floor with my magnetic boots, ensuring that I would not slide. When the jerk was past, I hurried to one of the viewing ports on the sides of the laboratory.

"Amazing," I said, watching the gray sphere beneath slowly slide away. I do not know that I would ever grow tired of merely watching travel in Outer Space.

I turned to Katherine and offered her a view. "You can see us leaving the Moon behind." Katherine stared out of the glass and whispered an amazed phrase.

While she gazed, I went back to the telescope. Earth would soon be beneath us. I could not wait to get home.

Chapter Seventeen,
Home Again

The *Star's Comet* arrived safely in its dock two days later. As it approached the platform, I wandered into the pilot's station. Star was sitting in his captain's chair, watching the pilot skillfully move the ship into its landing position. The main engines had slowed the ship to a stop, and only the small rocket thrusters were guiding us into the *Comet*'s semi-oval resting place.

Star Station was different than it had been when I left it two months ago. There was a large extension off of one of the sides of the platform, and floating on it was another Starship. It looked to be nearly complete, and workers in Spacesuits were climbing over it with welding torches and new panels to be placed. The name *Luna I* already shone on the side of the ship, painted in large black letters.

"Is that the new ship?" I asked Star, examining it. It looked very similar to the *Comet*, but I doubted that Star would make a replica of his first ship.

"That it is," Star said. "It's almost a copy of the *Comet* from the outside, but the inside is quite different. Nearly all of the scientific rooms have been taken out, to make more space for storage. It doesn't hold as much fuel either, since it's only going from the Earth to Luna for transport."

"Why is it the *Luna I?*" I asked, stressing the number.

"You're looking at the first of a fleet of these ships," Star told me. "I envision a nearly continuous trade between our worlds."

The *Comet* moved easily into its position in the middle of the platform. The holding clamps slowly slid into place around the ship, positioning it correctly. Finally the docking tunnel would be extended and we would be free to leave the ship.

Louis Pierre stuck his head out of the door leading to his communications room. "Monsieur Star, I have received the 'all clear' message from Monsieur

Edwards. He welcomes us back."

"Thank you, Pierre," Star nodded. He turned to the pilot and said, "Smith, I'm handing you control of the ship. When everything has been closed down, you have leave."

The pilot nodded and began flipping switches on his control panel. Star unbuckled himself from his seat and floated up into a standing position. He quickly left the room and marched down the stairs to Deck C. I hurried after him, carrying a bag in which I had tucked all of my belongings. I was quite eager to leave the ship and had been packed since we left the Moon's orbit.

There was already a large cluster of people waiting to disembark when we arrived. They were all staring at the door, waiting for it to be opened. Star and I joined the line and quietly waited alongside the others. Finally, the door opened with a short hiss, revealing two men who had unscrewed the locks.

A sudden exhilaration came over the crew, and they all pushed to be the first out of the door. I pushed a little too, wanting to keep my place in the crowd and not be pushed back farther by the eager crewmembers. Star struggled to maintain his own dignity, but allowed the excited crew to leave as quickly as they wished.

As I came out through the door, I recognized one of the men who had opened the door as Mr. Edwards, the commander of Star Station. I stopped long enough to shake his hand and to exchange several pleasantries, but the crowd soon swept me away from him. Edwards then caught Star, who managed to stay as the crew would not push their own captain.

We walked in a single mass down the long corridor and soon came to the massive main room in the middle of the station. As we came into it, however, another large crowd suddenly ran at us. Several sudden flashes blinded me, and the confusion continued to increase from that point onward.

The crowd was a large group of reporters. From the tags in their hats, they had come from newspapers from all over Europe and even America. Star must have gathered them to celebrate his triumphant return from the Moon.

The crewmembers had very differing reactions. Some of us immediately received the reporters, glad to give a quote and to be recognized. Others tried to dodge away from them, not wanting to be detained by the very fervent reporters. And a few were simply perplexed by the sudden attack and stood blankly, trying to decide what was happening.

I was caught by the arm by a reporter from a British newspaper. He dragged me out of the crowd and found a place away from the main fray to begin questioning me. He quickly said his name and the name of his newspaper, but I could not quite catch either of them. He asked me my name, and when I gave it to him, he immediately grinned.

"Looks like I got good luck today," he said, busily scrawling notes on a small pad of paper. "You're quite the celebrity down here. It's not every day someone becomes the rescuer of the first human empress of the Moon!"

I scratched my head, amazed at his energy. "Really?" I asked him, not quite sure how to respond to my newfound position.

"Oh yeah," he told me. "The whole story was plastered on the front pages from here to Timbuktu as soon as it came off of the wires. So would you answer a few questions we have for you down here?"

I smiled, pleased at myself. He suddenly repeated his question, forcing me to answer that I would. He asked me about every detail of the flight there, the initial landing, the discovery of the lunar caverns, and so forth. The questions came at blinding speed, and I did my best to answer them, despite the noise and flashes from several cameras.

Eventually the reporter had run out of questions. He left me, trying to find another interviewee in the large crowd, and I was left alone with my thoughts. First I watched him go, and studied the strange brown suit that he was wearing. It looked similar to a Star uniform, but was much more stylishly cut. He was also wearing shoes that had soles thick enough to hold magnets, which were probably also provided by Star. I wondered just how much Star was giving out to these people.

Suddenly another reporter found me and began assaulting me with questions. I answered them more easily this time, since many of them were the same that the first reporter had asked me. I spent more than an hour being questioned by reporter after reporter and posing for several photographs. Finally I escaped the main room and ducked inside the administrative wing of the station.

The secretary, the same one who had spoken with Mary long ago on my first tour of the station, smiled at me. "Busy out there?"

"Very," I said. My mouth was almost dry from all of the talking that I had had to do. I walked up to her, glancing at my shoes and glad that I had brought magnetic ones this time. "What are they doing here?"

"Sir Star sent a message to Mr. Edwards two days ago to organize a meeting with the press. It's been very chaotic here since they arrived this morning. They wanted to know everything about the station, but we only had so many people to grant tours. I've barely gotten any work done at all here."

I nodded, understanding how busy she must have been. She surprised me, however, by calling Star by his knightly title. It had been a long time since I had heard someone call him "Sir Star." He had been knighted just before we left the station, but very few crewmembers referred to him by that title.

"That must have been a lot of suits to give out," I said, remembering the clothes that every reporter seemed to me wearing.

"It was quite a bit," she said. "But they certainly weren't given out. I heard that Sir Star's clothing factory made the reporters pay upwards of one hundred pounds for them."

"Wow," I said. "That's quite a bit of money."

"Well, I'm sure they gladly paid it. The sales from the newspapers with stories about the expedition will more than make up for it."

"Is everyone that anxious for stories?"

"It's all we've talked about for the past two months," she told me, wide-eyed with disbelief at my ignorance. After a short pause, she looked down and added, "Except for the Queen's passing, of course."

I realized that Louis Pierre had a very necessary and important job and did not merely spend all of his time just sitting beside a wireless telegraph. Star was an enormous celebrity. He had come back from the Moon triumphantly, and now he was going to reap the benefit of his years of work. I could not help but be excited for him myself.

"Here," the secretary said, holding a newspaper out to me. She must have pulled it from a stack under her desk. I took it from her, and as I opened it, she said, "It's today's edition. I imagine that there will be several special editions once the reporters get back on the Sky Train."

I looked at the front page, marveling at the massive headline, "Star to Return to Earth Today!" There were several pictures of Star's manor and a long, thin illustration of Star's Tower. I scanned through the text, seeing that the newspaper certainly did explain him as a hero and celebrity.

"Speaking of the Train," she continued, "I imagine that it'll be heading down shortly. You best make sure that you're on it."

I thanked her and gave her back the newspaper. After quickly checking to make sure that I could escape from the administrative offices without being detected, I hurried to the numerous elevators that lined the wall opposite the large viewing windows. I caught one of the elevators just before it left, and squeezed into it between a large worker on the station and a crewmember from the *Comet*. We waited quietly as the elevator moved us up into a position next to the Sky Train.

When it jerked to a stop, the crowd inside the elevator squeezed out quickly. The workers from the station were all tired from a long day and the crewmembers of the *Comet* were excited to be home, causing both groups to be eager to get onto the train. I moved with them, doing my best to struggle in the thick crowd. Finally we came across the platform into a car on the train. Soon I was in a seat, buckled into place. I deactivated my magnetic shoes early and used my feet to hold my bag.

I began a barely patient wait for the Sky Train to leave the station. The crewman who had stood next to me in the elevator took the seat to my left while the seat on my right remained empty. I tried to place the crewman's face with a name, but I could not remember who he was. He was probably an engineer or someone who had stayed onboard the *Comet* for the entire expedition, so that I had only scarcely seen before now.

Suddenly a person filled the seat to my right. I glanced at him as he did, but I could not recognize him at all.

He smiled at me, attracting my attention, and asked, "You're Curtis Matricks, right?"

I nodded, and he gleefully began digging through his pockets. "I thought you were," he said. "Pretty big celebrity around here. I don't suppose you would mind…?"

As he finished, he took a pencil and a piece of paper from his pocket. I smiled and said that I would happily sign an autograph. I was amused at him, since I had rarely signed an autograph before, and none of those were very serious ones.

"My name's Martin Dreying," he told me, directing my writing. "That's D-r-e-y-i-n-g." I nodded and handed the paper back to him, filled with my signature and a short pleasantry.

"Thank you much," he said. He remained quiet for a moment more, but only a moment. Finally he asked me, "So, what was it really like, down there with the Selenites?"

I smiled at him. He said the last word with a mysterious hiss. As I began to tell him some tales, the door to the compartment closed. Soon we were on our way down to the surface of the Earth. All of the way I made him marvel with fantastic descriptions of the caverns under the Moon.

Eventually the dark sky became a warm blue color. Clouds passed around us as we lowered deeper and deeper into the atmosphere. Finally we came to a stop, inside the ground station next to Star's manor.

The man to my right groaned, upset that we had already arrived. He had certainly enjoyed my tales. As he unstrapped himself and stood to leave, he suggested that I put them in a novel. I smiled, doubting that I could ever write a book like that.

I unstrapped myself and stood up. I immediately fell back into my seat, however. Apparently, I had been away from Earth long enough to grow unaccustomed to its strong gravity. I tried to stand up again, and this time I was able to keep my footing.

I took up my bag and walked out of the Sky Train. The gravity seemed harsh at first, but I quickly familiarized myself with it again. It felt strangely good to be back in my natural gravity.

The station was as busy as ever before. I saw Star surrounded by a large mass of reporters. He was speaking loudly, explaining the adventures that we had undertaken. I dodged away from the great crowd and escaped as quietly as I could. Soon I entered Star's mansion and found a corridor in which to hide from the numerous reporters.

I came to an empty sitting room and waited there for several hours before venturing out into the lower parts of the house. When I finally did leave it, Mrs. Star met me on the stairs.

"Hello, Curtis," she said, smiling warmly. "Mason asked me a moment ago if I knew where you had hidden yourself. If you move quickly, you should be able to find him in the dining room."

I nodded and thanked her, then quickly ran down the stairs. I remembered just enough of Star's massive mansion to find the dining room, though I did need to turn around at least twice.

When I finally came into the dining room, I found Star calmly talking with Dr. van Sparchs. As I entered, they paused their conversation and greeted me.

"I should most likely be off, then," van Sparchs said, standing up from the table. "Good day to you both."

The German left the room eagerly. I doubted that I had seen him that enthusiastic ever before. As I took a seat next to Star, I wondered what had excited him so much.

"He's leaving for the Germanies," Star explained, almost as if he read my mind. "Kaiser Wilhelm has requested a personal meeting with him. It's certainly a blessing to be such a celebrity." He grinned broadly.

"You seem to enjoy it," I noted.

"Yes, yes I do," Star told me. "The *Comet* is packed full of Selenite artifacts. Many of them are destined for museums, but a large number of personal collectors approached me. I believe that this one shipload will pay off any debt I could have imagined."

"That's good to hear."

Star paused and straightened himself in his chair. "Have you been enjoying your newfound fame?"

I nodded, but said, "It seems to get in the way quite a bit."

"Don't worry. As soon as we leave again, you'll be back to just Head Astronomer," he consoled me. We both chuckled.

Star continued, "Speaking of leaving, have you planned what you will be doing until we do?"

"I haven't much thought about it," I admitted. "I hoped that I would be able to visit home for a short time."

"That would be a good thing to do." Star smiled and handed me a small envelope. "You leave Liverpool onboard the *Returner* tomorrow. A car will take you there in the morning. After that, it's just a train ride home."

I looked inside the envelope and saw the various tickets. My heart skipped a beat excitedly. "Thank you, sir!"

"You should probably send a telegram to your parents before you leave," he suggested. "And you may want to try to keep a low profile while traveling abroad like this. There is no telling what the reporters could do to you if they caught you."

I smiled, but inwardly shuddered at the thought of being bombarded with questions again. We chatted for a short while, and then I retired to one of Star's many spare rooms. I went to sleep that night smiling, glad to return to Earth.

The voyage from Liverpool to New York was a fast one. I kept to myself in my private suite onboard the *Returner*, leaving only when I wanted some fresh sea air or a quiet stroll around the decks. Whenever I did leave, though, it seemed that someone discovered me and begged for a signature.

When I arrived in New York, I was again overwhelmed by the massive city. Fortunately, everyone seemed too busy to notice me. I kept my cap low over my face and my coat's collar high on my neck to limit the possibility of someone recognizing me.

I hired a cab to take me from the port to the train station. The cabman did not recognize me at first, but after glancing at me a few times, he asked if I were Curtis Matricks. After I said that I was, he let out a thrilled laugh and told me that I was a big hero of his. I wondered how true his compliment was, but I took it graciously.

"I bet Earth feels pretty good after going through all that inside the Moon, huh?" he asked.

"It does," I nodded. He remained very chatty, but mainly explained his personal feelings about the Moon and did not ask many questions about me.

We quickly came to the station, and I paid the cabman a comfortable sum and left him. I succeeded in sneaking onto my train, giving the conductor my ticket quickly so that he did not bother to look at me long. In a few minutes, the train left the station, swiftly bringing me to Dayton. I was bothered a few times by conductors and stewardesses, but spent the majority of the train ride sleeping.

When the train pulled into Dayton, I was one of the first people off of it. When I saw the massive crowd that met me, however, I was shocked and nearly jumped back into the train.

The whole town and more had turned out to welcome me back. There was a small band that played joyously, numerous banners with my name written on it, and a cluster of people including the mayor, town constable, and my parents that immediately grabbed me as I came off of the train.

"What is all of this?" I asked.

"It's a welcome home party, Curtis!" my father told me.

"When we received your telegram, we were quick to put one together," my mother explained. "The mayor was very helpful and organized nearly everything."

I stood dumbfounded for a moment and considered arguing that I was supposed to keep my presence quiet, but then I began to enjoy the celebration. It was an interesting one and lasted for several hours. I was forced into a speech, and produced one off of the top of my head as best I could. After that, there was a large banquet and then dance in the town square in my honor. People with distant relations to me (such as my father's cousin's neighbor) swore that they had known me for my entire life. Numerous boys I barely knew began saying that we had been best of friends since early childhood. Every girl in the county seemed to attack me at once, requesting that I ask them to dance.

When it finally ended, I was completely worn out. My parents helped me into their old buggy, and we drove home in the dark. I leaned back in my seat, staring up at the stars and reciting their names in my mind to spend the time. Finally my eyes settled on the Moon, and I slowly went to sleep remembering all of the grand adventures that had happened there.

And so my story ends on a lonely, dusty road deep in the farmlands of Ohio.